"Maybe you're scared because I won't quit."

John heard Turner catch her breath. "What do you mean?"

"Haven't they all quit? The men in your life? Your father, your brother..."

John braced himself for her to hang up on him.

But she didn't. "You're very sure of yourself." Her voice was cool. "And of me."

He smiled tightly. *Oh, honey, you have no idea.* "You're anxious because I'm not going to quit until I have you in my hands."

"How do you know I'll let you get that close?"

"You'll have to."

"You want to arrest me." Was there a question in her voice?

"I *want* to get to know you," he said very gently. "I *have* to arrest you. It's my job."

"You can't do both things. You'll have to pick."

She was right. He knew that. But... "Maybe." *Maybe he'd gone insane.* "Maybe I can have both."

Acclaim for these novels

HOT

"A refreshing, funny, tug-your-heartstrings read that deserves a Perfect 10 . . . If you like *Hot* stories, this is just the book you need."   —RomRevToday.com

"A fabulous story! . . . A truly exciting and intriguing book, this was one that could not be put down until the end"   —TheRomanceReadersConnection.com

"[A] delightful crime caper . . . the story line is fast-paced and jocular . . . Filled with terrific twists, fans will appreciate Julia Harper's HOT thriller."
     —*Midwest Book Review*

"A fantastically written story filled with suspense, adventure, and—as the title suggests—steamy scenes. Julia Harper . . . has a flair for creating lovable and interesting characters who are hard to forget."   —BookLoons.com

"One of those books that is so good that it, unfortunately, is over long before the reader wants it to be . . . with unforgettable characters, slick dialogue, and a story that is both romantic and suspenseful. Julia Harper writes hot, sexy characters in fast-moving situations with searing realism."   —RomanceReaderatHeart.com

"A rousing romantic adventure that is certain to bring Julia Harper a large fan base. Wonderfully witty dialogue, vivid sense of time and place, a hero and heroine like no other; all of these add up to a stellar debut."
     —SingleTitles.com

"A funny, romantic comedy with a bit of action-adventure thrown in...will appeal to fans of Janet Evanovich."
—*Parkersburg News and Sentinel* (WV)

"This one is cute with a likeable heroine."
—BellaOnline.com

"A creative and even suspenseful story and a cast of quirky, small-town characters, HOT makes for a light and entertaining read." —NightsandWeekends.com

FOR THE LOVE OF PETE

"Hilarious...keeps the laughs coming."
—*Publishers Weekly*

"Reads like Janet Evanovich crossed with *The Sopranos*...you will be giggling as you cruise through the plot twists." —*RT Book Reviews*

"Madcap to say the least, *For the Love of Pete* is flamboyantly off-the-wall...[It] is a guaranteed good read, and will definitely put Julia Harper on more than one must-read list." —TheRomanceReader.com

"It's one of those books where you actually laugh out loud, it's so funny...I liked everything about this book."
—BookBinge.com

"A very enjoyable and fast-paced zany caper that doesn't disappoint from start to finish...Offering nonstop wacky fun and some adorable romance to boot, *For the Love of Pete* gets my love and a two-thumbs-up gesture."
—MrsGiggles.com

HOT

Titles by Elizabeth Hoyt writing as Julia Harper

For the Love of Pete
Once and Always

Titles by Elizabeth Hoyt

The Raven Prince
The Leopard Prince
The Serpent Prince
The Ice Princess
To Taste Temptation
To Beguile a Beast
To Seduce a Sinner
To Desire a Devil
Wicked Intentions
Notorious Pleasures
Scandalous Desires
Thief of Shadows
Lord of Darkness
Duke of Midnight
Darling Beast

Elizabeth
HOYT
WRITING AS
JULIA HARPER

HOT

FOREVER

NEW YORK   BOSTON

Forever
Hachette Book Group
1290 Avenue of the Americas
New York, NY 10104

www.HachetteBookGroup.com

Printed in the United States of America

First edition: January 2008
Reissued: February 2015
10 9 8 7 6 5 4 3 2 1

OPM

Forever is an imprint of Grand Central Publishing.
The Forever name and logo are trademarks of Hachette Book Group, Inc.

The Hachette Speakers Bureau provides a wide range of authors for speaking events. To find out more, go to www.hachettespeakersbureau.com or call (866) 376-6591.

The publisher is not responsible for websites (or their content) that are not owned by the publisher.

For HEATHER QUALE,
the only woman I know willing to wander
the backwoods of Wisconsin at
a moment's notice.

Acknowledgments

Thank you to my editor, Melanie Murray, for her enthusiasm, and to my agent, Susannah Taylor, for bearing with me.

HOT

Chapter One

*I*n Turner Hastings' opinion, the bank robbery didn't go truly bad until Yoda shot out the skylight. Which was not to say that the robbery hadn't had its problems up until that point.

It started out as a typically busy Saturday. Turner was working the drive-through teller station, peering out the bullet-proof glass at the customers in cars. It was almost noon—closing time for the First Wisconsin Bank of Winosha. Nasty old Mr. Johnson had just pulled up and begun fumbling with the plastic canister in the pneumatic tube when she heard the commotion behind her. She glanced over her shoulder in time to see two men rush the bank counter.

One was tall and spindly in that way some guys are. The kind of skinny where you can't help but wonder what, exactly, is holding up their jeans because they have no rear end to speak of. He was wearing a black Eminem T-shirt and a Yoda mask, and clutching a sawed-off shotgun in an uncertain way, as if he'd never held one before. The second man was short and hairy. He had the thick black stuff growing on his arms, the backs of his hands, his fingers, and of course, his chest. Unfortunately, he'd chosen to wear a yellow mesh tank, which only served to highlight all that abundance of fur. Perhaps he'd wanted to coordinate with the cheery yellow of his SpongeBob SquarePants mask. He held his shotgun with a bit more knowledge than Yoda, but under the present circumstances, that wasn't nearly as reassuring as it should have been.

"This is a floor! Everybody on the stickup!" SpongeBob screamed in a disconcertingly hoarse voice, little tube-socked SpongeBob legs swinging back and forth on the mask.

Everyone in the small bank paused, trying to digest those two sentences. Turner opened her mouth, thought better about it, and shut it again.

Marge, the only customer inside the bank if you didn't count the robbers, had no such inhibitions. "This is a *stickup*. Everybody on the *floor*."

And you really couldn't fault her, because she was right. Marge was short and bottom-heavy and wearing turquoise stretch capri pants with a big T-shirt that had glittery pink and orange flamingos on it. She was in her late fifties, which was an age, as she liked to tell anyone who'd listen, when she no longer had to put up with guff from men or boys.

Her correction seemed to make the robbers irritable.

"On the floor! On the floor! On the floor!" Yoda yelled redundantly, the mask's little sticky-out ears flapping.

Turner flattened herself to the floor behind the counter because, really, it seemed to be a good idea.

But that only made SpongeBob upset. "No, dickhead!

They'll hit the police alarm back there," he told Yoda. "We need to get them out here in the lobby."

"Okay. Yeah. Okay," Yoda said. "Come on out here, *then* get on the floor."

Turner crawled out after Ashley, the other Saturday teller. Ashley was looking peeved. Before the robbery had started, she'd been talking about her new leaf-green summer pantsuit. She'd found it on sale at the Wal-Mart up in Superior, and she obviously wasn't too thrilled to be crawling in it now.

Behind Turner at the window, she could hear Mr. Johnson's tinny voice through the speaker. "Can I have that in fives? No, better make it ones. And I need some quarters, too, for the washing machines up at the Spin 'n' Go. Make sure they're nice new ones. Last time you people gave me a bunch of sticky change."

Those inside the bank were all out in the lobby now. Turner lay on her belly and contemplated the manure-brown floor tiles. They needed mopping. Typical. Calvin Hyman, the bank president, who naturally wasn't working on a Saturday and thus wasn't in danger of having his head blown off—more's the pity—had saved money by cutting the cleaning to once a week.

"Here." A black plastic garbage bag was thrust in front of Turner's nose. "Fill this with, like, money."

She squinted over her glasses at SpongeBob. Did he realize that in order to . . . ?

"We're going to have to get back up to fill those," Ashley said, loud, exasperated, and nasal. "Why'd you make us come on out here and get down on the dirty floor if—ow!"

Ashley stopped talking to glare at Turner, who'd just kicked her in the ankle.

"Shut. Up," Turner hissed.

"Don't you go telling me to shut up, Turner Hastings. If you think—"

"Ashley, honey," Marge interrupted from her spot on the floor next to Turner, "just get the nice bank robbers their money."

Good idea. "I'm going to stand up and go get the money, okay?" Turner said to the robbers to give them plenty of warning. She didn't want to make them any more nervous than they already were.

"Yeah, yeah, okay. Hurry up," Yoda answered. She noticed for the first time that the mask's right ear had a tear in it. It'd been Scotch-taped back together.

Turner stood. She took the garbage bag gingerly and walked back behind the counter with Ashley. Behind them, Marge stayed on the floor. It sounded like she was muttering about dirt and men. Turner hit the release on her teller drawer.

Mr. Johnson's scratchy voice was still complaining. "Hello? Hellloooo? What's taking so long? I ain't got all day here, you know—some people have work to do."

Ashley huffed at her counter teller station and pulled out wads of cash.

Turner put a bundle of twenties into her bag and glanced carefully at the big round wall clock—11:56. Fudge. Ashley's boyfriend, Doug, came to pick her up for lunch every Saturday. And Ashley's boyfriend just happened to be a—

"Cop!" SpongeBob squeaked.

"What? Where?" Yoda swung around to look, his shotgun going with him.

Sheriff's Deputy Doug Larson pushed open the tinted glass doors of the bank and paused. The little silver star on his khaki uniform winked in the sunbeam streaming in from the big skylight. His Smokey-the-Bear hat had always seemed a little too big on him to Turner's eye, but that might've been because Doug had such a little pinhead. If you looked at him sideways, the back of his skull was totally flat. Something had to be wrong about that. A ludicrous expression of horror flooded Doug's face, and Turner could almost hear the *Oh, shit.*

Then Doug drew his gun.

Turner decided to duck behind the counter at that point, so she didn't actually see Yoda shoot out the skylight, but she did hear the *BOOM!* of the shotgun and the subsequent tinkling as glass rained down on them all.

Beside her, Ashley was whimpering, but that soon turned to a shriek. "Doug!"

Oh, Lord, thought Turner. *Please don't let Doug be dead.*

Then Ashley's hollering continued. "Doug! Dougy! Don't leave me! Goddamnit, Doug Larson, see if I ever let you take me out to the Ridge again!"

Turner blinked at that information slip. The Ridge was the local makeout spot. She chanced a look over the counter. Doug, as Ashley had already indicated, was nowhere to be seen. Smart man. He'd probably calculated the odds and gone looking for some backup. Or at the very least, a bigger gun. Meanwhile, Yoda and Sponge-Bob were still milling in the lobby. Yoda's right ear was dangling from the mask now. Evidently, the Scotch tape hadn't survived the excitement.

"What the hell did you do that for, you douchebag?" SpongeBob yelled. "Why didn't you shoot at the cop instead of the ceiling?"

"Hey, I was trying," Yoda said. "It's not as easy as it looks to aim a sawed-off shotgun—"

"Yes, it is!" SpongeBob retorted. And *BOOM!,* he shot out the front doors.

My, wouldn't Calvin just be miffed when he saw that? Turner's ears were ringing, and the bank filled with the acrid stench of gunpowder.

"Shit," Yoda muttered. "That's not fair. You've had way more practice, dude."

SpongeBob had turned away to shoot the doors. In doing so, he'd revealed a stunningly lush growth of back hair.

"Ew," Marge said from the floor, which pretty much summed it up.

"Fish!" Ashley yelled.

SpongeBob jumped as if someone had poked him in the butt. He swung around to stare at Ashley.

"You're Fish!" Ashley was waving a bubble-gum-pink fingernail at him, apparently unaware that it wasn't a good idea to identify a bank robber when he was actually in the process of robbing the bank. "I'd know that hairy back anywhere. I spent an entire year sitting behind it in sophomore social science. You're Fish."

"Am not!" SpongeBob said, confirming for everyone present that he was indeed Fish.

Wonderful. Turner grabbed Ashley's plastic garbage bag from her.

"Hey—!" Ashley started.

Turner shoved both bags at Yoda and SpongeBob. "Here."

"What are you doing?" Ashley shrieked.

Turner ignored her. She enunciated very carefully to the robbers. "Take the money. Run away."

Yoda lunged convulsively, grabbed the bags of money, and galloped out what was left of the front door. He was followed closely by SpongeBob.

"Can I get off the floor now?" Marge asked plaintively.

Outside, a car with a bad muffler roared away.

"I guess so," Turner replied. She looked around the little bank. Calvin's manure-brown floor was covered in sparkling glass, and a hot August breeze was blowing through the skylight and doors. Hard to believe that ten minutes ago it had been a normal Saturday.

"What'd you do that for?" Ashley demanded, fists on discount Wal-Mart hips. "You just handed them the cash. What kind of First Wisconsin Bank employee are you?"

"A live one," Turner replied.

Ashley looked disgusted. "At least I got one of those ink bundles into my bag."

Turner stared. "You did?"

"Yeah, why?" Ashley asked aggressively.

Turner just shook her head and went to the drive-through window. "I'm sorry, Mr. Johnson, the bank's closed now."

Sirens wailed in the distance, getting closer.

"Why, of all the—" Mr. Johnson began, but Turner switched off the speaker.

There was a squeal of tires from out in front and then the rapid slamming of car doors.

"Looks like the cavalry's arrived," Marge said to no one in particular.

"Come out with your hands in plain sight!" Sheriff Dick Clemmons's voice bellowed, amplified by the speaker on his squad car.

"Oh, for Pete's sake," Turner muttered. It hadn't been

a good day so far, and she was getting a little cranky. She walked to the doors and peeked through broken glass. Outside, two Washburn County sheriff's cars were skewed dramatically across Main Street. Predictably, a crowd had begun to gather behind them.

"They're gone," she said.

"What?" Sheriff Clemmons boomed, still using the speaker.

"They're gone!" Turner yelled.

"Oh." There was a crackle from the speaker, and then Dick stood, hitching up his black utility belt. The sheriff was a tall man with a sloping belly, and the belt had a tendency to slide below it. He looked a little disappointed. "Anyone hurt?"

"No," Turner replied in her best repressive librarian voice. She held open what remained of the shot-out bank door.

Dick strode up the walk in an I'm-in-charge kind of way, trailed by Doug, who still looked a little spooked. Turner couldn't blame him. It wasn't every day that a man got shot at by a Jedi Master.

The sheriff stepped inside the bank and squinted around. "Okay, now—"

"Doug Larson!" Ashley had caught sight of her boyfriend.

Doug sort of hunched his shoulders.

"Of all the low-down, ratty things to do," Ashley began.

"Now, honey," Marge interrupted. "You can't go blaming the boy for not wanting to be shot just so you wouldn't ruin a pantsuit from Wal-Mart."

"But he left me!" Ashley wailed, tears running down her cheeks along with a bunch of black mascara.

Marge began patting, Doug started explaining, and Sheriff Clemmons became authoritative. Then the paramedics arrived, crunching over the floor with equipment nobody needed. Two more deputies appeared, as did the volunteer fire department, most of whom had probably heard about the robbery over their scanners and wanted in on the action.

Turner watched all the people running around, talking, arguing, taking notes, getting in each other's way, and generally trying to look important. She thought about how easy it would be to rob the bank right at that moment when everyone was so very busy. She glanced at the surveillance camera in the corner, dumbly taping everything within the bank. Then she strolled to Calvin's big fake mahogany desk and pulled out the middle drawer. There, sitting in plain sight, was the red paper envelope that held the key to his safe deposit box. She stared at it. She'd never have another chance like this one. She knew because she'd been waiting for this moment for four years. Turner smiled a small, secret smile and palmed the key.

It was time for her own heist.

Chapter Two

The problem with playing hoops on a Saturday afternoon with younger guys was not that they were in better shape, but that they had no fear of death. None. At. All.

John MacKinnon feinted right, and when the tall blond kid guarding him shifted, he shot the ball over the boy's right elbow. There was a breathless moment of hope, followed immediately by crushing disappointment. The ball bounced off the rim, the sound echoing in the gym. It headed back into the key as four guys collided, trying to nab the rebound.

Not that he was out of shape. Far from it. He lifted weights twice a week, ran every day—well, nearly every day—and played pickup hoops on weekends. Lots of guys his age weren't nearly as fit.

The other team's point guard, a rangy college kid with abs you could bounce a quarter off of—damn him—caught the ball and ran down the court. Nine guys followed, thundering in a close pack.

But the thing was, once you reached a certain age—

say, forty—you became more aware of death. Of the potential of death. That little twinge, high on your left arm, or the stitch in your side that might be a forewarning of something more dire. You worried about what you ate. Thought twice about the deep-fried cheese curds and considered—actually considered—getting the tofu burger for lunch. Young guys, in contrast, were so busy thinking of pussy and beer that there wasn't a whole lot of room for anything else in their brains. Certainly not worry about trans fats and heart disease.

Someone elbowed him in the ribs. He shoved back, his sweaty arm sliding against an equally sweaty shoulder. The other player grunted. Served him right, the cocky young asshole. Score one for the old guy.

Just last month, Ted York had keeled over from a heart attack right in the middle of lunch with a bunch of desk jockeys from D.C., and wasn't that an awful way to go? The poor bastard had been eating a salad. Bet Ted would've ordered a bacon double cheeseburger if he'd known it wouldn't't've made a difference anyway. But that was the trouble with being over forty. You didn't know what—

John's pager went off with an obnoxious digital sound. One of these days he'd have to change the ring tone on the thing. If he could figure out how. Everyone stopped, and a couple of guys groaned. The ball bounced into a corner of the gym, and the blond kid went to retrieve it.

"Oh, man!" The rangy point guard bent over, hands on knees, panting. "Figures you'd get paged now, Mac."

"We were losing anyway," John shot back.

More grumbling, and a discussion of his mother's virtue or lack thereof. He ignored the back talk and dug in his gym bag for his pager, pushing aside the Glock to reach it. He read the number on the little device and swore softly. So much for hoops.

The game started again behind him.

John opened a plastic bottle of water and took a deep swallow as he punched in numbers on his cell phone.

The other end picked up. "FBI."

"MacKinnon."

"We've got a bank robbery in Winosha," Tim Holt, the Milwaukee ASAC—Assistant Special Agent in Charge—informed him without preamble.

"Where?" John picked up his bag and headed for the lockers.

"Winosha. Small town south of Superior on Highway 53. It's in Washburn County."

"Never heard of it." He shouldered open the men's locker-room door.

"No reason you should have," Tim said in his California surfer-dude drawl. "Not more than three thousand people all told, and that's at the height of tourist season."

"Yeah? Figures the assignment would be in podunk-ville." John pulled off his sweaty T-shirt and wiped his face with it before dropping it in his gym bag. "Who've I got?"

"McHenry's on leave of absence, Anderson's still on the Sun Prairie case, and Wilson's working surveillance this weekend." Tim didn't elaborate further, because he knew damn well John could draw the obvious conclusion.

Crap.

John finished stripping and rolled his right shoulder. It still ached from when he'd pulled a muscle shoveling snow back in April. It was the kind of injury kids in their twenties never sustained, and the guys at the office didn't let him forget it, either. Goddamn Wisconsin winter. Another problem with getting old: the body didn't bounce back from injuries as fast.

"Mac?" Tim queried.

"Yeah." John grimaced. "Give me Torelli."

"You okay with that?"

"Sure, I'm good. I'll call him."

"Fine. Paperwork's waiting for you here."

John said good-bye, punched the button to hang up, and dialed another number. He rubbed his shoulder while the other end rang.

"Hello?" A New York accent this time. Music played in the background, something kind of sultry and jazzy.

John grinned. Maybe Dante Torelli was with a girlfriend. *Ohhh, too bad.* "Torelli?"

"Yes?"

"We're on. Bank robbery. Meet me at the office at"—he glanced at his watch; it was 3:14. "Four o'clock."

John hung up without waiting for the reply and threw the cell back in his gym bag. He carried the bag into the showers and placed it on a nearby bench while he washed off the sweat. Then he dressed in old jeans and a light blue T-shirt. Damn, he'd have to change into something more businesslike at his apartment. Not that he'd be able to compete with whatever designer suit Torelli would decide to wear today.

He snorted and stuck the Glock at the small of his back under the loose T-shirt before grabbing his bag. Outside the gym, the August heat slapped him across the face, and he felt the sweat start again as if he hadn't just showered. He had transferred to Milwaukee from Philadelphia last fall and still hadn't acclimated to the

Wisconsin weather, despite the fact that he was originally from Lander, Wyoming. First the howling cold of the Midwest winter, and now the hostile heat of summer. Who knew it could be this ghastly hot so close to Canada, for God's sake?

John crossed the sticky asphalt parking lot to his black Chevy Silverado pickup and unlocked it. Naturally, it was baking inside. He popped both doors and watched the heat waves roll out from the interior. It was a wonder the steering wheel hadn't melted yet. Anchorage began to look like a good posting at times like this. He got in, took out the Glock, and tossed it on the passenger seat within reach before starting the engine.

Ten minutes later, when he pulled into his apartment-complex parking lot, the Silverado's interior was arctic-cold. He lived in a newer area built up in the late eighties, and his apartment building had the tasteful, bland look of that decade. He went in the so-called security door and hung a left in the hall to take the beige-carpeted stairs. He unlocked the door to his apartment—also done in beige—and tossed his keys on the little table by the door. The wall above the table was blank. Probably should've hung something there by now, maybe a southwestern print, but there never seemed to be time. Besides, the apartment had come furnished. Why mess with the decor when it wasn't really his?

On that depressing thought, he crossed the central living room to the bedroom. In the back of his closet he had a duffel he always kept half-packed. He hauled it out now and threw in a couple of clean shirts and slacks, then went back out to the kitchen and grabbed a box of granola bars—the old-fashioned kind that weren't too sweet—and some plastic containers of microwaveable stew. Meals could be real unreliable in small towns. John threw the food in his duffel and shucked off the jeans and T-shirt. He replaced them with khaki slacks, a navy polo, his brown leather shoulder holster, and a brown blazer. Then he pulled on bullhide Wilson boots with stitched swirls on the calves. Not that you could see the stitching, of course, with his slacks over them, but he knew it was there.

John straightened and stood for a moment, looking around his generic apartment, trying to remember if he'd forgotten anything. The AC kicked in, its mechanical hum loud in the silence. There were no plants to water, no cat to feed, no one to call. No one who would care that he'd be gone a few days. In fact, he could pretty much walk out of this apartment right now and never have to come back. He wouldn't be leaving anything important behind.

Man, his life sucked.

If he stood here any longer he was going to eat his own gun. John stuck the Glock in the holster under his left arm, picked up the duffel, and walked to the front door. He turned off the AC before he left.

Chapter Three

$\mathcal{I}$t was after four by the time Turner parked her tan '95 Ford Escort wagon on the curb by her little one-story cottage. Four hours. Four hours of being questioned and requestioned and waiting to be questioned yet again about the bank robbery. And all that time the contents of Calvin's safe deposit box had been lying in the bottom of her prim brown leather purse. No wonder her hands had begun to tremble just a bit.

Turner forced herself to get out of the car slowly. Deliberately. *Not* running in a scatterbrained panic up the front walk. The precaution proved to be a wise one. She was halfway to her front step when Ernestine Miller, her next-door neighbor, hailed her.

"Turner!" Ernestine puffed. "Turner! I just heard!"

Her neighbor hurried as fast as her fat little ankles would let her. Ernestine owned a police scanner and had no doubt been lying in wait for her. Turner paused for the short, round woman to reach her. She took a calm breath and didn't let impatience—or fear—show.

"Are you all right?" Ernestine asked, looking her up and down as if checking for bullet holes. "Did a gang of vicious bank robbers really take all of you hostage?"

"I'm afraid so," Turner replied. Technically, she supposed, there hadn't been a hostage situation, and she wasn't so sure the bank robbers were all that vicious, but she didn't have the time to debate that with her neighbor. "It was very frightening."

Not as frightening, of course, as standing out here in the burning sun, waiting for police cars to come screaming around the corner, but she didn't mention that to Ernestine.

"Well, I guess!" Ernestine looked thrilled to death. "Did they have guns?"

"Shotguns."

"And they blew up the doors!"

"It was awful." Turner stomped on the urge to just walk away from the woman. The last thing she wanted was to look suspicious, and in a small town, passing up the opportunity to rehash a real live bank robbery would look very, very suspicious indeed.

Fortunately, Ernestine didn't need much help with the conversation. "I bet they were one of those youth gangs you hear about on *Focus on the Family.* Probably from Superior . . ."

Five minutes later, Turner was able to tear herself away from the discussion by faking delayed shock and a headache. She walked sedately up her three wooden steps and slowly opened her front door. She even paused for a final wave at Ernestine.

Inside, she closed the door and locked it, noticing only at that moment that her hands had started shaking again. Turner frowned and stared at her palms until the palsy stopped. Then she dropped her purse by the door and ran on cautious tiptoes to her bedroom, even though no one could hear her. They hadn't noticed anything at the bank, so they couldn't possibly be after her already, but that didn't stop her from feeling that the full arm of the law was just around the corner, waiting to capture her. Her belly tightened.

They couldn't capture her. Not yet.

Turner pulled her old navy nylon suitcase out from under her bed and threw in a change of underwear, shorts, and a couple of T-shirts. She stared at the suitcase a moment. There was no way to tell how long it would take. She figured only overnight, but if there were difficulties . . . She tossed in more underwear, another change of clothes, and her small bag of travel toiletries. Then she went to the kitchen and gathered the scissors, her old pair of binoculars, a box of saltine crackers, some apples, and three jars of pickled herring. At the last minute she threw in a jar of olives, some Vienna sausages, and half a dozen bottles of water.

She dragged the suitcase to the front hall and dropped it there. By the door was a narrow coat closet. Turner opened it and stood on tiptoe to reach a cardboard box on the shelf inside. The box held winter clothes packed away for the summer. She set it on the floor and began rummaging until her fingers touched plastic. At the bottom of the box was a Ziploc bag containing one thousand dollars in cash. She pocketed the cash and returned the box to the closet.

Turner opened the front door and looked out. Her cottage was in the old section of Winosha on a street unimaginatively named Elm. The street looked serene in the heat, a typical hot August day. The cicadas buzzed loudly in the maple trees along the walk. No police cars marred her sleepy neighborhood. You couldn't tell that the town bank had been robbed only hours ago—or that she had finally made her move after four very long years.

She took off her glasses and set them by the vase on the hall table, then picked up her suitcase and lugged it down the walk to her car. Ernestine popped out her front door, but Turner waved and didn't break her stride. She threw the suitcase into the back seat of the Escort and was pulling away from the curb while her neighbor was still trotting down the walk.

Main Street took her by the bank again. Turner slowed like any other gawker. The two sheriff's cars were still parked out front, although they'd been moved to the side of the street. As she drove past, she saw Calvin Hyman enter the bank, his silver hair shining in the sunlight.

She shuddered and accelerated north out of town on Highway 53, turning up the AC to counter the sweat that had started along her spine. Outside of town, tall evergreens crowded in on either side of the road. They'd been planted after the forest here had been clear-cut. But the rows of evergreens were too straight, too ordered to ever take the place of a natural forest. They looked manmade.

Seven miles down, she exited on State 77. The shoulder was pale brown here from the drought, and she passed a forest preserve sign that warned, DANGER OF FIRE TODAY: HIGH. After another twelve miles, Turner took a right down County H and then a left on a dirt track. In the rearview mirror, clouds of tan dust bloomed, kicked up by her car. The dust would coat the outside of the Escort. Not that it mattered, since the Escort was essentially dust-colored anyway.

Tommy Zucker's house suddenly materialized out of the trees on the right—a surprise every time, even though she made this trip at least weekly. The house was stained a dark, almost black color that blended with its surroundings. She put the Escort in second and drove carefully up the primitive lane beside Tommy's house. Usually she parked the car in front, but today she continued around back to the shed where Tommy kept his excess vehicles. She killed the engine and listened to the stillness of the woods. A blue jay flew through the baking sunlight, attracted by the peanuts Tommy put out on his back deck.

He might not be here. She jerked slightly as the thought intruded. She'd driven out assuming that he'd be home, but Tommy had no schedule. She'd talked to him by phone only last night, and he'd not mentioned any plans then. What if the old man had decided to go to the lake today? And if he had—

"That you, Turner?"

She started, her car keys clattering to the floor. She bent to pick them up and glanced toward the sound of the call. Tommy stood in the open doors of his barn, khaki trousers hitched nearly to his chest, a faded T-shirt looking too big on his skinny frame. His thin white hair ruffled in a small breeze. A great sigh of air puffed out of her. *Thank God. Thank God Tommy hadn't left.* Shoot, she had to pull herself together. Turner got out of the car and walked to the old man, knowing there wasn't much use in calling him from here. He didn't like to admit it, but he was getting deaf.

"Hey, Tommy." She tried to keep her voice light. "Can I borrow the Taurus?"

The old man's eyes narrowed, but his words were the same grumble that he always used. "Nope, 'fraid not."

Just like that, all the tension was back in her muscles. It hadn't occurred to her that Tommy wouldn't want to help. "Why not?"

"Don't work." The old man gestured over his shoulder to the barn. "Think it's the battery, but it might be somethin' else. Don't like these new cars." New in this case was fifteen years old. "Wanna try the station wagon?"

The car in question was built like a boat and took forever to accelerate. Turner tamped down panic. "Can I have the Chevy?"

Tommy crossed his right arm over his chest to scratch at his left shoulder while he thought out her request. Finally, he said, "Well, I don't know. It's old, you know, like me. Might not start. And I hafta find the keys."

"Oh, it'll start. I'm counting on it."

"Humph. No way to know that. But suit yourself. Lemme get the keys." Tommy ambled back to the house.

Turner closed her eyes and tilted her face to the burning sun, trying to still her impatience. The lake. Think of the lake. The water was blue and calm and so very deep. She listened to the air flowing from her lungs and tried to steady it. She had to remain calm. Cool. Her goal was so close.

Tommy's footsteps sounded hollowly on the wood of the deck, and she opened her eyes. He came back carrying a bunch of keys tied together with a frayed piece of string. "One of these, I think. Maybe. Question is, which one."

Turner kept herself still and watched the old man carefully sort through the keys. Tommy was a slight man, no taller than five-eight, and as he'd aged he'd slumped a bit. Add to that some weight loss in the last few years, and he'd become frail-looking. His wrists were narrow and bony, the skin easily bruised. He probably didn't weigh much more than Turner herself, and she was a small woman.

He looked up and caught her watching him but didn't comment. "Think I got it here. 'Spose we can give her a try."

He gave an extra hitch to his khaki pants and led the way into the barn. Turner followed. Inside, the dark interior blinded her temporarily after the harsh sunlight. The air was still and hot and smelled of oil and sawdust. Lined up against the side were three vehicles: a huge station wagon with fake-wood panels, a lumbering late-eighties Ford Taurus, and the baby blue '68 Chevy pickup. The Chevy wasn't the most discreet of cars, but it wasn't like she had a whole lot of choice now.

"Okeydoke." Tommy wrenched at the driver's side door and it opened with a screech. "Oughter oil that."

Turner got in the passenger side and watched Tommy insert the key and start the engine. It made a horrible squealing sound.

"Starts right up," Tommy yelled over the revving. "That's because I take it out every month or so to keep her in shape." He'd apparently already forgotten his prediction that the truck wouldn't start.

He turned and cautiously, carefully, and very slowly backed out of the barn.

Once out in the sunshine, he switched the engine off

again. "Better put some oil in. These old trucks will run forever, but this one just about drinks oil."

He hopped down from the cab and disappeared back in the barn. Turner got out and fetched her suitcase from the Escort. Tommy had reemerged by the time she'd stowed the suitcase on the passenger floor. He slowly opened the hood and began tinkering.

Turner sighed and drove the Escort into the barn to take the Chevy's place. When she came out, Tommy was still under the hood.

She walked over and laid a gentle hand on his back. His shoulder blade felt sharp under her palm. The bone was covered with only a thin layer of skin; there wasn't any fat or muscle to spare. "I have to go now, Tommy."

"Eh?" He withdrew from the hood and looked at her, old blue eyes sharp. "What's the gol dern hurry?"

"I've got to do an errand for Rusty."

Tommy stilled for a moment, then slammed the hood down. "Okeydoke. Just remember to put oil in her every couple hundred miles or so."

"Will do." Turner got in the cab.

"I put some extra cans of oil under the front seat." Tommy slapped the hood and stepped away. "Take care now."

She nodded and backed out of the drive. When she looked back, he was still staring after her, the breeze gently lifting his grizzled hair. Turner made sure to memorize the image. It might be the last time she ever saw Tommy.

Chapter Four

$\mathcal{I}$'m pretty sure Fish has a first name," Sheriff Clemmons said slowly, not sounding sure at all. "Maybe Tom or Ned."

John watched the sheriff expressionlessly. *Ned?* Nobody named their kids Ned anymore, did they? The only Ned he could think of offhand was Ned Yost. Well, and Ned Nickerson, Nancy Drew's boyfriend. The name was wimpy even thirty-one years ago when he'd been sneaking reads from his sister's yellow-spined collection.

John tilted his paper coffee cup to catch the last nasty, stone-cold drop. It tasted like the toxic leavings in an old chemical oil drum, but it contained caffeine. Caffeine was the only thing keeping him upright at the moment. They'd been in Winosha four hours. Before that, it'd taken him and Torelli over five hours to get to Winosha, driving the agency's navy Crown Victoria. It was a damn good thing he had seniority, too, otherwise it would've been five hours of listening to idiot jazz. He was a Garth Brooks man himself. 'Course, Torelli had been looking a little twitchy by they time they hit Eau Claire. By that point they'd run through three Brooks tapes and a Johnny Cash for variety. And Eau Claire had been at least an hour before Winosha.

"I think Fish *is* his first name, sir," the deputy said.

John had already forgotten the younger officer's name, and the kid was turned just enough away so that he couldn't read his name tag. The deputy was big and corn-fed, with almost invisible blond hair shorn to within a quarter-inch of his scalp. The kind of cop that would be good at taking down a drunk and disorderly on a small-town Friday night but might need help filling out the paperwork on Monday.

"Don't be an idiot," Clemmons retorted. "Fish isn't a Christian name."

Good point. The reply seemed to temporarily baffle the sheriff's subordinate, and since no one else in the room was likely to know Fish's name—last or first—there was a silence.

They were all crowded into the meeting room in Winosha's small municipal building. The room was utilitarian, with a thin, dark gray carpet and cinder-block walls painted light green. Some female hand had tried to decorate the room by printing little pink cats in a row around the top of the walls, nearly at the ceiling. There were a couple of long tables, a pile of metal folding chairs, the TV, and a coffeemaker with an empty pot.

The fifth man in the room sat at the same table as John but didn't seem to pay much attention to the conversation. Calvin Hyman glanced at his watch in a manner he no doubt considered surreptitious. John didn't look at his own watch, but he knew it had to be getting on for midnight. Hyman was not only the First Wisconsin

Bank of Winosha president but also the town mayor, and he was apparently running for the state legislative seat, as well. The man was tall and silver-haired and looked just like a bank president and town mayor should. Distinguished. But he was wearing silly green snakeskin boots, and John couldn't entirely trust a man with such bad boot taste. Hyman had lectured them over an hour ago about the finer points of security at his bank, not that the security had done a whole lot of good in this case. Only one of the tellers had managed to slip an exploding ink device into a bag of money. Wherever they were, the robbers were traveling with lots of inked-up cash.

Hyman stood and shook out his trousers. "Well, about done tonight, are you?"

"No." John smiled at the man.

Hyman hesitated, then sat down again, visibly annoyed. John hid a grin and glanced at the screen displaying the bank surveillance tape. The little dark-haired teller was kicking the redheaded one again. They'd run the tape so many times he had the sequence of events memorized.

"What's she do?" he asked. He hadn't met either of the tellers in person; they'd been questioned and sent home before he'd arrived. That was first on his mental to-do list for the morning: requestion the witnesses.

The sheriff looked over, startled. "Who?"

John gestured to the screen with his empty coffee cup. "Ms. Hastings there. You said she works only Saturdays at the bank. What's she do the rest of the week?"

"Turner's the town librarian," Hyman answered.

John raised his eyebrows. "Really."

On the screen the woman rose slowly from the floor and took the black garbage bag from the robber wearing the SpongeBob SquarePants mask. She was a little thing, probably didn't hit five-foot-two. The redhead towered over her. But Turner had been the one to take charge. Later in the tape, she'd defuse things and get the robbers out of there. John lifted the cup to his mouth again before he remembered it was empty. The thing was, she looked exactly like a small-town librarian. The type of librarian who would've shushed the Beaver and Wally in the fifties, all prim and proper, her dress buttoned to her throat. He couldn't remember ever seeing a librarian look like that in real life. The woman behind the counter at his local library in Milwaukee had dreadlocks, multiple piercings, and a loud laugh.

Turner the librarian, in contrast, wore a plain, dark dress, either navy or brown, hard to distinguish on the black-and-white tape. She was petite, and the dress hung on her as sexless as a potato sack. There was no way to tell if there were any curves under there at all. It was about as revealing as a Taliban-approved burqa and it was frustrating as hell. She probably wore it for the sole purpose of bugging men like him. Then, too, she'd pulled her hair into a bun. Not a twist or a sexy coil, but an old-fashioned plain bun at the nape of her neck. And she was wearing honest-to-God, big horn-rimmed glasses. Where'd she find them? At a Goodwill? Did they even make glasses like that anymore?

For Pete's sake. She might as well be waving a red flag at him.

"She ever put a pencil in that bun?" he asked, scowling at the screen.

He heard a snort behind him from Torelli. The deputy turned to him, puzzled. Larson. That was his name. Larson.

"Yeah, now that you mention it, I've seen her do that at the library," Larson answered. "Why?"

John shrugged. "Hell if I know."

Torelli loudly sighed again and walked around him. "So you're sure that the other individual is a male called Nald?"

"That's right." The sheriff hitched up his utility belt. He was in his fifties with a gut that probably made running any distance impossible. Not that running was necessarily required for a small-town cop.

"His full first name is Nald?" Torelli asked, his voice dripping with disbelief.

"Maybe it's a family name, *Dante*," John drawled.

The sheriff looked between the two of them but decided not to comment. "Reginald is his first name, but everyone calls him Nald. He and Fish are known associates."

"Known?" John picked out the word. "They've got a record?"

"Not an official one. But they hang around together. We've had some break-ins during the winter on empty vacation homes. We thought that might've been them. Not much was taken. They're petty."

"Bank robbery's not usually considered petty," Torelli said in his dry New York accent.

It was almost midnight, he'd ridden in a poorly air-conditioned car for over five hours, the man was wearing a *suit,* for God's sake, and yet he still looked cool and neat. It just wasn't natural. Torelli was about thirty and had dark curly hair cropped short, swarthy skin, and a runner's build. He stood a couple inches shorter than John's own six-two. Maybe it was childish, but that fact pleased John no end. The younger man wore a dark charcoal suit with a narrow chalk stripe that was almost invisible. Underneath were a light gray shirt and a solid charcoal tie. His shoes were plain black and polished to a mirror finish. Either Torelli spent his entire government paycheck on clothes or the man had family money.

John had first met Torelli seven months ago when they'd worked a series of bank robberies around Milwaukee. He hadn't been impressed with Torelli's East Coast polish, and apparently the feeling was mutual. The younger man hadn't bothered to hide the fact that he didn't like his superior's laid-back investigative style. They had traded thinly veiled barbed comments, but John had thought the problem would rest there. Until he discovered that Torelli had gone over his head to complain to Chris Donaldson, the Special Agent in Charge at Milwaukee. Not a good team-player move. Donaldson hadn't been in Milwaukee all that long, and there'd been the real possibility that he'd believe Torelli's bullshit complaints. Fortunately, Tim Holt, the ASAC, had gone to bat for John. But the whole thing had left a bad taste in his mouth, and he'd made damn sure that Torelli hadn't worked with him again.

Until now.

"Tuna," Larson suddenly exclaimed.

Everyone turned to him.

A flush on the young man's narrow face bled into his buzz cut hairline. "That's Fish's first name. Tuna."

"Tuna Fish," Torelli said, deadpan.

"No wonder he took up a life of crime," John said. He glanced at the bank tape. Yoda and SpongeBob were making their getaway, and Turner was walking to the drive-through teller position to shut it down.

The door to the municipal room opened, and a woman

in her sixties came in. Her hair was flaming orange, and
she had an enormous mole on her left cheek. She'd been
introduced earlier as working for the town somehow.

"I thought you all might like something to eat," she
said cheerily. She set a cooler on one of the tables and
took out sandwiches wrapped in green and red cel-
lophane, a bag of Fritos, and some packaged cookies.
"I've got a cooler in the car with iced tea if you want to
get it, Doug."

The deputy nodded and left.

"Thank you, ma'am. That's very kind of you." John
stood and piled a paper plate with two sandwiches and a
handful of cookies.

Beside him, Torelli unwrapped a squished bologna
sandwich on white bread. He wrinkled his nose. John
carefully stepped on one of Torelli's polished Italian
shoes. The younger man stiffened but made no other
sign that his toes were being crushed. His face smoothed.
John removed his boot.

Larson came back with a big red plastic barrel
cooler.

"There, now." The woman began filling blue plastic
cups with iced tea. "I hope you all have found some
clues about the robbery?" She glanced up with a polite
but inquisitive expression on her face.

"Getting along fine, Louise," the sheriff replied rather
vaguely. "Thank you for the snack. We'll clean up when
we're done so you don't have to wait around for us."

Louise looked a little disappointed at her dismissal,
but she smiled and left the room.

John went back to sit in front of the TV. The bank
robbers were long gone on the screen, but he didn't have
the energy to rewind the tape again. He watched the af-

termath of the robbery for the first time as he unwrapped a sandwich—chicken salad—and bit into it. Too much salad dressing. It was mushy and bland, but they hadn't stopped for supper earlier and he was hungry. He took a second bite.

The redheaded teller was having hysterics on the tape, everyone crowded around her, which was probably her intention. Except for Turner Hastings. She was off to the side, watching, curiously apart.

"Iced tea?" Torelli handed him a cup and rested a hip on the table, idly watching the TV, as well.

"Thanks." John drank thirstily. The tea was freshly brewed and had a lot of ice in it. Just right. He took another bite of sandwich.

On the screen, EMTs started pouring through the bank door.

"What do you think?" Torelli asked, then answered his own question. "Sounds like a couple of kids bored with the heat. They didn't even get away with very much, according to Hyman."

John's mouth was full, so he shrugged.

In the surveillance tape, Turner walked to a desk and opened the center drawer. She took something out. Nobody paid attention to her. They were too busy with the other teller and the crime scene. John felt a little irritated. You'd think an EMT would at least ask her if she was all right.

"They've already checked these guys' families," Torelli continued. "And no one has seen the perps, at least not since the robbery. I can go by in the morning and question the family again, but there doesn't seem to be much point."

John watched Turner walk to a bank filing cabinet,

take out a key, and stroll into the bank vault. She didn't pause or hesitate. She looked like she had a perfect right to be there, and maybe she did. But then why . . . ?

"Maybe run down their friends, check out the school, doesn't sound like they attended much, but you never—" Torelli abruptly cut himself off. He stared at the tape, as well.

Turner opened a safe deposit box and upended the contents into her purse. Then she neatly replaced the box and locked it. She walked back to the bank filing cabinet and replaced what must be a safe deposit key.

"What's she doing?" Torelli muttered.

John didn't reply. He was too enthralled.

Turner strode briskly to the desk and put the other safe deposit key back into the center drawer. She closed the drawer. Then she tilted her face and for the first time looked right into the surveillance camera. Right into his eyes. Her mouth curved into a little lopsided smile, like that of a self-satisfied cat.

"Shit," Calvin Hyman exclaimed suddenly behind them.

And John realized three things. One, Turner, the little witch, had robbed the bank. Two, this case wasn't going to be nearly as simple as Torelli thought. And three, he had a raging hard-on.

Chapter Five

Calvin Hyman took out his house key and wearily started to insert it in his front door. The door was pulled open before he could complete the action.

Shannon, his wife, peered out at him, dry, teased hair framing her face like a demented halo. "Well, my goodness, that took forever," she chirped. "I was beginning to think you'd spend the night at the municipal building. Were you talking to Sheriff Clemmons all this time? Was Dougy Larson there? Did you have to give a statement?"

Calvin nodded curtly to all of the above as he stepped in and hung his keys on the pigtail by the door. There wasn't much point trying to get a word in edgewise this early on in the conversation. Besides, he needed to think about—

"And they sent FBI agents!" his wife exclaimed. "Who'd've imagined FBI agents?" Apparently not Shannon. Her voice was high and excited, and her pale blue eyes were wide and bright.

"Bank robbery's a federal crime," he explained to her slowly. "They had to call in the FBI."

"It's just like a TV show. Wasn't *CSI* about the FBI? Or was it *24*? Kiefer was a FBI agent, wasn't he? Did one of them look like Kiefer?"

For Chrissake. Did she have to flaunt her own stupidity? "No." He headed for the kitchen for a drink of water. "Nobody looked like Kiefer Sutherland. These are real FBI agents, Shannon, not actors."

"I bet they have two guns on them at all times." Shannon trotted behind him. "Did you see if they wore one on the ankle?"

"No."

"I saved some hamburger hot dish," she said, her mind fluttering to another topic. "It won't take a minute to microwave a plate."

It was nearly one in the morning, and the last thing he wanted to do was eat warmed-over casserole. But if he didn't eat it, Shannon's feelings would be hurt, and if her feelings were hurt, she'd pout. Shannon pouting was a terrible thing to behold. He sighed, gave in to the inevitable, and followed her into the kitchen, wincing. The house was new—he'd had it built only two years ago—but already the kitchen looked stuffed with pigs. Somehow Shannon had gone on a swine binge when it came to decorating. Ceramic jars in the shape of fat pink pigs' heads lined the counter. The curtains on the window over the sink featured frolicking pigs, and the wallpaper had rows of tiny dancing pigs on it. He'd never thought much about pigs before. If someone had asked his opinion of pigs two years ago, he would have shrugged and said that they seemed a nice enough barnyard animal.

Now. Now he loathed pigs.

"Here we are." Shannon set a plate in front of him at the butcher-block kitchen table.

Little pink pigs marched in a row along the plate's rim. A green mound took up the middle, and bright orange cheese melted atop the mound like hardened lava. The food was still steaming. Shannon had a heavy hand with the microwave.

"Have the FBI figured out where Fish and Nald got the idea to rob the bank?" Shannon was back with two pig coffee mugs.

Calvin frowned and looked up. "Idea? What do you mean? They were probably bored." That's all he needed: for the town to be looking for a criminal mastermind behind the bank robbery.

"Oh, come on." Shannon sat down opposite him and propped her elbows on the table, pink pig mug cradled between her hands. The curly tail was the handle, and she sipped out of the animal's back. "Everyone knows they couldn't have planned a bank robbery themselves."

"Why not? Doesn't take much brains to point a shotgun and grab some money." What did take brains was to seize the diversion of the bank robbery to steal the contents of his safe deposit box. If he hadn't seen it with his own eyes, he wouldn't have believed Turner Hastings had done it. What the hell had she been looking for?

"Still"—Shannon shook her head—"I can't see Fish and Nald coming up with the idea on their own. Eileen says they're lucky if they can figure out how to get out of bed most days."

"Is that what they're saying in town? That they had help?" Wonderful. Just what he needed. He tasted the hot dish on his plate and suppressed a sigh. She was using the low-fat cheese again. She might as well cook with orange plastic and have done. He reached for the salt shaker in the form of a pig face and shook salt from its snout.

"Sure. They must've had help." Shannon shrugged. "Of course, we won't know until Dick catches them. But that shouldn't be too hard, knowing Fish and Nald. All he'd have to do is stake out the porn section in the video store." She giggled at her own joke.

Calvin stared at his plate, thinking hard. "Maybe that's why the FBI men were so interested in Turner."

"Turner Hastings?" Shannon set down her pig mug. "What about her?"

"She stole the stuff out of my safe deposit box after the robbery."

"The safe deposit box!" Shannon shrieked, nearly taking out his ears. "Why didn't you say so before? Did she get my sapphire earrings? My mother's engagement ring was in that box!"

"Hush," Calvin moaned, wishing he'd just kept his mouth shut. It was way too late at night for this. "The safe deposit box was mine—"

"Calvin Hyman, when we got married you said you'd share all your worldly possessions with me. What do you need your own safe deposit box for?"

"It's for business papers. Nothing more." Thank God. Turner couldn't have possibly been after his papers, could she? Unless—

"Why would Turner want to steal your papers?"

Calvin stared at his wife a moment. True, he'd not been interested in her brains when he married her, but if he'd had an inkling of how dim she was . . . "I doubt she knew what was in it before she opened it."

"Oh. Well, then why would she do such a thing?"

He shrugged. "Revenge?"

"Revenge? She couldn't still be—"

"She took Rusty's arrest pretty hard four years ago."

"But you gave her that job at the bank!" Shannon was scandalized. "I just can't see it."

"They caught her on the surveillance tape, hon. Clear as daylight. She broke into the safe deposit box." And maybe she really had waited all this time for revenge. Extraordinary. He never would have guessed. Did she know enough to look for evidence? Had Rusty known? He shivered in the chill of the air-conditioned house. Calvin got up to put his plate on the counter near the sink. Surely Rusty had never suspected—

"Oh, I wish I could call Eileen!" Shannon exclaimed.

He glanced at the kitchen clock, which had pigs where the numbers should be. It used to grunt on the hour, but he'd disabled the sound. "It's already one-thirty. You'll have to wait for the morning."

"Well, darn it." Shannon put her mug in the sink.

A sudden mournful howl came from outside.

Calvin jumped. "Christ, Shannon. Did you forget to bring Duke in again?"

"He's your dog," his wife shot back. "I wanted to get a cute little Shih Tzu, but nooo, you had to get that big ol' thing."

"He's a purebred—"

"He smells. And he cost way too much. I don't know why we couldn't have got something pretty, like a Chin. Or a Pug. Have you seen Eileen's Pug? It's the most darling thing. We should trade that monster in."

Calvin sighed. Shannon was right. The dog, despite its impressive pedigree, had turned into a burden he just didn't have time for. Maybe he could leave him out for one night—

Another eerie howl broke the silence.

"Don't take too long," Shannon chirped. "We've got church in the morning, then that dinner where you can shake hands with local voters, and Monday the auditors come, don't they?"

"No." Calvin hesitated, hand on the doorknob. "I called them today. We've had to put back the audit." Thank God. The audit delay was the only thing that had gone right today. "The bank will probably still be a crime scene Monday, and we'll have to fix the doors and the skylight before we reopen."

"Still. Best get to bed," Shannon said, her voice drifting back down the hall to him. "I just can't believe little Turner Hastings could do such a thing."

Neither could Calvin. But obviously, he'd better start believing. Little Turner Hastings might just turn into a great big pain in the ass.

Chapter Six

I still can't believe Turner Hastings could've robbed the bank." Larson shook his head, looking bewildered in the glow of a streetlamp. "She's the town *librarian*."

John knocked on the door of the little white cottage. "Hard to argue with a surveillance tape."

They'd split up the work. Torelli was with Sheriff Clemmons, interviewing family and friends of Yoda and SpongeBob, while John and Larson had come out to talk to Turner. It had taken a couple of hours to get the search warrant, and now it was close to two in the morning. He'd bet anything that this street was usually quiet as the grave at this time of night. Tonight, however, at least four houses had lights on, and a couple of people were standing on their front porches watching him. John rapped on the door again for the benefit of the neighbors. No one answered. Not a surprise. He hadn't expected her to be home after what he'd seen on that tape. He tried the handle for luck.

What do you know? The door was open. He was conscious of a bizarre anticipation at the prospect of penetrating this woman's home. Maybe it was lack of sleep. On the other hand, maybe it was the aftershock of the sexual turn-on he'd felt before when he'd watched her steal from that safe deposit box. That feeling had truly come out of left field, and he was still trying to analyze it.

"She usually lock her house?" he asked Larson as he pulled out two pairs of latex gloves and handed one pair to the deputy.

"Don't know."

John nodded. "Okay. You know not to touch anything, right?"

Larson looked insulted. "Yes, sir."

John snapped on his gloves, pushed open the door, and flicked on the overhead light. The cottage couldn't be much more than eight hundred square feet all told. The front door opened directly into a living room with an old green couch, a nice bentwood rocking chair, a TV that was at least ten years old, and a couple of plants. The couch was one of those two-seaters with stiff cushions. It didn't look big enough to be comfortable for a man, at least not a large man. There was a faint, tantalizing aroma in the air that he couldn't quite place.

"She got a boyfriend?" John wandered over to the bookshelves on the other side of the TV. His boot heels echoed on the hardwood floor. Maybe the interest was simply because she was a woman and a fugitive. But that wasn't right. He'd dealt with plenty of female criminals before and never been turned on. Shit, he wouldn't be a law officer if crime made him hard.

"I don't think so," Larson said slowly. "No. Somebody'd know in Winosha if she was dating. I don't think she's seen anyone since she broke up with Todd Frazer."

"When was that?"

"Four years, maybe? He's married since."

"Yeah?" John cocked his head to read the titles in the bookshelf. Jane Austen, Edgar Allan Poe, Faulkner, Barbara Kingsolver, a whole row of Graham Greene. Huh. He took out *Our Man in Havana,* one of his own favorites. The pages were worn at the edges, and the edition was fifteen years old. She'd obviously read it more than once.

"What're we looking for?" Larson asked from behind him.

John put the book back. "Dunno."

The little cottage wasn't air-conditioned, and even this late at night it was stuffy from the daytime heat. He could feel the sweat start at the small of his back and trickle down his spine under his shirt and jacket. He glanced around the room. By the door was a small table with a mirror over it, probably so she could check herself before going out. He'd passed it when he'd walked in, but now he sauntered back to it. On the table was a blue-and-green-painted vase and a pair of tortoiseshell glasses. John frowned. They looked like the ones she'd worn on the bank surveillance tape. She must have more than one pair. He picked them up and peered through them, grunted, then handed the glasses to Larson.

"See anything?"

The deputy looked through the glasses, as well. "No. Should I?"

"They're clear."

Larson glanced again. "So?"

"Most people have prescription lenses in their glasses."

"Oh."

Why had she worn them? To make her look more intelligent? He'd heard that some women did that when they were working in male-dominated professions, but she was a librarian, for God's sake. He was conscious again of that heat stirring in his groin. Maybe it was the fact that she was so obviously playing a part. But he'd run across con artists before—that didn't jazz him. What was it about this woman in particular? He went back to the TV area. On the couch was a *Chicago Tribune* folded into a rectangle around the Saturday crossword puzzle. He bent to examine it without touching. She'd filled in the whole thing—in ink.

Larson was looking at the books now, his eyebrows knit over the titles.

John flicked on the TV. PBS. No surprises there. He turned it off again and went into the kitchen, turning on lights as he went. The kitchen was tiny, as expected, but neat. There was a colorful rag rug near the sink. A small white-painted wrought-iron table and two chairs stood against the wall. And a calendar with a European landscape hung next to the wall phone. John flipped through the calendar pages. Nothing was written on them. He picked up the cordless phone and pressed the redial button. The other end rang thirteen times, and then someone answered.

"What?" an old voice growled.

"This is Special Agent MacKinnon of the FBI. Please identify yourself, sir."

The line clicked off.

John raised his eyebrows and put the receiver back.

He opened the fridge door. It was full of mostly estrogen food: yogurt, lettuce, apples. But the milk was full-fat, which was interesting, if unhelpful. Not many people drank whole milk anymore.

"Check the call log on the phone for the last numbers she dialed and the last calls she received. You can try seeing if any of the numbers match ones she has in her speed dial. After that, search the cupboards and freezer," he ordered Larson. "I'll do the bedroom." For some reason he didn't want the other man with him while he was rifling through Turner's panties.

"Okay," the deputy said behind him.

John walked into the small bedroom and turned on the only light—a bedside lamp. There wasn't an overhead fixture in here. The bed was single. That made him smile. It was covered by what looked like a handmade quilt in all different colors. The odor was faintly stronger here, although he still couldn't place it.

He opened the closet door and took a small flashlight from his inside jacket pocket to illuminate it. Rows of dark dresses and skirts, the twins of the thing she'd worn in the tape. On the floor were five pairs of flat, dark shoes that all looked the same to him but undoubtedly would have subtle differences for a woman. He parted the dresses to look in the back. Way in the corner was a pair of red high heels.

He pursed his lips in a silent whistle and hunkered down to pick up one of the red shoes. The toe was cut away, the heel was thin and long, and the back was nothing but a tiny strap. 'Bout the most impractical pair of shoes he'd seen in a long time, and they were sexy as hell. He turned the shoe over, shining the flashlight on the sole. On the arch was the size, six and a half. He checked one of the plain Jane flats. Same size, so they were definitely hers.

He tapped the heel thoughtfully against his thigh. The shoes were at odds with the image Turner projected. From the little he'd heard and observed about the librarian, he couldn't see her wearing the red shoes in Winosha. What did she do, sashay around her house in them when she was alone at night? The mental image had him shifting uncomfortably. He'd always been a sucker for puzzles—for figuring out how people thought and what made them do the things they did—and for the life of him, he couldn't figure out what Turner was up to. Maybe it was simply that: she was a challenge to him. John frowned, put the shoe back next to its mate, and straightened. There was something more. Something he was missing.

Beside the bed was the usual small table. On hers were a utilitarian lamp, a clock, and a photo frame. John picked up the frame. The snapshot inside was obviously an amateur one—it was slightly out of focus. It showed a man in his sixties, a wide grin splitting his red face. In one hand he held a fishing line with a nice-sized walleye dangling on the end. The background was a lake. John slid the photo out of the frame and turned it over. Sometimes the developer printed the date on the photo, but not on this one. He slipped it back into place.

The bedside table had a single drawer. It contained a tube of hand lotion, some cough drops, a couple of pens, and a slim paperback book. John took out the book. The glossy cover was illustrated with the folds of a red satin sheet. He flipped a few pages and his eyebrows shot up. Good God, female porn. He had a sudden image of little Ms. Hastings curled in her narrow bed, reading this very book. She'd have on a man's T-shirt, and her hand would be creeping up under the hem to her—

"Find anything?" Larson called from the kitchen.

John nearly dropped the book. As it was, he had to clear his throat. "Nope. You?"

"Not unless you consider ten cans of sardines a clue." Larson sounded disgusted.

John smirked, dropped the book back in Turner's drawer, and closed it. "What about the call log?"

"The last call was from Tommy Zucker. Old guy, lives north of town."

"Good work."

John ambled across the room to her dresser. On it was a jewelry box with a few inexpensive necklaces and a tarnished silver charm bracelet. He pulled out a drawer and found cotton panties and plain white bras. Another drawer held socks, all neatly paired and rolled. He ran his hand under the clothes and around the sides of the drawers. In the sock drawer, his hand struck a cold piece of metal. John drew it out. It was a man's steel watch, the band expandable. He turned it over. On the back was engraved *"Russell Turner, 1955."* John walked back to the photo on Turner's bedside table. Sure enough, the guy holding the fish had a on a steel-colored watch. 'Course, it was impossible to tell from the small photo if the watch was the same one, but he'd be willing to bet a month's pay that it was ol' Russ holding that fish.

Larson appeared in the doorway. "Should I do the bathroom?"

"Yeah. Wait a sec, though." John flipped the photo around to face the other man. "Know him?"

"Yes, sir." Larson took a couple steps into the room. "That's Rusty Turner. He was Turner's uncle."

"Was?"

"He died about three, no four, years ago." The deputy scratched the back of his neck. "It was a big scandal. Mr. Hyman caught him embezzling from the bank and had to fire him."

"Really." John's eyebrows raised. "But Hyman didn't mind hiring Turner part-time?"

Larson shrugged. "Wasn't Turner's fault. Besides, it happened four years ago. Mr. Hyman's a forgiving man."

"But is Turner Hastings?"

"What?"

"Nothing." John put the photo back. "You finished in the kitchen?"

"Yes, sir. I'll get to the bathroom." The younger man backed out of the room.

John returned to the bureau and pulled out the second row of drawers. He found sweaters and jeans. At least she owned some casual clothing. The next drawer had pajamas—all in flannel. This woman was in dire need of a Victoria's Secret catalog. At the back of the drawer was a little denim drawstring sack. John opened the strings. Needles spilled into his palm from the sack. Pine needles. And all at once he identified the smell in her house: pine. Not the overwhelming artificial scent found in household cleaners, but the faintly acid green smell of fresh pine. He held his palm up to inhale, and suddenly he could picture the blue mountains of Wyoming. Carefully, he slid the pine needles back into the little sack, retied it, and replaced it in the drawer.

John looked around the room. The only thing left unsearched was a small desk in the corner. He pulled out the wooden straight chair and sat in front of the desk.

It was an antique, made of dark wood on turned legs, with two small drawers on either side and a wide drawer across the bottom. The middle section folded up and back to reveal a writing surface that could be pulled out, along with a row of pigeonholes.

John pulled out the bottom drawer. It was filled with loose snapshots, scattered like leaves beneath a dead tree. He stirred the pile with his index finger. Here was a black-and-white of a woman with a baby and a small boy. There, a young man in the black robe and mortarboard hat of graduation. Russell Turner was in several, his face always red, always smiling. John stirred the pile again and found a small photo of Turner herself. She looked maybe sixteen or seventeen, dressed in shorts and a halter top, sitting on the wide wooden steps of a house. She smiled shyly at him from the photo. Her eyes were tilted at the corners and green, like a cat's. John looked at the snapshot for several seconds, rubbing his thumb lightly over Turner's small face.

He replaced the snapshot, shut the bottom drawer, and pulled out the right-hand drawer. Inside were her checkbook and a box of blank checks. He turned to the balance in the checkbook. She was the type to meticulously balance her checkbook as she wrote a check. According to the last line, she had $1,056.73 in her checking account. He found a savings account, as well, with over five thousand dollars in it.

The pigeonholes held a box of paper clips, some pens and pencils, a calculator, and two unpaid bills, one from Visa and one from a gas station. On both credit card accounts the previous balance had been paid off. Unless Turner had a lot of outstanding debt not apparent here, she hadn't robbed Hyman's safe deposit box for the money. Interesting.

John pulled out the last desk drawer, the left-hand one, and found a small black datebook. He flipped through it and smiled. She'd obviously started the year with good intentions. January and February had lists and dates filled in, March and April had tapered off, and by August the pages were blank. He turned back to the front page, where the owner had the option of filling in pertinent information. Turner had still been in her good-intentions stage when she'd done that page. All the spaces were filled in—including the one for her cell phone.

Huh. John took out his own cell and punched in Turner Hastings' number.

Chapter Seven

The phone rang in the dark, and for a moment Turner was disorientated. Why wasn't she in bed? Where was the bedside table? Then she remembered. She'd robbed Calvin's safe deposit box, and she was in Tommy's baby blue Chevy. She sat up and rubbed a kink in her back. Although the Chevy's vinyl front seat was big, it was far from comfortable. She'd chosen a back lane to park in for the night, a little-used access road to one of the many small lakes that dotted the area around Winosha. It had the advantage of being remote and deserted, but at this time of night it was also pitch-black.

The phone rang again.

She pressed the button on her wristwatch to make it light up—2:34 a.m. Who could be calling her at this hour? She rummaged blindly in her purse and pulled out the hysterically ringing phone. The number displayed on the lit screen wasn't familiar, and she hesitated a moment before answering.

"Hello?"

"Turner Hastings?" The voice was slow and deep and very, very male.

She felt a shiver go down her spine even though the night was hot. The voice sounded official. "Yes?"

"This is Special Agent John MacKinnon of the FBI. I'd like to ask you a few questions."

She'd been expecting something like this, but all the same, it came as a bit of a shock that they'd contacted her so soon. Turner didn't let the shock enter her voice, however. She'd had many years to learn how to hide her mental state.

"So, go ahead." She'd read somewhere that they could trace cell-phone calls but that the trace wasn't very accurate. Even so, she didn't want to stay on the line too long.

"I was kind of hoping you'd come back to Winosha and we could talk here." The FBI agent sounded wry.

"I'm sorry, Mr. MacKinnon," she replied politely, as if she were turning down a telemarketer trying to sell her siding. "That's just not possible."

"The thing is, ma'am, we have a bank surveillance tape here, and in it you appear to be stealing the contents of Calvin Hyman's safe deposit box. Why don't you come in so we can clear this up?"

"I don't think coming in will clear things up at all, Mr. MacKinnon. You see, you're right. I did steal the contents of Calvin's bank box."

And she hung up.

Turner opened her suitcase and dug around for one of her jars of pickled herring. Waking up in the middle of the night always made her hungry. She was just unscrewing the lid when the phone went off again. She picked out a square of fish with her thumb and forefinger and delicately ate it while contemplating the ringing phone on the seat beside her. She probably shouldn't answer it, but it was very hard to resist. Curiosity had always been a problem with her.

"Yes?"

"Three things, ma'am." He really did have a sexy voice. Of course, he was most likely fifty and bald, with a paunch and bad breath.

"Yes?"

"One, we FBI guys prefer to be addressed as Special Agent so-and-so."

"I'll try to remember that," Turner replied, her voice grave. "Number two?"

"I really do wish you'd come in."

"I'm so sorry, Special Agent MacKinnon, but being arrested just doesn't fit into my plans for the night."

A moment's pause as the good agent processed her frank response. "Really? What exactly were you planning to do?"

She smiled in the dark. "I don't think it's in my best interest to answer that question."

"Ah. How about a cup of coffee?"

Turner held the phone away from her ear and peered at it. If she didn't know any better, she'd think . . . "Are you asking me for a date?"

"Could be."

Intrigued, she asked, "And where would you buy me a cup of coffee at this time of night? The Kwik Trip?"

"I'm sure the coffee is very good there."

"You obviously haven't tried it."

"There's that café in town—"

"Doesn't open until six a.m. This is a small town,

Special Agent MacKinnon. And anyway, wouldn't it spoil things a bit when you put the handcuffs on me?"

"We could save that for later."

She ate another piece of herring, carefully juggling both fish and phone. "Isn't asking for a date an odd way to go about capturing a fugitive?"

"It's not a technique I use too often."

"I should hope not." Turner frowned. "I'd hate to think that was how my tax dollars were being spent."

"Everyone always worries about their tax dollars—"

"With good reason!"

He sighed into the phone. "I take it that's a no?"

"I'm afraid so." Turner nibbled a piece of onion.

"What are you eating?"

"Pickled herring."

"Pickled *what?*"

"Herring." Turner rolled her eyes. Where was this guy from? "You know, the fish?"

"Pickled fish." His voice was deadpan, but she caught an undertone of horror.

She smirked. "Yes. It's very good."

"I'll just have to take your word on that, ma'am."

"Well, you can," she replied tartly. "Where are you from anyway, that you haven't heard of pickled herring?"

"Wyoming."

She had a sudden image of a cowboy in dusty boots and chaps, his hat pulled low over his eyes. *Stop that!* "You should try some local cuisine now that you're in Wisconsin."

"I think I'll stick to cheese curds."

"Chicken."

"Yes, ma'am. At least when it comes to pickled seafood. Not when it comes to other things, though." His voice was so low it was almost a growl. "You want to tell me where you are?"

She shivered. "Not really, no."

"Make this thing a whole lot easier."

"For you, maybe. Not for me." She frowned. Why was he bantering with her like this? "Are you trying to keep me on the line so you can trace the call?"

"That would be the smart thing to do." He seemed to mutter it to himself.

"Are you saying you're not tracing me?" she asked suspiciously. This wasn't how she would've imagined an FBI agent talked to a suspect.

"Well—"

"I didn't fall off the turnip truck yesterday, you know." People sometimes had such odd notions about small-town folk.

"No, ma'am."

"Are you laughing at me?"

"Wouldn't dream of it."

"Humph." She gazed sightlessly at the black night outside her windows. "What was the third thing? You said you wanted to tell me three things."

A pause, then his voice came back, dead serious. "I always get my man. Or woman."

Turner's eyes widened. She should laugh at him—the phrase was too melodramatic. But coming from him, with his deep, slightly drawling voice and that honest tone, she believed it. Panic gripped her. She punched the phone off and all but threw it onto the other seat. She hurriedly put the lid back on the jar of herring, started the Chevy, and tore down the back road in the dark with no idea where she was headed. She just needed to move.

It had been far too long since she'd had someone to talk to. *Really* talk to. Someone who related to her as Turner-the-woman, not Turner-the-small-town-librarian. She'd spent so many years waiting for one thing that she'd become vulnerable. The first time someone—a man—showed the slightest sympathy, seemed to know how to connect with her sense of humor, and she got all mushy. Mushy would land her in jail—or worse.

Best not to be mushy.

Chapter Eight

About the time they parked outside Todd Frazer's small real-estate office the next day, John began to worry that he'd made the wrong lunch choice. He and Larson had spent the morning talking to the redheaded bank cashier, a rather hostile young woman who hadn't helped his blood pressure. She seemed to feel that Turner's theft was a personal affront against her. Add to that her private relationship with the deputy—they had apparently just broken up—and the interview had been downright uncomfortable.

After that, they'd looked around for a bite to eat. When it came to dining options, Winosha offered the café that he'd had breakfast at—unappetizingly named the Greasy Grill—and pizza from the local gas station. He and Larson had gone with a couple of slices of pepperoni pizza washed down by a tankard of Diet Coke. Now John felt a burning sensation in his chest. Wonderful. The way the day was progressing, either he was developing a bad case of heartburn or he was building up to a heart attack.

Frazer's real-estate office was in a white prefab house with pressure-treated wood steps and railing. They'd already tried Frazer's house, but apparently the man was voluntarily working on a Sunday. John didn't like him already. A sign in the yard read, "BIG WOODS REAL ESTATE." He and Larson climbed the steps and entered the front door. Inside, the tiny room was so freezer-cold he could feel the sweat congealing on his back unpleasantly. The room was carpeted in industrial gray, a single desk positioned dead center. Two client chairs bracketed a suspiciously green plant against the outer wall. A young woman with long, straight black hair clipped on one side sat behind the desk. She looked startled to see them. Must not have too many walk-ins on a Sunday. Either that or Larson's uniform spooked her.

"Can I help you?"

"I'm looking for Todd Frazer." John showed her his identification.

Her eyes widened. "He went home for lunch." She looked past him to Larson, as if seeking a personal testimonial from the deputy that she wasn't lying.

"We must've passed him, then. Do you expect him back here after lunch?" John asked gently.

The woman glanced around the room vaguely. "Um, I think so."

"Good. We'll wait." John sat in one of the molded plastic chairs, ignoring the receptionist's look of alarm.

Larson inquired where the restroom was and left the room when it was pointed out. The receptionist stared at John.

He sighed. "Do you have any Tums?"

She jumped and looked down at her desktop as if there might be a roll sitting there that she hadn't noticed before. "No, I'm sorry. Do you want me to run out and get some for you?"

"No, thanks. I'm okay." *Not.*

The receptionist continued to stare. John suppressed an urge to bare his teeth at her and closed his eyes instead.

He and Torelli were booked into a local mom-and-pop motel because the two chain motels in town were full. Tourist season. He hadn't been in his room long—they'd got to the motel around three a.m. and been up at the crack of dawn. The mattress had been thin and lumpy, and he suspected that the pillow under his head last night had been cut from a piece of old foam. Add to that the clanking air conditioner—which despite its noise didn't produce much in the way of cold air—and he hadn't slept all that well. Perhaps his lack of sleep accounted for the incipient heartburn and the beginnings of a headache.

And then there'd been that phone call with Turner Hastings last night.

He'd been surprised at how husky Turner's voice had been. He must've subconsciously been expecting a higher, lighter tone since she was so small. Instead, she had the strained, low voice of a woman who'd been screaming. Or one who hadn't talked at all for a very long time. One who'd only now begun to come awake. That thought intrigued him. What had kept her from speaking, from living? She'd not been alarmed by his phone call. They could've been talking about the summer heat instead of federal charges that might very well put her in prison. She was a smart woman, he had to believe that, so she knew just how much trouble she was in. Yet it didn't faze her. That kind of reckless bravado shouldn't turn him on.

But it did.

Someone opened the outer door and John looked up. The man who entered was midthirties, slim, about five-ten, and wearing wire-rim glasses. He stopped and glanced at the receptionist, who rolled her eyes exaggeratedly at John.

The guy unconsciously repeated her earlier query. "Can I help you?"

Larson chose that moment to emerge from the back. Frazer, if that's who he was, looked at the deputy in confusion. "What's going on?"

John stood. "Special Agent John MacKinnon of the FBI, Mr. Frazer. I'd like to ask you a few questions, if you don't mind." He phrased it as a request but figured the other man was smart enough to know it was a command.

He was. "Well, sure." The confusion didn't leave Frazer's face. "Uh, Sylvie, hold my calls, will you?"

The realtor opened the door to an inner office. The space was mostly taken up by metal filing cabinets—three of them—and a big metal desk. Frazer went around the side of the desk and tried to reestablish authority in his own domain by settling into the swivel chair behind the massive metal furniture.

John strolled to the filing cabinets. Several framed photos were grouped on the wall above them. "I understand that you and Turner Hastings used to date."

"Yes." Frazer frowned, clearly puzzled. "We were engaged."

"For how long?" The photos were mostly of a petite

blonde with an overbite. In several, she held a towheaded toddler.

"Almost a year." Frazer glanced at Larson. The deputy stared stonily back. Not bad for a kid. "But that was four years ago. I've married Debbie since then. We've been married almost three years. Why are you asking about Turner?"

"Have you seen Ms. Hastings recently?"

"I wouldn't say recently."

John turned and looked at the man without replying.

Frazer flushed. "We attend the same church. I probably saw her there in the last month."

"When?"

"Four, six weeks ago?" Frazer looked at Larson again. "I don't remember. My wife would've seen her more recently. She takes Colin to the story hour at the library."

"Your wife knows you were engaged to Ms. Hastings?"

"The whole town knows." Frazer snorted. "It's hardly a secret."

"It doesn't bother your wife?"

"Debbie knows I love her," the man said simply.

John watched him a moment, then nodded. "Why did you and Ms. Hastings break up?"

"Look, this was over four years ago. Why do you want to know?"

Like the outer lobby, Frazer's office had two chairs in front of the desk for visitors. John took one. "You don't have any Tums, do you?"

"Uh, I might." Frazer pulled out a drawer in his desk, rummaged in it, and offered half a roll.

"Thanks." John took four and gave the rest of the

packet back. "Ms. Hastings was at the bank when it was robbed."

"Yes, I know."

"Apparently in the confusion following the robbery, she took the opportunity to open Calvin Hyman's safe deposit box and steal the contents."

Frazer cocked his head and then shook it as if checking his hearing. "What?"

John was pretty sure the other man had heard him. He chewed fruit-flavored chalk while he waited for Frazer to digest the news.

Finally, Frazer asked, "But why?"

"Well, that's sort of what we're trying to figure out."

"Are you certain?" The other man was still shaking his head. "I mean, could it have been someone else?"

"Nope." John swallowed the chalk slurry in his mouth. "Caught her on the bank surveillance tape."

"It doesn't make sense. I doubt she needs the money. And that thing with Calvin was over years ago."

"What thing?"

"The stuff with her uncle, Rusty Turner." Frazer glanced at Larson. "Surely you've heard about that?"

"Why don't you tell me your version."

"Well." Frazer scratched his jaw and sat up straighter. "Rusty Turner used to work for the bank. He was the vice president, in fact. He was a nice guy, everyone liked him in this town, but it turned out he'd been embezzling from the bank for years."

John raised his eyebrows.

"Calvin found out and"—Frazer shrugged—"he had to fire him. Calvin had no choice. Can't have a guy embezzling from any company, especially not a bank."

"What did Turner do?"

"Not much she could do, was there? Everyone knew Rusty had done it. I remember she was mad at Calvin. I suppose that was natural, but she got over it."

Did she? John stretched his legs and crossed them at the ankles. He folded his hands on his lower belly. "You said you broke up four years ago. Was it around the same time as the embezzlement?"

"A little later." Frazer frowned in thought. "After Rusty's funeral. I remember that."

"How did Mr. Turner die?"

"He had a heart attack." Frazer's eyes widened again behind his little glasses. "It wasn't murder or anything like that, if that's what you're thinking. He was in his sixties, had a history of high blood pressure and high cholesterol, from what I understood, and he just died one day."

"Keeled over from a heart attack," John murmured. He picked up a paper clip from Frazer's desk and slowly unbent it.

"Yes, if you want to put it like that," Frazer said stiffly. He seemed offended.

"So why did you and Turner break up?"

"I guess we just grew apart. You know how it is. You see less and less of a woman until you realize one day that the relationship died while you weren't paying attention."

Wasn't that the truth? John nodded. "Who finally broke it off?"

"I think Turner called me and let me know she was returning my ring. I suppose that was when we formally broke up. But it wasn't a dramatic confrontation or anything. By that point I knew it was only a matter of time, and she must have, too."

John smoothed the paper clip into a straight piece of wire. "Can you think of any reason she'd be angry with Calvin Hyman now?"

"No." Frazer spread his hands. "That's why it doesn't make any sense."

"Nothing at all?"

"No, nothing."

John was silent. He made a spiraling circle out of the wire. They could hear the clicking of keys as Sylvie the receptionist typed at her computer. Larson shifted in his chair, making it groan.

"I-I mean if it'd been four years ago," Frazer finally stuttered into the silence, "I could understand."

"Why's that?"

"She was pretty mad at Calvin at the time. I remember at Rusty's funeral she told me she thought Calvin had embezzled the money himself and somehow framed Rusty."

"And how did you reply?"

"What could I say?" Frazer sounded frustrated. "She was obviously upset over her uncle's death. People don't always say things they mean at times like that."

"You think she didn't mean what she said about Mr. Hyman?" John glanced up at the man.

"She couldn't have, could she? Calvin Hyman is the bank president. He's the mayor of this town. Politically and socially, he's very active. How likely is it that he'd embezzle from his own bank?"

"'Course you could say that about Mr. Turner, as well."

"Huh?"

John stood and flipped the paper-clip spiral onto Frazer's desk. "How likely is it that the vice president would embezzle from his own bank?"

Frazer stared up from his seat behind the desk, apparently forgetting his authority moves. "Calvin has everything. Why would he need more?"

John smiled. "In my experience, desire has very little to do with need."

Chapter Nine

Turner peered into the Chevy's rearview mirror and carefully snipped off a hank of straight dark hair. She was a bit anxious about cutting her own hair, but it wasn't like she could walk into Bea's Clip 'n' Snip on Main and ask for a cut and style. Not without being arrested, anyway. She'd had no choice but to take the scissors into her own hands, so to speak, and she was rather pleased with the result. Probably it helped that she wasn't trying for any particular style.

She trimmed the wisps at her temple and then looked at her wristwatch. 5:50 p.m. Calvin and Shannon should be leaving for the Lutheran church potluck dinner soon. It was held the second Sunday of the month, and the Hymans were regular attendees. At least they'd been for the last year. They'd started attending about the time that Calvin must've decided to make a bid for the state legislature seat. The current legislator was Mason Carter, who was retiring after his term ended because of poor health. Carter had already endorsed Calvin, and since the seat was traditionally a Republican one, Calvin was pretty much a shoo-in for it. Assuming everything went well and he got the Republican nomination in two weeks' time.

Turner sighed and checked the rearview mirror again. It looked like the left side of her hair was a tad longer than the right, but it was hard to tell in the little mirror. She shrugged and put away the scissors.

The sound of a car engine came from the rural lane. She instinctively slumped down in her seat, even though she'd made sure to pull the Chevy far enough off into the woods so that she couldn't be seen easily.

The car drove past.

She got out her binoculars, climbed to her knees, and turned to look out the back window of the Chevy. From this position she could just make out the county road the car would turn into. After a minute, a car drove past. Yep, that was Calvin's cream Cadillac retreating into the distance. She waited another ten minutes in case they forgot something and returned.

But they didn't. She pulled on her gloves, picked up a small paper bag, and got out of the truck. The day hadn't cooled off yet, and as she hiked up the lane to the drive she felt perspiration dampen her freshly shorn hair. The Hymans lived in a new house, a huge monstrosity with multiple gables, pale brick facing, and two-story pillars flanking the front door. It was on five acres of land outside of town. A long, grassy lawn rolled down to meet the road, brilliantly green in contrast to the surrounding brown weeds. The Hymans must have spent a fortune watering the lawn.

Turner walked up the gravel drive without worry that she'd be seen; the nearest neighbor was half a mile away.

She strolled around the back of the house and stopped dead. An enormous black-and-white dog was sitting in a chain-link kennel. Her heart leaped into her throat before she realized that the animal couldn't get out on its own. It was huge, like a giant Dalmatian, only with pointed ears. Maybe some kind of Great Dane? Whatever it was, it stared at her, tall ears pricked forward.

Turner sidled toward the brick patio at the back of the house. The dog stood up, pink tongue lolling from massive jaws. It looked hot, and no wonder—the kennel was in the sun. She snorted. Only Calvin would put out a dog without shade.

She waited for the dog to start barking at her, but it merely watched her approach the house. The patio had a teakwood picnic table and chairs and a fancy-looking gas grill. A set of French doors led to the kitchen. She examined the doors for a minute. Damn. Should've brought a hammer. Fortunately, several concrete pigs were placed artistically in the flower bed surrounding the patio. Turner selected a self-satisfied-looking porker—it was sitting on its haunches, grinning—and heaved him through the doors. The glass shattered with a spectacular crash. She glanced over her shoulder. The dog had its massive head cocked but didn't look particularly excited. Maybe he'd watched the house being burgled before. Turner picked up a spatula from the grill. She took a moment to knock out a couple of big pieces of glass from the doorframe and then stepped through.

The kitchen was vaulted with a distressed-beam ceiling and a thingy for holding copper pots hanging over the island. The theme had probably originally been conceived as French Provincial. But sometime between the planning and the execution, it had been attacked by a platoon of pigs. Pigs cantered down the wallpaper, frolicked on the curtains over the sink, and sat complacently on the counter in the form of ceramic jars.

Turner blinked for a second, then headed down the hall. She passed a bath, a great room with an enormous fireplace, the stairs, and an empty guest bedroom. The hall dead-ended, and she reversed to the stairs. On the upper level, the master bedroom sprawled over most of the second floor. She paused in the doorway to scan the room but didn't see what she was looking for.

The next room was pay dirt.

It was a study—Calvin's, she knew by the fishing-themed border that circled the room at head height. Not a single pig in sight. A dark desk with a bookcase/hutch contraption over and around it stood in one corner. Another table branched off it, with a computer monitor on top and the keyboard on a pull-out surface under the table.

Turner felt like crowing. She sat at the desk and flipped on the computer, then went through the desk while waiting for it to boot up. The hutch held a few books, *The Da Vinci Code,* a couple of Clive Cusslers, some fishing books, and a whole row of *Chicken Soup* for various and sundry souls. Brass navigation instruments were placed artistically at intervals—as if Calvin would know how to use a sexton. There was a framed photo of Calvin and a bunch of guys standing on ice and holding dead fish. She peered closer. Frozen dead fish. They must've been ice fishing. One of the men looked like a former Republican governor.

She made a raspberry and started pulling out drawers.

The middle drawer held paper clips, pens, staples, Post-it notes, and a key ring with four keys on it. In the back were papers, and she flipped through them but didn't find anything incriminating. She decided to check the computer before she went any further—after all, it was the most likely source of information. Calvin had fishing wallpaper on his computer with little cartoon fish jumping over the bow of a rowboat. She opened *My Documents* and found a list of files.

Ten minutes later, she sat back in frustration. She wasn't a computer expert by any means, but she knew as much as the average computer owner did nowadays, and she saw no trace of an accounting file. Shoot. Calvin had to have another set of books for the bank. How else could he keep track of the money he was embezzling? She'd gambled—and lost—yesterday when she took the opportunity to open his safe deposit box. She'd hoped it would contain a computer disc or even literal ledgers detailing the money he was stealing from the bank.

If he hadn't kept a concrete record . . .

No, she wouldn't go there. It did her no good at all to think that he had no record, no evidence of his crime. He must. And since he must, she would find it.

She opened more desk drawers. The right-hand side drawer held a black handgun. Sheesh. She hoped it wasn't loaded. The next drawer held files. She paged through household appliance warranties, medical records, a copy of his car insurance, and bills.

If you didn't keep accounting books on a computer, then where would you keep them? Not at his bank desk, surely. Even Calvin wasn't that confident. Besides, she'd searched there more than once and had never found anything besides the safe deposit key. That left this house. Another drawer held a file of brochures for fishing boats and motors, maintenance records for the Caddy, and the mortgage information for a lake cabin.

Surely he wouldn't keep it in the car. Shannon could run across it at any time, and Turner didn't think Shannon knew about her husband's illegal activities. At least she couldn't see Shannon—the biggest gossip in town—keeping silent about them if she did.

She pulled out the center drawer again, and her eyes hit the key ring. A cabin. Would Calvin hide the evidence there? It wouldn't be as accessible as the house, but it wouldn't be hard to get at, either. Who questioned a man visiting his own cabin? And in Calvin's case, a cabin would have the added bonus of not being under Shannon's daily control. He wouldn't have to worry about her finding suspicious books while he was away at work.

Turner picked up the key ring and examined it. Two of the keys were identical and looked like they fit an ordinary door lock. The remaining two were different. One was for an ignition, the other a small, narrow key.

She pocketed them all. She glanced at the wall clock, which took the form of a walleye circling a fishing lure. 6:45 p.m. The Hymans shouldn't be back for another hour or more, but she didn't want to take any chances.

She took a piece of printer paper and wrote down the address of the cabin listed on the mortgage papers. Then she stood and looked around the room. She had a strong urge to smash the computer and all the pretty sailing instruments. The Lord knew Calvin deserved it. But that wouldn't help her cause. Instead, she switched off the computer and replaced everything neatly, just to mess with his mind.

She backtracked to the master bedroom. Ew. The bedspread was quilted pink satin and had flying pigs on it. She upended the paper sack onto the middle of the tacky bedspread. Gold coins, jewelry, stocks, and a couple of certificates of deposit slithered around the spread. All from Calvin's safe deposit box.

Turner suddenly thought about the FBI agent who'd called her. What would he think when he saw what she'd done? Would he understand the message to Calvin? It gave her an odd feeling, knowing that MacKinnon was following in her footsteps, analyzing her every move. Not that it mattered. Her message was for Calvin, and he'd surely understand what it meant: *I'm not after your money. I'm after you.*

Turner smiled. She did a quick check of the rest of the house, just in case she was wrong about where Calvin would hide the evidence, but didn't find anything more incriminating than bad decorating taste. Half an hour later, she gave up and went back downstairs.

Outside, the dog must've lost interest waiting for her to return, because he'd laid back down on the concrete floor of his kennel, mailbox head on his crossed paws. He came to his feet as she exited the broken patio doors, and then he gave a tentative tail wag. Turner ignored him and began walking around the house.

Behind her, a low moan started.

She kept going.

The moan turned to a mournful howling. *Roooow. Roorooow. Rororrorwoooooow. Eek!* The howl ended on a strange high squeak.

Turner swung around. "Hush!" she hissed at the animal sternly. "Aren't you ashamed of yourself, a great big dog crying like a puppy?"

His jaw dropped open, huge tongue lolling as he wagged his tail at her.

Turner frowned at him and noticed an overturned red bowl by the door of the kennel. "What did you do? Flip your water bowl?"

At her words, the dog's entire rear end started wiggling. She sighed, unlocked the kennel, and reached in carefully for the bowl. The dog watched her, tail slowly wagging. She found the outside water spigot, filled the red bowl, and placed it within reach of the dog. It noisily lapped at the water.

She started walking away again.

Rooow. Rooowrowrooooow. Eek!

She turned around. The dog was staring at her, jaw closed, water dripping from its muzzle. It gave a tentative tail wag.

"What?" For God's sake, she was talking to a dog. The enemy's dog at that. Except it was very hard to see this animal as anyone's enemy. And what kind of jerk left a big dog out in the August heat without water? "Fine."

Turner marched over to the kennel and opened the chain-link door wide. The dog swiped her hand with his tongue and then made a bounding victory lap around the yard.

"Come on." She picked up the red bowl and set off down the drive.

The dog barked once and followed.

Chapter Ten

It was almost midnight by the time John made it back to the dinky Starlight Inn motel Sunday night. He parked the navy Crown Victoria in front of his room and got out slowly, almost expecting his knees to creak. It had been a long day, and he hadn't needed the late-night call to investigate the Hyman home break-in.

The row of motel doors and the cracked sidewalk beneath were illuminated by a bare yellow bulb. Moths and mosquitoes were swarming the light. Every now and then, an insect would hit the bulb with a *dink* sound. Poor bastards, doomed to a pointless death because of evolutionary wiring that no longer worked. There was probably a moral in there somewhere.

He unlocked his motel room. No modern card keys here. John shut the flimsy door behind him and turned the little knob lock—as if it would stop a determined three-year-old. The AC had cut off sometime during the day, and the room was oven hot. He toed off his boots and socks, stripped off his jacket and holster, laying the

Glock on the crummy bedside table, and then took off his shirt. He cranked the air-conditioning unit as far as it would go—which was not very. He needed a shower. He needed a beer. And he needed to talk to Turner Hastings. If he was smart, he'd start with the first, spend some time on the second, and forget all about the third. But he'd never been too bright when it came to women. He skipped directly to the third.

John took out his keys, wallet, and cell from his pocket, dropped them on the bedside table, stripped off his pants, and flung himself on the bed, wearing only his shorts. He stuffed the foam pillow under his neck, picked up the cell, and hit the speed dial.

"Mmm?" Her voice was so husky it was scratchy. He must've woken her.

Oh, man. His horny brain immediately flashed on her in a big soft bed, wearing a black silk shorty nightie—no, make it red—the shoulder straps sliding down her arms, her nipples poking at the fabric.

He shifted on the bed. "Did you have to throw the pig through the window?"

There was a silence on the other end. Then she said, "You woke me up. Again."

"I figured if I had to be awake because of you, you should be, too."

"You're angry."

"Oh, just a little. Do you have any idea how Shannon Hyman feels about pigs?"

"Well, I did see the kitchen. Pig wallpaper." She sounded more awake now, but her voice was just as husky.

He wondered idly if she was aware of the effect that

voice had on men. Probably not. "Would that have been on the way to ransacking Hyman's study?"

"Why, yes, it would." Bit of testiness there.

John grinned. Good. "That's breaking and entering, you know. Emphasis on the breaking."

"Hey, I was careful with Calvin's desk. I left it neater than when I first saw it."

"Yeah, but he liked it the way he had it, neat or not."

She snorted on the other end of the phone.

"And did you have to take the dog?" he asked. He'd nearly laughed in Hyman's face when the man finally realized that his expensive pet was missing. The guy had been furious, although John suspected it was more from the loss of money than affection for the animal.

"Yes, I did," Turner said.

"It's worth a lot of money," John replied gently. "Did you know that? It's some kind of fancy-ass purebred Great Dane. I wasn't even aware they came in different colors."

"Then Calvin should've taken better care of it."

"What are you going to do with a Great Dane?"

"I don't know, but at least I can make sure he has water and food and companionship."

"And how do you know that Calvin didn't give the dog companionship?"

"Because he's got calluses on his elbows from sitting in that concrete kennel run."

"Why don't you bring back the dog, Turner?"

"And he squeaks when he howls."

"Turner."

Silence. Was it his imagination, or could he hear her breathing?

"What were you looking for?"

"I can't tell you that."

"Can't or won't?"

"Won't."

John blew out a breath. God, this conversation was frustrating. "Where are you?"

She sighed. "You don't really think I'm going to tell you that, either, do you?"

John stared at the fly-specked ceiling. This was getting him nothing except blue balls. What did he think he was doing, anyway? He was acting like a high school geek with a crush on the pretty, smart girl who sat in the back of chemistry. "Are you targeting Hyman because you still blame him for turning your uncle in?"

He heard her suck in her breath. "You've been talking to people."

"Yeah. It's kind of my job. So. Are you?"

"What do you think?"

"I think yes."

"Smart man."

"And I think you loved your uncle very much."

She sighed, the sound carrying clearly through the ether. "Yes, I did."

"So much so that you planned a bank robbery to get back at his accuser."

She surprised him. She laughed out loud. The sound was husky and low and tugged at his loins. "Is that what you believe?"

"Didn't you?"

She made a noncommittal sound.

"I saw you grab the key from Hyman's desk and skip right into that bank vault like it was planned."

"Looks can be deceiving," she whispered.

"What's that supposed to mean?"

Silence.

He sighed. "Of course, you left the entire contents of the safe deposit box on Hyman's bed tonight, which would lead some to believe it wasn't the money you were after."

More silence.

"Did you see today's crossword puzzle?" he asked softly.

"What?"

"The *Wisconsin State Journal* crossword." He shifted and reached for the newspaper from the bedside table where he'd left it this morning, nearly eighteen hours ago.

"Now, when would I have had the time to do that?" She sounded grumpy.

He smiled. "I got stuck a couple of times. Fifteen down, four letters, messenger goddess."

"Iris."

"Really?" He pulled out the bedside-table drawer and found a pen. "How about Indian royal, five letters."

"Ranee. You must not do too many crosswords. They're always using *ranee*."

"Yeah?"

"Yeah. And the crosswords in the local papers are real easy. You should try the *New York Times* or the *Chicago Tribune*."

"Really. Didn't know that." He tossed the pen and newspaper aside. "You'll have to teach me proper crossword etiquette."

"I don't think that's a good idea," she said.

"Maybe not, but it'd be fun."

"Good night, Special Agent MacKinnon."

"John."

"What?"

"Call me John."

A pause. "Good night, John."

The line clicked because she'd hung up, but he said it anyway. "Good night, Turner."

Then he punched off and put the phone on his bedside table. God, he was tired. It had been a long, long day, and he was at the point where it was hard to think. He needed to think. Something about Turner and the bank president . . .

John snorted. Hyman wanted round-the-clock security for himself and his house now. He claimed that Turner was on a vendetta against him. The sheriff had politely pointed out that Turner probably weighed a hundred pounds less than the bank president, but that had only made Hyman madder. Sheriff Clemmons had finally had to confess that even if he wanted to put a twenty-four-hour watch on Hyman, he just didn't have the manpower for the job. Hyman had shut up about security fast when he'd been told he could hire private bodyguards. But he hadn't looked happy. That man surely didn't like being made a fool of.

Was that what Turner's goal was? To humiliate the bank president? Because it wasn't too bright of her to stick around after knocking over a bank. She had to have some kind of reason to stay in the neighborhood besides robbing Hyman. Of course, the woman wasn't stupid. Maybe she'd taken off after the Hyman house robbery. Heck, she could be on the way to Mexico at this very minute. But he didn't think she was all that far away. Whatever Turner was doing included the bank president, and John was pretty certain she wasn't done. He remembered the expression of rage—and maybe fear—on Hyman's face when he'd seen the contents of his safe deposit box in the middle of his bed. John was almost certain that the other man knew what Turner's reason was for leaving her present. He sighed and turned off the bedside light.

He only hoped she hadn't underestimated her adversary.

Chapter Eleven

*D*ude." Nald stepped into something deep and squishy and had to wave his arms a moment before regaining his balance. "This is gross. This is alien-spurting, brain-sucking, rotting-zombie—"

"Eyeball-exploding," Fish panted, expanding on the thought. "Scottish toilet-spewing—" There was a loud *plop!* as Fish hit a particularly wet spot and toppled over, his garbage bag of bank money landing in the water.

Nald zigzagged around the fallen form of Fish. He was following Fish because Fish said he'd once come to this swamp to hunt ducks with his uncle Earl and therefore he knew it best. It was Nald's opinion that only a duck who was brain-dead *and* a retard would bother landing here, because, as he'd already said, it was *gross.* Also, it was pitch-black—whatever pitch was—and you couldn't even see your own arm in front of your face. Hell, you couldn't even see your own *dick.* They'd been wandering around this bog for, like, hours now.

Nald wrinkled his nose. "And dude, it smells—"

"Yeah." Fish struggled upright. "Refrigerator-gone-bad smells—"

"You smell, dude," Nald pointed out, because it was true. Bank robbing seemed to have a bad effect on Fish's armpits. "You smell like a road-killed skunk."

"Gross. We wouldn't be in this swamp in the first place if you hadn't wrecked the Camaro." Fish kept talking about the damn car.

"Not my fault."

"Who was driving the car?"

"Me," Nald admitted. "But—"

"Then it is, too, your fault! The stupid car didn't drive itself into that tree."

"I was looking for cops," Nald said with dignity. "Coulda happened to anyone."

"Not unless they were missing most of their brain." Fish made an odd gagging sound. "Gross! I think a bug flew in my mouth."

"Yeah?" Nald asked, interested. "Did you swallow it?"

"No way, booger-brain!"

"Do you think we can use the money with ink all over it?" Nald had been worrying about this point off and on for the last two days.

"'Course," Fish said. "Who's gonna care?"

That's what Fish had said every other time he'd asked, but somehow Nald couldn't find the same confidence. "Yeah, but—"

"Look, a twenty's a twenty, even if it's purple."

"Whatever," Nald said, losing interest.

"People would use a twenty if it had puke on it," Fish insisted. "There's no limit, man."

"Dude, this, *this* is the limit." Nald pulled his foot up.

It lifted with a loud sucking sound. "I haven't seen anything this gross since that chainsaw movie where the guy lays that girl's head open and she's all *ahh! ahh! ahh!* running around with her brains falling out."

"Would you shut up?"

"And the mosquitoes." Nald waved an arm in front of his face and nearly took off his own nose with the garbage bag of money he held. "Ow! Damn! I think they're draining me dry. They're gonna find my shriveled body, looking like the mummy in that film with Tarzan in it."

"Tarzan didn't fight the mummy, you dickhead."

Nald was offended. He knew his mummy movies. "Dickhead, yourself. He did, too—"

"Oh, yeah, like he's in the pyramids with Cheetah—"

"Cheetah wasn't there—"

"Ee-ee-ee! There's a mummy, Tarzan!"

"I'm telling you, Cheetah wasn't in *The Mummy.*"

"You said Tarzan—"

"Didn't you see *The Mummy?*" Nald asked, amazed. "Remember those bugs that crawled right under your skin and ran around until they hit your brain and then you start screaming and clutching your head and going *uhg! uhg! uhg!* until you can't stand it anymore and ran yourself into a wall headfirst?"

Fish seemed to remember that part. "Gross."

"Yeah."

"Remember when the mummy ate one of those bugs and you could see it because his cheek was all rotted away?"

"Gross!" Nald yelled gleefully.

"Think you could actually eat a bug?" Fish could get deep thoughts like that sometimes.

"Naw." Nald shook his head in the dark. "Well, maybe if I was starving."

"Like a slug. Could you eat a slug?"

"Gross!"

"Or what about a cockroach? Would you eat a cockroach?"

"It'd be crunchy. Gross!"

"Yeah, it'd be, like, crunch, crunch—"

"Crunch, crunch!" Nald joined in the cockroach-eating sounds.

Then they were silent a moment, and Nald could hear Fish running into a tree.

"But *why* do we have to go through a swamp?" Nald asked, because this was another question that had been bothering him. "Couldn't we take the road? I mean, it's right over there." He waved an arm in the general direction of the highway but then almost lost his balance again.

"I already told you. We got to lose the dogs."

"What dogs? There ain't no dogs around for—"

"There're always dogs in movies," Fish interrupted. "To track the prisoners."

"Shit." Nald walked into something wet and sticky and spent a few minutes getting it off his face. Then he stopped and stared into space. "Prison? I ain't going to no prison."

"That's the plan, doofus. *Not* going to prison."

"But—"

"If the dogs find us we're toast, right?"

"Uh—"

"So can't let the dogs find us."

Nald knew that there was a problem with this argument, but since he couldn't quite put his finger on it, he gave up. Besides, no matter what he said, Fish would do what he wanted. When Fish got an idea in his head, there was no stopping him. Which, come to think of it, was part of the reason they were in a swamp in the middle of the night.

"Why do you 'spose he wanted us to rob the bank?" Nald asked, following that train of thought.

"What?" Fish seemed to be stuck in the muck. His shadow had sunk about a foot.

Nald grabbed an arm and pulled. "Why did he want us to rob the bank?"

"For the money, duh."

"But he didn't get the money," Nald pointed out.

"Not our fault."

"Yeah. We were at the pickup spot," Nald agreed righteously.

"'Sides, maybe he forgot." Fish gasped as the bog let him go with a *pop!*

"But would you forget to pick up money?"

"No. But see, we're smart. We've got priorities. We don't forget money."

"I guess." Nald had a funny thought. "How do we know he's a guy?"

"What?"

"I mean. . . ." Nald had to stop and concentrate. "The voice on the phone was all Tron-like."

"So?"

"So maybe it was a chick, like, in disguise."

"Ooo! A hot chick?" Fish sounded psyched.

"Yeah." Nald brightened. "Like Buffy?"

"Or Trinity. She could've been using a voice-altering spy thing."

"No, dude," Nald objected. "That'd be the Tomb babe."

"Nuh-uh, douchebag. The Matrix chick is way cooler than any Tomb Raider—"

"She's got no tits!"

"Oh, tits-man." Fish was scornful. "Like, you're looking at Pamela Anderson. As if!"

"Boner!"

"Douchebag!"

Then they fell in the lake.

Chapter Twelve

The birds were just beginning to sing the next morning when Turner's cell rang. She stretched and yawned and pushed a dog head off her hip. The dog yawned, as well. She winced. The Great Dane's breath was awful, but that couldn't account for all of the smell in the truck.

She stank.

Somehow she hadn't considered how she was going to keep herself clean when she'd taken off on Saturday. Sunday had been hot and muggy, and no doubt today would be just as icky. In the summer on days like these, she often took two or more showers, and now she couldn't take any. Her scalp was beginning to itch at just the thought.

The cell, which had been ringing continuously, finally stopped, and she felt a brief twinge of regret that the FBI agent had given up. Then she shook that thought aside and got out of the truck with the dog so that they could both do their business in the bushes. While she was squatting, the cell started again. This shouldn't have lightened her mood, but it did. She hastily returned to the Chevy.

"Hello?"

"What're you having for breakfast?" His voice was low and scratchy, as if he hadn't been awake that long.

She smiled involuntarily. "I'm planning on pickled herring."

"For breakfast?" He sounded appalled.

She rolled her eyes. "It's not like I'm close to a diner."

"I am. I had two eggs over easy, hash browns, bacon, and buttered rye toast this morning."

"That can't be good for your heart."

"Don't I know it. And coffee."

"The coffee would be nice," she admitted.

"See? You could come in and I'd get you a big cup. With refills on me."

"That is a tempting offer, but I've got things to do today." The Great Dane reappeared from the bushes and trotted up to the truck. She let him in.

"And cream." His voice lowered. "Lots of real cream."

Turner sucked in a breath. How did he know? "I have no idea what you're referring to."

"Yes, you do. But if you want to get straight to business, fine with me. Where are you?"

"Far, far away from you," she lied.

"Uh-huh." He didn't sound like he'd bought the lie. "But see, this is the thing. I have this funny feeling that you're still hanging around Winosha."

"A funny feeling, huh?" She dug a jar of herring out from her suitcase. The dog instantly came to attention at the prospect of food.

"Yeah. Kind of at the base of my neck. Sort of a tingling."

"Maybe you need to see a chiropractor."

"Go ahead, laugh at me. I like a mean woman."

She gasped. "I'm not mean!"

"Sure you are, honey."

"What—"

"I went to see your old fiancé yesterday, Todd Frazer."

Her eyes narrowed. What could Todd have told him? "So?"

"So you dropped that boy like a ton of bricks."

"The breakup was mutual."

"He didn't even know why, did he?"

She breathed hard for a moment. How dare he?

"Just as well," he drawled obnoxiously. "He wasn't right for you."

"Now, look—"

"Couldn't stand . . . to you, could he?" The signal was beginning to disintegrate. Her batteries were low. But she heard his last words clearly. "I can."

Then the phone died.

It was just like John to get in the last word, but Turner found herself grinning anyway. It was kind of fun to trade insults with the man. She hadn't talked so freely to anyone in ages. There was no disguise to maintain with him, no deception she worried about revealing. He already knew her secrets. It was oddly liberating. On that thought, she sobered. The FBI agent must know exactly how seductive his casual conversations were for her. He was trying to capture her. She couldn't lose sight of that fact.

Turner tossed the cell on the seat beside the dog. She'd

have to charge it later at a wayside or rest stop, but right now she just wanted to get away. She started the truck and drove until the lane came to a T and then took a right onto a bumpy dirt road. Back here, the dry green forest was deserted. There were no marked trails, and the roads to the boat docks were on the other side of the lake. She came to an access lane—really only two tire tracks through brown grass—and pulled over. From the road, the Chevy was hidden. Taking her jar of herring, a bottle of water, and the crackers, she got out of the truck with the Great Dane. She made her way down a slope through the woods to the water's edge. The dog went to investigate the weeds at the waterline.

Turner stood still a moment and looked out at the lake—Redfin Lake, with its deep, quiet blue water. So blue it was like seeing the sky inverted. So blue it made your eyes hurt to look at it sometimes. So blue it instantly calmed her soul. Every single time. A lone great blue heron near the opposite bank noticed her arrival and took off, flying slowly, long legs trailing. The wind stirred the cattails and sent a little ripple scooting across the water.

Redfin Lake wasn't big—more of a glorified pond. And because of that, not many came to fish here. But Rusty had liked it. He'd brought his battered old boat here nearly every Saturday and puttered into the shallows just outside the cattail bed. He could spend the entire day catching perch and bluegill and the occasional northern, although he hadn't much liked the latter; too bony, he'd said. He'd bring an old red-topped cooler full of braunschweiger and mayo sandwiches, a few ripe tomatoes, and a couple of cans of beer.

Turner sat on a dry rock near the bank and opened her pickled-herring jar again. They really tasted better on saltines. Somehow the vinegar, fish, onions, and dry, salty cracker combined to make a sublime mush in her mouth. She ate three before twisting the cap off the bottle of water.

The last time she'd been here, it'd been with Rusty. A perfect day in June, four years ago. It would've been before the trouble at the bank, before he'd lost his job and everything else. He was still happy, still carefree, like a little boy, even though he was sixty-three. She'd been impatient; she'd wanted to do something else that day, probably work, though she couldn't remember now. But Rusty had kept at her until she'd agreed to come along to the lake. She remembered that they'd packed turnips from the garden. Big ones, because it was late in the season. She'd wrinkled her nose when Rusty had eaten one. He'd waved the lavender monster in front of her face, laughing. *Come on, Turner, try one. Lets you know you're alive when you taste the bite of a big old turnip.*

She'd refused. Rusty had eaten the turnip himself with a sad, concerned look in his eyes, like he wasn't too sure what to make of her. And he'd never had another turnip, big or otherwise, after that day. She wished now that she had shared it with him. Such a little thing, but it would've meant a lot to Rusty. She watched a muskrat swim by and wondered: how could such an old man have lived so much better, so much bigger, than she? Sometimes it felt like since his passing she'd been locked up in a glass box, doomed to watch others enjoy their lives. Unable to continue with hers. When she'd refused Rusty's lavender turnip, had she been refusing life itself?

Turner stared out at the still, dark blue water. It gave no answers.

Chapter Thirteen

$\mathcal{A}$t least the old guy didn't come out with a shotgun, John thought that morning. Seven-thirty a.m. would be a bitch of a time to be killed. He hadn't even had his full quota of coffee yet. Torelli had insulted the waitress early on in their breakfast at the café, and they'd been damn lucky she'd come back with the check. Coffee refills had been out of the question. Instead, after his morning phone call to Turner, he'd had to swing by the Kwik Trip. He'd filled his travel mug with the black water they called coffee but hadn't had time to drink it yet.

"What do you want?" the old geezer demanded, glaring from behind his cracked door.

"Mr. Zucker?" John asked patiently. Zucker's phone number had been the last one listed on Turner's phone.

"Yeah, yeah, I'm Zucker." The old man waved a hand like he was swatting a fly in front of his face. "Like to be called Tommy, though."

"Fair enough. I'm Special Agent John MacKinnon of

the FBI. I wonder if we could take a look around your place?"

"What for?"

"We're looking for Turner Hastings."

"Ha! She ain't here, so you can just go on back to arresting real criminals."

And he shut the door in John's face. Behind him, Larson cleared his throat like he was trying to smother a laugh. John sighed and knocked again. A cardinal called from a nearby tree. It was another beautiful sunny day, and the weathermen were all excited because it might hit a hundred degrees by noon. And of course he was wearing a jacket.

"What?" the old man yelled.

"Open the door, Tommy, or I'll kick it in."

"Hey! You'll be needing a warrant for that, Mr. G-man."

"I've got a warrant."

There was a short silence, then the sound of the door being unlocked. Tommy's face appeared again. "Fine. But anything gets broke and I'm suing the government."

"Good. You do that." John stepped into the dim interior and looked around.

Tommy had either been a bachelor for a very long time or he had no use for cleaning house. Or both. The walls were stacked floor to ceiling with magazines, newspapers, and folded paper bags. Drop a match and the place would go up in flames in five minutes flat. At least it was air-conditioned. Larson poked a pile of paper and the top half slowly slid off, raising a cloud of dust. The deputy sneezed violently.

"When was the last time you saw Ms. Hastings?" John asked Tommy.

The old man mimed zipping his mouth shut and throwing away the key.

John arched his eyebrows. "Come on. It can't hurt to tell me that."

"So you say now, Mr. G-man, but I'm keeping my chopper zipped shut. You'll have to drag me into the interrogation room, put bamboo slivers under my fingernails, beat me senseless—"

"Yeah. Yeah. I get the idea." John scanned the room. Unless Turner was hiding under the stained furniture, she wasn't here. He wove his way through the stacks to check the kitchen. There was a musty smell about the place. Ancient grease, dust, and old man. He couldn't see the average woman staying here without at least spraying the air with that stuff that came in aerosol cans. Turner's house had been pretty neat; she'd have picked up Tommy's place if she were living here. In the kitchen, the only clean-looking thing was a small white casserole dish. It sat by itself on the counter. John went over to look at it without touching. He heard the old man enter the room behind him.

He questioned Zucker without turning around. "She make you stuff to eat?"

Tommy didn't reply, so John opened the fridge door. Sitting among the beer bottles and junk food was another white casserole dish, a twin to the one on the counter. It looked like it contained a fancy tuna casserole.

"What're you after Turner for, anyway?" the old man burst out, apparently unable to hold his silence any longer. "She's about the only one in this town I can stand. And she makes me real nice food, puts in vegetables and everything, so's I get my fiber."

"She robbed the bank," John said.

The old man made a rude noise. "Shows how much you government men know."

John ignored that and took a look in the bathroom and two other rooms just to cover all the bases, then went out the back door, trailed by Larson. There was a triangle of dirt drive back here with dust-covered grass in the middle. A big, leaning barn and a couple of outbuildings surrounded the drive. The outbuildings didn't look to be in use anymore.

Tommy had followed him outside. "Done yet?"

John shook his head and headed toward the yard. "I'm going to search the barn."

"Hey, hey!" The old man was right behind him. "You'll need a different warrant for that."

"Larson, show Mr. Zucker the warrant." John didn't break his stride.

Inside the barn, he found a row of cars. Tommy was obviously using it as a garage. A workbench with a nice collection of tools took up one wall. John peered in the cars. Two of them—a station wagon and a Taurus—were dusty. They looked like they hadn't been moved in years. The third, a tan Ford Escort, had dust on the outside but was relatively spotless inside. And Turner drove a tan Escort. John stood back to consult his notebook. Yep, same plates. Now the question was, what had she taken from Tommy's fleet in place of the Escort?

His cell went off, and for a moment he felt a wash of excitement. Then he looked at the number and realized it was Torelli. He punched the answer button. "MacKinnon."

"They're inbred."

"Who?" John hunkered to take a look at the car's undercarriage.

"Fish's relatives. If I have my notes right, his mother married her uncle."

"Check your notes again."

Torelli muttered something, then came back with, "I can check my notes all you want, but the result's going to stay the same. This is an inbred, illiterate, backwater—"

"Torelli," John growled.

"What?"

"You do realize this phone line is unsecure, don't you?"

Silence on the other end. John wondered for a moment if Torelli would hang up on him. The guy was too full of himself. He still couldn't believe that the younger agent had gone over his head on the last—

"We found the car they used to flee the bank. Sir."

"Well, good."

"They ditched it in a field and apparently left on foot from there."

"On foot?" John opened the door on the driver's side of the Escort, reached in, and popped Turner's trunk.

"On foot."

"What do you think their plan is?" The trunk was almost pristine. Jumper cables, a first-aid kit, and one of those dinky spare tires. He slammed it shut. "They must have another car stashed somewhere."

"I'm not so sure. You haven't seen these guys' homes and relatives."

"So you're saying they have no plan at all?" He pushed the driver's seat back as far as it would go and got in. Then froze. *Pine.* He could smell the faint aroma of pine.

Torelli's voice brought him back. "I'm saying I think it's a good possibility."

"Huh."

"Look. I don't think these guys could find their own ass with both hands, let alone plan and execute a bank robbery."

"We both know it doesn't take a whole lot of brains—"

"No one knows where they got the shotguns."

John paused in the act of opening the glove compartment. "Neither man owned one?"

"Nope. And Fish's uncle has shotguns, but they're all accounted for. None of them look like they've been fired recently. I checked."

John rummaged in the glove compartment. He pulled out the Escort's manual, two tampons, some pens, and a couple of road maps. Nothing else, not even those little ketchup packets that usually multiplied in glove compartments.

"What's your point?"

"Someone else supplied them with the shotguns and planned the robbery. And the librarian is missing."

"And that's why I'm searching her car at this moment," John shot back irritably. "Get over there and find out where Fish and Nald went. They couldn't have gone far on foot. Call me when you have something."

He hung up without waiting for Torelli's answer, knowing that he was being unreasonable. It was one thing for him to be chasing Turner, and quite another for Torelli to be after her. Torelli was a smartass gunning for a fast-track promotion. John didn't trust the younger man as far as he could throw him, and he didn't want him anywhere near Turner when she was brought in.

Turner might be behind the bank robbery—maybe—but she definitely wasn't a hardened criminal. Which meant he'd just have to make sure that he caught her before Torelli did.

Chapter Fourteen

 $\mathcal{W}$ e have to work on this howling business," Turner muttered to the big black-and-white dog.

It wagged its tail in reply and kept following her, her very own huge, hard-to-miss shadow. She'd made a brief attempt to leave it in the Chevy while she went to talk to Tommy, but the moaning howl it had sent up soon put a stop to that. So now she was sneaking through the north woods with a Great Dane in tow.

"And I need to get you a name."

Turner stepped out into the road leading to Tommy's house and then stepped right back into the woods. The dog—George?—went out and trotted back, too, loping good-naturedly. It probably thought she always did a do-si-do whenever she came to roads. In fact, she'd seen the sheriff's car in Tommy's drive.

Shoot. Good thing she'd decided to park the Chevy and walk through the woods to Tommy's place instead of driving up. She crouched next to the dog—Arnold?—and tried to think what to do next. The binoculars dan-

gling from her neck swung against the dog, and it licked
her face. Ew, dog breath. It was hot, even under the
canopy of the trees, and her back itched like something,
a twig or leaf, had fallen down her T-shirt. She needed
to talk to Tommy, get directions to Calvin's cabin, and
find out what he knew about it—like if there were close
neighbors watching it. She couldn't see much from here,
only the front of Tommy's house and the squad car. She
could retreat, go back to the pickup, and either leave
altogether or wait the intruders out. But then she'd have
no way of knowing when—or if—they left.

That decided it. Turner got up and crept farther into the
woods with the Great Dane. They began circling around
to the back of Tommy's house through the woods. There
was a small rise there, and she'd be able to see what was
going on better.

Fifteen minutes later, she settled against a maple tree,
careful not to sit in poison ivy. The dog—Howard?—
flopped down next to her, laid his mailbox head in her
lap, and sighed gustily as if he'd had a hard day. Below,
a tall man walked out of Tommy's barn and stood looking around in the sunshine. Turner brought her binoculars to her eyes and focused on him just as he turned in
her direction. She sucked in her breath. He looked as if
he was staring straight at her, and she froze like a rabbit
before a wolf.

He had a long face, made longer by the deep lines
bracketing his wide mouth. His eyes were heavy-lidded,
almost sleepy, but she knew that was deceptive. The man
was smart and could be quick when he wanted to. He
was hatless, his salt-and-pepper hair cropped to within
an inch of his scalp. From this distance there was no way
to tell, but Turner imagined that the man's eyes were

blue and intense. And she knew somehow, on a gut level, that she was watching Special Agent John MacKinnon down there.

His face turned as he spoke to someone else. Turner blew out a breath and lowered her binoculars a fraction, looking over them. Tommy had come out into the yard. Her lips twitched. The old man was probably haranguing John.

She peered through the binoculars again and watched the FBI agent's mouth compress impatiently at something the old man was saying. He pivoted, ambled to the squad car, and reached inside. Tommy trotted after him, his mouth still working. John came back up with a cup in his hand. He took a long drink from it while Tommy gave him what-for. No one could lecture like Tommy when he got into the swing of things.

John's plastic travel mug was the kind that came apart so a child could draw on a piece of paper that would be inserted between the mug and the clear outside. This mug had looping purple flowers and a great big pink heart on one side. Turner felt her stomach clench. Did he have children? A little girl must have made that cup for him. No boy would draw purple flowers. For all she knew, Special Agent MacKinnon might be married with five children.

She wrinkled her nose and lowered the binoculars. And what did she care if the FBI agent trying to find and arrest her was married? Her hand came within range of the huge dog head on her lap. The Great Dane swiped her with its tongue and then panted. For goodness' sake, she needed to give the thing a name. Turner dug her cell phone out of her pocket and pressed in the numbers. With her other hand she held the binoculars up again.

Down below, John, still talking to Tommy, unclipped his cell from his belt, and held it to his ear.

"MacKinnon," he said into her own ear. He sounded as if he were right beside her.

She drew in a shaky breath. "What did Calvin call the dog?"

Abruptly, he turned his back on Tommy and walked several paces away. His legs were long and lean, and she noticed he had on cowboy boots. He probably looked really sexy in jeans, darn him.

"Turner?" His voice was low and sharp, like he wasn't happy to hear from her.

Too bad. She ignored his question. "I need to give him a name. I think he's beginning to get a complex."

"Where are you?"

She was silent. She was afraid if she opened her mouth, she just might tell him. Or worse, stand and wave her arms. *Here I am. Come and get me.*

He sighed. "Hyman called him Duke."

"Duke?" Turner looked at the dog. He opened one eye, but she couldn't tell if he was responding to her voice or the name. "Like Marmaduke the cartoon? That's an awful cliché. Calvin doesn't have an imaginative bone in his body. No wonder the dog has no self-esteem. Have you seen him?"

"Turner, why don't you come in?"

He was a male siren. She could see him through the binoculars, rubbing his forehead wearily with one hand. She wanted to touch him, feel his warmth under her palm, lay her head against his chest and inhale. The urge to find out what he smelled like was almost a physical ache. Why, oh, why, after all the years alone, did it have to be *this* man who finally saw past her facade?

She shook her head. "He's definitely not a Duke."

"You can shower, get a change of clothes—"

"Maybe a Zeus."

"I can hook you up with a defense lawyer I know—"

"Or a Captain."

"You'd be safe—"

"Or Rafe."

"Turner—"

"I can't."

"What?"

"I can't come in." She bit her lip and was surprised at how close to tears she was. She had to swallow before she could go on. "I have to finish it. I can't come in."

She could see his frown through the binoculars, creasing between his brows, making the lines around his mouth deeper. Then his voice reached her, low and intimate. "I can't stop searching for you, either. You know that, don't you?"

Oh, Lord. "I know."

"It's my job. I'm going to find you, and I'm going to arrest you."

"You can try," she said with a bit of bravado.

"Turner." His voice was nearly a growl now, a clear male warning.

The female in her flaunted it. "I have something I have to do, and you're not going to stop me, Special Agent MacKinnon."

There was a silence on the other end. Then he blew out a breath. "I told you to call me John."

"John." Somehow his name came out almost a caress.

"See the *Tribune* crossword this morning?"

She felt the corner of her mouth curl. "You know I haven't."

"There was one that really stumped me. Something about Regan's father."

"Lear."

"What?"

"It's *King Lear.*"

"Huh. See, now that's where a librarian has an advantage over us FBI agents."

"Only the FBI agents who don't read Shakespeare."

"Which would be all of them." Was he smiling? She could see a tilt to his mouth through the binoculars.

"I'm sure that some of our government employees are Shakespeare fans."

"Maybe Torelli, but he's odd."

"Who's Torelli?"

"My partner."

"You don't sound too fond of him."

"I'm not. Doesn't mean I can't work with him to find you, though."

His voice was terse. This was business for him. He probably had a reason of his own to keep her on the phone. Maybe he'd sent someone into the woods to track her. She looked around in sudden panic. The dog raised his head at her movement. But no. John had no way of knowing where she was. Even so, calling him had been foolish.

She took a steadying breath. "I've decided to name the dog Squeaky."

"God, that's emasculating."

She smiled. "Squeaky. It fits him. Bye, John."

She hung up.

Chapter Fifteen

You ou lost Yoda and SpongeBob in a swamp?" John raised his eyebrows and poked at the Greasy Grill's notion of a Cobb salad. It was a mound of iceberg lettuce in a Styrofoam box with a few slices of processed cheese and some strips of pink lunch meat perched on top. His original idea had been to get something a little healthier for lunch today. That plan had backfired. All he could think of was Ted York, keeling over into his—

"We followed the tracks as far as we could," Torelli replied.

The younger agent was looking ragged around the edges. His razor-cut hair was plastered to his head at the temples, and his hand-painted paisley tie was loosened and rumpled. One lapel of his navy suit jacket was stained.

John would bet a good chunk of next month's paycheck that Torelli hadn't looked at himself in a mirror lately. He stopped himself from smirking. "Yeah?"

"Yeah," Torelli growled, then thought better of it.

"Yes, sir. The sheriff even brought in bloodhounds like we were in some kind of escaped-prisoner movie."

"I take it the dogs didn't do any good?"

"They milled around and eventually took off running." Torelli bit into his Reuben sandwich, narrowly missing dripping Thousand Island dressing on his tie. Cocky bastard, flaunting his young arteries.

John raised a questioning eyebrow.

Torelli shook his head, swallowing. "Rabbit."

"Figures." John forked up a piece of limp lettuce. "You doing any better finding out who supplied them with the shotguns?"

Torelli had just taken another bite, so John had to wait for his reply. They were in the meeting room of the Winosha municipal building again, the location chosen as much for its working AC as for the privacy. Sheriff Clemmons and Deputy Larson had said they would join them for lunch, but they were late. Just as well. John didn't want to step on local toes, but on the other hand, he could get a lot of this business out of the way faster with just Torelli.

The younger man swallowed, took out a small cordovan-leather notebook, and flipped through it. He consulted a page. "Nald lives with a maternal uncle out in the sticks on County Road G. We searched the shack they both inhabit, despite not having hazmat suits. Aside from years of junk, we found three handguns—only one in working condition—two rifles, and an air gun. Nald's uncle says he used to have a shotgun but he hasn't seen it in years and doesn't remember what he did with it."

John drank some iced tea from a Styrofoam cup. "So that might account for one shotgun."

"I don't think so. The uncle says he probably hocked the shotgun a long time ago."

"Still. Let's keep it in mind."

"Sure." Torelli shrugged.

"What did you find out about Fish—besides that his family is inbred?"

"You should've seen the place he lives in." Torelli shook his head, crunching a potato chip.

John's mouth watered. God, he hated salad.

Torelli flipped a page in his designer notebook. "Fish lives by himself in an efficiency apartment over the hardware store on Main. Another dump. He has a mattress on the floor, a hot plate, and a fairly new TV. That's about it."

"Good to know he has priorities," John muttered.

"Yeah." Torelli finished his Reuben, wiped his mouth with a paper napkin, and leaned back. "Anyway, no weapons. We did find a small stash of marijuana—less than half an ounce."

"Not useful." John gave up on the salad and stretched out his legs, as well. The metal folding chair he was sitting in squeaked. "So where did these guys—"

"Sorry we're late." The sheriff and Larson strolled into the room. The deputy was slurping from an extra-large paper cup.

"No problem," John said coolly.

He watched as the officers pulled out chairs and settled at the table. Clemmons plopped a brown paper bag on the table and unloaded what looked like a homemade roast-beef sandwich and a bag of chips. Larson sat next to him and unwrapped the foil from a huge bacon double cheeseburger, youthfully oblivious to the cholesterol count in such a monstrosity. He picked up his burger and took a big bite, grease oozing down his chin.

Larson swiped at the grease and looked up, catching John's eye. He blinked and offered the burger. "Want some?"

John waved a hand. "No. Thanks."

"Found out what vehicle Turner Hastings switched her Escort for," Larson said indistinctly around his second bite.

"Yeah?"

Larson nodded. "A light blue Chevy pickup, '68. Talked to one of the guys in town who works on cars on the side. Said Tommy brought it to him a year ago. Looked it up, and Tommy still has the Chevy's registration."

"Good work." John nodded. "Torelli and I were just about to discuss the bank robbers' means of employment."

Sheriff Clemmons stopped chewing, his brow furrowed. "*Are* Fish and Nald employed?"

"I—" Torelli started.

But the deputy got there first. "Doesn't Nald do some taxidermy with his uncle?"

Torelli looked confused. "Taxidermy?"

"Yeah." The deputy sipped from his straw. "You know, stuffed animals?"

"I know what taxidermy is, but—"

"And he's pretty good at it. Or at least his uncle is. You should see the badger they've got at the hardware store. It's sitting up with glasses on its nose and looks like it's teaching a class. And the students are chipmunks!" Larson slapped his thigh. "Funniest thing you ever saw."

"I can only imagine," Torelli began, New York accent thick and biting.

John cut in. "So what does Fish do?"

"Uh . . ." The deputy frowned at his burger, apparently stumped.

"Used to drive the school bus," Clemmons offered.

Larson glanced up. "Oh, yeah. But that was before—"

"Last spring." Clemmons shook his head. "Left the bus in gear and it got commandeered by Ralston Fish, worst nine-year-old delinquent you've ever seen and a cousin of our Fish. Anyways, Ralston drove the bus into the Kwik Trip store. Fortunately, he was only going about ten miles an hour at the time. No one got hurt, but the school board fired Fish nonetheless."

John contemplated this rural morality tale, carefully keeping himself from meeting Torelli's eyes.

The younger agent cleared his throat. "That means they're both unemployed"—he caught Larson's eye—"or at least not making a whole lot of money, in Nald's case. There can't be a fortune in taxidermy. They're prime patsies for Hastings—"

John opened his mouth, but the sheriff was ahead of him.

"I don't know if we should assume it's Turner masterminding this thing." Larson and Torelli stared at Clemmons, and the sheriff shifted in his seat, his face reddening. "I've known Turner a long time. Knew her mother and dad and Rusty Turner, too. She doesn't have any kind of police record, never been in trouble before in her life, not even a speeding ticket."

"She was on the tape—" Torelli began.

"Breaking into Calvin Hyman's box," Clemmons interrupted testily. "I know that. But that doesn't necessarily mean she got Nald and Fish to do the bank robbery."

"She did break into the Hyman house," John said quietly. "She admitted as much to me." He ignored Torelli's sharp look, focusing instead on the older man.

"Yeah, but she didn't steal anything valuable, and breaking and entering isn't a violent crime," the sheriff said. "Not like holding people at gunpoint."

"Yoda and SpongeBob were hardly very violent. They looked as likely to blow off their own heads as someone else's," Torelli scoffed, tilting back his chair so that it balanced on two legs.

"That's my point. They shot out the skylight and the doors." Clemmons' voice was sharp. "Those two idiots hardly had control of their weapons at all. We're lucky they didn't shoot someone purely by accident."

"Yeah." Larson shuddered. "Lucky I didn't have my head blown off."

"That's right." The sheriff nodded. "Whoever gave those two shotguns and sent them in the bank was taking a real risk that they would shoot some innocent bystander. I can't see Turner Hastings doing something that reckless."

Torelli brought the front legs of his chair down. "Hastings broke into the Hyman home, rifled through Hyman's desk and computer, and took off with the dog, of all things. That looks pretty damn reckless to me."

"She had cause!" Clemmons burst out.

Torelli raised his eyebrows skeptically. "What cause?"

The sheriff sat back and ran his hand through sparse hair. "Her uncle. You know he was fired for embezzling from the bank?"

Torelli nodded. "Mac briefed me."

"Calvin fired him, and Turner took it pretty hard at the time. I've always kind of wondered if the case had gone to trial if Rusty would've really been convicted."

"He was never tried?" John asked.

"Nope." Clemmons made a face. "Died of a heart attack before they could even set a date. 'Course, by that time he'd almost beggared himself on lawyers and bail. And he had only Turner to lean on. Her brother didn't bother coming home from California until the funeral."

"So she has even more reason to rob the bank and get back at Hyman." Torelli shrugged. "I'm afraid you're not making your case, sir."

John frowned. "Can you think of anyone else with motive to stage a robbery here?"

Clemmons snorted. "Sure. Any layabout in town."

"But no one specific?"

The sheriff opened his mouth, then shut it. "No."

"Then I think we should concentrate on Turner Hastings until we have another direction to go in." He didn't like saying the words, but he had a job to do, and all the facts pointed to Turner.

Torelli nodded. "She definitely has some kind of agenda."

"Yeah," John said grimly, "and it involves Hyman. Where else might she go?"

"Go?" The sheriff looked startled.

"She's searching for something. Where else might she look? Does Hyman have an office or a—"

"He's got a fishing cabin," Larson spoke up. Everyone looked at him. The deputy flushed. "On a lake somewhere."

"It's out by Rhinelander," Clemmons said wearily. "I can get you an address."

"Good." John got up to throw away the remains of his lunch. "Larson and I will continue with Turner Hastings. Torelli, keep looking for Yoda and SpongeBob."

"Where?" Torelli had stood as well. "We've already tracked them to the swamp east of town."

"They have to come out of that swamp somewhere, sometime."

"Yeah, but they could be—"

"Do you have a problem with that assignment?" John asked.

"No, sir." Torelli tossed the Styrofoam box his lunch had come in into the trash and walked out.

The sheriff raised his eyebrows. "Guess I'm with him." He, too, left.

John looked at Larson. "I didn't know Turner had a brother."

"I'm sorry, sir." The deputy flushed. "He lives somewhere in California. Like the sheriff said, he hasn't been back to Winosha in over four years. I didn't—"

"Don't worry about it," John interrupted. "Let's get his phone number. I'd like to talk to him."

Maybe Turner's brother could exonerate her. Or implicate her, for that matter.

Chapter Sixteen

The hardest part of being on the run was finding a comfortable spot to sleep at night, Turner had found. This was the third night—Monday—that she'd slept in the pickup, and already she was tired of it. She loved the vintage Chevy, but its vinyl seat was hard and narrow, and now she was sharing it with a dog. A really, really big dog.

Turner shoved at Squeaky's bony rear end, but the poor animal had nowhere to go. She'd tried pushing him onto the floor of the Chevy earlier, but he'd looked so pitiful down there, his enormous Great Dane body all bunched up in a smallish—for him—ball, that she'd relented and let him back on the seat. Now he had the driver's side and she was curled on the passenger seat against the window. Maybe they should try sleeping outside in the open. But no, they'd be eaten alive by mosquitoes.

Turner sighed and shifted. Her left leg was falling asleep. If only the rest of her could fall asleep as easily. She stretched the numb leg and thought about talking to Tommy earlier this afternoon. She and Squeaky had waited out John and Doug Larson before sneaking down to talk to Tommy. The old man had been tickled to death that she'd stolen Calvin's dog. He'd browned some hamburger meat for Squeaky and fed it to him with a loaf of stale bread. The Great Dane had wolfed it all down in about three seconds flat and looked for more, which had amused Tommy. Squeaky had ended up cleaning out Tommy's fridge of leftovers while Turner talked to the old man.

Tommy had not only known where Calvin's lake cabin was, he'd even been there. Turner had been startled by that statement until she remembered that once they'd all been friends, Calvin, Rusty, and Tommy. Long ago, back before Calvin had betrayed Rusty and destroyed him.

And her.

The cabin was on a lake near Rhinelander in the northeastern part of the state, basically on the other side of Wisconsin. By the time she'd left Tommy's and trekked back to the Chevy with Squeaky, it had been getting on to late afternoon. Turner had loaded the dog in the pickup and taken a back road heading south. She'd hoped to eventually hook up with Highway 8 and take it out to Rhinelander, but as it got dark, she'd begun to have more and more trouble keeping her eyes open. Eventually, she'd given up, pulled off the road, and called it a night.

Of course, now that she'd decided to give in to sleep, she couldn't. She shoved at Squeaky again. He was snoring. If only—

Her cell went off in the dark, making her yelp. Squeaky raised his big head and looked at her questioningly. Turner dug through her handbag, searching for the rectangular piece of plastic. When she found it, the number displayed on the little lighted screen was familiar, even though it had no right to be.

"Hello?"

"Where are you?" His voice was gravelly tonight, as if he were tired.

This time she had a face to go along with the voice. She pictured him lounging in an armchair, his jacket off, long legs sprawled, running a hand over his lined face. Would he have beard stubble at night, or not until morning?

She tried to make her own voice sharp, but it came out disconcertingly soft. "Do you know what time it is?"

"Just past eleven."

"That was a rhetorical question. Most people are in bed by now."

"Are you?"

She settled back against the Chevy door. Squeaky was snoring again on his side. "You know I'm not."

There was a short silence. "Come in. Then you could have a bed. Air conditioning, hot water—"

"You know that's not going to happen."

"Turner—"

"Who made your coffee mug?"

"What?"

"Your mug. The one with purple flowers and a big pink—"

"Tommy's," he said flatly.

She was silent.

He took a breath—she could hear it even through the phone. When he spoke again, his tones were tight and angry. "Where were you? I thought I searched that house and barn thoroughly."

"I wasn't there."

"Then where did you see me if not at Tommy's?"

"No." Turner grimaced. "I meant, I was at Tommy's, just not in the barn or house."

"Then where?"

"What does it matter? I won't go there again."

This time his silence waited her out.

She gave in with a sigh. "I was in the woods above the barn. With Squeaky."

"Shit." He sounded disgusted with himself.

"There was no way—"

"The entire time I was talking to you?"

"Yes." Now she felt guilty, and wasn't that ridiculous? "Did your daughter make it?"

Amazingly, he followed her train of thought back to the coffee mug. "No, a niece starting kindergarten this year made it for me. It was a Christmas present."

"Ah." It was crazy, but relief swept through her. He wasn't married. "I thought you might've had a daughter—"

"I do. My daughter is sixteen. I haven't talked to her in three years."

She caught her breath. He'd said it matter-of-factly, but there was no way he could feel so blasé about being estranged from a child. His child. Was he still married? "Why haven't you talked to your daughter in three years?"

"Long story or short?"

"I've got all night," Turner whispered. "Might as well make it long."

"It's not that long in any case." His voice was brusque, as if he was sorry he'd consented to talk about his daughter. "I married young, had one child, and then divorced. My ex remarried, then moved out to Washington state, and eventually her second husband adopted my daughter."

She was silent a moment, listening to crickets in the woods. "What's her name?"

"Rachel."

"That's a pretty—"

He interrupted her banality. "Like I said, she's out of my life. She hasn't spoken to me for years."

How that must hurt his pride. She didn't see him easily giving up anything that belonged to him, especially not the love of a child. "That must be hard."

"I don't want to talk about this," he said flatly. "How's Squeaky?"

Turner looked at the snoring dog. His head was resting on the steering wheel. She hoped he didn't drool. "Cramped."

He chuckled huskily. "Should've thought of that before kidnapping a Great Dane."

"I prefer to think of it as a liberation."

"Now you sound like an ecoterrorist," he chided. "What're you wearing?"

She blinked, caught off guard. "What kind of a question is that?"

"A kinky one."

"I don't think I know you well enough to play those kind of games."

"Don't you?" His voice was very low now, like a growl.

She glanced blindly out the truck window at the night. If he were close, she'd be frightened, and not just of being arrested. Why did he have to be so perceptive, so smart, so *appealing?* "I don't even know if you're married now."

"I'm not."

"You've never met me," Turner whispered.

"I've been through the panties in your dresser drawer."

What? She straightened. "You had no right—"

"It's my job," he clipped out. "You know that. The moment you opened Hyman's desk drawer, the moment you smirked at that surveillance camera in the bank, you set in motion events that can't be changed. By you or by me."

She clenched her fist into a ball. She knew all that, but to have him put it so bluntly was shocking. "You—"

He raised his voice over hers ruthlessly. "I'll be doing more than looking in your lingerie drawer soon, honey. I'm going to take you down. I'm going to be the one to put the handcuffs on you. No one but me."

She found she was gasping for breath, her chest felt so tight. "Why are you saying these things to me?"

"Because I'm the damned FBI, that's why. This isn't a game for me, it's my job. It's what I do."

"Then why are you talking to me?"

"I don't know." He sounded like he was biting off the words and crunching them between his teeth. "You made up the rules to this thing before I was ever on the scene. I'm just along for the ride."

"I should hang up on you."

"You should," he agreed, quieter now. "Don't."

"Why not?" She felt close to tears. "We're on opposite sides, so far apart we might as well be on different continents. Different worlds."

There was a silence from the other end, and she closed her eyes, simply listening to him breathe.

"I talked to your brother today," he finally said.

Her eyes snapped open. "Brad?"

"Yup."

"Why?"

"It's standard procedure to talk to the relatives of fugitives."

She made a rude noise. "Fugitive—"

"And he's your only living relative, isn't he?"

She shut her mouth.

He waited, then continued softly. "Besides your father, that is."

"You've done your homework." She drew a deep breath. "I don't think Dad really counts as family, since he moved away when I was barely three."

"Does Brad count?"

"Sure." She wrinkled her nose impatiently. "Why wouldn't he?"

"He says you hardly ever talk. The last he heard from you was a card on his birthday."

"So? We're both adults. What do you expect, daily phone calls?"

"Why not? I talk to my eldest sister at least once a week. More, if her teenagers are giving her hell and she has to vent."

This was the second time he'd mentioned his family. She hadn't pictured him with relatives of his own—it didn't click with her image of a tough FBI agent. Intrigued, she asked, "How many sisters do you have?"

"Three." He sounded like he was smiling. "One older, that's Lisa, and two younger, Sheryl and Karen."

"No brothers?"

"Nope."

"That must've been nice, growing up in a large family."

"Not when you're trying to get ready for school and there's three girls in the bathroom, putting on makeup."

"Even so—" She interrupted herself to yawn.

"You're tired."

"Sort of."

"I should let you go so you can sleep." But he didn't hang up.

She cradled the phone between her shoulder and cheek and let her head fall against the seat. Outside, the crickets were in full chorus, a sweetly sad sound.

"Goodnight, John," she whispered.

"Goodnight, Turner," he murmured in her ear.

She listened for the click and then hung up herself.

Through the windshield she could see a half-moon shining serenely in the night. The temperature had finally dropped, and she shivered and wrapped her arms around her shoulders. There was nothing more melancholy than gazing at the night sky all alone.

Chapter Seventeen

Calvin Hyman peered through the windshield of his cream 2006 Cadillac DeVille. He was looking for the turnoff, but the road was pitch dark because it was almost midnight. The only part he could see at all was in the V of his headlights, and even that was weirdly colorless, making it hard to identify anything. Everything else beyond the headlights was lost to the night. The turnoff was somewhere around here, he knew, but he hadn't been to the lake in years, and it was so goddamn difficult to—

There! He almost missed it, but he braked hard and swung into the dirt road, the Caddy kicking up gravel. He winced as a rock dinged off the door. With his luck lately, the door would be scratched. He'd have to check the paint later, maybe take it into the body shop up in Superior. There was no way he'd let the local idiots in Winosha within ten feet of his Caddy.

Calvin slowed the car to a crawl. The road was rutted, and he didn't want to lose the muffler on a pothole. He'd told Shannon that he was at a men's poker night, but it'd be just like her to examine the car for signs of duplicity. For some reason she worried about his fidelity, even though he'd never given her cause to doubt him. If she thought he'd lied, she would become hysterical, which was the last thing he needed right now.

God, the previous couple of days had been hell. First the bank robbery and all the anxiety that had gone along with that. And then, just when he'd begun to relax, thought the thing had come off and he was home free, no more disastrous audit hanging over his head—at least for the foreseeable future—he'd watched Turner Hastings rob his safe deposit box. He'd nearly stroked out right there in the Winosha municipal building. What the hell was she doing? He'd thought—no, he'd *hoped*—it was some kind of fluke. Old-maid librarian going off the deep end and turning to a life of crime. But even on Saturday night, watching the tape, he'd known it was no fluke.

And that had been before she'd broken into his computer at home.

There was no way to deny it now. The woman was out to get him. After four years, she was coming after him for Russell Turner's sake. Because of the sacrifice Calvin'd had to make four years ago. Things had gotten too close back then; the auditors had been asking questions, and someone had had to take the fall. He was genuinely sorry that it'd had to be Rusty, but who else would've been believable? The embezzling had to have been done by someone high in the bank. And besides, although he loved Rusty like a brother, no one could deny the man was getting on in years. He was ready to retire anyway.

He'd thought the whole thing had been over four years ago. And now Turner Hastings pops up, bent on some ridiculous revenge for Rusty, who'd been dead and buried all this time! If holding a grudge that long wasn't a sign of mental instability, he didn't know what was. That was probably why she'd stolen the dog, too. Turner Hastings clearly had a case of mental confusion at the very least. Too bad he couldn't just explain that to the sheriff.

She had certainly picked her time, too. The September primary was less than two weeks away. Carter, the retiring state representative, had assured him that the seat was his. Calvin was *this* close to being a member of the state legislature, for God's sake.

He felt like shoving that fact into the faces of all those people who had talked behind their hands about him when he was growing up. *Poor Calvin Hyman, have you heard his father just walked out? Poor Calvin Hyman, his mother was falling down drunk at the bar last night again. Poor Calvin Hyman, he's worn the same pair of dungarees for the last two years; the seat's just about worn out.*

Well, poor Calvin Hyman was the Winosha town mayor now. He was the bank president, a member of the Lutheran church, and on the school board. Poor Calvin Hyman was the most powerful man in town and soon—so damn soon he could almost taste it—he'd be the most powerful man in the district. He'd be a state representative. A member of the state legislature. How do you like *them* apples, you small-town gossips?

Soon. If only Turner Hastings didn't bring all his dreams crashing down at his feet.

The turn leading to the boat ramp loomed in his headlights. He checked the car clock. It was only 11:46, so he was still a little early. Calvin pulled the Caddy into a grassy area and turned off the engine. The car ticked as it slowly cooled. Outside, insects buzzed in the surrounding woods. He shifted in the car seat, his rear squeaking against the leather, wishing suddenly that he'd brought a magazine to read. Of course, he'd run down the car battery if he used the car light reading—

The passenger door opened without any warning and a large, bearded man got in, the overhead light illuminating him briefly. The light glinted off square black plastic-framed glasses. The man's bulk was intimidating, taking up more space in the car than it should. And he smelled. Calvin wrinkled his nose in the dark. The stink was made up of stale body odor, some kind of bug repellent, and cigarette smoke. The combination was reminiscent of dead skunk.

"You got the money?" Hank asked without inflection. It figured he'd get right down to the part that was in his interest.

"Of course." Calvin cleared his throat. "But I want to discuss terms first."

He saw the shadow of the other man's head turn in the dark interior of the car. "Terms? What terms you talking about? You want this girl killed, I want the money. What else is there to talk about?"

Calvin winced. God, Hank was crude. Of course, that was why he'd gone to him with this unsavory deal. A more civilized man wouldn't be able to pull it off. "I need to have an alibi when you do it."

"An alibi?" Hank snorted. "Like on TV?"

"Don't be insulting." Calvin half turned in the seat. "They might suspect me and—"

"Why?"

"Never you mind. Just make sure you plan it and let me know. I've got a dinner tomorrow—"

"No can do." Hank's voice was even and dull, almost bored. Like many chronic smokers, he had a pronounced rasp.

"Why not?"

"Look, you told me you don't know where she is, even. I'm supposed to find her—"

"She's got to be headed to my cabin." Calvin frowned, feeling impatient. This couldn't fall through now. It wasn't like northern Wisconsin was crawling with potential hit men. Hank was his only choice.

"And you don't even know when she'll show," Hank grunted. "This is gonna cost a lot."

"We already agreed. Five thousand dollars. Half now, and—"

"Nope. I want it all now."

"All?" Calvin heard his voice rise and lowered it, even though they were alone. He hissed, "Do you think I'm an idiot? I give you the whole thing now and you'll just take off."

"No, I wouldn't."

"Look." Calvin sighed. "I'll give you three thousand before, and after you kill her I'll give you the remaining two thousand."

"Three thousand."

Calvin felt relief flood his chest. "That's what I said—"

"No." Hank turned toward him, clothes rustling against the seat. His bulk blocked out the moonlight from the window. "Three thousand now, three thousand later."

"That's . . ." Calvin gasped, at a temporary loss for words. "That's outrageous!"

"That's where I stand." Hank sat back. He pulled a pack of cigarettes out of his shirt pocket and lit one without asking.

The smoke from the cigarette, combined with Hank's personal stench, seemed to fill Calvin's throat. He was going to suffocate if he couldn't get the other man out of his car soon. "Three thousand now, twenty-five hundred later."

Hank opened the car door. The overhead light switched on, revealing his straight greasy hair flattened to his scalp. His glasses were opaque in the glare, so it was near impossible to read his expression. He stood.

"Okay, okay." Calvin gripped the steering wheel. He wanted to let the other man get out of the car and then maybe run him over a few times, but that wouldn't be productive. He needed Hank. "Okay. Three thousand before, three thousand after. Sit down."

Hank slowly sank back down and shut the door. "Fine."

The light winked out again.

Calvin took a thick envelope out of his trousers pocket and handed it over. "I only brought twenty-five hundred because that's what we'd agreed on before. I can get you the other five hundred in the morning."

Without comment, the other man cracked the car door to make the light come on again. He slowly counted the money out, holding his cigarette between his first and second fingers. Calvin fumed. Christ, didn't Hank trust him to count the money correctly?

Finally, Hank stuck the wad of money into the front pocket of his jeans and gave the envelope back. He took a pull on the cigarette and blew more smoke in the car's interior. "Okay. But remember, I don't do anything without that five hundred."

"Fine."

Hank started to get out of the car.

"Wait! You need her photo." Calvin fumbled in his pocket.

"Oh, yeah."

Calvin found the snapshot and held it out. He'd had to really search to locate it. He'd finally discovered it in a stack of pictures that had been taken at a bank picnic a couple of years ago. Turner's face wasn't very big in the photo, but it showed her round glasses and her hair pulled back. That should be enough to identify her.

Hank took the photo without looking at it and put it in the same place as the money. He heaved himself from the car.

"Don't forget to let me know in advance," Calvin yelled after him. "You have my phone number—be sure to call me."

"Yeah, yeah. Soon as I get the five hundred." The big man waved a hand over his shoulder. He didn't turn around. The dark swallowed him, the glow of his cigarette end the last thing to disappear.

Calvin started the car and reversed to make a Y-turn in the road. This had better work. His future depended on it.

Chapter Eighteen

Turner had just passed the first Spooner exit on Highway 53 when her cell rang Tuesday morning. She glanced at her handbag on the seat beside her. No one had called her since the bank robbery Saturday, except for a certain FBI agent. She felt her heart jolt foolishly. On the radio, the Dixie Chicks were gleefully plotting Earl's murder. She'd been singing along—the Chicks and she seemed to have a common life philosophy these days—but now she stopped. Squeaky, lying on the seat beside her, opened one eye. The phone rang again. She really shouldn't answer it. Talking to John got her nowhere. And it couldn't be mentally healthy. He was trying to find her and arrest her, for goodness' sake.

Up ahead was a green sign for the second Spooner exit. Turner bit her lip and took it. She'd decided this morning to chance taking 53 south just so she could move faster. Now, of course, she was regretting the decision. She pulled to the top of the ramp, put the truck in first, and turned off the engine, silencing the Chicks in midyodel. She picked up her phone, still ringing, only to find that the number wasn't John's. In fact, the area code looked like—

"Brad?"

There was an exasperated sigh on the other end. "Took you long enough to answer, Turn."

She frowned. "Why are you calling?"

She was very visible at the top of the off-ramp. Sooner or later, John was bound to send out police alerts about her. Probably he already had. In any case, her instinct was to keep moving.

"Oh, that's nice," her brother said from the other end of the line. "I haven't talked to you since, what? Christmas? And the first thing you want to know is why I'm calling."

"Brad, why'd you call?"

Squeaky sat up and put one massive paw on the passenger-side windowsill. The poor animal probably needed a pit stop.

"Look," Brad said. "Some FBI agent with an attitude problem called my office six times yesterday."

"Six?" Turner blinked, then smiled, imagining John trying to get through Brad's firewall of employees. Her brother was a corporate bigwig in Silicon Valley, where nothing mattered but the product deadline and how the company stocks were doing.

"I finally took his call when he threatened to send a local FBI agent to bring me in for questioning. Although," Brad mused, "now that I think about it, I'm pretty sure he couldn't have done that. Not under California law, anyway."

"What—"

"He told me this ridiculous story about you robbing

a bank." Brian chuckled. "I mean, he has seen you, right? Your biggest thrill is doing the Sunday crossword puzzle."

Turner watched the highway. With the Chevy stopped, there was no wind, and the heat was intense. A semi with a huge photo of a potato chip bag on the side rumbled by. Beside her, Squeaky whined.

"Turn?" Brad had stopped chuckling.

"What?" She got out of the Chevy, slamming the door behind her. The dry heat blew into her face, wicking away any moisture.

"You didn't rob the bank."

"You know what happened to Rusty, Brad." She reached the other side of the Chevy and let out Squeaky. The dog bounded into the brown grass beside the road and immediately lifted a leg against a brittle shrub. If the plant wasn't already dead, it was a goner now.

Brad exhaled on an incredulous laugh. "You're not talking about . . . Come on, Turn. That happened, what? Five years ago? You can't still be angry at him, that's—"

She hung up on him and crossed her arms. Squeaky ran in wide circles.

"Hey!" she yelled at him.

The dog paused and looked at her, head up, ears erect, the perfect picture of a noble Great Dane. At least he listened to her.

"Okay," she called.

Squeaky went back to running in circles.

Her cell rang again.

She punched it. "What?"

"This is insa—"

She hung up.

A silver van with two canoes on the top pulled up to the stop sign where the off-ramp met the road. She watched carefully, but Squeaky didn't go near the road. A little boy in the van waved at the dog.

The cell rang.

"What?"

"Don't hang up, for God's sake!" Brad sounded frazzled.

"Why not?"

"Because I'm your brother."

Turner stared at the highway and frowned, trying to keep back tears. "You told me I was insane four years ago at Rusty's funeral, and you called me insane just now. You thought he'd done it, that he'd embezzled from the bank he'd worked at all his life. You just blew me off."

"I'm sorry."

"Are you?"

A sigh. "What do you want me to say, Turner? That I'm glad you robbed a bank? Look, I've got a friend in the DA's office. I can give him a call—"

"Brad—"

"Get him to recommend an attorney where you are—"

"Brad—"

"If you can't afford it, I'll cover the cost for now—"

Turner heaved a sigh and waited for her brother to wind down. She whistled to Squeaky. He cocked his head and looked at her. She whistled again, and he came galloping over.

On the other end of the phone, Brad squawked and sputtered. "What the hell is that? Why are you whistling in my ear?"

"I'm calling my dog."

"Dog? What dog? You never told me you had a dog."

"I have a dog." Squeaky thrust his muzzle into her hand, sliming it with dog spit. "Look, Brad, I don't need a lawyer. At least not yet." She opened the Chevy's passenger door and the dog leaped in.

"Yes, you do. When you come in—"

"I'm not coming in."

Silence. Inside the pickup, Squeaky rested his head on the windowsill and looked out at her.

"I don't understand," Brad finally said.

"I know." Turner walked to the driver's side of the Chevy and opened the door. Squeaky immediately rushed to that side, and she had to muscle him back so she could get in. "You've never understood. Rusty didn't do it."

"Didn't—"

"He didn't embezzle from the bank." She got in and shut the door behind her. The seat was hot enough to sear bare skin. Good thing she'd thrown a T-shirt over it to shield her legs. "He was innocent, Brad."

"Even if Uncle Rusty was innocent, that was four years ago. He's dead. What can you hope to do now?"

"Prove his innocence by catching the real embezzler, duh." She dug under the seat for a bottle of water and poured some into Squeaky's red water bowl on the floor.

"Even if you could—"

"Look, this is getting us nowhere, Brad—"

"Don't hang up!" She could hear her brother taking a deep breath. "Maybe I should've listened to you at Rusty's funeral. I'm sorry. I didn't realize his death and the accusations of embezzling had affected you so much."

"That's because you weren't here." She was surprised at how bitter that sounded. Brad was seven years older than she and had left home long before Rusty had died. Had she been angry at Brad all this time?

"I said I'm sorry. I can't apologize for having a life, though. California is where my career is, not the backwoods of Wisconsin."

"You could've listened." She knew she sounded childish, but she'd been alone a long time. Brad was her only family, as John had so kindly pointed out. Couldn't he have supported her just a little?

"I'm listening now, Turn, and I hear that you've been planning revenge for over four years. That doesn't seem very healthy."

"You think it's healthier to just forget?"

"Well . . . yes, actually I do."

"To let everyone think Rusty was a thief and a liar?" She spaced her words deliberately. "To let the man who set him up get away with it?"

There was a pause at the other end, then Brad said quietly, "What will you do afterward?"

"What?"

"After you get Hyman. It is Hyman you're talking about, right?"

"Yes."

"So after you bring him down, make everyone see he set up Rusty, what are you going to do then?"

"I . . ." She took a breath and ran a hand through her short hair. What kind of a question was that? "I don't know. Does it really matter?"

"Yeah, I think it does. You're burning bridges right and left, acting like this is the end of your life."

"Don't be—"

"You're not going to do a Thelma and Louise, are you?"

A laugh burst from her. "What gave you that idea? No, of course not!"

"Then maybe you should start thinking about the future. Your future. What happens afterward."

"I don't have time for that right now."

"Turn, you're only thirty-two—"

"Thirty-one," she interrupted. Brad always forgot her age.

"Sorry. Thirty-*one,* then. You've got most of your life still in front of you. Rusty wouldn't have wanted you to throw it—"

"You don't—"

"Shh. Listen for a moment." He waited.

"I'm listening." Turner pressed her lips together impatiently.

"Okay. Rusty loved you. He of all people wouldn't have wanted you to throw away your life on revenge for his sake."

"I'm not throwing it away!"

"Have you dated in the last four years?"

Turner winced. "It's not like there's an excess of eligible bachelors in Winosha."

"There's enough," he said gently. "If you wanted to date, you could. Is there anyone you can even talk to?"

She thought suddenly of the FBI agent. *Him. I can talk to him,* an idiot part of her brain whispered. "Why—" A sheriff's car went by on 53. Turner felt a jolt of anxiety. "Look, I need to keep moving. I have to go."

"Okay, good." Brad spoke rapidly as if he were afraid she would hang up on him before he could get out the words. "But think about what I said."

"Fine." She started the Chevy.

"And Turn—?"

"What?" Impatience was making her snap.

"I, um, take care."

She grinned. What a dork. "You, too, Brad."

She hung up and put the truck in gear. Squeaky sat up to stick his head out the window and let the breeze flatten his ears, until she got up to speed on the highway and he had to bring it in again. She wondered what, exactly, John had said to Brad to get him in such a dither. Her brother could be high-strung, but he didn't usually notice that much around him, including other people. He must be really worried to have called her. And the questions he'd asked about her future . . . Turner shrugged. She didn't have the mental energy to think about all that right now. She pushed aside the questions and the nagging uncertainty they produced. After she proved Calvin was a crook, she would deal with them.

For now, she'd concentrate on the job at hand.

Chapter Nineteen

Thank God for air conditioning. Whoever invented the stuff should be nominated for sainthood. John cranked up the Crown Vic's AC until it practically blew ice crystals in his face. Tuesday's late morning sun shone into the car and turned it into a solar oven. He didn't know how Turner was standing it in a '68 Chevy pickup. There was no way a vehicle that old had air conditioning.

He was on 53, driving south toward Rice Lake and State 8. He hoped he wasn't on a wild goose chase, but there wasn't much else he could do. He had to drive to where he thought Turner would go next. She was after Hyman—she'd admitted as much. She'd already searched his safe deposit box and his house. That left Hyman's lake cabin near Rhinelander. Ergo, he'd find her at the cabin.

Unless, of course, she'd given up her quest for revenge and had lit out for Las Vegas to start a new career as a showgirl. John smiled at the thought. Turner in a tall feathered headdress and not much else, a secret little smile on her lips. Then he frowned as another thought interrupted his fantasy. Or she could be heading in the opposite direction of Rhinelander for an entirely different motive. Because, when you got right down to it, he still didn't have a handle on what Turner Hastings was thinking.

John sighed and popped a Johnny Cash tape in the player. For now he'd just concentrate on what he did—

His cell rang. He fumbled it out of his pocket and pressed the answer button without looking. "MacKinnon."

"You've got my brother all worried now." Turner's tone was peeved.

John smiled at the sound of her voice. Talking to her was becoming strangely addictive.

"He called you, huh?" He wasn't surprised. In fact, he'd purposely pointed the man in that direction when he mentioned Turner had her cell phone with her.

"He was nearly hysterical. Brad was talking about getting me a lawyer."

John's eyebrows shot up. At least the man cared about his sister, even if he hadn't bothered staying in touch. "Well, now, that's not such a bad idea—"

"What did you say to him?" she demanded.

"Not much. I just informed him that his baby sister the librarian had robbed the local bank."

"I did not. I robbed Calvin, not the bank."

His lips twitched. "'Fraid most law-enforcement types won't see it that way—"

"Humph."

He raised his voice to finish his sentence. "And that includes me."

He heard her tense breathing from the other end and

wished she could've started the conversation with something else.

He sighed. "Where are you?"

He didn't know why he asked her the same question every time they talked. He knew she wouldn't tell him. But something inside him insisted he had the right to know. He deserved fundamental information about what space she occupied in the universe. And wasn't that the most ridiculous way to think about a suspect?

"It's none of your business," she answered wearily, as if she were as tired as he of the question.

He shrugged his right shoulder. It was aching again today, and Turner was pushing all his most basic buttons. "Actually, it is," he growled back. "My business, that is."

For a moment he thought she'd hang up, and he had a sense of impending loss. A sudden eerie howling came through the phone. "My God, what's that?"

"Squeaky," she yelled over the sound, just as it ended on what was indeed a squeak. "I left him in the truck. Shut up, you goof." He hoped that last was for the dog.

"His name fits him."

"He's a big baby." She sighed softly. "What's your favorite food, John? When you eat out, I mean? Where do you like to go? What do you like to eat?"

He wished she'd say his name more often. "It kind of depends on who I'm dining with."

"Just answer the question, Special Agent MacKinnon," she snapped impatiently.

"I'm pretty partial to steak."

She snorted. "Oh, that's a real surprise."

"Now, now. I also like little Mexican restaurants with cozy booths. The kind of place where they make the tortilla chips and the salsa themselves so it's fresh. Where they don't skimp on the peppers, either." He braked as the Crown Victoria came up behind a slow-moving semi.

"Ew, peppers." She sounded disgusted and reluctantly fascinated at the same time. "I bet you like the salsa really hot, too."

"The hotter the better."

"Places where they have sombreros and black velvet paintings hanging on the walls? And that liquor with worms in it?"

"Tequila." He glanced over his shoulder to change lanes. "I take it you don't like Mexican."

"Well, margaritas." Her voice was doubtful. "And if they have good shrimp dishes."

"Of course," he said solemnly. Who ate shrimp at Mexican restaurants? "So, what's your favorite food to eat out?"

"Sushi."

He winced. Figures it would be sushi with Turner. Raw fish—now, that was disgusting. "Where do you get sushi in Winosha?"

"I don't. I have to go to this little place in Madison. I found it when I went to college there. It has only two counter stools, and you can watch the chef make the sushi fresh. They have the most divine salmon, sliced so thin it's translucent pink."

To his mind, she wasn't describing a very appetizing place. But her husky voice was dreamy and slow, and John found he was getting hard just listening to her. "I'd like to try that place."

"Really?"

"Yeah."

"You like sushi?"

"We-ell . . ."

"That's what I thought." Her voice was brisk again. "How about Thai?"

"Now, that's more like it." He'd let the conversation stay casual if that's what she wanted.

"There's a really good Thai place in Madison, too. They make the best Pad Thai I've ever tasted, with tiny dried fish in it."

Gross. John bit the inside of his cheek to keep from chuckling. What was it with Turner and fish? "Ever had those little bitty Thai peppers? Hot enough to singe the hair on your—"

"Is that all you think of? Heat?"

"When I'm with you, it is." He said it before he had time to think, but it was true.

There was an awkward pause before she whispered, "You've never been with me. Not really."

His cock jumped at the smoky timbre of her voice. John flipped on his turn signal and pulled to the side of the highway before he drove head-on into a semi. "But I will be soon."

"You scare me." Her voice was so low he almost didn't catch the words.

"Why?"

She gave a little husky laugh. "Well, you are chasing me to arrest me."

"Yeah, but I don't think that's what scares you." He squinted through the windshield at the heat waves coming off the highway. "I think it's something else."

"What, then?"

He shrugged, even though she couldn't see. "Maybe you're scared because I won't quit."

He heard her catch her breath. "What do you mean?"

"Haven't they all quit? The men in your life?"

"I don't—"

He raised his voice to talk over her. "Your father left, your brother moved away just when you needed him most, Rusty died—"

"Now, listen—!"

"And your fiancé didn't even bother arguing when you said it was over."

On the other end, Turner breathed. John braced himself for her to hang up on him.

But she didn't. "You're very sure of yourself." Her voice was cool. "And of me."

He smiled tightly. *Oh, honey, you have no idea.* "You're anxious because I'm not going to quit until I have you in my hands."

"How do you know I'll let you get that close at all?"

"You'll have to."

"You want to arrest me." Was there a question in her voice?

"I *want* to get to know you," he said very gently. "I *have* to arrest you. It's my job."

"You can't do both things. You'll have to pick."

She was right. He knew that. But . . . "Maybe." *Maybe he'd gone insane.* "Maybe I can have both."

She caught her breath. "I have to go."

"Turner—"

But she'd hung up.

Shit.

John punched the *End* button and shoved the cell back in the holster on his belt. Then he noticed his hands were shaking. He stared for a moment at his own palms before barking a laugh. The more he talked to the woman, the more intrigued he became with her. A vigilante, for God's sake. But maybe that was it—the reason he'd been so turned on by her initially. She'd done the forbidden. She'd taken the law into her own hands. How often had he listened to other agents grumbling about the judicial hoops they had to jump through to see justice done? How often had he seen the longing in those other agents' eyes? The longing to just take a shortcut and bring a criminal down without the law. John had never been one of the guys who'd pined for vigilante justice, but he sure was fascinated by Turner's form of law enforcement, wasn't he? In a way, she was living every law officer's dream. She was going after the truth and damn the system. And he was going after her with more than professional interest.

He sighed and looked around. A red tanker passed, making the Crown Victoria rock in its wake. If he didn't move soon, he'd attract the attention of the highway patrol. John put the Crown Vic in gear and pulled out onto the road. Was she on this stretch of pavement, in front of him or behind, heading in the same direction? There was no way to tell. He had to simply keep going and trust it was the right way. But he hoped she was nearby, because he had to find her.

Soon.

Chapter Twenty

The problem with feeding a really big dog while on the run from the law was finding suitable food of a sufficient quantity.

Turner stood in the aisle of the Rice Lake Kwik Trip and contemplated her choices. She could buy Squeaky half a dozen stale donuts, which no doubt he would enjoy, or a box of saltine crackers. There was a bag of peanuts, but that might not be a good choice, dog-digestive-system-wise. She could go for the entire rack of beef jerky, but that would probably use a good chunk of her money and make her memorable, as well. She glanced at her watch. She'd already been in the Kwik Trip four minutes. Time to go. Saltines it was. She grabbed four bottles of water, the pack of crackers, and a hot dog off the little rotating self-serve heater thingy and took her bounty to the cash register.

"That it?" The mullet-haired teenager behind the counter looked at her purchases and then up at her.

"Yes," Turner replied. "Oh, and the gas." She gestured out the window at the Chevy pulled up to a pump.

Mullet swiveled his head to look. "Whoa. That your ride?"

"Um, yes."

"Cool pickup." He waved the saltines over the counter scanner. It beeped.

"Thanks."

"That a '66 or a '67?" He swiped a bottle of water and nothing happened.

"A '68, actually." Turner clasped her hands together to keep from grabbing the bottle of water from him and doing it herself. The boy was carefully smoothing the label now and trying to reswipe it. That never seemed to work, in her experience.

"Yeah? My grampa had a pickup like that." The bottle still wouldn't scan. He held it in his hand and gestured with it. "Only it was a Ford, and it was a '75 and it was black. But you know, other than that, it was real close to yours." He looked at her for a comment.

Turner smiled encouragingly. "Really? I wonder if you should manually enter the price?"

"What?"

She nodded to his hands. "On the bottle of water?"

"Oh. Yeah. Right." Mullet knit his brow and typed numbers into the cash register with one finger. He glanced at the total and laughed. "That's gotta be off. It says fifty-nine oh nine!"

Turner half smiled. Her life was slowly wasting away in this gas station.

"I mean, fifty dollars for a bottle of water?" Mullet laughed again, revealing a mouthful of fillings. "Can you believe it? I better void this out."

Oh, no. Voiding always took forever. Turner squeezed her eyes shut.

"Are you all right?"

She opened her eyes to see the boy staring at her with concern. He still had the bottle of water in his hand. She smiled. "Fine."

Her smile must've not been as friendly as she thought. He blinked and jerked his head back, then began working on the cash register.

Ten minutes later, Turner walked into the blinding bright sunshine. Squeaky was sitting in the truck with his head resting on the passenger-side windowsill. He lifted his head and grinned when he saw her, long pink tongue hanging from his mouth.

"Hi, baby," Turner crooned as she got in the truck.

She pushed his muzzle away from the paper sack Mullet had given her and put the pickup in gear, slowly rolling it to the parking spaces at the side of the gas station.

She opened the bag and reached in for the hot dog. "Look what I got you."

Squeaky took the hot dog delicately between his jaws and gulped twice. The hot dog disappeared, bun and all. He looked at her and wagged his tail.

"It's a good thing I got the crackers, too," Turner muttered.

She poured water into Squeaky's red bowl and got out her last jar of pickled herring. She'd already consumed the apples and the can of Vienna Sausages she'd packed Saturday night. She opened the jar and thought about the phone conversation she'd had with John this morning. How he'd talked about Mexican food. Fond as she was of pickled herring, after three days of it and not much else, she'd welcome Mexican with open arms. Even re-fried beans, possibly her least favorite food in the world, would be a change of pace at least. The next time she talked to John, she'd tell him—

Turner brought herself up short. What was she think-ing? She couldn't talk to John again—he was trying to arrest her. Despite the knowing words he'd murmured to her over the cell in his sexy, deep voice, the man wanted to put her in prison. The mere thought of him should send chills of fear down her back. Instead, the thought of John gave her chills of another sort altogether. She'd never actually touched the man, and yet the sound of his voice was beginning to provoke a Pavlovian response in her. Maybe he was right. Maybe it was his persistence that she found so seductive. She knew, somewhere deep inside herself, that once John had decided on a course he didn't waver from it, no matter the barriers. If John decided on her, he'd not walk away. Such determination, such strength was dangerously attractive. It had been a long, long time since she'd leaned on anyone, let alone a man. It was disconcerting to find that she had a weak spot—that *John* was her weak spot.

Turner wrinkled her nose at her herring. She was too old for this adolescent stuff, anyway. She'd hit thirty over a year ago, for goodness' sake. Her love life had al-ways been white-bread boring—not that she'd had much of one in the last four years. She dated safe, nice guys. The shy ones with bald spots and a love of books. She'd never played games like this one. And she'd never been attracted to dangerous men. Men who were out to get her—literally. Maybe this was some kind of kinky S and M thing in her psyche making a belated, post-thirty ap-

pearance. It figured it would be now, and with the FBI
agent who wanted to arrest her, of all people.

She shook her head at herself and realized that
Squeaky was staring at her herring. His eyes were intent,
following her fork from the jar to her mouth. A thread of
drool had started at the corner of his jowl.

"Want some?" She held out a piece of fish.

Stupid question. The dog snapped it up and appeared
to enjoy it, even with the vinegar. Of course, that might
have been because he hadn't taken the time to chew the
herring. She fed the rest of the jar of pickled herring to
Squeaky and then wiped her hands. Time to get back to
business and stop mooning over Special Agent MacKinnon. She'd already spent too much time at this gas station. Better get this over with before a state trooper saw
her. She got out her cell and hit the speed dial for a number she'd programmed in a while back but hadn't used
before. Squeaky licked up cracker crumbs from the seat
while she listened to the ring tone.

The other end picked up. "Office of the Federal Prosecutor. How may I direct your call?"

Turner cleared her throat. "Victoria Weidner, please."

"Just a moment." The line clicked several times, and
then another ring tone started.

Turner glanced at her watch. It was a little before one
o'clock. Darn. She hadn't thought to check the time before she called. Maybe Victoria was at lunch—

"Victoria Weidner." Her voice was the same as it had
been fifteen years ago.

"Hi," Turner began and then didn't know quite what
to say. Where to start?

"Yes?" Victoria asked impatiently.

She took a deep breath. "My name is Turner Hastings.

I live in Winosha. I don't know if you remember me. We were in the same class at Lincoln High School in Winosha nearly—"

"Turner." Victoria's tone was suddenly sharper, clearer. "Yes. I remember you. We were in sophomore chemistry together with Mrs. Knutson. What can I do for you?"

"I'd like you to help me look into embezzling at the First Wisconsin Bank of Winosha."

There was a hesitation at the other end. When Victoria's voice came again it was carefully neutral. "Wasn't that what Russell Turner was accused of?"

"Yes. He was accused, but he never went to trial." Turner kept her own voice steady with an effort. "Had he gone to trial, I don't believe he would've been convicted."

"I was sorry to hear of your uncle's death," Victoria said coolly. "But even if he were innocent, there's nothing I can do for you now. Since the case never went to court, the Office of the Federal Prosecutor—"

"I don't need your help with Uncle Rusty's case," Turner raised her voice to interrupt. "I want you to investigate a current case of embezzlement."

"What do you mean?"

"Uncle Rusty thought that Calvin Hyman was the one embezzling from the First Wisconsin Bank four years ago. I think he still is."

There was a short silence. Then, "Do you have any evidence of embezzlement?"

"No." Turner inhaled. "Not yet. But I hope to have some soon."

"What kind of evidence, exactly?"

"Uncle Rusty thought that Calvin must keep a separate set of books somewhere. I hope to find them."

"*Hope* to? You didn't find them in his safe deposit box?"

Turner caught her breath. Silly. She should've expected that Victoria would know about the robbery. "No."

"Then I don't want to know how you plan on getting them." Victoria laughed huskily on the other end. "Look, Turner, why don't you go to the sheriff with this—"

"No. I don't trust anyone local." She closed her eyes and marshalled her arguments. "Sheriff Clemmons was the one who took Calvin's word four years ago. Calvin Hyman is Winosha's mayor. Why would anyone local believe me over him?"

"Fine." The other woman sighed over the phone. "Then what do you want me to do?"

"I want to meet with you in the next few days. To discuss this and to show you the evidence."

"Okay." Victoria sounded like she was humoring her, but Turner didn't care as long as the other woman listened to her. "How about tomorrow?"

"That's too soon. I may not have the evidence by then." Turner frowned. "Can I see you Friday?"

"Nope. Sorry. I'm going out of town for a conference this weekend." There was the sound of flipping pages on the other end. "Wednesday or Thursday are the only days I have open this week."

"Can I get back to you?" She hadn't expected to set up an actual time to meet during this call. Now she felt flustered and off balance.

"Fair enough. Do you want to tell me where you are now?"

Turner glanced out the window. Mullet was outside the Kwik Trip now, smoking a cigarette. He studied the Chevy as he blew a stream of smoke from his lips. She frowned uneasily. "I don't think that would be a good idea."

"Just a thought," Victoria said smoothly.

But Turner's attention was on the convenience-store attendant. As she watched him, Mullet tossed his cigarette aside rather cavalierly, considering he was standing at a gas station. He looked up and his eyes met hers, and then he quickly glanced away.

Her pulse accelerated.

Chapter Twenty-one

*J*ohn was trying to unwrap a greasy taco one-handed when his cell rang. He cursed and grabbed for the phone on his belt. The Crown Victoria swerved and the taco spewed ground meat, shredded cheese, lettuce, and taco sauce down the front of his jacket and white shirt. Served him right for trying to eat and drive at the same time.

John sighed and punched the *Answer* button on his cell. "MacKinnon."

On the other end a woman gasped.

He smiled. "Turner?" He'd talked to her only a couple of hours ago, but maybe she'd worked up the courage—

"John MacKinnon?"

The smile died on his face. It'd been three years and her voice had matured, but he'd recognize it for the rest of his life. No matter how many years had passed.

"Rachel."

There was silence from the other end.

He frowned as the implication of her call sunk in. The

last time he'd talked to his daughter, she'd said she never wanted to see him again, and he figured she'd meant it. "What's going on? Are you okay? Is your mother okay?"

She sighed with adolescent exasperation. "Of course everything is okay, John."

He winced at the pointed use of his first name. If their relationship was better, he'd insist on Dad, or at least Father. But he'd given up the right to be called Dad when he'd let Amy's second husband adopt Rachel. "Why did you call?"

"Can't I call just to talk?"

"Yes. Yes, of course you can call me just to talk." John signaled to pull over to the side of the road. He needed all his attention for this conversation.

"Well, so . . ." She paused.

He grabbed a paper napkin from the bag of tacos and tried to repair his shirt and jacket. "So. How's school?"

"It hasn't started yet."

Oh, yeah. John winced again. "Ah."

"We moved." Her voice had lowered. "Did you know that?"

"Yes." His tie had a big grease stain on it. He gave up, wadded the napkin into a ball, and threw it back in the bag. "Your mom gave me your new address."

"You still talk to her?"

"Now and then." Actually, he was the one who did most of the communicating. If it were up to Amy, the contact would've died a long time ago. "Mostly about you." *Only about you.*

"Oh."

"Do you like your new house?" He stared out at the dry grass beside the road. Further up the shoulder the trees started, dry, as well. The whole area was ripe for a forest fire.

"Yeah." She cleared her throat.

He pulled out his wallet and flipped to the photo of Rachel. It was a school photo Amy had mailed him over a year ago after much pressure. Rachel smiled widely at the camera, her straw-blond hair hanging over her shoulders. Her cheeks had thinned since childhood, but they were still full. Three years ago she'd called them *chipmunk cheeks* and hated them. He'd thought them cute. But then, he was biased. He was her father.

"I want to ask you about Mom," she said in his ear.

That brought his attention back to the conversation. "What?"

"I want to know why you guys broke up."

"Hasn't your mom told you?" he asked cautiously. Surely Amy hadn't missed the opportunity to defame him.

"She says it was all your fault. That you were never home."

"That's about right." More or less.

"So you just got tired of Mom? Of us?"

"Divorce is never that simple. You know that, Rachel."

She was silent for a moment. Then she burst out, "Did you have an affair?"

"No." Where had she gotten that idea?

"There wasn't another woman? Some chick? You never cheated on Mom?" Her voice was high with suspicion.

"No," John said. "Look, I don't know what Amy has been telling you—"

"She doesn't tell me anything. That's the problem."

He stared at the photo a moment, rubbing his thumb over the corner. He hadn't seen her in the flesh in three years. "What do you want from me, sweetheart?"

"I want the truth. I want to know why you and Mom divorced."

"Rachel, look. There's never any one reason for a divorce. Bottom line, your mother and I felt that we'd be better apart."

"So you just got rid of me?"

"No!" He grimaced. He noticed that she'd dropped the *and Mom* in her equation. She must have been feeling abandoned somehow. He glanced at the highway. Turner was out there somewhere in her light blue Chevy, and he needed to find her. Rachel couldn't have picked a worse time to call if she'd tried. "No. I wanted to stay in your life. It was you who—"

"If you wanted to stay in my life, you would've stayed married to Mom."

"That didn't happen." Good Lord, she was stubborn. He took a deep breath. "I like talking to you, Rachel. Can't we find another subject to—"

"No. I want to know about the divorce. There's no other reason for me to talk to you."

Well, she certainly knew where to hit him to hurt the most. "Don't you think we should have this discussion with your mother present?"

"She'd just stonewall."

With good reason. John ran a hand through his hair. "I don't want to—"

"I'll hang up."

Christ. "Look, I'd love to see you. I'm working on a case right now, but why don't I fly out to see you when—"

"I told you, we don't have anything else to talk about."

"Rachel—"

But a click in his ear told him she'd hung up.

"Shit!" Something close to panic flooded his chest. Rachel had finally—finally!—reached out to him. He couldn't let her go like that. John fumbled with the buttons on the cell phone, trying to bring up the last number called, when suddenly the phone went off in his hand. Wild relief swept through him.

"Hello!"

"We've got a lead on Hastings," Torelli said.

John blinked and brought his focus back to the job even as his hope drained away.

Torelli paused on the other end of the phone. "Mac?"

"Yeah. Yeah, I'm here." He'd have to call Rachel back later. He started the Crown Vic. "Where is she?"

"A service-station attendant reported a pale blue '68 Chevy at the Kwik Trip in Rice Lake."

He'd passed Rice Lake about three miles back. Damn. He thought she'd be ahead of him by now. "East or west of the exit?" He glanced over his shoulder to check the traffic. A line of semis was coming up, but there was a sizable break after that.

"East."

"Okay, I'm on it." John swung into the highway, cutting across both lanes and doing a wide U-turn.

"Should I call in state troopers?"

"No!" The speedometer needle climbed to seventy and kept going. "I don't want anyone else there."

"Your call." Torelli's voice was disapproving.

"Damn right it's my call," John snapped. "No one else. That's an order."

"Fine." Torelli hung up.

John glanced at the cell long enough to find out that Rachel had called from Amy's home phone, and then he flung the cell on the passenger seat. His daughter might think that she had the final word, but she was wrong. She'd given him an opening after three long years, and he'd be damned if he'd let it go. As soon as he could, he was reestablishing the connection.

Right now, though, he had to pay attention to his driving.

John glanced at the dash. He was doing over ninety now. He needed to get to Turner and stop this nonsense before she was hurt. And he couldn't trust Torelli not to go over his head again and call in outside law enforcement. Cops who didn't know Turner and might think she was dangerous. Cops who might shoot first and ask questions later. That was a recipe for disaster if ever there was one.

The Rice Lake exit came up fast on his right. John hit it, barely slowing as the Crown Vic barreled up the off-ramp. He glanced to his left at the top, didn't see anyone coming, and turned right without stopping.

The Kwik Trip was on the left up ahead, two lines of gas pumps with a red-roofed convenience store behind. Two cars were at the pumps: a maroon sedan and a navy minivan. He could see the light blue Chevy parked to the side of the convenience store. But a line of cars streamed past in the opposite lane; he couldn't turn.

John waited, stopped dead, the turn signal clicking, and swore steadily under his breath.

A break came in the traffic. The Crown Vic's tires squealed as he accelerated into the gas station just as the Chevy reversed. Shit. She was going in the opposite direction. If he could drive in front of her, block the pickup from exiting the gas station—

At that moment, the maroon sedan pulled in front of him.

John hit the brakes hard. The Crown Vic shuddered as it stopped inches from the other car's bumper. The maroon sedan's driver flipped him off and began backing up. And Turner Hastings drove past, green eyes stark in a white face. As she passed him, John had one thought.

She'd cut her hair.

Chapter Twenty-two

Oh, Lord. Turner's heart felt like it was going to pound right through her chest. She swung the Chevy out of the Kwik Trip and onto the overpass road, tires squealing on asphalt. Squeaky grunted as his body was flung against the passenger door. His paws scrabbled to keep his seat.

Her breath was coming short and quick, and her hands shook on the steering wheel. Turner shifted through the gears as fast as she could and pressed down hard on the accelerator. Was John following her? She glanced at the rearview mirror, but the truck bounced over a bump in the road and she couldn't see clearly. She flung the truck into a turn and then into another, speeding down a residential street.

It'd been John. She was sure even though she'd caught only a glimpse of him as she fled the gas station. He'd been driving a plain dark blue sedan, not the sheriff's car she'd seen at Tommy's. If she'd hesitated even one moment more, if she'd not been suspicious of the mullet-haired attendant staring at her and decided to leave the gas station, John would've caught her. As it was, she'd had to hang up on Victoria while the other woman was still talking. She'd call her later and apologize.

But she couldn't think about that now. Now she had to get away from John.

And what was worse, a small part of her, a tiny bit hiding in a corner of her heart, had wanted to be caught. To at last have the opportunity to see John up close. To inhale his male scent and look into his eyes when he was talking to her. To watch the expression on his face. And to finally have this whole mess over with. No more running, no more fear, a chance to rest. If he caught her, she'd no longer be in control. It wouldn't be her fault if she didn't find the evidence against Calvin. It'd be an honorable failure.

But she wouldn't give in to that seductive lure—the honorable failure. She would not fail. She must not. She must keep on, no matter how hard it got. Now was not the time to rest. Not yet. She still owed Rusty, still had to clear his name and put Calvin in jail.

Beside her, Squeaky whined. He had a hind leg braced on the floor, and his rear end was half off the seat. The poor animal didn't look at all comfortable. Turner glanced in the rearview mirror again. Nothing. Had John set up a roadblock outside of town? Were there other agents after her?

She was on an odd little lane now, near the outskirts of town. Up ahead she could see a decrepit old house with several sheds and a collection of rusting cars huddled around it. She made a quick decision and swung in the drive, bumping over ruts and maneuvering behind the house. She put the truck in neutral and looked around.

She couldn't see the road from back here; the house and old cars hid it. And as far as she could tell, the Chevy wouldn't be visible to someone searching from the road, either.

Turner killed the engine just as her cell began to ring. It'd slid to the floor under her feet during the wild drive. She picked up the palm-sized piece of plastic and stared at it. She knew he couldn't pinpoint where she was just by talking to her. Even so, some superstitious part of her wanted to fling the phone as far away as possible.

Instead, she answered it. "What?"

"Slow down. I'm not chasing you." His voice was angry and his breathing rough, as if he'd been running.

She laughed, the sound coming out like a bark. "Yeah, right."

"I'm not going to cause an accident by chasing you through a small town, Turner. Just slow down, dammit. Don't kill yourself running away from me. I'm not following you."

"And I'm supposed to believe that after—"

"It's my job, goddamnit!" He sounded like he was at the end of his rope.

Well, so was she. "I hate your stupid job!" Squeaky laid his ears back and looked worried at the tone of her voice.

"We've been over this before—"

"I didn't rob the bank," she burst out. "Can't you leave me alone?"

"No." She heard him take a breath. "No, I can't."

"Please."

"Don't." His voice was low. "Don't beg me to do something I can't."

Turner stared out the window at the dingy backyard.

Nearby, the frame of some kind of car was rusted a uniform clay-brown. It sat in a bed of tall grass like the fossilized skeleton of a dinosaur. Tears blurred her vision.

John spoke again in her ear, his deep voice slow and intimate in the afternoon sunshine. "I can't leave you alone, and I can't let you get away. From me or the law. I can't sit back and make the exception for you, no matter how I feel personally. I can't change what I do or who I am."

"Then stop calling me." The tears trailed down her cheeks now, and she swallowed in order to talk clearly. "Stop following me. Stop talking to me about your daughter and Mexican food and the daily crossword puzzle. Stop whispering in my ear at night in the dark—"

"You're under a lot of stress—"

"Stop making me feel!"

"I can't."

"Yes, you can," she said shakily. "Get another agent assigned to my case."

He sighed. "I can't do that, either."

"Why not?"

"I can't, and I wouldn't even if I could. You're mine, honey."

"Oh, Lord." She rolled her head back on the seat, staring at the old ceiling of the truck, letting the tears run down her face and into the neckline of her T-shirt. "I can't do this anymore."

"Why not?"

"This isn't going to work."

"You've been alone too long." His voice was soothing. "You need to come in."

A sob burst from her. "No. You're hurting me. You—"

"Don't cry," he whispered. "It kills me."

"I can't stop." She was still shaking from the adrenaline that had surged through her arteries when she'd fled him. It was too much. Finally, too much. It seemed she could no longer dam all the emotions she'd held back for four long years. Squeaky whined and put his mammoth head on her lap.

"I don't want to hurt you," John said.

"But you are." She stroked Squeaky's velvet ears and tried to think of a solution. There wasn't one. There wasn't any good outcome to this. "We can't continue like this. I'm jumping at shadows as it is. I can't live like this—"

"Then stop. Tell me where you are."

She half laughed, half hiccupped.

"I'll come get you," he said.

She licked the salt tears from her lips and stared out at the dinosaur car. A red squirrel had climbed the top and was sitting there, tail swishing back and forth.

"Oh, John."

He sighed in her ear. "Is it really worth it?"

She closed her eyes and thought about Rusty. How could she explain? She took a shuddering breath, trying to still the tears so she could somehow tell him. "My mom died when I was seventeen, did you know that?"

"Yes."

Of course. He must have a file on her by now. He probably knew her bra size and her grades from high school biology. She thrust that thought from her mind.

"Mom had cancer. It took a while—about a year—for her to go. A long year. She was in and out of the hospital, getting the chemo." She swallowed again, remembering.

"Dad had left when I was a toddler. I already told you that. So it was just us, Mom and me. And Uncle Rusty."

John was silent.

"Anyway." Her throat felt swollen from the crying. She cleared it. "It was pretty bad, her cancer. The whole hospital thing. Rusty had this big old Victorian house on the edge of town, and he let us move in with him because Mom . . ." She inhaled sharply. "Mom wasn't able to do much, for me or her. She felt too sick most days. Rusty and I split the cooking and chores." She laughed a little, her voice scratchy. "Uncle Rusty had been a bachelor all his life. Most of the time we had Swanson's frozen dinners on his nights to cook. Swedish meatballs or la-sagna. Or bratwurst sandwiches when he hadn't planned ahead—they were his favorite. He did his best. He did the best he was able."

"Turner—"

"And when Mom died . . ." Her voice trailed away.

"I'm sorry," he whispered.

Squeaky nuzzled his jaw into her palm. She forced herself to continue while she stroked his long nose. "Most of our money was already spent by that time. Hospital bills. Uncle Rusty paid for the funeral and the plot and headstone."

"Baby." John sounded pained.

She shook her head and gulped even though he couldn't see. "Brad was already gone. Away at school and then starting his first job, so it was just Uncle Rusty and me. He was in his late fifties, and yet he never made me feel unwelcome. He never said anything about hav-ing his life turned around, virtually adopting a teenager at his age. He was so . . . kind. I wish you could've met him, then you'd understand."

"I wish I'd known him, too," John said gently.

"He didn't do it. He didn't steal from the bank." She steadied her voice, making it sure. "And he didn't deserve what happened to him. Rusty worked all his life at that bank. He was only two years away from retirement. He was planning on getting a cabin at the lake, maybe a new boat. He was going to go fishing every day."

"Turner—"

She closed her eyes. She had to get this out. "When Calvin accused Rusty and then fired him, he killed something in Uncle Rusty, long before he actually died. Rusty was humiliated that anyone would think he'd done the things he was accused of. He stopped smiling. Stopped laughing."

"I'm sorry." She could hear him blow out a breath. "I'm sorry. I understand your uncle meant a lot to you."

"He did."

"Have you thought what Rusty would say about what you're doing?" John asked. "Would he want you to live your life this way?"

She half smiled. John was so good at this. So good at presenting the sane alternative, so good at listening without condemning. He must've brought in scores of fugitives with that slow, deep voice and sympathetic manner. And she was almost—*almost*—tempted by him. "No, of course not. Rusty wouldn't have wanted this for me. He was a gentle, kind man and he loved me."

"Then—"

"But that's not the point," Turner said softly. Firmly. "I'm the one who chooses my actions, and I choose to make sure his name is cleared. Because he was the way he was. Because he loved me."

"Christ," he muttered, like he was frustrated. And angry.

Her own anger welled, even though he was only doing his job. She wanted to cut through all the pretense, all of his motives and her motives to the core feelings beneath. To the man beneath the FBI agent. The man she'd been talking to in the last few days.

She inhaled slowly. "You tell me not to try to change you, and in the same breath you ask me to change who I am."

"Turner—"

"No, John. Listen. I believe in righting wrongs. I believe in standing by the people I love. And I believe that evil people shouldn't be allowed to get away with their crimes. That's who I am."

"I believe all those things, too," he answered. "The difference is that I'm a professional. Leave Hyman to the FBI."

"I did," she said softly. "They had four years to bring Calvin to justice, and no one lifted a finger to investigate him."

"Okay, what if I promise to investigate the embezzling at the bank?"

It was so tempting to give in. But . . . "You'll still need evidence. You would've needed just cause and a warrant to search Calvin's safe deposit box, wouldn't you?"

"Yes." He said it tightly.

She smiled. John didn't lie, even when it meant losing the argument. "And you wouldn't have got the warrant just on my suspicions, would you?"

He swore under his breath.

"I'm going to find that evidence." She didn't have to add that she wouldn't be waiting around for a warrant.

"And I'm going to make sure Calvin Hyman goes to jail for what he did to Rusty."

"What about when you go to jail?" he asked softly, his deep voice rumbling. "I'm not going to stop, you know. Not until I arrest you."

She glanced out the window of the Chevy half expecting him to be standing there, her own personal nemesis. "I have to go."

"No, you don't." He sounded tender. And frustrated. "You're running away again. For such a fearless woman, you sure can be chickenshit sometimes."

A surprised laugh burst from her. "I am n—"

"But that's okay for now," he continued over her, his voice sure. "Because sooner or later I'll catch up."

Oh, Lord. "Good-bye, John."

"Good-bye. Like the hair." And he hung up.

She sat staring at the cell in her hand for a moment. Hair? Then she remembered that she'd cut her hair. Hacked it, really. John had seen her for maybe a half-second, and in that miniscule moment of time, he'd noticed she'd changed her hair.

Turner shivered. She didn't know whether to feel flattered or frightened.

Chapter Twenty-three

*D*ude, I think this is the wrong way to Minnesota," Nald panted.

"Oh, like you're Mr. Direction Guy," Fish said without bothering to turn around. "What? Have you got one of them GPS things up your ass?"

It was hot. It was *bitchin'* hot. It was so hot that the asphalt was melting on the road and sticking to his shoes in black globs. It was so hot that ants would fry on the road, if any ants came out of their little bitty holes. Which they didn't. It was so hot that Nald could feel his balls itching with sweat.

Hot.

"Well, I know that Minnesota's to the west," Nald said. "Like, if you look at a map, it's left of Wisconsin, and that's west—"

"What's your point, douchebag?"

"I don't think we're heading west, dude."

Fish stopped dead in the middle of the road and turned around to face Nald. A tick was crawling up the side of his face. He looked truly disgusting. His hair was all flat and greasy and gross from the swamp water, and there were little white lines on his face where the sweat had cleaned the dirt. Gross. Also, his nose was red and peeling from a massive sunburn. Of course, that might be partly because of the poison ivy Fish had run into yesterday. Fish was real allergic to poison ivy. His arms were dripping yellow gunk like he was a nuclear-waste zombie.

Gross.

"We're heading west," Fish said, squinting into the afternoon sun.

Nald stopped, as well, and took out the piece of teri-yaki beef jerky he still had left from the store they'd knocked over this morning. "East. Jerky?" He held out the jerky which only had a small amount of pocket lint on it.

"West."

Nald took a bite and chewed. "East. Do you think that counter lady recognized us?"

"How could she, booger-brain? We switched masks."

Sometimes Fish was a real criminal mastermind. Cunning. Like this morning. He'd pointed out that the cops would be looking for them. Would have, like, those bulletins they sent out. *Be on the lookout for two scary bank-robbing dudes. Armed and way dangerous.* So he said they'd confuse their pursuers by switching masks. Fish would be Yoda and he, Nald, would be SpongeBob. Which was fine with Nald, because even though Yoda was a cooler character, the Yoda mask had lost an ear, which sorta cut down on its coolness factor.

"Yeah, but she looked at us kinda funny," Nald said

through the jerky. It was old jerky and took a lot of chewing.

"That's because she was so terrified of us, man," Fish said.

Nald was doubtful. "You think?"

"She started shaking, didn't she?"

"Yeah, but she was making funny noises like she was having a fit or something."

"So we scared her into a fit. What else do you want?"

"I dunno." Nald finished the jerky. "Too bad all she had was this jerky and a couple of cans of Yoo-hoo."

"What do you expect?" Fish made a spitting noise, but nothing came out. The tick fell to his chin. "Small town and all. 'Sides, you're forgetting the cheese curls."

"Yeah." Nald perked up. "Those were good."

"And they're a dairy group," Fish pointed out righteously. "Nutritious."

"Yeah. And jerky's protein." Nald squinted, trying to remember the nutrition charts from first grade. It was hard, because he'd spent most of first grade discovering boogers. "That just leaves vegetable."

"Cheese curls." Fish scratched a poison ivy welt on his arm. Yellow gunk oozed out.

"You just said they were dairy," Nald objected.

"And vegetable."

"How can cheese curls be dairy *and* vegetable?"

"Because," Fish said slowly, like Nald was a retard or something. "They make them out of corn. It says so right on the bag."

"Huh." Nald felt a little uneasy. He'd had no idea he was eating health food all these years.

"So let's get going." Fish turned around. He had a tick crawling up his back, too.

Nald trotted after him. "Yeah, but we're going east."

"Are not, dickhead." Fish tried to run his hand through his hair, but it was stuck to his head. He found the tick on his face, picked it off, and flicked it into the bushes. Another tick emerged from behind his ear.

"Are, too, moron," Nald said.

"Are not!"

Fish stopped, turned, and threw up his hands. His face got really, really red. "We. Are. Walking. West!"

Nald folded his arms. "Nope."

Fish stood, arms outstretched for a moment, and then his stumpy little body began to shake. "WEST!" he cried. He threw down the black garbage bag of money, which was kinda raggedy on the edges, and began jumping up and down on it. "West! West! West!"

Nald wrinkled his nose. He'd tried to stay upwind from Fish most of the time, but the wind must've shifted, because a real powerful stink was burning his—

"WEST!"

"SKUNK!" Nald yelled.

"Where?" Fish hollered, his body still hopping up and down.

"There!" Nald pointed to the big gray animal emerging from the woods. "That's the biggest badass skunk I've ever seen."

Fish stopped jumping and looked. "That's not a skunk, you turd."

"Yeah? Then what is it?"

"I dunno, but it's not a skunk."

"It's got a white stripe."

"It's gray."

Nald watched the animal. It was staring back at them out of tiny black eyes in a little flat head. A corner of its lip was lifted like maybe it wasn't too happy to see them. "Probably an old skunk."

"Don't be a dickhead." Fish looked like he was about to start jumping up and down again. "Skunks don't get old. They get run over."

"It's a skunk, dude."

The gray skunk lost interest in them and started digging in the dust near the road.

"It's not a skunk. It's a raccoon."

"Not a raccoon. No mask."

"Well, it's not a skunk, either. Does that thing look like Pepé Le Pew?"

Now that Fish mentioned it, the animal didn't look all that much like Pepé Le Pew. It looked more like—

"It's Bucky Badger!" Nald cried in triumph.

"No way!" Fish did a double take.

"Yeah! Bucky Badger. Isn't he cute?" Bucky was turned around, his little furry ass wiggling as he dug furiously.

Fish looked scornful. "How do you know it's a he?"

Nald stared. "Because Bucky's a boy, dummy. Don't you know anything?"

"I meant this badger. How do you know it's a boy?"

"Does it look like a girl?" Nald pointed at Bucky in outrage. "Duh!"

Bucky turned around and smiled, showing little yellow teeth. Definitely a boy.

"Where's his dick, then, boner?"

"You're a dick. Bucky's dick is under all that—that"—Nald waved his hand wildly—"fur."

"Dick yourself." Fish sneered. "I don't see no dick. I think it's a fairy badger."

"Bucky's not a fairy!"

"Is, too!"

"Is not!"

"Is, too," Fish shouted. "He wears that little red sweater and struts around with his naked ass hanging out. Tinkerbell."

Nald felt ready to cry. How could Fish say that about Bucky Badger? "He wears the Wisconsin sweatshirt."

"So? Then why doesn't he wear the Wisconsin sweatpants, huh?"

"Maybe he's hot."

"He's hot, all right." Fish pursed his lips horribly beneath his beet-red nose and made kissing noises. The tick sat on his cheek like a beauty mark. "He's a fairy!"

"Is not!"

"Fairy! Fairy! Fairy!" Fish swished around the road. "Bucky's an airy-fairy!"

"Douchebag!"

"Fartbrain!"

Then Bucky attacked.

Chapter Twenty-four

$\mathcal{I}$t was almost ten that night by the time John found Calvin Hyman's lake cabin near Rhinelander. Hyman had given him the directions, but it had taken John an hour, driving up and down back lanes, to even get in the right area. Then he'd had to peer at mailboxes, most badly marked, to try to read numbers in the gathering gloom. He'd driven past the place twice, finally back-tracking and getting out of the Crown Victoria to verify the number on the fire-engine-shaped mailbox.

Now the lane leading down to the cottage was dim in the dusk. The bushes along the side hadn't been trimmed in a while. Branches scraped the sides of the car as he drove by in second gear. The cabin itself was on a grassy slope that led down to the lake. John parked the Crown Vic and got out to look around, absently rotating his right shoulder. It ached from sitting in the car so long.

A bird called sleepily from the woods as he tramped toward the cabin. It was nice, a newish two-story brown clapboard with a wraparound screen porch. A two-car garage stood kitty-corner to the cabin, with a gravel circle drive between the two. Down by the lake was some kind of shed, probably a boathouse. Behind the cabin was a mowed clearing with a sagging volleyball net.

He mounted the wooden steps and noticed a spider's web strung across the screen door. If Turner had been here, she hadn't gotten in that way. He left the cobweb on the porch door and circled the cottage. The screen windows would be easy to cut, but he didn't see any tampering. In back, the windows were dusty. He had to stretch to peer inside. Turner would need something to climb on to enter through the windows.

Satisfied she hadn't gotten this far, he returned to the Crown Vic and carefully maneuvered it into the grass behind the cabin. He backed around the volleyball net until the car bumped a tree on the edge of the woods, then killed the engine. He had a nice view of the back of the cabin and the gravel turnaround from here. The moon was out, but it was just a thin crescent. There wasn't enough light to reveal the car. At least, that was what he hoped.

John propped his arm on the door and watched the back of the cabin. Where was she tonight? Nearby, he was sure. He'd spent a fruitless couple of hours searching the teeming metropolis of Rice Lake for Turner after he'd lost her at the gas station. She must've left town headed this way, but he hadn't seen her, and there hadn't been any more reports of a light blue pickup in the area.

He pushed the button on his watch to make the face light up. 10:23. It was only a little after eight in Washington state. He fished out his cell and dialed his ex-wife's number. Across the miles, the phone rang. The answering machine picked up. John hesitated, then punched the *End* button without leaving a message. What could he say? If Amy or Dennis, her husband, got the message, they wouldn't bother replying. And besides, he wasn't sure Amy knew that Rachel had called him. He didn't want to break his daughter's trust when she'd only recently reached out to him. At least, that was what he was telling himself. Maybe he was just a flat-out coward, too afraid to talk to his little girl who wasn't so little anymore.

He snorted and leaned his head against the seat. It'd been a shitty day all around. God, why not? He gave in to temptation and punched the speed dial.

Turner answered at once. "John."

He sighed, the muscles in the back of his neck already relaxing. "Yup."

"Where are you?" Her voice was low, almost whispering.

His groin immediately tightened. "That's a change of pace. You asking me where I am."

"Are you going to answer me?"

"No."

She sighed, the sound lost and lonely in the dark. "I can't tell you where I am, either."

He shifted in the car seat, wishing he could push it back into a more comfortable position. But he had to be ready to drive should she show up. "How's Squeaky?"

"He's sleeping. He got anxious in Rice Lake."

He smiled. "Squeaky got anxious? How about you?"

"I got anxious, too," she admitted.

"I'm sorry." His lips compressed. "Did you get something to eat for dinner?"

"Saltines and Spanish olives."

He laughed.

"You?" she asked.

"DQ. I got a bacon cheeseburger basket and a vanilla shake."

"That's not good for you. Nothing but fat and salt."

She sounded disapproving, and his heart ached. "Yeah, but it tasted good. And there was a thing of cole-slaw in the basket."

"I don't think that counts. They put it in a condiment cup."

"True."

They were silent a moment. John could hear her breathing, and he closed his eyes. God, he wanted to be beside her right now. Touch her, inhale her scent, brush his lips over her hair. The thought of her with him was oddly seductive. He opened his eyes again and rolled down his side window. The leftover air-conditioned cold had dissipated from inside the car, but the outside air had begun to cool and there was a breeze.

He tilted his face to see the night sky. "Are you outside?"

"Um. Yes." She sounded sleepy, her husky voice blurred.

His cock began to throb. "Can you see the stars?"

"Yes."

"Do you know where the North Star is?"

"Polaris," she murmured. "I can see it. And Ursa Minor prowling around it."

"That's the Little Dipper to me."

She laughed. "Do you see Cassiopeia?"

"The one shaped like a big W, right?"

"Yes. And next to her is her daughter, Andromeda."

His mouth twisted. "Whoops. You've found me out. I don't know where that one is."

"Do you see the two biggest stars in Cassiopeia?"

"Uh-huh."

"Follow them down," she instructed slowly. "The next biggest star is Andromeda's right foot. She's kind of in the shape of a long, narrow triangle. There are three stars leading right from her foot, do you see them?"

He wasn't sure, but he didn't tell her that. "Yes."

"And on the opposite side of Cassiopeia is Cygnus, the Swan. It's in a shape of a cross. Sometimes it's called the Northern Cross. Do you see it?"

"Yes," he lied.

"And Vega is there, too. It's a very bright star, closer to the horizon. Vega's in the Lyra constellation. Do you know that one?"

He wasn't bothering to look. He leaned his head back and listened to her husky voice murmuring in his ear. She could be reading the phone book for all he cared. "Yes."

She chuckled, a low, sexy sound.

"What?"

"You don't see it, do you?"

He smiled. "No. How did you know?"

"Because no one has ever heard of Lyra." She sounded triumphant to have tricked him.

"You made it up?"

"No. It's an obscure constellation. I only know it because of the myth."

"Tell me," he commanded softly.

"Lyra is Orpheus's lyre. One of those little harps they had in ancient Greece."

"Uh-huh." He could fall asleep just listening to her hypnotic murmur.

"Orpheus was a wonderful musician, the greatest of all time. When he played, the birds stopped singing to listen and the wild animals followed him as if they were enchanted."

"Pretty good."

She laughed again. "Yes, pretty good. He fell in love with a woman named Eurydice, and she with him, and they were married. But then Eurydice was bitten by a snake and died. Naturally, she went to Hades, and Orpheus was inconsolable with grief."

"That's a sad story."

"Yes, but I'm not done. You see, Orpheus was so in love with Eurydice that he braved the underworld to get her back. He journeyed to Hades and after many travails stood before the god of the underworld himself. Orpheus played for Pluto, and the god was so moved by the beauty of his music that he did what had never been done, before or since. He let Eurydice leave death." She paused.

He made a listening sound.

"But there was one catch," she whispered in his ear.

"There always is."

"Yes, there always is." She sounded sad now, and John stirred uneasily. "Orpheus could lead his wife to the upper world, but he must not look back at her while he did this, not even once."

John grimaced and waited for the inevitable.

"So Orpheus led Eurydice through the caverns of Hades, but she wasn't allowed to talk until she reached the surface. And although Orpheus knew she must be following him, he didn't hear anything. He grew more and more uncertain, until he couldn't bear it anymore. He turned around."

"She disappeared."

"No," she said slowly. "That was the worst part. She was there, standing right behind him, and Orpheus saw her for just an instant before Pluto took her back."

"Poor son of a bitch." John rubbed a hand over his eyes. "But I can understand what made him turn around to check."

"Really?" Her tone was curious. "I would've thought you'd have no sympathy for Orpheus losing control."

"Yeah, but see, he couldn't hear her."

"So?"

"So, a woman's voice is the most distinctive thing about her to a man. He hears it day and night, after all."

"I detect some male chauvinism in that remark." She sounded amused.

"You shouldn't. I'm serious." And to his surprise, he was. "Women talk more than men, generally speaking. A guy gets used to his woman telling him what to do, chatting about her day, just gabbing."

"Gabbing?"

He grimaced. He knew he wasn't explaining this well. "Yeah, gabbing. Women do it all the time. Constantly. Even you. It gets to be soothing. Normal. He knows everything's all right with the world by the sound of her voice."

"I don't think I've ever heard this particular theory before." Now she was laughing at him.

He continued anyway. "Ol' Orpheus must've been pretty disconcerted to know his wife was right in back of him but wasn't saying anything."

"I'm still not sure that's a compliment to my sex."

He closed his eyes. "Oh, it is. A man can get hard just listening to the right woman's voice." God knew he was.

A laugh burst from her. He could tell he'd startled her. *"What?"*

"You heard me."

"I can't believe you're telling me this."

"Believe it. A low, raspy woman's voice is a turn-on every time. Makes a guy think of the bedroom and what that voice might say there."

"Jeez. Do you guys think about sex all the time?"

"Pretty much." John grinned. She sounded so prim. "But I know that women think about it, too."

"You're awfully confident."

"Yeah, maybe I am. Come on, admit it. You've thought about what it would be like to kiss me." John was conscious that he'd just crossed one of his own boundaries. Had he crossed one of hers, as well? How far would she let him go?

"I'm not going to answer that." Her voice was soft, almost a whisper.

"That's as good as an admission." He grinned in triumph. "I think about it. How your mouth would feel under mine."

"I-I can't do this, John."

"We're just talking," he coaxed. "Talking on the phone. Nothing scary about that."

She either laughed or sobbed, it was impossible to tell which. "Everything about you scares me. Even talking on the phone."

He closed his eyes. He was so hard, so frustrated. It wouldn't take much, the state he was in, but he wasn't going to give in to that need right now, no matter the urgency.

"We should work on that fear," he said instead.

"I-I need to go."

It was an excuse, he could tell. Dammit, he'd lost her. He beat down the frustration, the impatient need to hold on to her voice. But there was no point tonight. He was a hunter who knew well the importance of timing. Better to let her go and hunt again on the morrow.

"Good night," he said tenderly.

"G-good night, John."

He punched the *End* button and grimaced into the dark. It was going to be a long, long time before he slept.

Chapter Twenty-five

The ringing of her cell jolted Turner awake early the next morning. She flung her arm out in reflex and hit her hand on the dash painfully. "Ow!"

Next to her, Squeaky lifted his head and yawned, revealing a cavernous mouth and long yellow teeth. The phone rang again.

Turner sat upright and looked around. She'd spent the night in a pull-off between Woodruff and Rhinelander. She hadn't dared approach the cabin so soon after seeing John in Rice Lake. After that near-miss at the gas station, there could be no doubt that he was following her. That fact was going to be a stumbling block to her plans. By now they—the FBI, police, whatever law-enforcement agencies were working on her case—must be aware that Calvin's cabin was her destination. They'd have it staked out, probably. How was she going to—

The phone sent up another annoying digital ring.

Turner grabbed it and answered. "Hello?"

"I hope I haven't woken you," Victoria said, sounding very wide awake herself.

Turner sat up straight and ran a hand through her short hair. It felt matted.

"Oh, no," she lied. "I'm glad you called. We need to set a time to meet." She looked at her watch. Good grief, it was only seven a.m. Who called people at this time?

Evidently, Victoria. "Good. That's what I thought, as well. Does 12:30 tomorrow work for you?"

Tomorrow was Thursday, and Victoria had said in their last phone call that she couldn't meet Friday. Tomorrow would have to do.

"Yes, that's fine," Turner replied. She'd have to get into Calvin's cabin today somehow and find the evidence. "Where?"

"You could come to my office."

Turner felt unease creep up her spine. Victoria seemed helpful, but she didn't really know her that well. And the other woman had asked about Turner's whereabouts in the last phone call. On the other hand, she didn't have any other contacts in the Federal Prosecutor's Office. She was taking a calculated risk.

Still, best to be cautious. "No, I'd rather see you somewhere more neutral."

"Fine," Victoria said smoothly. "I can meet you at a restaurant or coffee shop."

"Well . . ." She tried to think of a Madison restaurant with an open floor plan. Her mind was blank.

"Or I'm not too far from the capitol square," Victoria suggested. "We could meet on the north side."

"Yes." Turner relaxed a little. The capitol square was big and open. She'd be able to spot Victoria and look for any police before approaching her. "That's perfect."

"Good. Tomorrow at 12:30."

"Okay."

"Bye." Victoria broke the connection.

Turner hung up thoughtfully. Victoria had known about the bank robbery and Calvin's safe deposit box. The other woman might assume that Turner had masterminded the robbery, as the FBI seemed to think. She might very well be in contact with John and the other FBI agents. There was a real possibility that Turner would be walking into a trap when she met Victoria. But what choice did she have? She'd already weighed the odds. Victoria knew her. She would be far more likely to believe her accusations against Calvin than would a stranger in the Office of the Federal Prosecutor. In the end, the benefits outweighed the risks. Turner shook her head. She could spend all day debating this, and her decision would still be the same. Better to get on with what she had to do. Beside her, Squeaky tried to stretch but was hampered by the steering wheel. He whined.

"Me, too," she muttered to the dog.

She got out with Squeaky and leaned against the Chevy while he investigated the calf-high yellow grass by the side of the road. The sun was out again today, hot and dry and too bright already. A crow flew out of the woods, cawing, and Squeaky paused to watch it.

Her thoughts turned to the phone conversation she'd had with John last night and the frustration she'd heard in his voice at the end. How had that happened? They'd started out talking about stars and myths, each of them far apart physically, each looking at the same night sky. They'd avoided more explosive topics, like John's determination to find and arrest her and her opposing determination to avenge Uncle Rusty. How had talking quietly with him led to talk of kissing him? That had just not been her. She wasn't the type to be turned on by pursuing FBI agents.

Even when she'd had a boyfriend—and she could count the guys she'd linked up with on one hand—the sex had been plain vanilla. Most of the time she didn't even come during intercourse, and it had never bothered her. She could take care of herself all by herself. Few of her boyfriends noticed, but the ones who had seemed deeply threatened by her self-sufficiency. That had led one ex-boyfriend to give her the number of a sex therapist when they'd broken up. He'd handed the slip of paper to her with his brow wrinkled in honest concern for her so-called impairment.

She'd thanked him and thrown the number away at the first opportunity. Sex just wasn't that important to her. It involved body fluids. And getting really, really close to another human being, both physically and emotionally. There were embarrassing noises and smells, and a horrible lack of control over one's own body. Heck, you were supposed to, in theory, have a very intimate event—*an orgasm*—with another person right there in the same room with you. Right there *in* you. How that could possibly be appealing to anyone was beyond her. Sometimes she wondered how someone could relax under those circumstances. She just wasn't that much of a sharer.

And yet, last night she'd been totally turned on by just the sound of John's voice. Turner shivered. Wasn't that kinky in some vague way? God alone knew what would happen if John ever actually put his hands on her. She'd probably spontaneously combust. And wouldn't *that* be messy? What was it about John that let her relinquish control? Was it the situation? The adrenaline rush of being on the run, the near miss at the Rice Lake Kwik Trip?

A hawk circled high overhead, searching for a hapless mouse or songbird for breakfast. She wished—she really wished—that she could pin her arousal on the situation or the adrenaline. But she couldn't. When she imagined John and her, alone, touching each other . . . Turner squirmed, her face heating. Her reaction was very different. It wasn't the situation. It was the man.

And wasn't that a terrifying thought?

Squeaky flushed a turkey just outside the tree line. The big, dark brown bird did a flapping run into the woods, and the dog gave chase enthusiastically. Turner could hear them crashing through the tall coniferous forest. She took the cell phone out of her pocket and looked at it. The urge to call John was almost overwhelming. She wanted to hear his voice. To ask him how he felt this morning.

No. No. No. She was an adult woman. Over thirty, and sophisticated, like those women in the *Sex and the City* reruns. Only in small-town Wisconsin. No. She wasn't going to call John, and she wasn't going to encourage him. No matter what he could make her feel, sexually and emotionally. Their relationship was just not healthy. Besides, she wasn't entirely certain she could say anything without stuttering and blushing. She put the cell away again. Back to business. She had to find Calvin's cabin and figure out a way in.

"Squeaky!" she called. Would the dog even know his name by now?

There was a crashing from the trees and Squeaky

bounded out of the forest, mouth agape and grinning. He ran up to her and tried to put his paws on her shoulders.

"No." She gently knocked him aside and fished his red water bowl out of the truck. "Did you catch the turkey?"

He wagged his whip-thin tail and gulped the water she poured into his dish. A colony of burrs clung to his backside near his tail. Turner picked them off. She'd have to check him for ticks later. Taking care of a dog was proving to be more complicated than she'd initially figured on. Squeaky looked up from his bowl and showed his gratitude by slobbering water down her front. She picked at her T-shirt and sighed. She needed to find a place to wash up, anyway.

Time to get back on the road.

Chapter Twenty-six

*O*h, man. He was getting too old for this.

It was nearly seven-thirty a.m. when John climbed from the Crown Vic's front seat. He moved slowly, like an old man. An arthritic old man. An arthritic old man who'd been beat up the night before. He actually heard his joints creak. Maybe it was time to seek out a boring desk job.

He stretched and then swore when his damn shoulder cramped up. God, he was just falling apart. He massaged his right shoulder while he limped to the edge of the woods to take a piss. In the light of day, the Crown Vic stood out clearly. He'd have to find a better place to park. He was stuck here without food or a place to shower until Turner showed, and he needed a shower bad. Maybe he should go into Rhinelander, clean up and eat. But then he risked missing Turner, and he couldn't—wouldn't—do that.

His cell went off in the car where he'd dropped it the night before. Could Turner be calling him this early? He loped back to the Crown Vic and found the cell on the passenger seat. Crap. It was Torelli. Just who he wanted to talk to first thing in the morning.

He answered the phone. "MacKinnon."

Torelli didn't waste time on a greeting. "We've got another lead on Turner Hastings," he said, his East Coast accent strong this morning.

"Yeah?" John leaned into the Crown Vic and found his coffee mug in the console holder.

"A woman named Victoria Weidner, works in the Office of the Federal Prosecutor in Madison, called the office in Milwaukee just now. They transferred her to me."

John knit his brow. "What did she call about?" He lifted the coffee mug to his lips and drank the cold swill left over from yesterday morning. He shuddered at the bitter liquid.

"Hastings contacted her."

John lowered the cup. "What?"

Torelli ignored his surprised interjection. "Apparently, Turner Hastings wants to meet with Weidner and show her evidence that Calvin Hyman has embezzled from the Winosha bank."

Why, that little witch. If she had evidence, why the hell didn't she trust him with it? "Why Weidner?"

"Weidner grew up in Winosha. She and Hastings know each other from high school."

Huh. "And Weidner turned her in?"

"She is a federal prosecutor," Torelli said neutrally. "She read about Hastings in the newspaper and figured she should alert us about her."

"Some friend." John sighed and ran a hand through his hair. Good thing he had it short, otherwise it might frighten the squirrels after his night in the car. "When are they meeting?"

"Tomorrow. Twelve-thirty hours on the north side of the capitol square in Madison."

John squinted at the early morning sun. "Why the delay?"

"I don't know."

"She doesn't have the evidence yet," John answered his own question.

Torelli was silent, waiting.

"Okay," John said. "I still think she has to show up here, sometime today or tonight. Rhinelander is four hours from Madison, and she needs to search Hyman's cabin to find that evidence before she meets with Weidner."

"Yeah," Torelli said. "That fits with what Weidner said. She indicated Hastings didn't have the evidence yet."

"Good."

"Do you want me to contact the Madison police to stake out the capitol tomorrow?" Torelli asked.

"No."

"Mac—"

"That's an order," John growled.

He could hear the other man sigh over the phone. "We know she'll be in Madison at twelve-thirty hours tomorrow. You can't let this chance slip away." Torelli didn't mention the Kwik Trip incident yesterday, but the disgust was strong in his voice.

Damn it. He couldn't let Torelli go rogue on him now. "Listen. She needs to come to Rhinelander first. I'll catch her here, before she ever gets to Madison."

"And if you miss her again?"

"I won't."

"You did before."

Asshole. John took a breath. "If I miss her, I can still be in Madison in less than four hours."

"But—"

"This isn't open for discussion, Torelli."

The younger man muttered something under his breath. It was probably just as well that John didn't catch the words. Then, "Yes, sir."

"I don't want outside help."

"Yes, sir."

"No calling in the locals."

"Yes, sir."

"And no going to the SAC behind my back," John said in a low, lethal voice. "Got it?"

"*Yes,* sir." Torelli sounded as if he were spitting through gritted teeth.

John smiled grimly. As long as Torelli obeyed him, he didn't care how pissed off the other man got.

"Good. Keep me informed." He pushed the *End* button before his subordinate could respond.

John poured out the remains of yesterday's coffee onto the sparse grass. God, what a crappy way to start the day. Now there was no chance of going into Rhinelander. He knew Turner had to show up right here sometime in the next twenty-four hours. He sighed and stretched. At least he had the box of granola bars he always carried with him. And he'd bought a couple of bottles of water yesterday. He popped the trunk and rummaged for the box. He'd have to move the car. Too noticeable in daylight. That meant staking out the cabin by squatting in the woods with all the ticks and mosquitoes and other wildlife. Not to mention the heat. Oh, joy.

He found the box of granola bars and pried it open. He was way too close to this case. He knew it and, what was worse, Torelli knew it. If Torelli went over his head, he might not have a credible defense this time. Had he requested the help of the state patrol yesterday, Turner probably would've been captured. John knew that. He could plead anxiety for citizen safety and the FBI's normal reluctance to involve other agencies as reasons for not calling in the state patrol. But that defense got real thin when it came to Madison and Turner's meet with the woman who worked in the Federal Prosecutor's Office. The fact was that he should involve the Madison police, and he would, normally. But this wasn't a normal case.

This case was about Turner.

He tore open a peanut butter granola bar and crunched into dry oats and peanuts. What was it about Turner? She wasn't spectacularly beautiful. In fact, she was ordinary-looking, in a petite, girl-next-door sort of way. And yet he hadn't felt this intensely about a woman in ages. The women he'd dated in the years since his divorce had usually been nice enough, but there'd been something missing. A deeper level of connection that he hadn't seemed to be able to reach with any woman. A part of him had feared that he'd missed his chance altogether. That he'd spend the remainder of his life essentially alone. And he'd been reconciled to that idea. Mostly. Although now that he had a chance at a woman he felt he could truly communicate with, he sure was pursuing her, wasn't he?

John smiled wryly. Maybe he hadn't been that reconciled, after all.

She fascinated him. Turner seemed to have spent the

last four years carefully hiding her attractiveness under glasses and the facade of a clichéd small-town librarian. She went out of her way to blend into the background. The exact opposite of what most women wanted. The average guy would've overlooked her. Hell, if he'd met her in any other way, *he* would've overlooked her. He didn't give himself credit for being particularly sensitive. But he hadn't overlooked her. From the moment he'd seen that secret little smile caught for a second on the bank surveillance tape, he'd been drawn in by the puzzle of her. What kind of person had the strength of character to lie in wait for a chance at revenge for so many years?

He wanted to open her up, dig around in her psyche, find out what made her Turner. He wanted to spend time asking her questions, picking apart the details of her life. How long had she had those red heels at the back of her closet? Why had she become a librarian? Was it a disguise, or had she found her profession convenient when she'd decided on a course of revenge against Hyman? Why had she cut her hair now? There was something essentially erotic about his need to pursue. To capture and reveal her. He was the predator, and she was his wily, seductive prey. The game they played was a sexual one. He could feel it, and he thought she could, as well.

The problem was that she was obsessed about her uncle's death. That obsession, the fact that she'd waited four years, for Pete's sake, to enact her revenge, was typical of her character. It was part of what fascinated him about her. But it was frustrating, as well. He felt like he was competing against a dead man, and that fight he couldn't win.

John sighed and looked around the clearing in back

of Hyman's cabin. Okay. First order of the day: move the car so he wouldn't be immediately obvious when Turner arrived. He'd have to find a spot in the woods to wait where the ticks weren't so bad. Then he would call Turner. Because he wanted to find out how she felt about last night. He wanted to see how she was this morning. And he needed to ask her where she was. Even though she wouldn't answer.

He needed to ask her anyway.

Chapter Twenty-seven

*F*ry 'em." Luther Hindenburg tapped a nail-bitten finger on the Formica table for emphasis. "That's what I say. Fry 'em on the first offense. Not the second or thirty-third, for fuck's sake. And none of this waiting around for years on appeal. If a guy gets the death penalty, he oughta be cold meat by the following evening."

There was a rumble of agreement down the long row of folding tables. Calvin swallowed a bite of gluey pancake and opened his mouth.

But he was beat to the punch by Harvey Johnson, waving a sausage on a fork. "And why's it so damn hard to convict these guys? Pedophiles that've raped dozens of kids, and slimeballs that've killed their entire family? I tell you why. Defense lawyers. Where's it say these guys have a right to one of them slick attorneys?" Harvey shoved the entire sausage in his mouth and chewed aggressively.

Calvin knit his brows. "Well, technically, the Bill of Rights—"

"If they can't afford to pay one of those bottom-feeding scum-suckers, these criminals ought to get up and defend their own sorry asses in court." Harv banged his fist on the table, hitting a puddle of pancake syrup and coming away sticky. Not that he noticed. "I'd like to see that."

A round of nodding heads and mumbled assent.

"Yeah." Luther laughed. He was completely bald—probably shaved his head—and owned the hardware store in town. Luther could sling a newly repaired lawn-mower into the back of a pickup without breaking into a sweat. "Can you see some murderer trying to explain himself? *I didn't mean to do it, really. Her head got in the way of the shotgun.*"

Loud masculine laughter reverberated through the hall.

It was Tuesday morning, and they all sat in the former Elks Lodge in Winosha. The Elks Lodge was now used mostly by the Kiwanis Club, since the last two Elks were ninety-two and ninety-four, respectively. It was a dark-timbered building with a concrete floor. At one end was a podium. Over the podium was a dusty mounted elk head, so old the fur was molting onto the floor in tufts.

This was the annual Kiwanis Club pancake breakfast fund-raiser and he, Calvin, was the guest of honor. He was a little vague on what, exactly, the Kiwanis were raising money for, but he was certain of his part here: make a speech that would get out the vote. Fortunately, he would be preaching to the choir. As far as he knew, the Kiwanis in Winosha were one hundred percent Republican, except for Ed Riley, who lived in the woods and never bothered attending meetings.

"That's exactly why I feel," Calvin finally got his two cents in, "that when I'm elected, there must be a three-strikes law instituted in this state. And I will do my level best to see such a law enacted. Furthermore—"

"Yeah, Cal, but what about them defense attorneys?" Harvey asked rather pointlessly. Harv was a small man, only about five-four or so, but he enjoyed picking arguments. Fridays he'd get drunk at the bar and try to take out a tourist or two in a fistfight. That was in summer. In winter he drove his snowmobile through town after midnight. The next morning the wobbly tracks could be seen between the bars and his home.

Calvin summoned up his best we're-all-boys-here smile. "Of course I agree with you, Harv, but—" The cell phone in his breast pocket started vibrating against his chest. Calvin winked and reached for it, never breaking eye contact with his audience. "But what you got to keep in mind is all the representatives from the blue districts that I'll be contending with once elected. Like Madison."

Everyone chuckled except Harv, who looked annoyed. "Yeah, but wasn't Madison—"

Calvin glanced down at the vibrating cell in his palm. *Good God.* "Excuse me." He gave an all-encompassing smile. "Important call." He rose.

"But—" Harv started.

Calvin ignored him and walked away. He found the back door and pulled it open as he answered the cell.

"What is it?" he muttered into the phone.

"I'm here," Hank grunted from the other end.

He frowned. "Where?"

"Here."

Why did ex–special forces guys think it was macho

to use as few words as possible? Was it something they taught in the military? Or was it because only nonverbal, almost insane men chose to go into the special forces? Ones like Hank. At least he'd called finally. After giving Hank the extra five hundred dollars yesterday morning, Calvin hadn't heard from him since. He was beginning to think the man had disappeared into Canada.

He took a deep breath. "Where is here?"

"The cabin."

Calvin rolled his eyes. Was that so hard to say? "Good. Is, ah, the package there?"

"What?" Hank blew out a long exhale. Probably smoking again. Filthy habit.

Calvin checked over his shoulder. No one about. The back of the Elks Lodge led out onto a concrete patio, crumbling at the edges. Beyond that was a small strip of mowed grass, then a wooded area. "The *package*. The one you went to find."

"You mean the girl?"

"Yes."

"Why don't you just say the girl?"

"Because," Calvin said through gritted teeth. "I'm at the Kiwanis annual pancake breakfast."

"Oh."

"Well?"

"I forgot the question now."

Calvin sighed and did a neck roll. Hank always said he'd been in the Rangers and told stories about Afghanistan, but really, were the Rangers that hard up that they'd take on a guy like Hank? Not that it mattered. Even if Hank had never been in the Rangers, he had killed people. You only had to look into his dead eyes to believe that.

"Is she there?" Calvin asked.

"Nope."

"You're sure?"

"Yeah, I'm sure. Checked the cabin and woods. There're some tire tracks in back—"

"Shit!" Calvin exclaimed. Had the idiot missed her?

"But they belong to a car. Not a truck. She hasn't been here."

"Good. Then you wait."

"You don't even know if she'll be here." Hank's smoker's voice didn't raise or lower. He kept the same level tone always, so it was hard to tell if he was mad.

"She'll be there."

Silence from the other end.

Calvin gritted his teeth. "You don't—"

The door behind him opened, and Luther stuck his head out. "All right out here?"

Calvin twisted his mouth into a smile. "Sure. Sure." He tilted his head, indicating the phone. "You know how the guys in Madison are." He twirled a hand, miming long-winded.

Luther's eyes widened. "Good. Just checking. Herb said you can start your speech any time."

Calvin nodded, the smile still stretched on his face.

The door closed.

"Who was that?" Hank wanted to know.

"Doesn't matter. You don't move until that girl shows up. Do you understand?"

"Fine."

"Not even to get a Big Mac."

"Yeah. Yeah. You don't have to tell me my job."

"Well, good then." Calvin blew out a breath. "Remember, you still have three thousand coming. Be a shame to lose that much money because you couldn't hold out."

"I can hold out." The other man's voice should've been angry, but it was just as robotic as before. "I held out in Afghanistan, you know. I can hold out here. I've got water and jerky and my rifle."

"Okay."

"This baby'll blow your head off at two hundred feet—"

"Ah—"

"And I always go for the head shot, you know."

Too much information. "Good."

"Not all snipers do."

"Ah." Calvin hesitated. "Be sure and call me when it's time."

"Yeah. Yeah."

Hank broke the connection.

Calvin hung up and pocketed his cell phone. Then he took out a linen handkerchief and carefully blotted the sweat running down his face.

So close. So damn close.

Chapter Twenty-eight

It was midmorning by the time Turner found the back road near Rhinelander. She slowed to look for the number to Calvin's cabin and shifted down into third as the road became rougher. Beside her, Squeaky was taking his morning nap, unperturbed by the jolting of the pickup.

Rhinelander was a tourist destination, and most of the lake cabins looked like the yuppie idea of roughing it. She drove past a drive decorated by a bare wood arch festooned with deer antlers. The mailbox read 1408. She was looking for 1475, and the numbers were rising. Time to park the Chevy and do some reconnaissance. She chose the next drive. It led to a bright green bungalow decorated with ornamental birdhouses around the front steps. A sign over the door read OUR HAPPY HIDE-AWAY. The grass beside the drive was midcalf length and dry as straw. Even taking into account the drought, she doubted that it had been cut in the last month. Nobody home.

She got out of the pickup and waited for Squeaky to jump down, then slammed the door. Turner checked that she had her cell phone and a bottle of water and set out with the dog trotting along happily. Squeaky was always up for a walk. She followed the road but kept close to the tree line in case she had to duck into it. Squeaky loped in and out of the forest, disappearing for minutes at a time only to reappear, head and tail high, wearing a doggy grin. They crossed three drives before they saw anyone else. A gold SUV passed them, kicking up dust in the road. Turner repressed the urge to break stride and kept walking casually. When she was within several lots of Calvin's cabin, she walked into the shade of the trees and stepped more carefully. She wore a black T-shirt and jeans, but the paleness of her arms and face would stand out to anyone looking.

And she had to assume John was looking.

The trees were tall here, mostly pines, but some shorter aspens and birch, as well. The deciduous trees were already turning color, despite the fact that it was only August. They must have been stressed by the drought. Beneath her feet was the decaying leaf litter from the previous fall. It should have been moist, but the heat and sparse rain had made the forest floor dry. The leaves rustled and sent up puffs of dust that gritted in her mouth. Spiny branches from the understory scraped her now and then, subtle hurts that were not initially painful but then welled blood in pinpoints on her skin.

Turner looked into blinding sunlight on the opposite side of the road. A fire-engine mailbox stood there with the number 1475. She huffed out a breath of air and backed another step into the forest. Then she squatted, watching Calvin's mailbox and the lane that led to his cabin. It was still. As far as she could see, the lane was deserted. She felt something on her arm and looked down. A tick was slowly crawling toward her shirt-sleeve. Ew. She flicked it off and went back to watching the lane.

The rumble of a vehicle engine drew near and a red pickup drove by.

The problem was that she couldn't assume that John wasn't there just because she couldn't see him. That would be—

A big shape came up fast on her right. Turner gasped, twisted to face it, and fell on her rear.

Squeaky skidded to a stop beside her and cocked his head.

"You big idiot," Turner muttered to the dog.

He seemed to take her words as a compliment. He wagged his tail and tried to slobber on her face. She ducked just in time. She was getting good at it. Squeaky was very affectionate.

"Okay," she said to the Great Dane. "I'm not going to learn anything sitting here all day. We better go check out the cabin."

She stood carefully and laid a hand on the dog's collar. If she could, she'd leave him behind. But then he'd start howling and that she didn't need. Better to bring him with her. She waited a moment longer, watching the road and listening. The only sounds were Squeaky, panting softly beside her, and the wind in the treetops. Nothing was on the road. Turner stepped out and walked swiftly across, expecting a shout at any minute to signal that she'd been spotted.

None came.

She made it to the side of the road and walked into the

trees without breaking her stride. Then she paused, hand on her chest. Her breath was coming more swiftly than a quick stroll across a road should warrant, and she was sweating. She took two steps forward and her cell went off, making her drop to the ground in reaction.

"Shoot! Shoot! Shoot!" Turner fumbled the cell out of her pocket and pressed the *Answer* button. "Yes?"

"Where are you?" John asked.

Was he in earshot? She concentrated on steadying her breath. Then she said low, "You know I'm not going to tell you."

"Yeah. But I have to ask anyway."

She closed her eyes and leaned against a tree trunk. "I know." Out of nowhere she felt tears prick at her eyelids. "What are you doing this morning?"

"You know I can't tell you that." His voice was gentle. "What did you have for breakfast?"

She wrinkled her nose. Oh, yeah. Breakfast. "Nothing. Squeaky and I forgot to eat."

"I can't imagine Squeaky forgetting."

She looked at the big dog. He'd been circling the tree, nose in the leaf litter, but now he came back to her and plopped on the ground with a groan. "Well, he hasn't complained, at least. What did you have?"

"Granola bar."

"Ick."

"It's not that bad." He sounded a little defensive. "It's peanut butter flavor."

"Double ick." She wrinkled her nose. "Is that what you usually have for breakfast?"

"Nope. Only on the road. Mostly I'm a Wheaties man."

That she could see. She smiled. "So how do you start your morning at home?"

"The usual. Shave, shower, breakfast."

"Every day?"

"Sure, every day. Unless, of course, you'd stayed over the night before." His deep voice was intimate in her ear.

She inhaled. "You're making quite a leap."

"Am I?"

"I—"

"I see you staying at my place someday, don't you?"

She swallowed, unsure of what to say. "John . . ."

"Someday soon."

"Anyway, how would that be different?" She watched a red-headed woodpecker circle a tree. She couldn't believe she was sitting here. She couldn't believe she was listening to this.

"First of all, we'd probably still be in bed."

"On a weekday?"

"Maybe not a weekday."

"You know that's not what I'm talking about." She wriggled a little on the leaves. Squeaky looked up. Good thing he was a dog and didn't know when she was blushing. "I meant afterward."

"That's what I'm talking about. Afterward." His voice was teasing. "First we'd spoon for a bit, and then I'd get hard again because you'd be naked—"

"John—" she warned.

"And then we'd—"

"After we get up!" She cringed and looked around, hoping her voice hadn't been too loud.

"Spoilsport. Okay. *After* we get up, I'd naturally make you pancakes with fresh strawberries."

"You know how to cook pancakes?"

"Hey, you're dissing me." He was laughing now. "There are pancake mixes."

Okay, she'd concede that, but . . . "How do you know I like pancakes?"

"Two words. Whipped cream."

She laughed. She couldn't help it. Squeaky took that as a sign that he should lay his head in her lap. "How did you find out I like cream? I never mentioned it."

"The only milk you have in your fridge is whole. And besides, you're a cat."

"A cat?" Her brows knitted. "Where did you get that idea? I don't even like cats."

"FBI secret. And cats often don't like other cats."

"Uh-huh. Are you a cat, too?"

"No, baby. I'm the big bad wolf out to get you."

She couldn't tell if he was teasing or not, and she had the uneasy feeling he wasn't. She didn't want to go there, so she tried a different question. "Why did you decide to become an FBI agent?"

"Special agent."

She rolled her eyes. "Special agent. Why?"

"All the usual reasons. Love of country. Desire to put bad guys away. And you get to carry a really big gun around all the time."

"You're blowing me off. What's the real reason?"

He was silent a second. A faint tapping came from his end of the phone. "I don't think anyone has ever asked me that."

"You're stalling," she said gently.

"Yeah." He laughed quietly. "My dad was a police officer. I guess law enforcement's in the genes." The tapping came again.

"So why not local law enforcement? Why aren't you a cop?"

He sighed, then said abruptly, "He was killed."

She watched the woodpecker complete his circle around the trunk of the pine in front of her, leaving a row of holes behind. The bird inched up and started another row.

"I was in college," John said so low in her ear it was almost a whisper. "My first year. There was a bank robbery, and Dad was off duty. He drew, but the robbers got the drop on him. Shot him three times in the gut."

She sucked in her breath at the violence of the words. The woodpecker suddenly flew.

"He bled out before they could get him to the hospital."

"I'm sorry."

"It wouldn't have mattered, anyway. Gunshots to the stomach tend to be fatal." He stopped talking, and Turner listened to his breathing over the wire.

And that faint tapping in the background.

Her eyes widened as she looked at the row of horizontal holes in the pine in front of her. It was a woodpecker. On John's end of the phone. He was sitting near a woodpecker. Like the woodpecker she'd been watching.

He was in the same woods as she.

She silently lowered the phone from her ear and looked around. She couldn't hear tapping. John's woodpecker was out of her earshot. She raised the phone back to her ear and heard his voice. Plus the woodpecker in the background.

". . . why I probably went into the FBI instead of the local police. The feds are the ones who investigate bank robberies. And I dunno, the elitism may have played a part."

"In what way?" She gently shoved Squeaky's head off her lap and stood. Calvin's cabin was to her right. She grasped the dog's collar, cautiously walked a couple of steps, stopped, and listened.

"Guess I wanted to be the best at what I do."

"That makes sense," she replied absently. She couldn't hear the woodpecker yet. She moved further into the forest.

"So why did you become a librarian? Was it cover for what you're doing now?"

"What?" His odd question brought her back to the conversation. "No. What gave you that idea?"

"You've spent the last four years like a nun, haven't you? Or an undercover op."

"Don't be silly." She had to concentrate, but his words were distracting. A nun? She almost tripped, but caught herself in time. She took a breath and continued walking.

"When's the last time you went out on a date, honey?"

"I—" Her mind went blank. She couldn't think of when she'd last dated. She rounded a stand of birch.

"Got any close friends? 'Cause I couldn't find any when I looked."

"That's ridiculous!" She caught herself and lowered her voice. "I have plenty of friends. There's my assistant at the library, Kate, and Missy and Hope from church—"

"Do they know about the red shoes in your closet, Turner? Did they know your glasses were fake?" His voice was tender now, and it scared her.

Almost as much as the realization that she could no longer hear the woodpecker over the phone. She stopped and swiveled her head without moving her feet. The trees were secondary growth, their trunks only three or four feet around, but that was enough to hide a man.

"Do they know you do the *Chicago Tribune* or *New York Times* crosswords but don't bother with the local papers?" John continued relentlessly.

She could glimpse the back of the cabin now. He must be close. She tried to still her chest, regulate her breath. Overhead, the tree leaves rustled in the wind, branches creaking.

"Do they know you like to read Graham Greene and that you make tuna casseroles for Tommy?"

She took two careful steps.

"Do they know you've planned on revenge for four years, huh, Turner? Do they know how relentless, how strong, how goddamn driven you are?"

Oh, Lord. He was ten paces away. She could see the back of a man's head, one shoulder, and a bent, trousers-clad leg that ended in a tan cowboy boot. It had to be John. He was sitting under a big pine, his left hand holding the phone to his ear. It was a miracle he hadn't heard her yet. And how was she going to get in the cabin with him sitting there?

Beside her, Squeaky whined.

Chapter Twenty-nine

$\mathcal{D}$o they know you like that, Turner, these friends of yours? Do they know you like I do?" John demanded.

On the other end of the phone he could hear Turner's harsh gasp. He grimaced. He was pushing her with his questions, he knew, but this had to end soon. She couldn't take it much longer. Hell, he couldn't take it much longer. The trees over his head moaned in the wind, as if in agreement.

"You may be right," she said in his ear.

"What?"

"I may not have any real friends anymore. You're right."

She sounded eerily close. He frowned. "That's not—"

"But that doesn't matter."

"Turner—"

"Bringing Calvin to justice is what matters. I'm sorry, John."

"Wait—"

"I'm sorry." She clicked off.

John swore and shoved the cell in his pocket. At almost the same moment, a bizarre sound started in the woods. A crying wail, but deeper, almost a howl. It went on in an undulating moan until it abruptly ended on a high squeak. There was a pause, and then the crying began again.

It was the Great Dane Turner had stolen. He was howling in the woods nearby. That meant she was here, somewhere close. John stood and turned in the direction of the sound. Out of the corner of his eye, he saw someone step into the clearing. Shit, she was getting bold. What did she think she was doing?

Except the person in the clearing was a man. Holding a rifle. John froze, watching the big man stride confidently across the mowed grass at the back of Calvin's cabin. The intruder hadn't seen him. He seemed to be concentrating on Squeaky's howls. John couldn't see the dog from where he stood, but the other guy must be able to. The dog cut off in midhowl. Almost immediately he began a staccato barking. The woofs were deep and menacing, despite Squeaky's unfortunate name. Where was Turner?

"Shut up," the man said. He said it without inflection, his voice strangely even. Then he raised his rifle to his shoulder and sighted down the barrel. "Shut up, dog."

Squeaky continued barking.

Well, shit. John unholstered his Glock and aimed it at the man's back. "FBI. Put down—"

He didn't have time to finish the command, because the son of a bitch whirled and fired into the woods at him. *Crap*. The shooter had to be a certified lunatic.

John dived and squeezed off four rounds at the same time, the crack of the Glock loud in his ears. He fired twice more from the ground and then belly-crawled around the side of the tree trunk he'd been sitting next to. He chanced a look. The shooter was nowhere in sight. Impossible to know if he'd hit the man, but considering the distance, probably not.

John raised his voice. "FBI. Throw down your weapon!"

The answer was another gunshot that chipped the bark over his head. The shot had come from the front corner of the cabin. John aimed and squeezed off three rounds to keep the asshole there.

Squeaky was moaning now. The loud shots had probably terrified the dog. Strange that he hadn't run away. John did a kind of crab crawl to another tree, his shoulder protesting all the way. The lunatic with the rifle snapped off two more rounds. A sapling in front of him shattered.

His cell phone rang.

He swore and fumbled for it, cutting off the ring tone. *"What?"*

"John? John?" Turner's voice was the highest he'd ever heard it. She sounded near hysterics. "Oh, God, are you all right?"

"Hi, honey. I'm kind of busy right now."

The shooter peered around the side of the cabin and John sent three more bullets his way, just to keep him occupied. Splinters of wood exploded from the corner of the building.

"But are you hurt?"

"No, I'm fine." John shifted to try to crawl to a closer tree. The leaves to his right jumped in the air from another shot. He flattened again. "Turner, listen, you need to get out of here."

"But—"

"This guy's got a screw loose. He's shooting at anything that moves. Tell me you're driving away from the cabin."

"I'm in it."

"In the cabin?"

"Yes."

John closed his eyes briefly. "Fuck."

"What?"

"Sorry. That's not what I wanted to hear."

He raised himself to his elbows and fired two fast shots. Immediately, a shower of wood chips hit him from the tree he was peering around. Good. The shooter was still at the corner of the building.

"Okay," he said to Turner. "Can you see the guy shooting?"

"No. I'm on the floor in the kitchen."

He glanced at the rear of the cabin. There were four screen windows in a row. "Is the kitchen at the back?"

"Yes."

"Grab something and wave it in the window."

There was a pause, and then a broom appeared at the bottom edge of the middle right window.

"I see you," John said. "I want you to move to the last window in back. To your right as you face the back of the house. Can you do that without being seen from the front?"

"Yes." She sounded out of breath. "But what about you? He's shooting at you, John!"

The shooter did another peekaboo, and John got off a round at him.

"I'm an FBI agent, honey." He rolled to his side, ejected the spent clip from the Glock, and shoved an-

other one in before rising to his elbows and firing once
more at the corner. "Have a little faith."

"But—"

Crap. The shooter hadn't returned his fire. "Move!
Now!"

John got to his feet and made a crouching run at the
cabin. The shooter's silence might be a ruse to draw him
out, but he had to take that chance with Turner in the
cabin.

He made the back corner of the cabin without being
shot and flattened himself against the dusty shingles.
"Turner? Why aren't you at that window?"

"I'm—"

A gunshot sounded loud inside the cabin.

Christ, no.

John fought down panic. He peered over the windowsill and saw a man's bulk in the kitchen. He shoved the
cell in his pocket, backed up two steps, and fired five
rounds in rapid succession into the kitchen, his shoulder jolting with the recoils. The glass in the window exploded, some of the shards driving themselves into the
outer screen. He squinted through the mess. The shooter
inside was slumped against the kitchen doorway. To
John's left, the screen on the end window burst suddenly
outward, and Turner tumbled to the ground. He gave her
one piercing glance and saw no blood. *Thank you, God.*

He turned back to the room and found the man's
shape was gone. *Well, shit.*

"Run, goddamnit!" he bellowed at Turner.

She gave him a white-faced stare and then took off.

He holstered the Glock, grabbed the window screen,
and pulled it off the window. Then he put both hands on
the windowsill and vaulted into the kitchen, his shoulder

bitching like a mother. A piece of glass embedded itself in his left palm.

He crouched and silently drew the Glock again, listening. The cabin was quiet. The kitchen was square with a rustic wood table and four chairs, two of them now overturned. Turner's broom lay underneath one of the chairs. Broken glass from the window made a mosaic on the floor. He didn't see any blood spatter.

John took two swift steps to the inner kitchen wall near the doorway, the glass crunching under his boots. He flattened himself and listened again.

Nothing.

He drew a quick breath and stepped around the corner, leading with his Glock. Outside the kitchen was a hallway. He scanned left, then right, listening. All he heard was his own harsh breath. To the right was a large doorway, probably access to a living room or some kind of entrance hall. But Turner had come out from the back corner window. Had the shooter followed her there?

John turned left down the hallway. The first door was to his left, and it was closed. One of the windows along the back of the cabin would be in there. He backed up a step and kicked the door open, going in low. The door crashed against the wall. It was a bedroom. There was a single bed and a closet on the right. John crossed to the closet and checked. Nothing but hangers. He hunkered by the bed and flung up the bed skirt, prepared to fire if there was any movement. The space underneath was empty.

He went back out in the hall again and kicked in the next door. Another bedroom, single bed, the screen missing on the window where Turner had leaped out. But—

A crash came from the front of the house.

John whirled and strode to the hallway, holding the Glock in both hands in a shooter's stance. The son of a bitch must've been in the front room all the time, waiting for him to move away so he could flee the cabin.

The hall led to a big open area, a den or family room. He swept the space with the Glock, checking behind the sofa and chairs before running out on the porch, where he found footprints in the dust. John scanned the woods outside and then crouched to look at the dusty porch floorboards. Two sets of footprints going in, a woman's and a man in boots. One set leaving. The man's. The shooter had gotten away.

Nearby, Squeaky began howling again.

John walked around the cabin, gun held by his side. A humongous black-and-white dog stood by the edge of the woods. The dog spotted him and switched to staccato barking. He was tied to a tree. No wonder Squeaky hadn't run at the sound of the gunshots—she'd tied the dog up as a diversion for him. John swore and dug the piece of glass out of his left palm with the fingernails of his other hand. Blood spurted from the wound.

"Guess she abandoned both of us, bud."

Chapter Thirty

Turner jammed her foot hard on the brake. The Chevy shuddered to an abrupt stop, and she had to brace one hand on the dash to keep from catapulting into the steering column. She'd turned onto a forest access road several miles away from Calvin's cabin. She switched the engine off, grabbed her cell, and quickly punched in John's number. The other end began to ring.

Come on. Come on. She felt her chin tremble involuntarily, either from the aftereffects of adrenaline or, more likely, fear for John's life.

Fifteen minutes ago she'd been standing in Calvin's cabin. A thrill of undiluted horror had coursed down her spine when she'd realized that those were gunshots she was hearing outside. And that John was out there alone with whoever was shooting. Up until that moment she'd been excited in a fearful kind of way. It'd been almost a game. A game to outwit John and enter the cabin while he was watching it. In fact, she'd just been congratulating herself on getting in when the shots shattered her smugness.

After that, everything had happened so fast. The assailant had invaded the cabin and fired at her. She still didn't know how he had missed, he'd been that close. John had ordered her out and then ordered her to run. She hadn't liked it. It didn't feel right to run away when she knew he was going to confront a man with a gun, but she was afraid that if she stayed she would distract him. So she'd run and abandoned him to face down a possible killer.

And now he wasn't answering his phone. He might be a FBI agent, but people were killed in the line of duty every day. Oh, Lord—

"MacKinnon."

She closed her eyes and took a deep breath of relief. For a moment she couldn't speak, her throat was so constricted, and then she managed to get out, "You're okay."

"Me and Squeaky." He sounded almost lazy.

Turner's eyes widened, and she looked at the empty seat beside her. "Oh, my goodness. I forgot him!"

"Shh. He'll hear you. It'll hurt his feelings."

"Is he okay?"

"Well, we've established that he likes peanut butter granola bars."

Turner winced. "You didn't."

"Hey, he was hungry. You didn't feed him this morning, remember?"

"Yeah, but—"

"Did you find what you were looking for in the cabin?"

"No," she admitted. "I'd barely got in when the shooting started."

"Huh. Nice diversion, by the way. Staking Squeaky out and leaving him to howl so I'd go investigate."

She grinned shakily. "Thanks."

"No prob." His voice was dry as dust. "What were you looking for, exactly?"

"A computer. Or a disc."

"Yeah?"

"I didn't see any, but I only looked in the front room and the kitchen—"

"Okay." She could hear him opening a door. "We're searching for a second set of books that documents Calvin embezzling from the bank."

She caught her breath. "Yes. Are you, um, offering to help?"

"Maybe. What if he doesn't keep a second set? What if he has no records?"

"Then I'm out of luck, aren't I?" She'd tried not to think about that possibility too much over the last four years. Assuming there wasn't evidence of his crime didn't get her anywhere. "But I think he does. He's very meticulous at the bank—he likes to document everything and gets upset if something isn't written down. Or entered into the bank's database."

"Okay." More rummaging sounds.

"Did you arrest him?"

"Who?"

"The guy shooting."

"Nope." He grunted as if moving something. "Got away."

"At least he didn't hurt you."

"Mmm. Y'know, this image you have of me—that

I'm easily bruised—is starting to erode my masculine self-esteem. I may need therapy."

"I didn't mean—"

"Yeah, I know. Your dog is howling outside again."

Turner smiled. "He must like you. He misses you already."

"Me or the peanut butter granola bars."

"You do realize that those aren't good for him, don't you?"

"And pickled herring is?"

"Maybe you can get him some real dog food. But make sure it's a name brand, like Purina or Iams. I don't trust those generic—"

"Turner—"

"And I've heard you're supposed to get a special kind of food for big dogs. For their joints."

"I'm not keeping Squeaky," he said flatly.

She straightened in her seat. "You're not going to send him to the pound, are you?"

"Of course not—"

"Or a kennel? He'd too big for a kennel."

"He belongs to Hyman—"

"You're going to give him back to a criminal?"

"And his name is Duke."

"John!"

She heard his impatient exhalation. "He belongs to Hyman. You can't just go around stealing dogs whenever you feel like it."

"Calvin left him out without any water."

"For one day."

"I—"

"No, listen for a moment," he said in a hard voice. "Hyman has no animal-cruelty complaints against him.

I looked. The lack of water may have been a onetime lapse of judgment, for all you know."

"But—"

"Listen," he growled.

Turner compressed her lips.

"Hyman may have done everything you've said he's done," John said in a low, intense voice. "He may have embezzled from the bank, he may be a thief. Heck, he may be a mass murderer, for all I know. But he didn't abuse his dog."

"He didn't have water!"

"Okay, let's say he did, Turner. Let's say he did abuse Squeaky. What the hell do you think the police are for? You make a complaint, they investigate, and if it's valid, the case is turned over to the courts. That's how it's done in America. It's a good system. It keeps us from anarchy. Bottom line, you don't have the right to take the law into your own hands."

She grimaced, knowing he was right. "I don't want you to give Squeaky back to him."

There was a masculine sigh from the other end. "I'm not seeing anything here."

Not a subtle change of subject, but she still needed to know. "Have you gone through the drawers in the bedrooms? It might be only a disc with information—"

"I know how to search a house, honey."

"What about the garage?"

"I'll check the garage and the house once more, but right now I'm not seeing it."

Turner swallowed. The evidence had to be at the cabin. There wasn't any other place—

"Are you going to come in now?" His voice was tender, the tones unnervingly seductive.

She stared out at the surrounding woods. Some of the trees near the access road had been cut. Dismembered logs lay in sawdust blood, impotent and dead. Even the underbrush had been crushed under heavy machinery.

"I can't," she whispered.

"Jesus." Disgust was strong in his voice. "Didn't a word of what I just said get to you? You're done acting like a vigilante. Why aren't you coming in?"

"I've told you. This is important. I can't give up just because the going gets rough—"

"Yeah, well, what if the going gets lethal?"

She frowned. "What?"

"Who do you think that son of a bitch was after?"

She hadn't considered the matter. There hadn't been time. "I—"

"He had the place staked out long before you got here. I found six cigarette butts under a tree."

"That's—"

"He went into the cabin after you."

"Me?" She felt like laughing, but her throat was dry. "Don't be silly. I'm a librarian."

"You're no longer just a librarian. You've abandoned your camouflage, decided to take the law into your own hands. Everyone knows you're a hunter now."

"For goodness' sakes—"

"Listen to me," he growled. "That guy wanted to kill you. He had a sniper's rifle and he was staked out in the woods waiting for you."

She pressed a trembling finger to the spot between her eyebrows. This just wasn't believable. "But you're the FBI agent. Maybe he followed you here. Do you have any enemies?"

"Plenty. But that's not who this guy is. I want you to come in—"

"No!"

"Goddamnit! You were almost killed today. Are revenge and ego worth your life?"

She gasped. "Ego?"

"Yeah, ego. Don't you have a bit of it tied up in this thing? Turner Hastings, who's so much smarter than everyone else—"

"Oh! You—"

"Fools an entire town into thinking she's the meek librarian—"

"That's—"

"Doesn't need the cops or the FBI. Can investigate and bring in a thief all by herself."

Turner breathed deeply through her nose. She suddenly noticed that a small, slim lizard had crawled on top of one of the logs in front of her. It was light brown except for its tail, which was electric blue. She stared. The lizard flickered and was gone. Maybe she'd imagined it. A blue-tailed lizard? It seemed so unlikely.

"I think you're the one with a hurt ego," she said very quietly. "You're the big tough FBI agent who can't catch one little librarian."

John was silent on the other end. She'd finally said too much, pushed him too far. He'd leave now.

Then he sighed over the phone. "You might be right. Maybe my ego is hurting. But you still need to come in."

Why did she feel such relief that he hadn't hung up on her? "Why would the shooter be after me, John?"

"You're a very smart woman, baby. Don't play dumb now. Hyman must've hired him."

She swallowed. Calvin the bank president? The mayor of Winosha? "That's not possible. Where would he find a hit man in Wisconsin?"

"You'd be surprised. Do you understand now why you have to come in?"

"No."

"Jesus Christ," he exploded. She'd never heard him lose control before. He sounded enraged. "I'm about to pop a vein here. You've got a hit man after you, Turner. This guy didn't even stop when I identified myself. He had no fear of killing a FBI agent. Don't do this to me."

"I'm not—"

"Your life is in danger, goddamnit! Do what I say for once."

"I—"

A siren sounded on John's end. "Crap. The local yokels are here. Just what I need to make my day perfect."

Turner frowned at her watch. "It took them long enough. I called 911 half an hour ago."

There was a short silence.

"You called the police." His voice was expressionless.

"I didn't like you in there alone with that lunatic."

"I'm a friggin' FBI special agent and you called the cops to help me."

"FBI agents get killed, too."

"Special—" John blew out a breath into the phone. "I don't have time for this. They're getting out of their cars. Where can I meet you?"

"I can't."

"Meet me, Turner."

"I'm sorry."

"Don't you dare hang up—"

But she pressed the *End* button.

She let her head drop to the seat back. She felt so tired. Exhausted, like she'd been up for days. God, what a mess. She'd lost Squeaky, there didn't seem to be any evidence of Calvin's guilt, and she'd been shot at. And she'd ruined things with John. Totally and irrevocably. He wouldn't be calling her anymore with the morning crossword or to ask what she'd eaten for breakfast. It was a wonder that he'd put up with her this long. Her eyes blurred, and she felt the tears trickle down her face to drip into her T-shirt. She didn't bother to wipe them off. There wasn't anyone to see, and she wasn't sure she even cared anymore.

She stared at the severed logs in front of her, but the blue-tailed lizard didn't reappear.

Chapter Thirty-one

Turned out that Crown Victorias weren't really made for transporting Great Danes. Sure, the dog could fit in the back seat if he were actually lying down. But Squeaky spent most of his time in the car standing half-crouched in the back seat. The dog alternated between staring out the front windshield at Highway 51 as he whined softly under his breath and anxiously panting down John's neck, occasionally dripping drool.

"You're a real pantywaist," John said to the dog, glad nobody could see him talking to a dog. "You rode with Turner in a truck. What's so bad about a sedan?"

Squeaky whined and licked John's ear.

He winced and brushed at his ear. "And no ear licking. Guys don't do ear licking. Not with other guys, anyway. You've been hanging out with a woman too long."

He could hear Squeaky moving restlessly around in the back seat, despite the small space. Maybe he needed to pee. The dog whined again, fetid breath blowing on the side of John's cheek.

"Okay, okay. I'm pulling over."

The dog must've sensed that they were stopping, because he barked, which nearly deafened John's right ear. He slowed, turned in to a historical-marker rest stop, and got out of the car. Squeaky maneuvered between the front seats and bounded out the driver's-side door. He hustled over to the historical marker and peed on it.

John sighed and leaned against the Crown Vic. He'd spent several lost hours with the local cops at Hyman's cabin, wrangling red tape and paperwork. At any point he could've turned Squeaky in and notified Hyman that his dog had been found. But he just couldn't bring himself to do it. The dog felt like Turner's, even if Hyman had the legal right to the animal.

Now Squeaky was running in widening circles, nose to the ground.

What the hell was he going to do with a hot Great Dane? This was not going to look good on his annual evaluation. Although, if Turner had to steal a dog, she'd picked a nice breed. At least she hadn't gone for one of those little yapping things. Squeaky was a fine dog with a handsome square head and a deep chest. A man's dog, despite the awful name she'd given him.

The cell rattled on his belt. He unclipped it and checked the number, hoping, but didn't recognize it. "MacKinnon."

"Can you talk now?" a peeved teenaged voice asked him.

A wide grin spread across John's face. "Sure, sweetheart. What do you want to talk about?" He was just so damn relieved that his daughter had called back.

"You and Mom."

He closed his eyes as his heart sank. This again. "Have you asked your mom since we last talked?"

"Yes." Rachel sounded really frustrated, as if she were at the end of some rope. "Mom won't talk to me. She just goes on and on about how you were never there, that you'd leave us during dinner to go out on a case and how she hated that."

"Well, so maybe that's your answer," John said. "Hard to have a relationship when someone's gone all the time. And she's right. Early in my career I did have to leave at the drop of a hat. Still do, matter of fact."

"And that's it, huh? You and Mom broke up because you missed a few suppers? What were they—Mom's special tuna surprise? Yeah, I can see where that'd really get her panties in a twist." Nobody could be as sarcastic as a sixteen-year-old girl.

John winced. "Rachel—"

"Oh, come on, *John*. What's the big secret? Are you gay? Were you out at a boy bar when you should've been home with the wifey and kid? Were you—"

"Rachel, that's enough," he snapped.

There was silence from the other end. And then a tiny sob.

Oh, God. What the hell was he supposed to say to this daughter he hadn't even seen in three years? What did she want from him?

He took a steadying breath. "No, I'm not gay. And no, I wasn't hanging around in bars or picking up one-night stands of either sex when I was married to your mother."

"Then—"

"I think you owe me an answer, as well. Why are you so interested in this now?"

"What do you mean?" she burst out, all adolescent self-righteousness. "Don't I have a right to know about my parents' marriage? Don't I have a right to know why my father abandoned me?"

He'd give her high points for verbal histrionics, but he wasn't going to let her yank him around emotionally this time. "I'm not your father anymore."

There was a gasp on the other end.

John ignored it and continued deliberately, "Not legally. That was your decision, not mine. You chose to cut me out of your life three years ago when Dennis formally adopted you."

"So now you don't even—"

"Rachel," he stopped her. "Try to see around that great big chip you have on your shoulder for a moment. I love you. I always have and I always will. But I'm not a punching bag you can flail at any time you get the urge."

Panting breaths from the other end. At least she hadn't hung up on him. Yet.

"Now," John said quietly. "Are you having some kind of problem with Dennis?"

Dennis had been the guy Amy had left him for. True, it was kind of hard for John to see him in a neutral light, but he had thought the guy was okay. For an adulterous asshole, that is. Otherwise he never would have agreed to let the jerk adopt his only child.

"No!"

"He hasn't hit you—"

"No!"

"Or touched you in an uncomfortable way?"

"That's so disgusting! Accusing Dennis of molesting

me is really low. No wonder Mom left you. Your mind is just full of sewage. God, I can't believe—"

"Yeah, yeah," John cut her off. "But if you were being abused, you'd want me to ask, wouldn't you?"

There was a short, furious silence. "He isn't hurting me."

Squeaky had disappeared into the cattails in the ditch next to the rest stop. John could see only the reeds moving and a splash now and then. The dog was probably going to be a muddy mess when he came out.

He sighed. "Then why this sudden curiosity about me, Rachel? You told me three years ago that if you never saw me again in your life it would be fine with you."

"I did not!"

"I have it engraved on my brain, sweetheart." And he did. He could still see her furious little face, twisted with hatred, mouthing those terrible words. Words that had made him bleed internally, somewhere in his gut. Internal wounds were so hard to stanch. Sometimes he thought he still bled.

"I can change my mind, can't I?" The words were muttered in a sullen tone, but they were like birdsong to his ear. "I just want to know what happened with you and Mom—"

He started laughing. He couldn't help it.

"What's so funny?" Oh, the teenage indignation.

"Sorry. It just struck me how tenacious you are." A trait she'd probably gotten from him, but he wasn't going to say that. "It's a good quality in an FBI agent."

"Oh, like I'd ever want to become an FBI agent. You all are the Gestapo of the government. I've read about how you spied on Martin Luther King Jr. in the sixties—"

"Now, now," John said mildly. "That wasn't me personally. Besides, I was still in diapers when that happened."

"Even so—"

"You know, one of the first rules of interrogation is to get on the subject's good side."

Rachel was silent a moment, presumably mulling that one over. John watched Squeaky emerge from the cattails. Yup, he was covered to the withers in slime. The dog looked deliriously happy.

"What about good cop/bad cop?" Rachel asked.

"Can't be both when you're interrogating alone, can you?" John replied cheerfully. "Sure, you can try roughing up the subject, but studies have shown that more information is obtained more quickly when the questioner acts like the suspect's buddy."

"Huh."

John grinned. "So. What about that boyfriend?"

"I don't have one." The words were grudging, but John would take them anyway.

He crossed one leg over the other at the ankles and settled his butt more comfortably against the Crown Vic. "Why not?"

"They're all such turds in this new neighborhood. It's like if you don't give head on the first date, they don't want to be bothered with you."

Good God almighty. He'd faced down gunfire from strung-out gang members with much less fear than he felt now. It was a wonder his hair wasn't standing on end. But he'd asked for this.

"That must be difficult," he replied cautiously.

"Yeah, well, not really. I've got better things to do than stroke the ego of some little perv."

"That's good to hear." *Understatement.* "Are you still in track?"

"Yeah. We've started practice."

"Good." He could picture her flying down the track, her blond hair streaming behind her. He had a sudden ache near his heart.

"So is that enough?"

He frowned. "Is what enough?"

Heavy sigh. "Did I butter you up enough? Are you going to tell me now why you and Mom broke up?"

"Rachel, we've been over this—"

"And you haven't told me!"

He inhaled deeply to get his voice under control. "Ask your mother. If she wants to talk about it, I'll be happy to—"

"I've already told you, she won't talk."

"Well, maybe there's a reason for that." John swore under his breath. He hadn't meant to say that.

"What do you mean?"

"I'm not talking about this with you."

"Fine." She sounded close to tears. "Then there's no point in continuing this conversation, is there?"

"Rachel—"

But she'd already hung up on him. Again.

"Shit!" He tossed the cell into the car, not caring if it hit the seat or not.

Squeaky took that as a sign he should bound up and jump on him, muddy paws and all.

"Down, goddamnit!" John shoved the beast away, nearly toppling him to his back.

The dog cowered, tail between his legs. Oh, wonderful. Now he was an animal abuser.

John sank to his haunches and put his head in his

hands. Jesus, what next? Rachel wouldn't listen to him. She was charging toward a revelation about her mother that she wasn't ready to handle. And he didn't know how to stop her. She was just pigheaded enough that she'd keep pushing and pushing until she found out the ugly truth. His daughter had already discarded one parent. What would she do when she found out her mother wasn't nearly as saintly as she believed? And Turner, the other female in his life, was just as stubborn in her own way. Determined to bring Calvin Hyman down come hell, high water, or hit men, all on her own. She was so isolated that she had no one to help her, no one to fall back on. She didn't even trust him, and that hurt worst of all.

Hot, smelly breath blew against his face, and a tongue swiped his ear.

"What did I tell you about guys and ear licking?" John muttered to the big dog.

Squeaky grinned and wagged his tail. Apparently all was forgiven, or at least forgotten by his tiny canine brain. Too bad it wasn't that easy with the women in John's life. He sighed and stood. He still had to get to Madison today so he could be there at the meet tomorrow between Turner and Victoria Weidner. He opened the Crown Vic's front door and let Squeaky in and then climbed in himself, starting the car and easing into the traffic on 51.

He had a sense of helplessness. Some guy with a rifle was trying to kill Turner, and he didn't even know where she was, wouldn't see her until tomorrow. And what if the killer found her first? There wasn't a damn thing he could do to save her while riding around in a dark sedan with a Great Dane in the back seat. She'd effectively tied his hands by not letting him close. At least Squeaky had finally settled in. John couldn't see his head in the rear-view mirror, so he must've found some place to put it.

They were nearing Portage now, the last town before Madison, and he supposed he should pull off to get some belated lunch, or—he glanced at the dash clock—early supper. He signaled to exit the highway. On the right of the Portage off-ramp was a McDonald's, but he wasn't sure he could stomach a Big Mac right now. He drove further into town past a strip mall and into a mess of construction. It looked like they were repaving the whole road at once. The air was full of dust and the roar of heavy machinery. Shit. John slowed, looking for a way out. Up ahead was a sign advertising ALICE'S KITCHEN, and he headed for that. On the left was a mom-and-pop motel in garish pink. He glanced at it as he crawled by.

A light blue Chevy pickup was pulling into the parking lot.

He'd almost missed it; his mind was so busy. As it was, he nearly ran down an orange-vested construction worker. Adrenaline jolted into his veins. He had to get back there. He'd bet his next paycheck that Chevy was a '68.

Chapter Thirty-two

*O*h, dear, it was tempting. Turner sat in her pickup and stared at the little motel on the outskirts of Portage.

Portage was a small town just north of Madison, off Highway 51. She could easily make Madison today, but then she'd have to find a place to spend the night where the baby blue Chevy wouldn't be seen. Somebody was bound to be looking for her in Madison. She didn't entirely trust Victoria not to have alerted some authority of their meeting.

Which was maybe why the motel was looking so tempting. There were ten pink bungalows, each trimmed in either peppermint green or white. Beside the motel office—also pink—was a white wishing well planted with purple petunias. Red-hatted gnomes sat on the edge of the well, fishing. The place was adorable verging on tacky, but it wasn't the decor that made her mouth water. It was the marquee sign out front proclaiming, ALL NEW BATHS. A bath. She nearly moaned. Or a shower. She wasn't picky, so long as it was wet. And clean. She hadn't had a real bath since Saturday, and today was Wednesday, so that made . . . Good grief! Four days without a bath. The very thought made her body itch all over.

Her cell rang loudly beside her, and she ducked reflexively before grabbing it off the seat and answering.

"Hello?"

"At least you're not in jail yet," a voice said irritably from the other end.

"Brad? Is that you?"

"Yeah, it's me. Who else would be calling you, Ms. America's Most Wanted?"

"Um . . ."

Fortunately, Brad wasn't waiting for her reply. "Are you still wandering around Wisconsin?"

Turner looked at the little motel outside her truck window. "Yeah, I guess I am."

Brad sighed loudly in her ear. "Look, when you get done with this early midlife crisis, I was wondering if you might want to come visit me."

"Visit you?"

"Yeah. Hop a plane, eat three peanuts, and get off in California, where I'll be waiting at the airport. Visit me."

Turner raised her eyebrows. Brad had never invited her out to see him. She didn't even know if he lived in a condo or a house or what. "I—"

"It wouldn't have to be for long." Brad spoke quickly, as if he were nervous she might hang up on him. "And you don't have to answer right away. You know, think about it a bit while you're breaking into safes or whatever you desperadoes do in your spare time."

She couldn't think of anything right now besides

bringing Calvin down. Although how she was going to do that without any evidence . . . She dragged her mind back to Brad and the conversation. "Thank you. I will."

"Good. Fine."

There was an awkward little pause.

Turner cleared her throat. "What, exactly, brought on this urge to see me?"

"Well, you know . . ." Brad trailed off.

"No, I don't know," she said gently. "Tell me."

"I've been thinking." He cleared his throat. "After I called you yesterday. That, you know, we haven't seen too much of each other lately, and, um, maybe we should. See each other, I mean. Get to know each other again. After all, you're my only living relative."

"I guess we could try."

"Yeah." Brad sounded relieved. "Just, you know, try it for a while. No pressure."

"Okay."

"Great. And try not to get in too much trouble, please, Turner?"

Her face twisted. She couldn't really make that promise, but Brad sounded so worried. "Okay."

He said good-bye, and she went back to staring at the motel. Would it really make a good impression on Victoria if she had to argue her case all grungy? Hard to claim that you were in your right mind when you stank—and Turner had the sneaking feeling that she did indeed stink. That decided it. She hopped down from the pickup and went in the pink office.

Ten minutes later, she emerged with a key on a ping-pong paddle. Painted pink. Apparently, they'd had problems in the past here with people absent-mindedly walking off with the room keys. Something that was almost impossible when the key was attached to a pink ping-pong paddle. Turner got in the pickup and drove it the short distance to her bungalow parking spot. Fortunately, the parking lot for the cottages was in back. The pickup wouldn't be easily seen from the road. She jumped down from the truck and went around to the passenger side to lug out her suitcase. Inside the bungalow, she shut and locked the door and let the suitcase drop at her feet. The room was already cool. The air conditioning must've been running all day.

She tiptoed to the bathroom and squeezed her eyes shut before looking. If she'd just spent fifty dollars on a room with a yucky shower stall . . . But no. Turner grinned. The bathroom was, as advertised, fully refurbished. In pink, true, but everything was shiny and very, very clean. Complimentary herbal shampoo, conditioner, and body lotion stood on the sink.

Humming happily to herself, she stripped naked and turned the shower on full blast. She twisted the knobs to hot and stepped in. Ahhh. Nothing was as wonderful as getting clean after being filthy. She washed her hair twice and scrubbed a washcloth all over her body like a loofah. When she finally stepped out, her skin tingled. Turner dried herself and then wrapped a towel around her head. She wiped a spot clean in the mirror and applied all of the complimentary body lotion in the eensy little bottle. She took the towel off and almost laughed when she saw her short hair sticking up. She'd forgotten her hairbrush in the suitcase sitting in the outer room. Smiling, she ran her fingers through her hair and opened the bathroom door.

And stopped dead because she had almost run down Squeaky. The dog was whining and wagging his whole body, he was so glad to see her. But that wasn't what sent the thrill down her spine.

John was lying on the bed, propped against the headboard. His blue eyes were calm and watching her, it seemed, without expression. On the bedside table beside him was a gun in a holster. He'd taken off his jacket, as well, and rolled up his white shirtsleeves, but otherwise he was fully dressed and looked totally at ease.

Except for the handcuffs that stretched his arms above his head.

Chapter Thirty-three

The second thing John noticed about Turner was the way her cat eyes immediately flew to the door. Even while petting the Great Dane's ears, her gaze was taking in the room. No doubt about it, the woman wanted to run. Good thing he'd taken the precaution of shoving the dresser in front of the motel room's door. True, it had felt like it was made of matchsticks when he'd lifted it, but the dresser would still take her a moment to wrestle aside if she tried to make a run for it. Of course, she'd have to get dressed first. Because that was the first thing he noticed about her.

Glory hallelujah, Turner was nude. Maybe this was his reward after a freaking bitch of a week.

"Why are your hands cuffed to the bed?" she asked.

Squeaky gave her one last lick and settled back down in the place he'd found for himself: the floor of the alcove closet. He could just fit if he curled into a ball. John tore his eyes away from Turner's breasts, soft and white and with shockingly dark nipples. His cock was already throbbing.

"I thought it might make it easier for you."

She looked wary, like a wild thing ready to run. Her slim legs were braced apart, and she held her arms slightly away from her sides. "Easier for what?"

"To talk." That was what he'd gambled on, anyway. If he made himself nonthreatening to her, maybe she wouldn't run. Of course, the flip side to that equation was if she did run, there wasn't a damn thing he could do about it.

A gamble.

"Talk?" She made a sudden swift move that had his heart leaping painfully in his chest, but she only grabbed his jacket and wrapped it around herself. Technically, she was covered. But the sight of her, with bare legs and the jacket only coming to midthigh, was a wet dream come true. He was never going to look at that jacket in the same way again. He nearly groaned.

He didn't, though. He kept his voice calm. Light. As if they were still conversing via cell phone. It was important that he not scare her. "Yeah, talk. I think it's about time we spent some time together and figured this thing out."

"And the handcuffs?" She pointed with her sharp little chin. Her hands were occupied keeping his jacket closed around her nude body.

"I figured you'd find me less intimidating this way. I'm not wearing my Glock." He pointed with his own chin to the bedside table, where his holster and a hand-cuff key lay. "I can't chase after you if you decide to leave."

She exhaled on a laugh. "You've got to be kidding."

"Baby, do I look like I'm kidding?" He rattled the metal cuffs against the headboard.

"I've wondered what your expression would look like when you said that." Her scratchy voice had lowered.

"What?"

"Baby." Her gaze was on his crotch, where she was probably getting an eyeful.

Oh, man. He had to clear his throat before he could speak. "That wasn't what I was wondering about you."

She raised her green eyes and took a step closer. Was she conscious of her move? "What did you wonder about me?"

"Your taste. What it would be like to kiss you on the lips."

She stared at him as if sorely tempted, and he sure as hell hoped she was. But she didn't move closer. She just stood there flexing her narrow hands on his coat lapels.

He exhaled. "Why don't you sit down?"

"I ought to leave." Her straight, dark eyebrows knit. "How do I know you haven't called for reinforcements?"

"I haven't."

She nibbled at her bottom lip as if debating whether to believe him.

"We're all alone," John said softly. "Just you and me."

Her gaze flew to his. Her eyes were narrowed, suspicious.

John waited, breathing in and out slowly, concentrating on the flow of air to his body. He met her eyes calmly and, he hoped, reassuringly.

"Okay." She sat on the far corner of the bed.

He suppressed his smile. True, she looked ready to fly at any moment, but he'd just won the first round.

"Bet it was nice to have that shower," he said.

She snorted. "Obviously, I'm not meant for a life on the run when I can be caught because I stopped to bathe." Her voice had a bit of wry self-disgust, and her soft mouth had twisted.

He smiled. It would be wonderful to touch her, but just watching the expressions move across Turner's face was oddly satisfying in itself.

"You're not doing so bad. You managed to escape from an experienced FBI agent twice."

"Only to be caught the third time." Her eyes narrowed again and the outer corners tilted up, making her look more like a cat than ever. "How did you find me?"

He shook his head. "I can't let you know all my techniques, can I?" Dumb luck, in this case. "So what do you plan to do now?"

Was it his imagination, or did the color rise in her cheeks? "What do you mean?"

"You don't have the evidence, do you?" A soft canine snore started in the corner. They'd bored Squeaky.

"No."

"Then what can you do?" He crossed his legs on the bed, and her gaze slipped down to follow the movement. "Is there another place you can look?"

He carefully didn't mention her arranged meeting with Victoria Weidner the next morning. That was his ace in the hole. If this didn't work, he could still catch her in Madison. But he was hoping she'd tell him about the meeting herself.

She didn't. "I don't know."

"So what will you do?"

"You want me to give up, don't you?"

"Not give up, exactly." He grimaced. "If Hyman really is embezzling from the bank, we'll get him eventually. Don't worry about that."

"But it'll take time, won't it?" She stared at him with what seemed like fading hope in her eyes. "You'll need warrants and a special investigator and some kind of evidence just to start. That's assuming the FBI even decides to investigate. And all that time Calvin will be hiring expensive lawyers and destroying whatever evidence there is."

He sighed. "Turner—"

"No. I'm right, aren't I, John?"

He shifted. This handcuffing-himself-to-the-bedpost business wasn't such a good idea, after all. He wanted to touch her, hold her, keep her from running. Of course, he could get out of the handcuffs if he wanted to—he had the second key sewn into the band of his watch. But he wanted to maintain the illusion of vulnerability.

Not to mention it would take some time to get the handcuffs unlocked. "It might go down that way, but there's always a chance—"

"A chance? A chance isn't good enough."

"That's how the system works."

"No. I'm sorry, I can't wait for a chance that might never come."

She stood up, and he straightened reflexively. Or tried to. The handcuffs prevented him from moving his upper body much.

"Stay."

She'd turned away to her suitcase, but now she stilled and looked at him over her shoulder. "Why?"

"Because I want you to."

"What are you saying?"

He put as much intensity as he could into his gaze.

"Stay with me. Forget about Hyman and the bank and everything else. Just for tonight. Stay with me."

"John—"

"Just the two of us. Here. Let whatever is going on outside stay outside. Just for tonight."

She looked at the door. "You're stalling."

"No—"

"You're waiting for some kind of backup and you—"

"No, goddamnit!" John lunged against the stupid handcuffs and nearly tore his arm from the socket. "Shit!"

She was by his side immediately. "I can't believe you actually handcuffed yourself to the bed."

"Yeah, well, it wasn't my brightest moment."

"I don't know." Her mouth was wry. "It kept me here, didn't it?"

He closed his eyes. "Stay with me."

"You've hurt yourself."

"Turner—"

"I can't stay, you know that."

"Why not?" He opened his eyes to find she was even closer than before.

He inhaled. There it was: the green scent of pine, even under the flowery perfume of whatever soap she'd used. He was smelling Turner—her special scent. She stared at him mutely. He could see yellow slivers in her green eyes, she was that near. Finally. God, he couldn't let her disappear again.

"There's nobody outside. It's just you and me—"

"John," she said in her low, sexy voice. "It's impossible. You know that."

"Why? No one need ever know."

"That's—"

"It's only you and me. Forget everything else."

"I can't." She ran a hand through the drying spikes of her hair. "You want to arrest me. I want to get Calvin. This won't work."

"Just for tonight."

She laughed softly. "You're crazy."

"Maybe. But I need you so much, baby."

She sighed and looked away.

"Please." Christ. He was begging.

"How do you undo these?" She was touching his shoulder lightly now, her fingers gentle.

He was losing her, he could tell. An uncharacteristic panic filled his chest. "Don't leave me. I want—"

She turned her face and her mouth was suddenly inches from his. "What do you want?"

If he lived another forty years, he'd never forget the erotic huskiness of Turner's voice whispering that to him. *What do you want?* You, he wanted to say, I want you, now and forever. But he settled for something a lot less intimidating.

"I want you to kiss me."

Chapter Thirty-four

A kiss.

Such an innocent request. Unless the person making the request was a man with desperation in his gaze and an almost palpable tension in his body.

A man like John.

Turner stared into his eyes. The irises were a strange kind of blue, so pale as to make his pupils stand out in sharp contrast, with a thin, dark blue ring around the outer edge. They were the kind of eyes that made some people uneasy because they were so light. But at the moment it wasn't his eyes that were making her uneasy. And excited. It was the look they held: part need, part compulsion. John wanted her very badly.

He hadn't given up on her. That had been the first thought she'd had when she'd seen him. Somehow, despite all the times she pushed him away, despite her prickly self-sufficient personality, he'd stayed. He'd come after her. It wasn't logical, but she felt triumph. Triumph and heat. She wanted this man, too.

She shifted on the bed. The jacket she was wearing had ridden up a little when she'd sat down next to him, and her bare bottom was in contact with the bedspread. On top, the jacket covered her decently, but underneath . . .

Why was she still here? She should have taken advantage of his chivalrous urge to handcuff himself to the bed. She should have been out the door fifteen minutes ago. Instead, she was leaning over him, so close she could feel the heat radiating from his chest.

So close she could scent him.

Ah, that. She felt her eyelids droop half-closed. That was what she'd wanted to do the first time she'd actually seen John, only two days ago at Tommy's place: to smell him. And now she could. It was almost intoxicating, his aroma. He smelled like a man. A delicious, wonderful man. Not sweaty or smoky. Not even any identifiable odor like cologne. She smelled just him.

His essence.

Turner swayed forward, tantalized by that scent, and found her mouth was almost on his. It seemed so natural, so right, to give in to his plea.

She kissed him.

She brushed her lips over his, warm and firm, and then brushed again. She felt his beard stubble at her cheek, and he opened his mouth. His tongue stroked her lips and she parted them slowly, cautiously, to let him in. A groan whispered against her lips, and then he darted his tongue into her mouth. She gasped. She could taste him. Coffee and something else she couldn't identify. He darted in again, and she stroked his tongue with hers, feeling the texture. She drew back a little and looked at him.

"Come closer," he murmured.

His eyes were half-lowered. Passion should have softened his face, but instead it had deepened the lines around his mouth and hardened his jaw. She inched closer until her hip bumped his side and leaned down, delicately, deliberately biting his lower lip. He watched her kiss him, his eyes still open. Then she licked his bottom lip, licked all around his mouth, slowly, thoroughly, with him watching all the time. She broke the kiss with a small, wet sound, intimate in the still room. She raised her head and paused, looking at him.

He didn't comment.

So she lowered her head and fit her open mouth over his. Immediately, he angled his face and thrust his tongue into her mouth, more strongly this time. She caught it and sucked until he groaned.

He pulled his head back. "I want you closer. Climb on top of me."

She arched her eyebrows but did as he asked. First she knelt on the side of the bed, and then she swung one leg over him, hiking the jacket up a little. Her bare bottom was now just below his pelvis, partly on his thighs. She sat still for a moment, adjusting to the feel of his trousers against her bare legs. Her hands held the jacket—his jacket—closed across her chest, but then she looked into his eyes and let go. The jacket fell partially open.

His gaze dropped to her pubic hair and her parted sex. His eyes narrowed, and his face became almost saturnine.

She leaned forward and placed one hand on his chest. The other cupped his jaw. And she kissed him again with tongue and lips, moaning with the voluptuous freedom. She could do anything—anything she liked—with this man. For tonight.

Just for tonight.

She drew back a little and bit his chin, scraping her teeth against his stubble. He inhaled but didn't say anything. He tilted his head back. She softly, gently licked his throat and felt his Adam's apple move as he swallowed.

"The key is on the bedside table." His voice was gravelly. "Unlock me."

"No."

She sat up and watched him. His brows were drawn together over his blue eyes, and his jaw flexed like he was grinding his teeth. She smiled. And began unbuttoning his shirt. It was a white oxford, nothing special. She slipped a finger underneath the placket and slowly drew a button through the little hole. She felt the corner of her smile tilt up. John had chest hair.

"Turner—"

She parted the shirt between the next two buttons and leaned down to poke her tongue through the hole. She could taste a bit of salt, feel the hair tickling her tongue.

"Jesus." It was a low growl.

She spread both palms over his pectorals and felt his heat through the shirt cloth. The trousers where she sat were probably damp by now, but she didn't care. She brought her hands together in the center of his chest and trailed them down to his pants. And paused. He inhaled sharply. She gently unbuckled his worn leather belt and left it hanging. When she pulled the zipper, the rasp was loud in the room. Carefully she opened the fly to his trousers and almost giggled.

Navy boxers.

"What's so funny?" he muttered.

"I figured tighty-whities."

"Ouch." But his voice was distracted. Because even through the boxers, he was standing outside the fly.

"Raise your hips," she ordered.

She had to get on her knees to accommodate him, but she was able to pull the trousers and boxers down to midthigh even so. Then she sat back down on his bare legs and almost gasped. His hot skin against her wet flesh felt wonderful. And decadent. It had been so long. And usually this was when she started getting the willies. Instead, she just wanted to . . .

She bent and licked across the head of his cock. She heard his harsh gasp but didn't bother looking up. His cock was beautiful, tight and veined with a shaft that was thicker than the head. It was quite thick overall, actually. His pubic hair was dark with a sprinkling of gray that she found sexy somehow. She licked again, tasting him, and then she took him into her mouth and sucked. Just the head, while she played with the shaft and his balls.

Another gasp. "Turner—"

She hummed with him in her mouth.

"Christ." His voice was guttural. "Condoms in my back pocket."

Well, now, that was interesting news. He'd been that sure of her, had he? She looked up, his cock still between her lips, and narrowed her eyes at him. His cheeks had flushed and his face was harder than ever; his pale eyes sparked with a hunger that echoed her own.

"Would you prefer that I didn't have them?"

He had a point. And besides, she really wanted him

inside her. She dug under his thigh until she found a square packet and unwrapped it. She carefully fitted the condom over his erection. She expected him to ask her again to let him go, but he didn't. He just watched her handle him with intense ghost eyes, his arms strained over his head. When he was covered, she inched forward until her vulva lay over his cock. *Oh, Lord.* She shuddered at the feel of him beneath her. *Sooo good. Oh, so good.* She moved slowly, grinding herself back and forth along his length, made slippery by her fluids. She reached his tip and aligned it with her clitoris, then flattened herself against him and sought his mouth with hers.

His tongue was rough, his kiss almost violent. He hadn't made a murmur as she pleasured herself on him, but she knew he must be at his limit. She ground down again.

"Put me in you, baby," he growled against her lips. "Fuck me."

She shuddered at his coarse words. She tore open his shirt, spreading the halves so she could have access to his bare chest, before rising and positioning him at her entrance.

Then she lowered herself.

The first inch or so slipped in easily, but then she had to push. She braced her hands on his chest, felt the hairs beneath her palms, and bore down. It had been years, and John was thick, maybe thicker than any man she'd ever had before. She gasped. She felt each inch of his flesh invading hers, parting and stretching her.

"Easy," John whispered huskily. "Easy, baby. Take it slow."

She slid up on his cock and sat again, taking a little more of him into her. Repeated the movement. And again. He thrust up at her on the fourth try. She moaned as she felt him enter her entirely, his length sliding home and filling her.

"Is it okay?" John gasped. "Are you okay?"

"Yes. Yes, I—"

But her words were lost as he thrust within her. She had to lean forward and clutch at his shoulders again, he was humping up at her so roughly. His erection shoved back and forth inside her.

He watched her beneath nearly closed eyes. "Kiss me."

So she kissed him as she rode his pelvis and his penis. She thrust against him and kissed him until his mouth went slack beneath hers. And then she had to raise her head to look.

To watch John as he came.

It was such an intimate thing, watching a man fall apart, literally lose himself in her. John's face was flushed, his teeth gritted. He closed his eyes and grunted. Then she felt him jerking within her. His shoulder muscles beneath her palms were bunched and rock hard as he convulsed.

A feeling of tenderness—of love—filled her. Tears beaded in her eyes.

He grunted again, and his thrusts became weaker until he went lax beneath her. Turner kissed him, little light kisses that just touched his face. He was still in her, partially hard, and she didn't want to separate from him.

He sighed, his eyes closed. "You didn't come."

"Don't worry," she said quickly. "It doesn't matter. I—"

"It matters to me." He opened his eyes and smiled at her. The lines around his mouth had finally softened.

She was embarrassed now. As if she'd failed at some test that everyone else passed easily. "No, really—"

"No, really, it does matter to me."

He bumped her with his hips, and she gasped at the feeling. She was sensitive down there after his lovemaking.

"I thought so," he whispered. "Now, as I see it we have two options."

She stared at him, half-shy, half-aroused. She couldn't believe they were talking about—

"You can climb up here and sit on my face," he drawled conversationally. "And I can lick you until you scream."

Her eyes widened. There was no way she was going to—

"Or you can move on me like you were doing before I entered you."

She wanted to hide her face. "I-I can take care of it myself—"

"I know you can, baby." He'd lost his smile. "But I want you to do it with me."

Oh, goodness. She couldn't do this. In front of someone else? She just couldn't.

But John was watching her, waiting. And she wanted to please him. She closed her eyes and tilted down until her clitoris was in contact with him. He was still inside her, not quite hard, and she knew if she moved too much he would slip out. And somehow she wanted him in her when she . . .

This was so intimate it was almost unbearable. She ground against him, knowing that he was watching her, knowing that he could see every emotion cross her face. She leaned farther and the tips of her breasts accidentally brushed his chest. She gasped. His chest hair scraping against her sensitive nipples was . . . She brushed her breasts against him again and ground faster, pushing out of her mind the reasons why she couldn't do this. Instead, she thought about John, about how she had felt when he'd come in front of her.

"That's the way, baby." She heard his voice through a haze, encouraging her. "Do it for me."

She felt like fire, like a storm building. She felt . . .

"You're so beautiful," he murmured. "So sexy. Come for me. God, you're making me hard again."

She knew she must not look elegant or pretty right now. She was moving almost frantically on him, her face contorted uncontrollably.

"I've never seen anything in my life as erotic as you are right now." His voice was relentless. "I'm going to have to make love to you again. Once won't be enough. Come for me, baby."

There was moisture on her upper lip, and she was making sounds. It didn't matter. All that mattered was . . .

"Turner."

She moaned, her voice loud in the room, and opened her eyes as the feeling broke and crested over her. Overwhelming. Nearly frightening. And she found John watching her, his face hard again and possessive—and something else. But she couldn't fully analyze his expression, because she was arching and panting and coming. Coming in front of him, her eyes helplessly locked with his. She knew suddenly that there was no going back from this point. Her world would never be the same again—her life had just been roughly turned upside-down, and maybe she liked it that way, all cock-eyed and crazy and off balance, as long as John was with her. *John.*

Tears ran down her face.

Chapter Thirty-five

"Which way would you pick to die?" Nald panted as he stumbled over a root. Why did there have to be so many trees in the forest? "Four giant snakes attack you and each gets, like, an arm or a leg, and they pull back and forth, back and forth until your arms and legs rip off midair and your little stumpy body falls to the ground and you're like, *ah! ah! ah!* unable to move until one of the snakes bites off your head, or—" He shoved aside a branch. It whipped back and hit him in the face, nearly taking out his eye. "Or you're attacked by a huge purple squid thing and it shoots one of its arms down your throat and you're like, *urk! urk! urk!* and then the arm grows more tentacles inside you and explodes out your stomach and back all at once?"

"What the fuck are you asking me this for?" Fish muttered from in front.

"It's a question—"

"I know it's a question, douchebag!" Fish stopped and whirled, one shoulder down and the other up like that hunchback church dude. His yellow mesh tank was hanging in strips from the neck, thanks to Bucky, and he had deep scratches all over his hairy belly.

Nald had always thought that Bucky, as a team whatchamacallit—mascot—was a little wussy. No more, dude. Now, as far as Nald was concerned, Bucky was one baaad mascot. But if you mentioned Bucky at all, Fish started twitching. Which was why he'd found a new subject. "Well, I—"

"I don't need questions! I don't want questions! Why are you asking me questions?"

Nald stopped to think. They'd come to a little clearing in the woods that was covered in these tall green plants. 'Course, most plants were green. The morning sunshine was really bright. It shone kinda pretty through the long leaves of the plants, though. "Well, it's like talking—"

"D'oh!" Fish screamed. "Of course questions are like talking! What are you, a-a—"

Nald scratched his chest and watched Fish's eyes bug out even more. If Fish did much more eye-bugging, his eyeballs were going to fall right out of his head. He decided to help Fish. "A cool dude?"

"No!"

"Bad dude?"

"No!"

"Wicked dude?"

"No! No! No!" Fish screamed, totally losing it. "You're the biggest, dumbest, smelliest fuckass on the entire planet!"

Nald felt insulted. "Hey—"

Fish flung wide his arms, banging the falling-apart bag of money against a long-leaved plant and knocking it over.

"Why? Why? Why?" he screamed. "Why me? Why am I lost in a fucking forest with a fucking guy, carrying fucking inked-up money and being fucking attacked by fucking wild animals? How could my fucking life get any more fucked up than this?"

"Well, you could—" Nald started.

"It's not a fucking question!" Fish bellowed.

"Then why'd you ask it?" Nald bellowed back.

"I didn't!" Fish screamed, just before he fell over and disappeared into the tall plants. The plants waved frantically, like they were having a spaz-attack, and then Fish reappeared, still angry. "I can't fucking believe—"

"Hey," Nald said. "These plants look kind of familiar—"

"That I took you along—"

Nald plucked a branch. The long leaves looked like a hand with too many fingers. Where had he seen—?

"On a fucking bank heist—"

Nald sniffed the plant.

"When I could've—"

"Weed!"

"Huh?" said Fish.

"Weed!" Nald waved the plant branch in front of Fish's face.

"I know that's a weed, you dumb—"

"No," Nald explained patiently. "Not *a* weed. *Weed*."

Fish slumped his head into his hands. "I'm in the woods with fucking Rain Man."

Nald got impatient. "Weed. Grass—"

"Grass isn't a weed," Fish objected.

"This grass is!" Nald thrust the leaves beneath Fish's nose.

A look of wonder dawned across Fish's face. Kind of

like the time they'd gone to the topless *and* bottomless girlie show in Superior and a redhead had come out on stage and bent over backward and put her hands on the floor behind her. A look that said, *The world is a strange and beautiful place.*

"We're standing in a field of weed!" Fish shouted.

"Yup," Nald said.

"It's enough weed to smoke for years!"

"Yup," Nald said.

"It's enough weed to make us rich!" Fish said, doing a little hopping dance.

"Yup," Nald said.

"And it's all ours!"

"Nope," another voice said, and it was accompanied by the *cha-chink* of a shell being chambered into a shotgun.

Nald slowly turned around.

A short, round woman with long gray braids stood behind them. She had a shotgun at her shoulder.

"That's my weed," she said.

Nald started to smile, because she was only an old woman, and besides, most women liked him. But then she fired the shotgun, busting that thought all to hell.

BOOM! A whole row of plants lost their heads.

Nald ducked and felt his own head to make sure it was still there.

"Run!" Fish yelled, which was the smartest thing he'd said all day. Maybe all week.

Nald galloped for the woods.

Behind him, the shotgun went *cha-chink* and then *BOOM!*

"Head for the highway!" Fish panted. He darted past Nald, even though his legs were much shorter. His garbage bag of money seemed to have a hole. Tufts of paper cash were flying out behind him, catching on the underbrush and getting trampled underfoot. "Run!"

Cha-chink. BOOM!

Nald ducked and zigzagged through the trees, heading for the light that meant the highway. He was gulping air.

Cha-chink. BOOM!

A twenty from Fish's bag plastered itself across Nald's eyes. He brushed it away into the woods. He was almost at the light—

BOOM!

Nald hit the ditch right behind Fish and kept going. They ran up the small incline to the highway, and Nald passed Fish like he was standing still. He ran like his feet were on fire. He ran so fast it took him a while to hear Fish yelling behind him.

"Stop! Shit! Stop, man!"

Nald stumbled to a halt, his chest heaving for air and a stitch starting on his side. He turned to look. Behind him, Fish was on his back on the highway, his arms and legs kicking in the air kind of like a newborn baby.

But that wasn't what made Nald stare.

No, it was the money he was looking at openmouthed. Because all along the road behind him, for quite a ways, really, was a cloud of cash. The twenty-dollar bills floated in the air, being blown higher in swirls by the playful breeze, alighting in the tops of trees like a flock of green starlings and sticking to the gluey asphalt on the road.

Nald suddenly realized that his garbage bag felt light. He looked down at the tattered rag in his hand and opened what was left of it. One purple-ink-stained bill lay at the bottom. He lifted the bag to peer at it, and as he watched, the bill rose like a miniature helicopter and flew into the air to dance with its brothers. It looked kind of happy.

Then the cop car drove by.

Chapter Thirty-six

*J*ohn woke when Turner left the bed early the next morning. Thursday morning. Actually, it wasn't the first time he'd woken. She'd gotten up several times during the night to visit the bathroom, and each time he'd been aware of her movements, of where she was in the room and the rate of her breathing. But this time after she came back from the bathroom, she began dressing.

He lay still and watched her. Last night, after they'd made love, after Turner had come so heartbreakingly on him, after she'd lain against him, recovering, she'd carefully unlocked the handcuffs and freed him. He'd finally been able to put his arms around her. To hold her close and spoon with her all night, the luxury nearly overcoming him. The cuddling, for him at least, had been almost as satisfying as the sex.

Now she pulled on panties, slipping the pale pink cotton fabric over her hips and adjusting the band at her waist. She picked up a white bra from her suitcase and put it on. It was funny how women always bent from the waist to fit the cups over their breasts when they put on a bra. He could see the curve of her back and the little bumps of her spine as she leaned over. John watched and found her motion erotic in a tender way. It was a feminine action—putting on a bra—and a very intimate one. Only when a man was a woman's lover was he allowed to see her perform that mundane task. It made his heart ache.

Squeaky got up and stretched, his long forelegs braced before him. He yawned loudly, then padded over to greet her.

"Shh," Turner whispered at the dog. She glanced worriedly over at him in the bed.

A twinge of irritation ran through him. Did she think he was some kind of idiot who'd sleep while she ran away from him? Ran without even saying good-bye? He waited until she'd finished dressing and had gathered her things. She was pulling the bureau from in front of the door when he spoke.

"Stay."

She startled. She really had thought he was still sleeping obliviously. John narrowed his eyes in anger.

Turner glanced at him over her shoulder. "I can't."

He watched her soft lips firm. Her cat eyes slid away from him, hiding guilt and some other emotion. His own tightened. "I've been running after you with all the finesse of a Keystone cop. I've let you slide through my fingers, turned aside when I could have caught you, pulled my punches so I wouldn't hurt you. But now there's someone else after you who won't pull his punches. He wants to kill you, and I'm not going to let that happen."

"I—"

"Even if that puts your little plans all out of kilter," he finished, his voice even.

She still couldn't meet his eyes. "I know that—"

"No, you don't know." He levered himself up to sit in the bed. "I'm not playing by your rules anymore, Turner. If you walk out that door, all bets are off as far as I'm concerned. I'll bring you down when and where I want. Whether you're ready or not."

"John—"

"Come back to bed," he commanded. "Now."

"I can't."

"Damn it, Turner, yes you can!" He couldn't remember the last time he'd lost control of his temper like this. And then he did: it had been on the phone with Turner, not two days ago. "Don't give me that crap about your uncle and how Hyman has to pay. It's your life at stake now."

"It's more than that," she burst out.

"What are you talking about?"

"This," she gestured jerkily at stomach height with her hand, "Between you and me. It's gone beyond Uncle Rusty. That's why I have to leave."

"You're not making any sense."

"I know!" She was looking a little ragged around the edges. Her eyelids were smudged as if bruised.

"Tell me what the problem is." He tried to lower his voice and wasn't altogether successful.

"I can't do that, either."

"Turner—"

"I can't, John!" She sounded wild.

Were those tears in her eyes? John frowned and threw back the covers to rise, uncaring of the fact that he was nude.

"No!" She put both hands up as if to ward him off. As if she feared he might hurt her.

As if she feared *him*.

He froze. She might as well have punched him in the gut with that little gesture. "What is it? Tell me."

"I can't—" She rubbed her eyes. "I can't stay with you here, John. I have to leave—"

"For God's sake, why?"

"Because every time I look at you—" She broke off, staring with wide cat eyes that flayed him open with their pain.

"What?" he whispered.

"I *feel*."

Then she was gone.

Feel? Feel what, for God's sake? What the hell did she mean? John stared at the closed door, debating whether to go after her now even though he was still naked. But she was already worked up. If he caught her in the parking lot, they'd just have the same argument, but this time in public. Shit. He ran his hand through his hair. If—

His cell rang shrilly, breaking his trance. John swore. He hunted around the bed and found his trousers crumpled on the other side. The cell rang again from the case on his belt and he tore it off. Squeaky whined. Shit. She hadn't even bothered to take her dog, who, from the way he was pacing, needed to go out.

"Okay, okay," John muttered to both the animal and the phone. He punched the *Answer* button and tucked the cell between his shoulder and ear as he yanked on his pants. "MacKinnon."

"Sleeping in?" Torelli drawled.

If he'd been in the same room, John just might've

taken a swing at the younger man's smug face. "What is it?"

"We've got SpongeBob and Yoda. Sir."

"About time." John took two steps and opened the bungalow door. Squeaky nearly knocked him over rushing out. "Where'd you find them?"

"Actually," Torelli cleared his throat, "it wasn't me who pulled them in."

John grinned tightly. First good news he'd heard today. "Oh, yeah? Then who beat you to it?"

"A part-time sheriff's deputy from Sawyer, the next county over, was patrolling a back road. He saw these two guys running along the highway, throwing money into the air and screaming."

"Into the air." John craned his neck out the door to look for Squeaky. It'd be just his luck to lose the dog, as well. "They were throwing the bank money away?"

"Apparently."

"What are they, insane?" Shit. Where was that dog? There was no sign of him, and the highway was only fifty yards away. John walked around behind the bungalow.

"I guess. The deputy says they're covered in bug bites and scratches and they may have been attacked by a rabid badger."

"Christ. Where did they manage to find a badger?"

"I—"

"Never mind." John shook his head. "So when will you get a chance to question them?"

Behind the bungalow was a mowed field and then the highway. Squeaky was running back and forth in the field. Thank God. At least he hadn't lost the dog.

"Sometime this afternoon, I hope," Torelli replied. "There seems to be some kind of paperwork holdup over there in Sawyer. They're dragging their feet about bringing them to the sheriff's office here. And they say SpongeBob and Yoda might need rabies shots."

"Well, geez, Torelli," John drawled. "The next county over must be all of—what?—fifty miles away? Any reason you can't get off your ass and book on over there?"

There was a short silence from Torelli's end. "I just didn't want to step on any local toes. Sir."

"Good thought," John conceded. "But the sooner we question these idiots, the sooner we can close this thing."

"Speaking of which," Torelli said. "How're you doing finding the runaway librarian?"

"I'm doing just fine."

"Don't need any help?"

"No." Squeaky came bounding up with something dead in his mouth and plopped his prize at John's feet. Wonderful. It looked—and smelled—like a skunk in the greasy stage.

"Because I can still call in the Madison police," Torelli persisted.

"Shit, no," John said to both his subordinate and the dog. He grabbed Squeaky's collar and hauled him away from the dead skunk, which he clearly considered breakfast. God, dogs were disgusting—

"What?" Torelli sounded startled.

"I said no," John grunted. It wasn't easy yanking a Great Dane away from something he wanted. "We've been over this already. No outsiders."

"But—"

"And call me as soon as you've questioned Sponge-Bob and Yoda." John took a firmer hold on the collar and pulled. Squeaky sat down and bowed his head, the collar slipping to right behind his ears and pushing them forward. He looked like a donkey refusing to move. "They sure as hell didn't plan that bank robbery, and they might tell you who put them up to it."

"I thought our theory was that the librarian did it."

"The librarian's name is Turner Hastings, and no, we no longer think she masterminded it."

Silence from the other end.

John stopped hauling at Squeaky but kept his grip on the dog's collar. Squeaky collapsed in a boneless, but very heavy, heap. "Torelli?"

"Yes, sir. Can I respectfully point out that you seem to be getting awfully close to this suspect?"

John tilted his head back. The damn dog smelled, Turner had run away from him—*again*—and Torelli was pushing every single one of his buttons. All this before his morning coffee. It was enough to make a big bad FBI agent whimper. "No. You may not point it out, respectfully or otherwise. I'll call you after the meet in Madison. I want some answers by then, got it?"

"Yes, sir. Got it."

"Good." John hung up the cell and looked down at Squeaky.

The dog thumped his tail.

John sighed. "Come on. We both need a shower now." He slapped his thigh.

The dog got up and, after one last yearning look at the odorous carrion he'd bagged, followed without protest. Which was a good thing, because after they both had a bath, they needed to eat and get on the road to Madison. Today was the day he would arrest Turner. No matter her feelings.

Or his.

Chapter Thirty-seven

So how you all doing?" Calvin said, nice and hearty, as he entered the county sheriff's office Thursday morning. He carried a cardboard container with four coffee cups from the Kwik Trip and a bag of donuts.

Doug Larson perked up at the sight. "Gosh, thanks, Mr. Hyman," the young deputy said, accepting a paper cup of hot liquid.

"Calvin. Please. Call me Calvin, Doug." He smiled benevolently. "After all, with a little luck, I might be your legislative representative soon."

"Yeah, that's right." Doug grinned and selected a jelly-filled donut from the white paper bag. "I'm sure you'll be elected, Mr. Hyman. Everyone from Winosha will be voting for you."

"That's what I like to hear." Calvin slapped the younger man on the back while covertly casting a glance around the room.

It was a typical small municipal office: cinder-block walls, battered green metal office furniture, old oak doors leading to an outer reception room, and a high ceiling with exposed ductwork. The sheriff was lounging behind his desk, feet up, talking on the phone. Clemmons had nodded when Calvin had entered the room, but he hadn't stopped talking. Flanking the sheriff's desk was another desk that must have belonged to the deputy sheriff normally. Right now, though, it'd obviously been taken over by the FBI agents. The younger agent—what was his name? Something spic—sat on the corner, also on a phone, this one a cell. He looked none too pleased with whatever the person on the other end of the phone was saying to him.

Calvin picked up a cup of coffee and carefully pulled back the little plastic tab on the cover. He took a scalding sip and smiled. God, the coffee was awful at the local Kwik Trip. "Had any breaks in investigating our little bank robbery?"

"Oh, yeah. We had an important one just this morning. The gunmen have been caught." Doug was opening a little plastic tub of nondairy creamer and so didn't catch Calvin's expression. Which was a good thing.

Calvin had to clear his throat twice before he could talk. "Oh?"

"Yeah." Doug finally got the creamer tub open and poured it into his cup. "Over in Sawyer."

"Really? That's not too far away."

"Tell me about it. They were just, like, walking along the road. And flinging money in the air, according to the deputy. Can you imagine? This deputy drives by on patrol and sees money flying through the air and two guys yelling or something. Naturally, he stops to see what's up, and there you are. Two bank robbers nabbed just like that."

"Good. Good."

"Wish I could have that kind of luck sometime," Doug muttered into his coffee cup.

Calvin felt the smile stretched across his face begin to freeze. He wanted to wrap his hands around the deputy's neck and shout at him until he found out what was going on.

Instead he widened his smile even more. "I bet you've questioned them."

"Oh, no." Doug waved his jelly donut at the sheriff, still talking on the phone. A blob of jelly fell to the linoleum. He didn't seem to notice. The FBI agent glanced over, apparently attracted by the movement. "Sheriff Clemmons is working that out now. Seems they got bitten by some wild animal."

Calvin had been thinking about his own problems, and this non sequitur caught him off-guard. "Who?"

"You know." Doug stared. "The bank robbers? The ones in masks? Tuna Fish and Nald. I guess they'd been slogging through the woods all this time, and let me tell you, those guys are not woodsmen."

Calvin frowned. "So—?"

"So they got attacked by something. A bear or a wolverine. Do we have wolverines in Wisconsin? Maybe it was a skunk." Doug laughed with an unpleasant braying sound. "Anyway, they gotta be looked at by a doctor."

"I see."

A measure of relief swept through Calvin. Those two bozos hadn't been questioned. At least not yet. But that still left the other matter that had been bothering him: Turner Hastings.

"Wonder if they'll need those shots you get in the

stomach?" Doug was musing. "You know those big-ass ones for, like, rabies?"

Oh, he certainly hoped so. Calvin smiled. "The sheriff's office is to be commended in resolving this crime swiftly. It's good to know that our tax dollars are being used so effectively. I'll be sure to bring the matter up in my next speech."

Doug looked a little doubtful. "Well, they were by the side of the road and all—"

"And your law-enforcement personnel were quick to apprehend them."

"'Course, it was the Sawyer County sheriff—"

"Yes. Yes." Calvin broadened his smile. God, what a fool! Couldn't he just take the credit for the job like a normal man? "It was a job well done all around, no matter who actually made the arrest."

"Well—"

"But I suppose Turner Hastings is still on the loose?"

Doug brightened. "Yeah, but not for long."

Calvin's heart dropped painfully. "What?"

"Can't exactly tell you, it's a department secret." Doug winked and shoved the rest of his jelly donut into his mouth. He said rather indistinctly, "But take it from me, we'll have her by this afternoon."

That was not what he wanted to hear. Calvin smiled painfully. "Really? Well, I shouldn't be surprised. This is the best sheriff's department in the state, after all—"

Doug's chest puffed up.

"—but I find it hard to believe that you'll be able to get her that soon." Calvin arched his eyebrows skeptically. "*This* afternoon?"

"Yeah, this afternoon. Today." Doug caught some of

the doubt in Calvin's look. He leaned forward earnestly and lowered his voice. "No, I mean it. Special Agent MacKinnon will be picking her up."

Not if Calvin could help it. "But how?"

"We've got a tip. We know where she'll be."

He could see the younger FBI agent watching their conversation as he listened to the phone. Doug wasn't aware they were under scrutiny, because his back was to the man.

Calvin felt sweat bead his upper lip. "Where she's *going* to be? You don't even know where she is now?" He forced a careless laugh. "I'm sorry, Doug, but that doesn't sound particularly convincing, now, does it?"

"No, really—"

"What have you got? An anonymous tipster?"

Doug seemed to feel he had to defend his department. "She's totally legit."

"She?" Calvin chuckled again. "Some old biddy getting her panties wet calling in tips to the police."

"No, no." Doug leaned forward earnestly. "It's a woman in the Federal Prosecutor's Office in Madison. Her name is Victoria Weidner."

"Really?" Calvin let a trace of respect show. His heart beat painfully fast in his chest. Shit. A federal prosecutor talking to Turner Hastings. That he definitely couldn't allow. "But how do you even know she'll show?"

"She will."

"How do you know?" Calvin just kept from shouting the words.

Doug's brows knit in surprise at his vehemence.

He inhaled and forced himself to open a creamer tub and pour it into his coffee cup as if the conversation didn't matter. The FBI agent was shifting on the desk corner as if his phone conversation was winding down. Time was running out to get the information out of Doug.

"I mean," Calvin said casually, "if she's just meeting this woman, she might spook at the last minute. Or decide not to meet her, after all. There's a lot that can happen between now and tonight."

It was a shot in the dark, but it hit home.

"They're not meeting tonight," Doug said triumphantly. "Hastings is going to meet the woman in front of her office building at twelve-thirty. That's only—" The deputy glanced at his wristwatch. "Geez. That's less than three hours from now. No way will she miss it."

"Ah." Calvin fought to keep his dismay from his face. Good God, less than three hours. Did he even have time to get hold of Hank? And if he did, was Hank within three hours of Madison? He frantically tried to calculate the time between Rhinelander and Madison, all the while keeping a disinterested expression on his face.

Doug was still babbling, oblivious to the bombshell he'd just thrown at Calvin. ". . . he seems to be really with it. Guess that comes with the territory, FBI special agent and all. And you know, I've been thinking." The younger man actually blushed. "I might try for the FBI myself."

"Really?" Calvin muttered.

"I mean, you know, try for it." The deputy stuck his hands in his pocket, looking remarkably like a twelve-year-old boy. "Not that I expect to get in or anything, I'm not that—"

The younger FBI agent snapped his cell phone shut and stood. He strolled toward them.

"Good. Good." God, he had to get out of here and

phone Hank. Tell him where Turner would be and make sure she was eliminated before she could talk to the federal prosecutor. "Well, this has been interesting, Doug, very interesting, indeed, but I need to go." Calvin's chuckle sounded sickly to his own ears. "No rest for the wicked, you know."

"Oh, right. Yeah, right." Doug blinked. "I should be getting back, too . . ." His voice trailed off as he glanced over his shoulder, apparently trying to figure out what, exactly, he needed to get back to.

But Calvin hadn't the time for this. And the FBI agent had almost reached them. "Don't want to stand in the way of the law."

He pretended not to notice the FBI agent and raised his hand in a farewell wave to the sheriff, still on the phone. Calvin hurried out of the building. On the sidewalk in front of the sheriff's office, the sun hit him in the face. He took out a hankie from his breast pocket and wiped the sweat from his forehead and upper lip.

Then he opened his cell phone and punched in Hank's number.

Chapter Thirty-eight

$\mathcal{T}$urner carefully painted her right little fingernail black. She recapped the bottle of nail polish, holding her fingers stiffly so she wouldn't smear them, then flattened her hands and blew on the nails to dry the polish while she looked around the parking garage.

Madison had grown since the last time she'd been here. There were more malls on the outskirts of the city and some new buildings she hadn't recognized in the downtown. She'd driven in on East Washington early this morning, following the boulevard into the isthmus between Lake Mendota and Lake Monona. The capitol building was on the isthmus, smack between the two lakes. It sat on its own city block, a square white classical building with a dome. She'd circled the area, getting tangled in one-way streets for a bit before deciding to park.

She had needed to alter her appearance, anyway. Even though Victoria Weidner had agreed to meet her, she still wasn't altogether sure of the other woman. Victoria did work for the Federal Prosecutor's Office, after all, and technically Turner had committed a federal crime by opening Calvin's safe deposit box. Love of the law might very well have won out over their tenuous high school connection. There was no way to know if Victoria had contacted the local police or even John's FBI office. Turner reminded herself that this was probably a trap.

Hence, a disguise was in order to enable her to look around the meeting place before Victoria got there. Turner had already made one stop at an army surplus store on her way into town. Now she locked the doors of the pickup and changed into the clothes she'd bought at the store. Overhead, sparrows flew in and out of nooks in the ceiling of the parking garage, but that was the only sign of life around her. In the middle of the day, the garage was dim and grimy and deserted. At one point she had heard footsteps echoing and she'd frozen, her mind a blank. Then the sound receded and she was able to breathe again.

John's warning about the man who had been at Calvin's cabin was uppermost in her thoughts. John had said the man was sent to kill her, and she believed him. She'd been shocked at first that Calvin would go to such lengths, but once she'd had time to think about it, his hiring a killer made sense. Hadn't Calvin betrayed his best friend to cover up his crime? It was only a small step further to try and have her killed.

Turner finished changing, put the black nail polish in her purse, and unzipped the army green duffel bag she'd gotten at the surplus store. She stuffed a change of clothes into the bag, put her purse in, as well, and got out of the pickup.

Outside the parking garage, the sun was nearly blinding, bleaching the colors of the city and radiating off the sidewalk. It was hard to believe anyone could try to kill her in this bright light, on such an ordinary day. Nevertheless, she looked around her as she walked and kept well away from the buildings, where someone might hide in a doorway. The few pedestrians she passed looked like businesspeople on their lunch break. But couldn't the killer seem ordinary, too? The problem was that she hadn't gotten a good look at his face in the cabin. He'd been only a dark shape before the awful blast of the rifle. If he stood in front of her right now, she wasn't sure she'd recognize him.

And wasn't that an encouraging thought?

Turner made it to the capitol square and strolled slowly, scuffing her feet. The Office of the Federal Prosecutor was in a nondescript brick building to the south. It was marked only by a discreet street number in small letters on the outside. No name, no way to tell what was housed within. She glanced at her watch. It was just before twelve. She had plenty of time to scout the area and think about what she would say to Victoria.

The City had planted big swathes of purple petunias and scarlet salvia on the capitol lawn. She stopped and squatted by the flowers while she tried to marshal her thoughts. She needed to convince Victoria of the seriousness of her accusations. That Calvin had not only embezzled from the Winosha bank but that he'd been doing it for years. That the last time he'd felt the pressure of the law, he'd diverted it by sending the police after Rusty. That he'd probably hired a hit man to kill her now.

All this without any proof at all.

A woman walked by with a little black pug dog on

a lead. The dog dawdled to sniff at her, and the woman pulled it away. Turner felt a sudden longing for Squeaky. Were he and John getting along all right? Did the big dog miss her? She hadn't even asked about him last night, and that thought produced a guilty feeling, as if she'd been a bad mother. John had originally said he'd take Squeaky back to Calvin. Why hadn't he? Was it just that he hadn't had time yet, or was he conceding to her wishes and saving Squeaky for her?

She sighed and watched a big bearded man shuffle past. He had greasy-looking glasses, and a cigarette dangled from his lips. He also had on an overcoat, despite the burning heat. She held her breath and looked down at her toes, hiding her face. But he only flicked the cigarette stub at her as he passed. It fell in the petunia bed and smoldered against the dry mulch until she stomped it out with her shoe. The bearded man crossed the street and disappeared into a tall office building on the corner.

She hadn't handled that well this morning, her parting from John. He'd been angry and maybe a little hurt. Maybe a lot hurt. But it'd been a moment of panic on her part. She'd had to get away from him. Get away from the heat of his body, lying next to hers, and away from the intense mental pressure he put on her. Just thinking about how she'd come last night, with him watching her, her body and emotions totally on display, made her burn with . . . what? Adrenaline? Terror? Certainly an erotic awareness that made her breath rasp and her palms sweat. Because while she'd been uncomfortable last night, scared of revealing herself in front of him, she'd also been completely turned on. She'd never had an orgasm like that before. Definitely not in the presence of another person.

God, she was messed up.

And now John was angry with her. Angry and out to get her. She didn't underestimate his resolve to catch and arrest her, especially after this morning. He had said he wasn't pulling his punches anymore. She shivered a little, thinking about what he would do if he caught her. She remembered the last glance she'd had of John. He'd been naked and furious with her, his pale blue eyes cold and contemptuous.

She blinked back tears. Nothing was left of the sweet bond she and John'd had. She'd stomped on it this morning as surely as she'd just crushed that cigarette. And now that she'd finally pushed him away, was finally free to concentrate all her efforts on avenging Uncle Rusty, now she felt bereft.

Like she'd lost something before she had fully realized its worth.

And why should that make her cry? She'd just got done thinking about how uncomfortable he made her feel, as if she had no control over her body or emotions. She didn't like feeling that way, she never had. Being with John was uncomfortable. It was tiring. And she found out things about herself that she didn't like knowing. For instance, that she was an essentially selfish person who didn't seem able to form a normal, adult relationship with a man. Not to mention she strongly suspected something was wrong with her sexually.

She swiped at the tears on her face. So, good. She'd killed the budding relationship with John. That was a good thing, right? No more finding out icky truths about herself. Maybe what she really needed was therapy.

But she didn't have the time to think about all this right now. Victoria's office building was across the street from where she sat. It had a small paved courtyard, maybe fifty feet square in front, with wide terraced steps leading down to the sidewalk. Turner glanced again at her watch. 12:25.

And right on time, a slim woman with long dark hair emerged from the tinted glass doors at the front of the building.

Chapter Thirty-nine

*H*e couldn't see her. Damn it. He couldn't see Turner.

John stood just inside the tinted glass doors, scanning the courtyard in front. Somewhere on one of the floors above his head were the offices of the federal prosecutor and Victoria Weidner's office in particular. Behind him, just inside the building, was a typical security setup: a metal detector, a scanner belt, and a couple of guards—a young woman who hardly looked older than a teenager and a graying man with a paunch. He'd already briefed both the security guards and Ms. Weidner about how Turner's arrest would go down. Ms. Weidner had just strolled out into the sunshine in the courtyard to wait for Turner. From this vantage point he should be able to see Turner.

But he couldn't.

Two women were sitting on the low brick wall surrounding the courtyard. One African American, the other a platinum blonde. The women were eating lunch and talking animatedly. Across the street, various people strolled by the state capitol and a grungy youth—hard to tell the gender—slumped by a flower bed. A slight man with a little potbelly and a suit was walking briskly across the courtyard, headed for the doors. A couple of kids were skateboarding on the wide, shallow steps leading to the courtyard. The potbellied man pushed through the glass doors and slid a glance at John out of the corner of his eye when he saw him inside. John nodded in return and the man kept walking.

She might have decided not to show. He'd been blunt with her this morning, and she'd appeared on the edge of a nervous breakdown. Not exactly how a man hoped his lover would look the morning after a night of his best efforts, but Turner was nothing if not tough. That was something he'd learned about her in remarkably little time. She might be small in stature, but he'd seen war veterans with less mental stamina. If she didn't show up for the meet, it wouldn't be from fear of a confrontation.

Or from any fear at all.

And that's what worried him the most: she seemed to have no physical fear. Hell, she didn't even display mental fear. The only apprehension Turner showed was emotional, and that rarely. And the emotional mistrust was just with him, come to think of it. God, her dread of him hurt. It was like someone had reached in and wrapped a fist around his gut and squeezed. How could it hurt this much when he'd known her only a couple of days? Her mistrust had made Turner cut him out of her life. Like a dangling thread on a sweater. Snip, snip, and into the trash.

It bothered him that she hadn't seemed to be as affected as he by their lovemaking. He'd been stunned by how good it was to feel her move on him, how right it had felt to be in her. It had been like finally finding shelter after huddling out in a snowstorm for a long, long time. Yet this morning she'd literally run out the door. As if she were ashamed of what they'd shared the night before. Christ, and wasn't that a blow to his male pride? Wasn't it the *woman* who was supposed to be worried about the morning after?

John snorted. If—

The grungy young kid that had been sitting on the sidewalk across the street got to his feet. The kid was the right height, the right shape to be Turner in disguise, but he'd seemed a long shot. He would've tagged the blond coed who'd just sat down on the capitol lawn to eat an apple as a better bet.

But it was the boy who got up, so John watched him. And when the kid moved, started slouching across the street, he knew.

It was Turner.

That was the thing about disguises. You could change the face fairly easily—and he sure hoped the rings through her lower lip and eyebrows were fake—and you could change the clothes, but it was damn hard to change the walk. Turner was doing a good impression of a kid, but she walked like a woman. Too much swing in the hips, a slightly lower center of gravity. That simple. It was Turner.

John watched her stroll closer. She'd flattened her short hair and made it dingy with either dirt or some kind of powder. She wore faded black high-tops, overlarge camo pants torn away just below the knee to make baggy shorts, and a black T-shirt with jagged orange writing on it. Various string bracelets decorated her arms and one ankle. But the pièce de resistance of her costume was the tattoos. She'd covered her arms from wrist to shoulder in black, curling tattoos.

The corner of his mouth kicked up in admiration even as something in him was dying.

He really hadn't wanted to arrest her. Especially not in such a public place. Turner was going to be humiliated. He'd have to cuff her hands behind her back. It was standard operating procedure. Shit. What a crappy job he had.

Shit.

John reached for his handcuffs and prepared to kill what was left of their relationship. He watched Turner approach Ms. Weidner. The assistant to the federal prosecutor still hadn't copped to the fact that the young boy was Turner. She was scanning the sidewalk in both directions. In fact, John saw the exact moment Turner spoke to her. Ms. Weidner's head whipped around as she stared at Turner. John started to push open the tinted glass doors.

And then all hell broke loose.

A crack sounded, echoing in the canyon of the office buildings. A woman screamed. The blonde on the lawn looked up.

And both Turner and Ms. Weidner went down.

Jesus fucking Christ.

Chapter Forty

So where do you want to go for lunch?" Victoria asked.

Turner was opening her mouth to answer when the other woman seemed to trip and fall against her. At the same time, there was a loud *Crack!* Turner stumbled backward under Victoria's weight and they went down together, Turner on the bottom. She hit the brick pavement hard, banging her elbow and rear end painfully, as she scrambled to think. Was Victoria tackling her to arrest her? Adrenaline stampeded through her veins. Then she heard the second shot.

Crack!

It echoed around the courtyard. Someone was shooting. The two women who'd been eating on the wall scurried to duck behind it, skirts riding immodestly high. Victoria rolled off her, and Turner looked around wildly. She couldn't see the shooter. One of the women against the wall was crying, hysterical hiccupping sobs that echoed loudly in the courtyard. The skateboarding kids still bumped down the steps, oblivious.

"Get down, goddamnit! Get down!" John yelled.

The skateboarders didn't hear. Turner swiveled her head at his voice, strangely unsurprised that he was here. He crouched against the building, his gun held in one hand. He was looking up, scanning the rooftops around them. He glanced in her direction and his eyes met hers.

She could see the pale blue of his eyes, hard and angry as he shouted, "Are you hurt?"

Crack!

A brick in the pavement beside Turner exploded, sending up chips that stung her bare legs.

"Are you hurt?" John yelled again.

Crack!

She shook her head mutely. "What should we do?" Turner whispered to Victoria. It was fifty feet to where John hunkered against the building. Fifty feet to safety. If they ran, would they make themselves a better target? But lying here in the middle of the courtyard, they were sitting ducks. She had to assume the shooter was after them. It was only a matter of time until he hit her.

Victoria moaned.

"I think we should try to run," Turner said and turned her head to Victoria.

The other woman clutched her upper arm, her face twisted in a grimace of pain. Blood seeped between her fingers. "Run for the building," Victoria gasped.

Oh, Lord. "She's been shot!" Turner screamed. "John, she's been shot!"

What an idiotic thing to say. How could anyone not see that Victoria was shot? She pulled her T-shirt over her head and wadded it into a bundle that she shoved against Victoria's shoulder.

Crack!

The skateboarders finally seemed to hear. One took off running; the other stood and gaped.

"Go!" Victoria rasped.

Turner dragged her eyes away from the wound and looked at her gray face. "What?"

"He's shooting at you. You're making me a target."

Turner stared, trying to assimilate Victoria's words.

Crack!

A rapid series of shots exploded behind her. Then big hands wrapped around her waist, dragging her, dragging her fingers from Victoria's wound.

"No!" Turner shouted. "I have to help her—"

"You can't help her," John said in her ear harshly. "You'll only get shot."

He half lifted, half dragged her to the front doors of the building. A young woman police officer was crouched to the side, firing shot after shot from her handgun. Turner couldn't see where she was aiming.

John thrust Turner inside. "Stay away from the windows."

Then he turned and went back outside. Back to where the gunfire was. He had to save Victoria, too, but Turner felt a selfish urge to recall him to safety.

A gray-haired policeman took her arm firmly. "Come sit down over here, miss." He all but shoved her onto a marble bench and stood over her, apparently so she couldn't escape.

Not that she cared. John was still out there. What was he doing? Had he seen the shooter? Had he been shot?

She whimpered and clasped her hands between her knees. *Oh, please let John be safe.*

And, as if in answer, the policewoman came bursting through the tinted-glass doors, supporting the two women who had been lunching by the wall. John followed behind, holding Victoria.

He sent a piercing glance at Turner, then addressed the policeman standing over her. "She's been shot. Have you called 911?"

"Yeah." The policeman helped lower Victoria to the floor. Her eyes were closed now. Maybe she'd fainted. "The EMTs are on the way."

The policewoman was talking in a low monotone into her shoulder radio. Turner noticed that the woman's hands shook.

John looked back outside again. He still held his gun in his hand. "He's stopped shooting. I think he's left."

The older policeman's head jerked up. "Wait for backup."

"He's probably leaving the area," John said, tight and hard.

"Yeah, and you getting shot won't stop him."

John grimaced, still watching outside.

Sirens began wailing, growing rapidly closer.

The policeman straightened from where he was checking one of the women lunchers and moved cautiously to the windows. He kept well to the side. "Any more shots?"

John shook his head. "No. The last one was when I reached Ms. Hastings." He seemed to come to a decision. "Watch my back."

Then he was out the door again.

Turner stared down at her hands. She had bloodstains

on her palms. She flexed her hand, feeling the tackiness of the blood. If she hadn't asked Victoria to meet her, Victoria would never have been hurt. Victoria would probably be eating right now, maybe meeting someone for lunch.

John came back through the doors. He was followed by a group of police officers and EMTs. He was talking to them, maybe explaining something or giving them orders, but Turner couldn't make out the words. And she didn't care, anyway. He wasn't shot like Victoria. That was all that mattered to her.

Then John was squatting in front of her. He looked in her face and frowned. "I need a paramedic over here."

"I'm okay," Turner muttered, but he ignored her.

A young woman rushed over and began taking her blood pressure.

"I'm okay," Turner said again, this time to the paramedic.

The woman had flat cheekbones with acne scars. She smiled professionally. "Just checking. Doesn't hurt to check, does it?"

"No, I guess not."

John strode over to talk some more with the police, but he glanced her way every couple of seconds. He still frowned at her. Victoria was wheeled out the doors on a gurney, an EMT running beside holding an IV. Turner caught only a glimpse of her, but the other woman's eyes remained closed and her face gleamed with sweat.

"Is she going to be okay?" Turner asked the paramedic.

"Your friend? The bullet went straight through and we're dealing with the bleeding. She should be fine."

More people came into the lobby. These were in civilian dress, but they had the bearing of law enforcement. One slight young man bent his head close to John and showed him a crumpled piece of paper. John nodded as the young man talked.

"Here." The policewoman thrust a bottle of orange juice into Turner's hands. Where had she gotten it? "Drink some of this. It'll make you feel better."

"Thank you." She hated orange juice, but Turner carefully unscrewed the cap and took a sip.

The paramedic smiled and began putting things back in her box. John looked at Turner and his frown deepened. He cut off whatever the young man was saying and handed him a set of keys. He grabbed a paper bag from another officer, then strode toward Turner.

"She okay?" he asked the paramedic.

"Yes. A little shaky, but that's mostly emotional," the woman replied as if Turner weren't there. "Make sure she finishes that orange juice."

"Gotcha." John nodded. "Thanks."

"No problem." The paramedic smiled quickly and moved off to help with the two women lunchers.

"Put this on." John took a denim jumper dress out of the bag. It looked like something a kindergarten teacher would wear.

Turner gazed at it stupidly. Where in the world had he gotten it? John said something under his breath and stood in front of her, partially shielding her from the rest of the room. He took out a long-sleeved white T-shirt and only then did she remember that she was wearing just her bra. He put the white T-shirt on her and then stuffed her into the denim jumper. Turner lifted her arms passively, like a child being dressed by its mother. The dress was several sizes too big, but it covered everything, including the baggy shorts she still wore. The final touch was a big straw hat John jammed down low on her head.

"Let's get out of here." He took her arm in a firm grip and helped her stand. She was surprised at how wobbly her legs were.

They walked past the knots of police officers and emergency personnel and through the tinted glass doors. Outside, the sun still shone brightly as if nothing had happened. Except that in the middle of the courtyard there was a smear of blood.

Chapter Forty-one

Turner looked like she'd aged twenty years in the last hour. Like she'd never smile again in this lifetime. John swore under his breath. He would've given his right hand to go back an hour in time and erase the whole awful sequence of events.

He gripped Turner's arm firmly and hustled her across the courtyard at almost a run. He felt exposed out here, even though he'd been assured the area was secured. The cops had found the shooter's firing position, complete with cigarette butts and a computer-printout photo of Ms. Weidner, but he didn't want to take any chances on the asshole returning.

The Crown Vic was already at the curb when they reached it. The Madison detective got out looking irritated. "You didn't tell me about the dog."

"Sorry," John muttered. Squeaky had fallen off his radar. He bundled Turner into the passenger-side seat and walked around to the driver's side. He caught the keys the detective tossed at him. "Thanks."

"Sure." The man glanced at Turner curiously, then ran up the steps to the courtyard, back to where the excitement was.

John got in the car, hit the locks, and pulled away from the curb. In the back, Squeaky whined and Turner put up a hand absentmindedly to pet him. Then she seemed to notice that her hand was streaked with blood. She pulled it back again and sat silently. She didn't ask where he was taking her, didn't say anything at all, in fact. He drove out of Madison and got on I-94 heading east. Once in a while he glanced at her, but each time she was either staring out the window or looking down at her hands, wiggling her fingers.

It wasn't until they'd reached the outskirts of Milwaukee over an hour later that she stirred. "Am I under arrest?"

He frowned. "No."

"Why not?" She asked the question like she was inquiring whether it would rain later in the day.

"Because." Because he'd decided to play by his own rules now. To hell if that pissed off the brass.

He could feel her looking at him as he drove. "It was my fault Victoria was shot. You should arrest me."

"No." He signaled to pass a semi. "No, it wasn't your fault that Ms. Weidner was wounded and no, I shouldn't arrest you."

"But—"

"Look, it was that motherfucker on the rooftop that shot Ms. Weidner, no one else." He knew he was letting some of his own frustration and guilt overflow into his words, but he couldn't stop it. "He's the one who hurt her. Period. But if you want to talk blame and who's at fault and shit like that, then you can start with me. I'm in charge of this case, and I knew that you had a hit man on your tail. I could've—hell, should've—stopped Ms. Weidner from meeting you in such a public place. But I didn't, did I? And now she's at the hospital."

Turner was silent for a minute, and he figured he'd shocked her with his blunt words.

But then she gave a little sigh. "You swear a lot when you're upset, don't you?"

He blinked. "Yeah, I guess I do."

"It isn't your fault, either, John," she said softly. "You had no way of knowing the hit man would be there."

That was debatable. As a professional, he should have anticipated the possibility. Should've made damn sure the area was safe. That slip-up would be added to the long list of things that would haunt him for the rest of his life. But he wasn't going to argue this with Turner right now. He was just glad she was talking again.

He glanced at her. "How are you doing?"

She ignored his question and frowned. "How did he know who to shoot? I mean, I know this isn't the best disguise, but from a distance—"

John was already shaking his head. "The police found a photo of Ms. Weidner on one of the nearby roofs."

Turner stared at him. "Victoria? He was after Victoria? I thought it was bad luck he'd hit her instead of me."

"No." He didn't like disabusing her, but she had to know. "I doubt he was after Ms. Weidner. We're pretty certain you're still the primary target."

"So it was a mistake that he hit her?"

John shrugged. "Looks like it."

"Then why have a photo of Victoria?"

"To identify you."

"When I walked up to her, he knew it was me. But how—" She waved that question aside. "You knew I was going to be there."

"Yeah, I did." He glanced at her. "Ms. Weidner phoned us yesterday morning."

She grimaced. "I was afraid of that, but it was a risk I had to take."

He nodded. Turner was a frighteningly logical woman. And a driven one.

She seemed to have lost interest in the shooter. Or perhaps it was just exhaustion from everything that had happened today. She glanced around the neighborhood he was driving through. "If you're not arresting me, then where are you taking me?"

He signaled for a turn. "Home."

He felt her look at him as he pulled into the apartment complex parking lot. He parked the Crown Vic, got out, walked around to her side, and opened the door.

She looked up at him. "I suppose this is normal for the FBI? Taking suspects to their homes?"

"Funny. You know it isn't." He shut the car door behind her and let out Squeaky.

She watched the dog water a tree sapling. "Do they allow dogs here?"

He whistled for Squeaky and grabbed his collar when the dog bounded up. "They do now. Does he have a leash?"

"No. I haven't had time to get one."

"Need to get the dog a leash," John muttered as he hauled Squeaky up the walk.

He let them in the outer door and led the way up the stairs. Turner was silent beside him. When they got to his apartment door, he had to juggle Squeaky before he could get the key out and unlock it. He went in first and let go of Squeaky's collar so he could do a quick walk-through.

Turner was staring at the hall table when he got back to the entryway. She glanced at him curiously. "Do you always search your apartment when you get home?"

"Uh, no." He locked the door behind her and gestured for her to precede him into the apartment. "Do you want something to drink?" He tried to think if he had anything to drink.

"No, thanks. Actually," she was staring down at her hands again, "could I use your shower?"

"Sure." Jesus. When was the last time he'd cleaned the bath? He hoped there weren't any hairs in the drain. "It's over here."

He gathered some clean towels—thank God he'd done the laundry—and showed her the bathroom. She smiled and shut the door in his face.

John went back to the living room and found that Squeaky had made himself at home on his couch. He frowned down at the dog. "We need to talk about this."

Squeaky replied by lifting his front leg and rolling over to expose his stomach.

"Nice, but I still want you off." John gently shoved the dog.

Squeaky sighed and lumbered off the couch. He did a circle on the carpet and lay down right in the middle of the traffic path. John squinted at the animal but decided to leave him. He had a feeling he could spend the rest of the day chasing the dog from place to place, and he had more important things to do. He took out his cell and first called the Madison detective who'd brought the Crown Vic around for him. He listened to the report of the investigation with one ear. The other was tuned to the faint sounds coming from the bath. She'd started the shower.

His second call was to Torelli.

"Hello?" the younger man answered the phone.

"We've got a leak." John didn't bother identifying himself.

"What?"

He told Torelli about the shooting that morning in short, succinct sentences.

"Shit," Torelli muttered, and it occurred to John that he'd never heard the younger man swear before.

"Someone had to've leaked the meet information," John said. "This guy knew the time and who Turner was meeting. He had a photo of Ms. Weidner."

"I'm not the leak."

John's eyebrows shot up. It surprised him that Torelli thought he was accusing him. Now he suddenly wondered. "Yeah?"

"Come on, Mac. You can't seriously think I would jeopardize an investigation by letting information like that out."

John was silent. He walked over to the bathroom door, listening to the sounds inside. Was Turner—?

"I can't believe this!" the younger man burst out.

She was crying. He could hear the sobs faintly over the sound of the shower. Shit. He ought to leave her alone. Turner was a very private person, and she would no doubt be embarrassed that he knew she was weeping.

"You've had it in for me since the Bertram case. Just because I took some concerns of mine—"

"Look, Torelli, I've got to go." John hung up on him in mid-speech.

The cell began ringing again immediately, but he tossed it on the couch. Whether or not Turner would be unhappy to see him, he couldn't stand out here and listen to her cry alone.

He opened the bathroom door.

Chapter Forty-two

The blood wouldn't come off.

Turner stood under the hot spray from the shower and scrubbed at her hands like a demented Lady Macbeth. She had crusted, now-black blood under two fingernails, and it just would not wash away. She didn't realize she was sobbing until John pulled back the shower curtain and grabbed her arms.

"Stop it," he said. "You're hurting yourself."

"I can't get it off," she replied. And despite the fact that her words were obscure, he understood her.

"I'll do it." He took the washcloth she'd been using away from her.

Standing there in the shower fully clothed, he washed her hands. She watched his face. His hands were gentle on hers, but his expression was grim, his eyes shadowed. He resoaped the washcloth and washed her hands again.

"Okay?" He looked at her, waiting for her approval. His white oxford shirt clung to his body, soaked.

Turner knew that if she said the blood was still there, he'd wash her hands again. And again. He'd wash as many times as it took to absolve her of the blood. Her throat swelled with emotion. Had anyone in her life ever taken care of her so tenderly? He seemed to know what to do for her even when she couldn't figure it out herself. She felt a twinge of guilt. She didn't deserve this care. She hadn't earned it. But he was waiting for her reply, so she nodded, mute, to his question.

John's face relaxed a little. "Good."

He stripped off his shirt and tossed it to the bottom of the tub. Then he picked up the washcloth again.

Turner was suddenly shy, standing there, fully nude before him while he still wore his khaki pants. "You don't have to—"

"I know," he cut her off. "Please?"

The lines around his mouth were so deep, grooved by bad memories. As if he'd been through an awful experience. And he had. The shooting had happened to him, as well. He'd probably seen the whole horrible incident and not been able to do a thing about it. For a man like John, that would have been like hell.

"Yes." She nodded her assent and then closed her eyes because she couldn't bear to watch as he touched her body.

She felt the cloth return to her hands, this time softly. It rubbed in gentle circles over her right palm, sensitive from the previous abrasion. She inhaled, imagining that she felt each loop of the washcloth. Concentrating on that feeling and nothing else. The cloth smoothed up her arm in ovals. Then it left her. John took her arm to guide it under the spray of water, lukewarm now. She felt the water hit her, little pinpoint strikes, and run off.

She imagined the fear and guilt trickling from her with the water, swirling in the tub and vanishing down the drain.

John took her left hand and repeated the process with that arm. Then the washcloth moved to her neck. He stroked it down her throat, and she tilted her head back to give him access. He washed her shoulders and breasts and then her belly, circling softly around her navel. She sucked in her breath, her lower stomach trembling. He rinsed her body in long sweeps of spray. She realized that he must have detached the showerhead because she didn't move. She merely stood in the tub, a passive mannequin, letting him wash away her sins. A mannequin had no feelings, neither guilt nor rage nor fear. Not even love. Right now it was good to set all those emotions aside, feel nothing, and let him take care of her.

He worked his way down her hips and legs and she never opened her eyes. He washed the bottoms of her feet and between her toes and then rinsed them. She felt him move behind her. Then his hand was in her hair. He guided her head back and slicked down her hair with the water, using his fingers to work shampoo into her hair. Turner smiled then. His shampoo was a cheap brand and smelled like strawberries, a childhood scent. He rinsed her hair thoroughly and she prepared herself to return to the present. To open her eyes and step out of the shower and resume her adult responsibilities.

"Wait," he whispered. "I'm not done."

His fingers touched her face.

She drew in a silent breath. She felt the brush of his fingertips on her lips, the most sensitive skin on her body. Goose bumps rose over her arms and she knew her nipples had spiked. He stroked around her mouth, firmly yet lightly, massaging, washing her face with only water and his fingers. He worked his way up her cheekbones and then stroked down again over the bridge of her nose. He delicately outlined each nostril. He brushed his fingertips lightly over her closed eyelids. Her eyelids fluttered at the unfamiliar contact and he did it again, his touch oddly soothing. He finished by framing her face with his hands. He rubbed his thumbs back and forth over her forehead, as if he were erasing the ghastly memories.

Then his hands fell away.

She remained standing, her eyes closed as if she were in a trance. She'd never been touched so intimately, with such a sense of possession. The thought flitted through her mind that she ought to be afraid. Were it anyone but John, she would be. But he seemed to have a right to do what he had done. To touch her as he liked. They'd entered a stage of intimacy that she'd never reached before with anyone else.

His hands returned to her face again, one on either side. This time his lips moved over her face, retracing the places his fingertips had been. She tilted her head back, and finally, he caressed her lips with his. He kissed her softly, much more softly than he had last night. At the same time, the kiss had an assuredness that hadn't been there before, either.

She opened her mouth and he deepened the kiss, drawing her body to his. He was naked—he must have removed his clothes while her eyes were closed—and he was aroused. But he didn't force his arousal on her. It pressed into her belly, but the touch was matter-of-fact. She wrapped her arms around his waist and held him as he held her. That seemed to be the signal he'd waited for.

He broke away. Turner opened her eyes just as he lifted her into his arms. He set her on the bath mat briefly, wrapping a towel around her body and one around her hair, then lifted her again. He carried her into his bedroom, a monochrome room with a gigantic bed, and set her down on the pulled-back sheets. He dried her, then pulled the covers up over her before drying himself.

Turner lay on the cool sheets and watched him. He was still erect. His expression was shuttered as he rubbed the towel over his chest and legs, and she was reminded of the fact that this man was an FBI agent. He was used to taking charge and making decisions in a world foreign to her.

When he pulled back the covers, Turner held out her arms to him in invitation. She wasn't feeling especially sexy, despite his care in the shower, but he obviously was. And she wanted to give back to him some of the tenderness—the closeness—he'd shown her. John lay down on his back and pulled her to his side. She snuggled against him and traced her hand down his chest toward his belly. But he caught her hand in his before she could touch his cock. She tilted her head to see his eyes, raising her eyebrows.

He drew her hand out from beneath the covers and kissed her knuckles. "Later. Let's take a nap." His fingers twined with hers on his chest, and he closed his eyes.

Turner stared a moment more at his face and then she, too, closed her eyes.

Chapter Forty-three

*C*alvin Hyman pushed a cold, limp french fry around his plate and listened with only half an ear to his campaign manager.

"We have this election just about wrapped up, Cal. I'm feeling very confident," Stan was saying, "but there're some things we really have to keep an eye on. The primary is in only a week, but the opposition is moving up in the polls I looked at today."

"What?" Calvin straightened, pulling his mind from whether or not Hank had made it to Madison in time. "I thought this was in the bag. I've got Mason Carter's endorsement, for God's sake. Why would I be losing ground in the polls?"

"Mason Carter's endorsement is gold, Cal, pure gold," Stan said patronizingly. The man had a frizzy gray comb-over and an odd little mustache. You'd never know to look at him that Stan had all the humanity of a Nazi death camp guard. "But our opponent is young, good-looking, and talks like he's already in office. And he relates to people really well."

"I relate to people."

Stan winced. "Of course you do, Cal, of course you do. I'm not saying you don't relate. It's just that we need to work a little more on your perceived persona. Loosen up a bit. Maybe wear jeans once in a while. Kiss some babies." Stan caught the arm of a passing waitress. "Can you warm up my coffee, sweetheart?"

They sat over an early supper at the Greasy Grill on Winosha's Main Street. The place boasted only a one-page menu, encased in a plastic sleeve. It listed an unimaginative array of sandwiches and burgers that had a tendency to come out of the kitchen oddly alike. But it looked good to patronize local places—made him seem like more a man of the people—and he could greet a lot of potential voters in the busy diner. As Calvin glanced at the door, Sheriff Clemmons and that young FBI agent walked in. The FBI agent scanned the diner, and his lip lifted in a curl as if he had smelled fresh shit. Probably expected bruschetta and French chardonnay in a northern Wisconsin diner. The sheriff nodded when he caught Calvin's eye.

Cindy, the aging diner waitress, came back with a glass carafe of coffee and slopped some into their cups. "Hey, Cal." Why was everyone shortening his name suddenly? "Shannon came in about half an hour ago, looking for you. She was kind of excited."

Shannon looking for him was nothing special. She probably wanted money to buy a gilt pig planter. Calvin smiled reassuringly. "Thanks for letting me know, Cindy. I'm sure it's not important."

"You're probably right." Cindy pivoted, her white

orthopedic shoes squeaking. "She said something about the bank."

"What?" His voice was loud enough that Cindy started and splashed coffee on her waitress uniform. Stan looked up and frowned in disapproval, but Calvin had other things on his mind. "What about the bank?"

Cindy scratched her orange permed hair. "Well, I don't really know. She just said something about the bank. Maybe that they caught the robbers? Does that sound likely?"

Yes, it did. He tried to relax his shoulders. He already knew that Nald and Fish had been caught. Really, it'd been only a matter of time with those two.

"Problem, Cal?" Stan was watching him.

"No, no." Calvin made himself take a sip of coffee. "No, I was just caught off guard is all. I guess I'm jumpy about the bank since the robbery. Good thing they caught those two bozos."

He smiled again just as the sheriff sauntered up. "'Spect you all heard about the shootout in Madison."

Calvin felt a spurt of glee. At last something was going well today. He knit his brows in artificial horror and leaned forward: The Candidate Concerned. "No, what happened?"

Clemmons pulled a chair up to the table and sat down. "Seems there was a shootout practically on the capitol square."

"No!" Cindy was still lingering, her coffee carafe forgotten on one hand.

Clemmons nodded. "'Fraid so. Young woman in the Office of the Federal Prosecutor got herself shot."

"I just think it's awful the way they let any old person get a gun," Cindy started in, waving the coffee carafe precariously. "Why, I bet it was one of them foreign students that go to the university there in Madison. They oughtn't let them have firearms, you know?"

"Which is why you need to vote for Calvin here come the preelection day," Stan jumped in. He ignored the fact that Calvin was in reality for gun-owners' rights. "We need to get these lunatics off the streets of America, and Calvin Hyman stands for tougher criminal sentencing and a fast-lane death penalty."

"Actually," Sheriff Clemmons began.

Calvin interrupted him impatiently. "Was anyone else hurt?"

Clemmons paused to take a sip from the coffee cup he'd carried over before drawling, "Nope."

Shit. Hank had failed. Turner was still alive. Calvin struggled to keep his expression normal. How was he going to fix this? Especially with his election campaign in trouble? How—

But Cindy snapped her fingers suddenly. "That's what Shannon wanted you to know."

Calvin frowned, his panicked thoughts interrupted. "What?"

"The bank auditors," Cindy chirped cheerfully like the robin of his personal doom. "They're moving the audit up to tomorrow."

Chapter Forty-four

Turner felt the masculine warmth against her back and sighed deeply. Contentedly. She hadn't felt this warm, this safe since . . . since she couldn't remember. She was like a cat curled by a fire, purring. Which was a ridiculous image since she wasn't a cat, no matter what John said, and this certainly wasn't her home.

That thought made her open her eyes.

The room was dim. She could see a bedside table, the type that might be in a modest motel room, with a metal adjustable lamp on top. Next to the lamp was a digital alarm clock that read 8:16 p.m. They must've slept the afternoon away. Two books, a paperback on top of a hardcover, sat beside the clock. The spines were facing away so she couldn't read the titles. She looked at them thoughtfully for a minute before curiosity got the better of her. She pulled a bare arm out from underneath the covers and picked up the paperback. It was a Robert B. Parker. *Cold Service.* Underneath, the hardcover read, *Days of Defiance: Sumter, Secession, and the Coming of the Civil War.* Hmm. That sounded rather erudite for an FBI agent. She turned the paperback over and started reading the blurb on the back.

The male arm lying over her stomach tightened.

"Do you like Robert B. Parker?" John's voice was slow and rusty. He sounded sleepy still.

"Not really." She put the book back and rolled over in his arms. "He writes guy books."

John watched her with eyes that had bags underneath them. His face was creased from the pillow, stubble shadowed his jaw and lower cheeks, and his salt-and-pepper hair was mussed. He looked so sexy she could hardly contain herself.

He raised his eyebrows. "Guy books?"

"You know. Guns. Fisticuffs. Women with big boobs."

"Huh. And what do you make of my bedside table?"

"You like history and detective stories?"

"Anything else?"

"No. Should there be anything else?" Her eyes dropped to his lips.

Both she and John were nude and lying intimately close. She could feel the hair on his thigh against her calf. Maybe he was too tired? But then he moved his leg and that theory bit the dust. By the feel, he definitely wasn't tired.

"Sure," he said. "You can find out all sorts of things from people's bedside tables."

She bumped her hip casually against him. "Like what?"

His pale eyes narrowed. "Lots of stuff gets found on bedside tables and in them—"

She tried to keep her face blank as she ran through the

contents of her own bedside table. There wasn't much in it besides gummy cough drops.

He started listing. "Guns, drugs, bunny-rabbit-shaped vibrators—"

Her eyebrows shot up. "Bunny—?" At least she didn't have a vibrator, bunny-shaped or otherwise.

He nodded. "Diaries. Female porn—"

"Female . . ." She suddenly remembered the paperback book in her bedside table. The one with the threeway story inside. Oh, good gravy, how embarrassing. He hadn't read it, had he? She cleared her throat. "And what would a trained FBI special agent make of such material?"

"Funny you should ask." He stroked his hand up her arm and fingered the sensitive skin at the juncture of her neck and shoulder.

She arched her neck to give him access.

"A detailed study," he said in a deep, intimate voice, "of a certain female porn book I found recently, revealed that the average woman likes really big dongs. In multiples."

He *had* read her book. Turner tried to look sophisticated. "It's only a fantasy, you know. I doubt the average woman really wants multiple, uh, partners at a time."

"You relieve me," he murmured into the side of her neck. The vibration tickled. "But there's still the question of dong size. I was taken aback by the dimensions quoted in said female porn. One of the guys sounded like the victim of growth hormones gone wrong."

She raised her eyebrows in amusement. "And this came as a surprise to you?"

"Nooo." He drew back. His hand was at her breast, and he gave her nipple a little pinch. She arched involuntarily as sparks of arousal shot through her. "But I'm disappointed that women are so superficial. I'd somehow considered them the more romantic sex."

Turner rolled her eyes. "Oh, like men aren't interested in breasts."

"Well, yes." He frowned sternly, rubbing his thumb over her nipple to emphasize his words. "But not every man is that interested in size—"

"Oh—"

"And a guy could get a complex after reading about giant dongs."

"A complex? Like an inferiority complex?" Turner widened her eyes. "I really don't think you have anything to worry about in that area."

"Why, thank you kindly, ma'am." John grinned. "I do aim to please."

She opened her mouth to retort to that rather self-satisfied statement. But he leaned down and kissed her, and the words fled her mind. His lips were firm and only a little moist. He moved them sensuously over her mouth, nipping at her bottom lip. Turner sighed, and he took advantage of her open mouth to push his tongue into her. It was thick and textured like suede, sweeping against the roof of her mouth, tasting of coffee and man. He thrust in and out, always just escaping her own tongue, until she moved restlessly. She tilted her head and caught him, sucking on his tongue, running her hands across his smooth back.

His muscles rippled as he rolled. Suddenly he lay over her. He settled his hips on top of hers and pinned her to the mattress. He thrust his thigh between her legs, forcing them apart, and she felt his body hair on the soft skin inside her thighs.

It made her vulnerable. Open. And that knowledge excited her.

He nudged again, and she widened her legs still more. He had his thigh pressed against her so close that the lips of her vulva were spread over his hard flesh. He shifted and rubbed against her there.

She broke the kiss. "John, I—"

She gasped because he'd pressed down on her, directly on her clit.

"Too much?" he asked, as if he were inquiring about the amount of wine in her glass.

She licked her lips. What he was doing to her felt so good, she didn't know where to look. He was right in her face, and he knew what he was doing to her. How could he not? Her entire pelvis was heavy with heat and desire. He must feel her wetness down there on his skin.

"Turner," he said, his tone quiet and dark, "is it too much?"

"I . . ." She licked her lips again. "I-I don't know."

He watched her and moved his leg again deliberately. She felt the hair on his thigh abrade her most sensitive skin as he slid through her vulva. She couldn't help it—she wriggled against him.

"I don't want to hurt you," he murmured. "Does it hurt?"

Oh, my. She blinked and tried to concentrate on his words. It was difficult. "What?"

"Some women are more sensitive than others," he explained, his words seductive in the still room. "Some can't stand direct contact on their clitorises. Others can. Can you?" He nudged against her.

"I . . . yes. Uh, yes." She wasn't even sure what she was saying.

But John knew what she meant. "Good. Then you'll like this."

He reached down and touched her flesh, adjusting her against his leg matter-of-factly. Suddenly the pleasure was much more intense. Could he do that? Just touch her there so casually? She had the feeling that she wasn't up to John's level of sexual sophistication. Wasn't he embarrassed at all? Of course, he wasn't the one about to—

Oh, she didn't know where to look.

"Keep your eyes open, baby," he crooned. "I want to watch you."

Watch me? She shivered at the thought. "But—"

"Shhh. Just feel." He propped himself on his elbows, presumably so he could put both hands to her breasts. "It feels good, doesn't it?"

Yes. It felt too good. She was in danger of losing control of her body, of herself. Of everything.

"Feel," he whispered like some dark incubus, making her forget all she knew about herself.

"I—" She couldn't do this. She was so wet down there that each movement of his leg made soft squishing sounds.

He squeezed her nipples—both at once—and pressed down hard with his leg. If he hadn't been holding her down, she would've come right off the bed. She couldn't . . .

"God, you're sexy," he murmured so low it was almost a growl.

She felt a surge of arousal.

"I'm going to remember you like this forever," he whispered, his voice rasping with erotic need. "Your nipples red from my fingers, your neck arched back, tender and vulnerable. And my leg riding your pussy."

Oh, Lord. No one had ever talked to her like this before. So roughly, so explicitly, using such words. It shouldn't turn her on, but it did. It did. She watched him, watching her through eyes so slitted she could barely see the blue, and felt her excitement rise.

"I can feel your heat, baby." His nostrils flared and he looked almost cruel. "And your liquid. I'm going to fuck you soon. I'm going to put my cock in your heat and make you come again. And I'll be watching you the entire time—"

"John." She fell apart. Simply fell apart.

She shuddered, incapable of stopping her body from sliding over the edge into pure bliss. She spread her legs wider and arched into his hard thigh, unable to see or care. Her breath came in harsh gasps, and when she opened her eyes again, he was still watching her. He looked satisfied. He pushed up and knelt between her limp, wide-spread thighs. He reached over to the drawer on the bedside table, took out a wrapped condom, and glanced up at her again.

"Are you ready?" he asked conversationally as he tore open the packet. "Because I'm about as hard as I've ever been in my life. I almost came just from watching you. You're that sexy to me."

She blinked and wet her lips, her eyes drawn to his penis. It stood up between his thighs, nearly purple, thick and hard against his flat belly. He carefully sheathed his cock, letting her watch him prepare himself for her. She actually shivered with erotic anticipation.

Then he did something that made her widen her eyes.

He dipped two fingers into her vagina and spread her own essence on his cock. She must have made a sound. He looked up as he deliberately rubbed his fingers into her sensitive flesh again.

"I'm making sure I'm ready for you." He fisted his hand over his erection and slowly stroked the liquid up and down the outside of the sheath.

She watched, mesmerized.

"Because once I'm in you, baby," he said softly, "I want it to last a good long time. I'm going to ride you hard. And you're going to come again with me in you this time. You're going to know who made love to you tonight. I'm going to leave you weak and exhausted and thoroughly fucked."

Her eyes widened even as she clenched internally at the slow words. "I—"

He leaned down, holding his body above hers with one arm. "Watch."

And she helplessly obeyed. Her eyes followed his to where his cock just touched her body. She watched as he guided himself into her with one hand, feeling and seeing that first ravishing breach.

"Are you watching?" he grunted.

"Yes," she breathed.

"Do you feel me?"

She moaned in reply. It was almost too much—seeing and feeling what he was doing. She wanted to close her eyes. But they stayed open, connected to John.

"Good. I'm with you now." He glided into her on one long slide to emphasize the point.

She moaned, feeling the invasion of his flesh into hers. Her hips tilted, and she drew her knees up on either side of him.

"Hold on," he whispered.

He withdrew almost all the way, then rammed his entire length home again. He continued in a hard, fast rhythm that shook the bed and made her feel each thrust vibrating through her. Her head arched in reaction as she clung to his shoulders. It was too much. He wasn't giving her any time to adjust. To combat the exquisitely pleasurable sensation. To keep herself whole. He was—

"Don't turn away." He caught her face between his palms on a grunt, his hips still in motion. His face was sheened with sweat, his mouth drawn on almost cruel lines. "Stay with me."

"I can't—"

He reached between their bodies and touched her at her most sensitive place. He pressed down with his thumb. Firmly, never breaking contact as his penis slid in and out of her roughly, drawing the hood around her clit taut on every thrust.

"I—"

"Feel." His gaze pierced hers. His thumb rubbed ever so slightly.

She gasped, and then suddenly he was kissing her without any finesse at all, his tongue thrusting into her mouth as his cock thrust into her below. Powerfully, possessively. And all the while his thumb bore down on her.

She broke from the kiss with a gasp, grabbing for his butt and pulling it into her, grinding her hips up to his, his hand caught between their bodies. "Oh, I—"

So close. So very close.

He thrust hard and fast, with her fingers still digging into him. She saw stars. A million points of light sparkling behind her eyelids, and she knew she was gasping.

Had lost all control of her body, of her mind—again. And she didn't care. It felt that wonderful.

She could hear John laughing, a loud, joyful sound, but that soon stopped.

Because he came himself.

Chapter Forty-five

"Oh, man," Fish groaned.

"Like, this is, like, torture or something, dude," Nald whimpered.

They were in a little room at the Sawyer County sheriff's office. The air conditioning was out. The walls were blank. There wasn't anything in the room except a table and four folding chairs and them. They wore el stupido orange jumpsuits. Somebody had said their clothes had been burned after they'd stripped, but that had to be a joke. A really sick joke. And he and Fish had on, like, chains. Like, dungeon chains. Chains from one ankle to the other so they had to shuffle if they walked, and chains that tied their hands to a belt-chain at their waists. Totally medieval. They clinked when they moved.

Obviously, the Sawyer County cops considered them very dangerous dudes.

But that wasn't what had made Nald whimper. Nope, what was really the icing on the long-john donut, so to speak, was a guy who'd just walked in the door carrying a big paper grocery bag. The guy was in a dark suit and he had some kind of gel in his hair, so he was probably a certified fruitcake, but right now, Nald could not've cared less.

The guy had food. He could smell it.

The guy set the bag down on the table and began unpacking it. First came some sandwiches with the bread sort of squished so you could tell it was the good kind. Then he took out a big bag of Lay's BBQ potato chips and some cans of Yoo-hoo. Nald held his breath when the guy stuck his hand in the bag again. The hand came back out with a long white box. Could it be?

Nald was so excited he closed his eyes and prayed. *Pleeeeeeeaase!*

He peeked with one eye. It was! He opened both eyes to gaze reverently at a big box of Little Debbie Zebra Cakes—those funny-shaped cakes with the hard white icing and black stripes. Nald stared in awe at the fruitcake guy. He had perfect taste in food. He was amazing.

For a fruitcake.

The man sat down in a chair behind the table and glanced at them. Now that he was no longer unloading food from the bag, he looked a little mean. He'd pushed back his suit jacket and there was a big black gun under his arm. Nald shifted from one butt cheek to the other in his chair. The man took out an itsy-bitsy tape recorder and set it on the table. He pressed a red button.

"My name is Dante Torelli," the man said without showing any embarrassment for having such a goofy name. In fact, his lips hardly moved. Which if you thought about it, was a weird way to talk. "I'm an FBI special agent."

Nald licked his lips and tried to figure out if he was

supposed to be scared at this news. Maybe the FBI guy was going to beat them up with a rubber hose or something. Although why they would use a rubber hose when a tire wrench was a whole lot harder was a good question.

But Fish had an inquiring mind. "Why're you special?"

The guy blinked. "That's what we're called. Special agents."

"Why?" Nald asked.

"Because. That's what an FBI agent is called."

"So you're not any different than other FBI guys?" Fish clarified.

"No."

"Then why did you say you were special if—" Nald started.

The guy slammed both his palms down on the desk. Fish jumped. Nald gulped. The guy blew out his breath. Then he smiled. You could tell he was trying to make his smile friendly, but it wasn't. It was more like scary. Nald smiled back just to let him know the smile was a nice try, even if it wasn't really working. Maybe if the guy liked him, he'd give Nald a Little Debbie Zebra Cake.

"So, gentlemen," Mr. FBI man said. His smile slipped, and he forgot to put it back on again. "I want to ask you a few questions about the bank robbery."

Fish stiffened. "Nuh-uh. We're not gonna talk without a lawyer present. Think we've never seen a cop show before?" Fish snorted loudly to show how unlikely *that* was.

"Yeah," Nald nodded righteously. "I've watched every episode of *Reno 911!*"

"First thing you do, you get a lawyer," Fish said.

"Yup."

"Otherwise it's a no-go. We clam up." He sat back and stared at the FBI dude.

Nald tried to fold his arms, realized he couldn't, and settled for sitting back in his chair, as well. He hoped his stare was as tough as Fish's.

A tiny muscle popped out on the FBI guy's jaw as if he were pissed at them. Then he reached over and snagged the bag of BBQ potato chips. He tore open the top, stretched it wide, and took out one—just one—potato chip, confirming for Nald that the man was indeed a fruitcake. What real man eats chips one at a time?

"Well, that's just too bad," Mr. FBI Fruitcake said, sort of waving the chip.

Nald would've sworn he could smell BBQ and grease across the table. His stomach rumbled.

"Uh," said Fish. He looked less smart now, because drool was running down his chin.

"Looks like . . ." the FBI dude ate the chip and rustled around in the bag for another, "I've got at least an hour to kill. Sure you don't want to talk?" He asked that last bit through a full mouth of potato chips.

"Uh," Fish said again. Maybe his brain had, like, fried from the smell of chips.

The FBI agent ate another chip slowly, and Nald followed the guy's hand to his mouth. He could almost taste that chip, salty and crisp and all mashed up in his mouth. Nald whimpered.

The agent looked up, like an idea had just occurred to him. "Would you like one?"

"Uh!" Fish said and made a grab for the bag. But his hands were chained to his waist and he could only move them the length of his elbows. The potato chip bag was out of his reach.

The FBI guy made a tut-tut sound, like an old grandma when you'd tracked through the house in muddy shoes. "You know there's things I'd like to discuss, Mr. Fish. I'd be more than happy to share my lunch with you while we talk."

"Aww," Fish kind of moaned, and his chin quivered. You could see that giving up those chips was costing him, but he'd always said there was a code of honor among thieves.

Nald swallowed. He was pretty unsure about the code of honor. If thieves were so honorable, then what were they doing robbing people?

The FBI guy picked up one of the sandwiches and popped the plastic triangle thingy it was in. He took out a sandwich half and sort of waved it, too. Right in front of their noses. A pale pink sliver of bologna showed where the sandwich had been sliced. It glistened in the fluorescent light.

Nald lunged for it.

The FBI guy jerked back the sandwich real quick and raised one eyebrow like he was the Duke of Dork. "Do you have something you'd like to say, Mr., ah, Mr. Nald?"

"Yeah, I'll spill." Nald wriggled his fingers. He could almost feel that sandwich in them.

"Wha—" Fish started, but the FBI dude handed over the sandwich half.

Nald hunkered down because his arms could reach only to chest height, and bit into the soft white bread. It was the best thing he'd ever tasted.

"You're going to rat me out for half a bologna sandwich?" Fish yelled.

"It's got Miracle Whip," Nald defended himself, mouth full of mushed-up bread and bologna.

"Turd!"

"Douchebag!"

"After all we've been through—"

"Yeah, like that swamp!" Nald laughed, but then some bits of bologna flew through the air and landed on the desk and made him look less cool, so he stopped.

"Give me some of that!" Fish yelled at the FBI guy.

"You'll need to—"

"Yeah, yeah, I'll tell you everything, too," Fish muttered. He got the other half of the bologna sandwich. Nald was already eyeing up the rest of the sandwiches. One looked like chicken salad. Lots of Miracle Whip in that.

FBI guy took out a pen and a yellow pad of paper. He clicked the end of the pen and held it over the paper. "So, who planned the robbery?"

Fish got a crafty look on his face. "How about some Yoo-hoo?"

"Talk first, Yoo-hoo second."

Fish pouted.

"Well, it was a guy called us up—" Nald started.

"Might've been a girl," Fish reminded him.

"Ooo, right. Like that Trinity chick." Nald nodded.

"Yeah. Yeah." Fish had finished his half of the sandwich and was drooling again.

"Sooo," the FBI agent said real slow. Nald noticed that he hadn't written anything down on his notepad. "You're saying that Trinity from *The Matrix* planned your robbery."

Nald squinted. Was this guy dumb or what? "No. No. The voice was all Tron-like. You know, disguised. It could've been a chick like the Matrix chick—"

"Or a dude," Fish put in.

Nald nodded. "Or a dude."

The FBI guy put one elbow on the table and rubbed his forehead with his hand like he had a headache. Probably they were talking too fast for him.

"It. Was. A. Dude," Nald said real slow.

"Or. A—" Fish started.

"Chick. Yeah, I know." The FBI dude waved a hand and sighed. "Okay, how did this person contact you two?"

"Nope." Fish sat back.

The FBI guy looked up. "What do you mean, *nope?*"

"We already told you one thing," Fish said. "I want a Little Debbie."

"A Little Debbie cake," the Fruitcake said slowly, like they were the ones having a problem following the conversation. "You want a Little Debbie cake for telling me a man or possibly a woman called you, but you don't know which."

They nodded so fast that their chains clinked.

He took out one potato chip and held it up. "This is what that piece of information is worth."

"Aw, but—" Nald started.

Mr. Fruitcake broke the chip in half and gave them each one half.

Fish stared down at his half a chip. "Man, that's cold."

But he ate his chip and so did Nald.

"C'mon." The FBI agent wiggled his fingers at them like he was a spaz. "Give me something I can use."

"Well." Fish looked at Nald. "We got this phone call one day."

"Yeah! We were watching *South Park* in the basement of your uncle's house. It was that episode when Kenny got killed."

"Doofus!" Fish yelled. "Kenny gets killed in every episode!"

"I know that, bonehead. But this was the juicy one—"

"Oh, yeah!" Fish was excited. "With spit—"

They both doubled over laughing so hard Nald's gut ached. When he looked up again, tears were running out of his eyes and the FBI dude was tapping a finger slowly on the table.

"Enlightening as that little exchange was, gentlemen," he said. "I still don't know what was said during the phone call. I want you to tell me every word."

"Oh, yeah. Right." Fish frowned real hard, thinking. "Okay, the phone rings and I pick it up and I say *hey*."

"No, you didn't." Nald shook his head.

"Did, too!"

"Did not."

"Did, too. I always say *hey* when I answer the phone."

"Not this time. You were pissed, remember, because you couldn't get the bag of cheese doodles open. So you said *what* instead of *hey*."

"Oh, yeah—"

"Gentlemen," the FBI dude interrupted. "I'm getting older even as we sit here. What did the caller say?"

"Um. He—"

"Or she," Nald reminded Fish.

"Yeah, he or *she* said, *what.*"

"No, that's what you said," Nald pointed out. *"What."*

"Yeah, but he—or she—said *what,* too. And then I said *what* and it was *What? What? What?*"

Nald shook his head. "Should've hung up on them."

"Gentlemen!" the FBI dude said loudly. Nald sort of flinched. For a fruitcake he was kind of scary. And he was fingering the gun under his arm. "What did the caller say after the whats?"

"Um . . ." Fish thought carefully. "Would we like to get a lot of money?"

They both looked at the FBI guy.

He stared back. "And?"

Maybe the guy was a retard.

"We said yes," Nald told him.

"Duh!" Fish pointed out. "Of course we'd like a lot of money!"

"Who wouldn't?" Nald nodded.

"I mean, only a real doofus wouldn't want a lot of money."

"And we are not doofuses."

Mr. FBI closed his eyes. "Did he—"

"Or she," Nald reminded him.

"Or she," he repeated through his teeth. "Say anything else? When the robbery was going to happen? What weapons to use? How to do it? Anything?"

Fish screwed up his face in thought. "He—or she—said we could come get the shotguns at the quarry. We got directions, 'cause we hadn't been out there in a while."

"And we were s'posed to do it on Saturday," Nald reminded him.

"Yeah, that caller person was a real butthead about Saturday."

"We said, why not Monday?" Nald put in.

"We're more awake on Mondays," Fish explained. "But nooo."

"Had to be that Saturday," Nald finished. A thought occurred to him. "Hey, is that a clue? Like a Scooby-Doo clue?"

"We deserve a Scooby-Doo treat!" Fish yelled. He opened his mouth like Scooby-Doo and begged.

Nald laughed and did a Scooby, too.

The FBI dude must not watch Scooby-Doo. He was staring at them, the muscle under his eye jerking. Then he suddenly got up and walked out of the room without even saying good-bye. But that was okay, because he left the Little Debbie cakes behind.

Chapter Forty-six

*J*ohn awoke Friday morning to the worst smell he'd ever encountered in his life. He opened his eyes and saw Squeaky, ears up, tongue out, panting by his side of the bed. Man, what had the beast eaten? His breath smelled like carrion. The dog must've seen he was awake. He backed up two steps, whined, and lunged forward again, hot doggy breath washing over John's face.

"Okay," John muttered. He sat up, and the dog barked.

"What is it?" Turner mumbled beside him.

"Your dog." John looked at her.

She lay on his usual side of the bed, taking up both pillows. Her face was flushed with sleep, and she had an adorable cowlick on the side of her head. The sheets were around her waist, exposing soft, pale breasts with relaxed nipples. He already had a morning erection, but the sight of her hardened him further.

He leaned down to kiss the nearest nipple. "Good morning."

She smiled at him sleepily, just as Squeaky began barking in earnest. John swore.

Turner frowned. "I think he has to go out."

"Yeah, I guessed that."

He sighed and sat up again, looking for his trousers. Then he remembered: he'd left them on the floor of the bathroom the night before, soaking wet. Fine. He got out of the bed and crossed to his dresser, found a pair of sweatpants, and put them on. By this time, Squeaky was nearly bounding around the room.

John put on his athletic shoes and looked at the dog. "Shit. We still don't have a leash for him, do we?"

Squeaky sat and swept the beige carpet with his whip-thin tail.

"Sorry," Turner said from the bed. "Do you have a clothesline?"

He looked at her. "A clothesline?"

"Okay. How about a belt?"

"That I do have." He got out a worn leather belt and looped it through Squeaky's collar. It left him only about a two-foot lead, but it'd have to do. He pointed at Turner. "Stay there."

She smiled as Squeaky hauled him away. But ten minutes later, when he got back to the apartment, he found her in the kitchen. She was already dressed in one of his T-shirts and the baggy jeans dress from yesterday and looking in his fridge.

He muttered to Squeaky as he unhooked him, "You're cramping my style, pal."

The dog ran over and stuck his head in the fridge to take a look. Turner pushed him away absently. "Do you have any anchovies?"

"Uh, no." John went to the sink to fill a cooking pot

with water. Mental note: stock up on fish of all kinds. He put the pot on the floor, and Squeaky began to drink from it in big slurping gulps that splashed water everywhere.

Turner gave a little sigh. "How about an omelet?"

An omelet? John tamped down panic. Seventeen years with the agency and he had no idea how to cook an omelet. He cleared his throat. "I can do scrambled eggs."

It was her turn to give him a look. "No. I meant I could cook an omelet. Do you want one?"

He grinned. "If you're making it, sure."

She flickered a smile at him and took out his carton of eggs. Briefly, he tried to calculate how old the carton was but then decided that life was too short. If the eggs were bad, he'd know soon enough. He got out coffee beans and ground them, watching her from the corner of his eye as he prepared the coffee. She looked better this morning. Yesterday afternoon in the car there had been a fragile edge to her that had scared him. She'd seemed ready to fracture at the slightest touch. This morning her face still had a drawn look about it, but she was more serene. He'd like to think the improvement was from his lovemaking the night before, but it was probably the long hours of sleep that had done the most good. That and the catharsis of crying in the shower. He had the feeling she didn't often allow herself the luxury of crying.

Turner opened a cupboard, found a skillet, and frowned at it. The pan looked fine to him, but it probably had something wrong about it that only a female could identify. He added new skillet—Turner's pick—to his mental list of things to buy. She evidently decided to use the pan anyway. She set it on his stove and switched the appliance on. John turned to the sink to fill the coffeemaker carafe and nearly tripped over Squeaky, who'd opted to lie down smack in the middle of his galley kitchen.

He toed the dog. "Move."

Squeaky shot him a mournful look, got to his feet slowly, and slunk into the breakfast nook, where he could still keep an eye on them. The dog slumped into a heap and groaned. Turner, fortunately, was ignoring the animal. She'd found a bowl and was scrambling the eggs with a fork. On the corner of the counter next to her was his phone and answering-machine setup. John noticed the light was blinking on his answering machine. He hit the button before it occurred to him that it might not be a good idea.

A series of hang-ups made him relax until the fourth message. There was audible breathing, then a sigh. "John, I need to talk to you. Please call me." A hesitation, then, "This is your daughter." Click.

The answering machine informed them that the call was from Monday afternoon. Rachel must've called here first and, when he hadn't returned her message, tried his cell. The only other message was from the Madison police department, letting him know that Victoria Weidner was out of surgery and expected to recover without any problem.

"That's good to know." John got out a loaf of bread from the fridge and started lobbing slices at Squeaky.

"Yes." Turner didn't look up, but her back had stiffened during the message. "I thought you didn't talk to Rachel?"

He noticed that she'd remembered his daughter's name. That pleased him, but he still fought to keep the defensiveness out of his voice. "Yeah, well, she called me a couple of times in the last few days." He really, really didn't want to talk about his dysfunctional relationship with his daughter right now.

"Does she usually refer to you as John?" she asked in a neutral voice.

"Yup. I think she's doing it to irritate me." The coffee was half-dripped. To hell with it. He needed caffeine for this conversation. He pulled the carafe out and poured himself a cup while the machine hissed at him. "It's working. I'm irritated."

"Ah." She'd poured the eggs into the hot pan, and now she hovered over it, holding a spatula. As far as he could see, an omelet was scrambled eggs cooked like a pancake. "What does she say when she calls you?"

Christ. If it were anyone else, he'd blow them off for getting too personal. But this was Turner—he wanted her to get personal. Even if he didn't like the results.

He sighed. "She wants to know why her mother and I broke up."

"Doesn't she know?"

"She knows the official version."

"Which is?"

"I was busy, spent too much time away from home, we grew apart. Yada yada yada." He took the milk out of his fridge, sniffed it, and decided to take his coffee black. Better add half-and-half to his list.

"And the unofficial reason?"

"She was fucking another guy."

She looked at him, eyebrows raised.

"Sorry." He took a sip of his coffee. It tasted better with milk, but at least it was hot. And caffeinated. "It really wasn't as one-sided as that. We had grown apart. We hardly talked, in fact. When I came back from an assignment and saw this guy's razor on my sink, I kind of figured she'd made her choice. And she had. She'd decided to find somebody that was around more, listened better. She ended up marrying the guy. His name is Dennis, and he adopted Rachel." John shrugged. "I was a rotten husband."

"I find that hard to believe." She folded the omelet in thirds and slid it onto a plate.

"Do you? It's true. I was a lot younger then. I think . . ." He cleared his throat. "I'd do better now, both as a husband and a father."

Her hand paused for a second, but she didn't comment. He'd take that as a good sign, at least for now. Turner smoothly divided the omelet in half and slid the second half onto another plate. John snagged the loaf of bread and a jar of peanut butter, and they went into the breakfast nook. Squeaky immediately perked up at the sight of food, even though he'd just been fed.

"So," Turner said as she sat down. "Why can't you tell Rachel what you've told me? Leaving out the profanity, of course."

"I don't think it's any of her business."

She frowned. "Why not?"

"Her mother's sex life? Do you really think that's an appropriate thing to talk about with a sixteen-year-old girl?"

"She's asking, isn't she? She obviously feels that there's more to the story than what she's been told. Besides, as the story stands, you're the villain of the piece. That isn't right."

"It's a small price to pay to keep her happy."

"But is she happy?"

John forked up some of the omelet while he thought

about that. The omelet was pretty good. He could get used to this.

"She isn't, is she?" Turner must've figured that he wasn't going to answer. "Or she wouldn't be calling you."

He shook his head slowly. "I don't see how crushing her illusions about her mom is going to solve anything."

"But—"

"I'm a big guy. I can take being the scapegoat for the marriage falling apart."

She frowned and opened her mouth again. He could tell she wasn't going to let it go. He interjected a change of topic before she could start again. "How're you doing after yesterday?"

Turner's mouth closed, and she looked at him out of narrowed cat eyes, clearly debating whether or not to let him change the conversational flow.

Finally, she sighed and looked down at her plate. "Okay, I guess. I'm not sure how I'm supposed to feel."

He nodded and flipped a bite of omelet at Squeaky. The dog had been watching. He caught the piece deftly and returned his gaze to John's plate.

"It can take a while to assimilate a shooting," John said. "That's why a lot of police departments have in-house therapists to talk to cops who've been involved with a shooting."

"That makes sense." She hesitated, pushing at the egg on her plate with a fork.

"But?"

She sighed. "Don't get me wrong. I feel awful about Victoria . . ."

He looked at her, but she was staring at her plate.

"It's the other stuff," she whispered.

He ate some more omelet while he waited for her to gather her thoughts.

She suddenly pushed away from the table and walked to the window, looking out. His apartment backed up on another building. He had a nice view of an industrial-sized air conditioner.

She stared at the air conditioner. "It's just that I've spent so long on Calvin and the bank embezzling. It's taken up all my life for years and now it's just . . . gone. I feel kind of set adrift."

"Uh-huh."

"But it's also almost a relief."

He frowned. "What do you mean?"

She threw up her arms. "There's no evidence. I've looked and looked, but there just isn't any. And now Victoria's out of the picture. I've lost. Honorably." She lowered her arms slowly and repeated the phrase. "I've lost."

John finished his omelet and sat back with the coffee mug in his hand while he debated. She needed to get over this revenge thing, and as she'd said, this was an honorable out. She'd done her best, truly tried every route. Maybe he should be grateful she was willing to let it go. Finally. But would the whole thing come back to haunt her in a few months or years? Right now, she was still in shock. Even the most hardened warrior found it difficult to rejoin the battle after a defeat. And Turner was a warrior of her own sort. Would she regret not bringing Hyman down? Was her loss Hyman's victory?

She came back to sit at the table. "I don't know what to do next. Maybe there isn't anything to do. I just don't know."

He stared into his mug. The black coffee had a sheen of oil on the top.

She folded her arms across her chest. "I was so sure that there must be some evidence. I just never really considered the possibility that there wasn't any for me to find."

"It's a logical assumption that there'd be something."

"I've wasted four years of my life." She bit her lip, blinking her eyes as if holding back tears. "Is that stupid or what?"

"It wasn't a waste," John said softly. "You wanted justice for an uncle you loved."

She grimaced ruefully. "A lot of good it did me." She swiped the heel of her hand across her eyes.

John sat forward. "Tell me where you've looked."

She glanced up at him as if surprised. "You already know. The safe deposit box. His house. The cabin. Everywhere."

"You didn't have a lot of time at the cabin, though."

"You searched it, too."

"Yeah." He frowned. "There must be somewhere else."

"John—"

He looked at her.

"I don't know if I want to get on that train again." She sat forward, as well, and rested her elbows on the table. "Spend another four years of my life searching for something that's not there."

"What if it is there?"

She shook her head.

"Can you just give up?" He looked in her cat eyes, so sorrowful and confused. "What if there's still some place you haven't searched?"

She was silent a minute. He placed his hand over hers and held it. Her hand felt small and delicate beneath his, but he knew her strength.

"I wondered once if he kept discs in his car," she finally said slowly. "That big Cadillac he drives around."

John shook his head. "Then why send a hit man after you?"

She smiled for the first time that day. "Maybe he's pissed at me?"

"Definitely." He grinned back. "But it's more than that. The evidence—whether discs or a computer—must be somewhere he hasn't been able to get to easily."

"Why do you say that?"

"He's been trying to keep you from finding it." John tapped the back of her hand with his forefinger. "If he had it in his car or house, he'd simply destroy it. Problem solved."

"So, maybe it's at the cabin?"

"Or somewhere else we haven't thought of yet."

She compressed her lips. "You're assuming he kept evidence at all."

"Yeah, I am."

Her brows knit in thought. Squeaky came and laid his head on her lap, eyeing the remains of her cold omelet still on her plate. She absently fed him a piece.

"Does Calvin have family?" John asked.

"There's Shannon, his wife, and he has three sons, all in their thirties."

"Where are the sons?"

"The eldest is in Washington state, and the younger two somewhere on the East Coast. Do you think he'd send them the discs?"

John grimaced. "Too far away. He needs to get to the books easily. Who else is there? Does he have friends?"

Turner snorted. "He had a photo on his desk of him with the last governor of Wisconsin and a bunch of other guys. They were standing in the snow, holding frozen fish."

"Frozen fish?"

"You know. Ice fishing."

"Huh." John frowned. Ice fishing meant—

"What?"

He looked up at her. "He must have an ice fishing house."

"I thought ice fishermen just went out on the lake and sat on a bucket, hunched over a hole in the ice."

John grinned tightly. "Can you see Calvin hunched over a hole in the ice exposed to the cold?"

She shook her head slowly. "No."

"Then he's got an ice fishing shack. And I'm betting it's a nice one."

She stared at him, her eyes widening with hope.

Chapter Forty-seven

Turner glanced around as John pulled his enormous pickup truck into the drive of Calvin's cabin. It was just after two in the afternoon, despite the fact that he'd driven like a demon all the way up.

Part of the delay was because she'd insisted they stop by a discount store so she could run in and get a pair of shorts and a T-shirt that fit her. Wearing the denim jumper was like walking around in a giant bag. After that, John'd had to swing by his office, write out a warrant that included every potential possibility, and then find a judge friend in Milwaukee. He'd roused the poor man from bed—it was his vacation—and then bullied the judge until he'd signed the warrant to search Calvin's cabin and grounds.

Turner just hoped that the theorized ice fishing shack was at Calvin's cabin. John seemed pretty confident. All the way up to Rhinelander, he'd been intent and focused, a wolf who'd caught the scent of running bunny rabbit. But she'd been stalking Calvin for many years now, gotten her hopes up too many times before. She couldn't help feeling like this was going to be just another dead end.

John got out of the truck. Squeaky nearly broke a limb scrambling over the seat and bounding out after him. Turner shut the door to her side just in time to see his irritable look at the dog.

"Howl," she reminded him.

They'd initially thought to leave Squeaky behind in the apartment, but he'd started singing as soon as they shut the door. It was kind of flattering, in a way. Turner thought he must not have done the howling thing with Calvin and Shannon. Calvin would've just gotten rid of the dog if he'd been that much of a nuisance. But all the same, she'd have to look into doggy therapy when this was over.

John narrowed his eyes at her comment, but he seemed resigned.

"Where would Calvin keep an ice fishing house?" Turner asked.

He shrugged. "I didn't see an ice fishing house in the garage when I searched it before. He must have it down by the lake somewhere."

He whistled, and Squeaky came galloping up to accompany them down the grassy slope to the lake. It seemed as if the trees had turned more yellow since the last time she'd seen them, although that could be her imagination. She'd been here only a few days ago.

By the lake there was a fiberglass dock and a ramp for backing a boat into the water. A kind of shed was off to the side. As they neared, she could see the shed was a larger building than she had thought—about fifteen feet square. Bigger than most utility sheds, but smaller than a car garage. It was painted dark green and had a single door, no windows. They came up beside it and stopped. Squeaky ran to the building and lifted a leg against the corner.

"Bingo." John gestured to what looked like runners on the bottom of the shed. He caught her confused look. "He must haul it out on the ice in winter on those."

"Ah." The light dawned along with excitement. "Gotcha. So this is it?" Surely it couldn't be this easy. She'd expected armed guards, secret codes, and locks at the very least. Instead, they'd just walked right up to the thing. It wasn't even hidden.

At least the lock was there. "Looks like it." John was examining the heavy padlock on the door. "I'm going back to the car for the bolt cutter. Stay here."

"Okay."

Turner walked out on the dock to watch the lake. A slight breeze rippled the water, and the sunshine reflected prettily off the liquid surface. Although, judging by the yard of dried mud on the bank, rain would have been better for the area than the sun. It was a nice lake. The trees crowded close to the shore, reflecting in the water like a tourist postcard. Sometimes she forgot how beautiful northern Wisconsin was—you got kind of used to it. Then she'd see something like this lake and it would just take her breath away.

She heard a rustle in the bushes behind her, then the click of dog claws on the dock. Squeaky came to stand beside her. He bent his big head down low and sniffed at the water.

"Don't even think about it," she told the dog.

He looked at her innocently, pointed ears forward, and wagged his tail.

"Turner?" John was standing on the bank with a long, efficient-looking bolt cutter.

And it was efficient. Within seconds, he had the padlock off and the ice fishing shack door open. Inside was what looked like a tiny family room in a seventies ranch house. The floor was carpeted in indoor–outdoor brown Berber. There was a beige couch and matching armchair and even a bar with a microwave and battery-run refrigerator.

"Nice," John commented.

Turner had to take his word for it. She'd never been in an ice fishing house before. John strode over to the bar and started searching behind it. Turner investigated the couch area. Beside it was a square, cut-out section of the carpet with a metal ring on one side. Presumably you could lift up the square and cut a hole in the ice underneath. Then all you had to do was sit back and fish from the couch. Turner snorted. Only Calvin would—

"Turner." John's voice was low and almost expressionless.

She hurried to his side. He had a laptop up on the counter, and she felt her heartbeat accelerate. He switched the computer on. She held her breath as the screen turned blue. Five minutes later, he'd accessed a file prosaically titled "Bank." Rows and rows of figures came up, with dates attached going back ten years.

"That's it," Turner breathed.

She leaned over John's shoulder, checking the numbers, correlating the data she'd figured out on her own. It was far more money than she'd estimated. A fortune. Calvin Hyman had stolen more than three million dollars in ten years from the First Wisconsin Bank of Winosha.

Where the heck was it all? He must have it stashed some-where. His house and car weren't worth that much.

"Is it enough to get him?" she whispered.

"Oh, yeah," John said with relish. "Looks like Hy-man's kindly documented all of his activities at the bank. This'll put him away for a very long time. Good thing I took the time to include a computer on the warrant."

Turner closed her eyes. After four years, she knew she should feel elation—even vindication—but the only emotion she could identify inside herself was . . . no emotion. She was numb.

John turned off the laptop and packed it up in a black case with handles. He turned to the door. "Let's get this—"

From outside, Squeaky barked once. Then a rumbling sound started, low and menacing. Turner's eyes wid-ened. She had never heard Squeaky growl. Someone was outside the ice fishing house.

John froze. "Stay here," he mouthed.

He handed the laptop case to her and took out a big black gun from underneath his jacket.

"John," Turner whispered urgently, clutching the laptop. Oh, Lord. Had the hit man followed them? She didn't want him going out there alone.

He frowned at her and gestured abruptly with one hand. The signal was clear: be quiet.

No—

He stood to the side, back to the wall, and cracked the door, peering around the edge. There was a silent hesita-tion, then he spoke one word. "Torelli."

Torelli? But wasn't that John's partner? *Thank good-ness.* Turner heaved a sigh of relief. Not a hit man. She hugged the laptop to her chest and stepped forward so she could see through the cracked door.

Outside, a slickly handsome man in a suit stood absolutely still, flicking his gaze between John and Squeaky. The dog was stiff-legged, tail and head unmoving as he growled in a low, constant undertone. The hair all along the base of Squeaky's neck was ruffled. The man had a gun similar to John's in his slightly raised left hand. His dark suit looked really out of place in the north woods of Wisconsin.

"I take it this is the kidnapped dog?" Torelli drawled. Turner had to hand it to him. He was taking being menaced by a 120-pound Great Dane with aplomb.

"What're you doing here?" John asked. He didn't sound that welcoming, considering the man was his partner.

"You mind calling the dog off?" Torelli's voice was casual, but his face wasn't. "And it would be nice if you put your gun away."

John didn't move. "Answer the question."

Torelli's face went blank. "I figured out who masterminded the bank robbery, Mac, so I came running to tell you. You are in charge of this investigation, after all."

John muttered something obscene.

"John," Turner murmured. Why was he being so obnoxious?

Torelli caught sight of her, peering around John's shoulder. "Is that the librarian?"

John stiffened. "You're not going to arrest her."

Turner saw a look of surprise cross Torelli's face—right before someone shot him in the back.

Chapter Forty-eight

 tay back," John yelled to Turner even as he tried to figure out where the gunshot had come from.

The trees around them were still. Whoever had hit Torelli was well hidden. At the sound of the shot, Squeaky had taken off running, tail between his legs, and disappeared somewhere into the woods. The shot had knocked Torelli facedown on the ground. But as John watched, he levered himself to his elbows and made a valiant effort to crawl to the safety of the ice fishing house. Blood soaked the back of his jacket, a shiny wet spot on the dark blue fabric. Hard to tell how serious the wound was. The younger man was a stubborn bastard.

A stubborn bastard who had better live.

John swung his arm out from the shelter of the door and laid down a covering fire for Torelli. When his gunfire wasn't returned, he said a prayer and took a chance. He ran out, expecting to be hit at any moment, and grabbed Torelli under the armpits.

Torelli swore.

John ignored him and kept dragging. Pulling on Torelli's arms probably put stress on his back wound. Tough. He was a little painted duck in a shooting gallery out here. John hauled him bodily into the ice fishing house, dropped him on the floor, and kicked the door shut behind them.

Torelli was still swearing.

"You're welcome," John said, peering through the crack of the door. Where had the shooter gone?

"John, he's hurt," Turner murmured reproachfully. It figured she'd take Torelli's side. She was trying to remove the bloody jacket.

"Thanks," the younger agent grunted. John noticed that he'd stopped swearing even though maneuvering his arms through the jacket armholes had to hurt like hell. "Dante Torelli. You're Turner Hastings."

"Yes."

"She didn't mastermind the bank robbery," John said without looking away from the door.

"I know."

That merited a glance. The back of Torelli's shirt was soaked in blood.

"Here." John stuck the Glock in the small of his back and took off his own T-shirt. He threw it to Turner along with his cell phone. "Call 911. Get us some backup and an ambulance." He looked at the younger man. "What do you mean, you know?"

Turner tucked the phone under her chin and talked quietly as she folded the T-shirt.

"I questioned SpongeBob and Yoda this morning." Torelli grunted as Turner pressed the T-shirt into his back.

The wound looked like it was high on the younger

man's right shoulder. Thankfully, it didn't seem to have compromised the arm much—Torelli was at least using it. He didn't know if Torelli would be able to help, but for the moment, he would take what he could get.

Meanwhile, Torelli kept talking, though his tone was strained. "The guy who set up the bank robbery contacted them by phone. He used voice-disguising software. Fish and Nald have no idea who it was." He paused dramatically, the prick.

John glanced over. "You're going to have to bind the T-shirt to his back. Here." He took out a pocket knife and tossed it to Turner. "Cut his jacket into strips."

Torelli groaned. "That's a Hugo Boss."

"Serves you right for wearing it in the field," John said. "What about SpongeBob and Yoda's caller?"

"They couldn't tell me much else. I don't think they knew much else. I've seen dry toast with more brains than those two have between them—"

"The caller?"

"He wanted the robbery on Saturday." Torelli hissed as Turner wound a strip of fabric around his chest.

"Better make sure it's tight," John told her.

Torelli grimaced.

Turner nodded. She'd dropped the cell—open on the ground—while she worked on Torelli's bandage. But her pale face told it all. She looked terrified.

She glanced at John. "The ambulance may be awhile. They said there's a big fire in Tomahawk."

"Shit," John said.

Torelli ignored the byplay and continued, "I thought there must be a reason for the date. I checked. There wasn't any special delivery of money on that Saturday or the Friday before. In fact, quite a chunk of money was transferred from the bank that Friday. But on Monday there was an appointment to have the bank—"

"Audited," Turner said.

Torelli glanced up at her. "Yeah. The only reason to do the robbery on Saturday was to delay the audit on Monday."

"And the only person who would care about the audit on Monday is someone who'd been embezzling from the bank," John said.

"Calvin." Turner's lips compressed.

"Yeah," Torelli said.

John didn't particularly like the way he stared admiringly at Turner. "So why're you here if you know Turner didn't plan the robbery?"

"Because Hyman is missing."

"What?" John looked away from the door again. "What do you mean?"

Torelli shrugged, then grimaced. "He's gone. As of this morning, according to his wife. And the Smith and Wesson he has registered is gone, too."

"Shit."

"Yeah. I tried calling you, but your cell was down." He glanced at the phone lying on the floor. "You must've been driving between towers. Anyway, I contacted the office in Milwaukee, and they said you were on the way here. I figured there was a chance Hyman would show up here, too, and thought I should give you some backup. Guess I figured right about Hyman. Sorry the backup plan didn't work as well."

John shook his head, his gaze back outside. "You think it was Hyman who took a shot at you?"

"Who else could it be?"

"The same asshole that was shooting up Madison yesterday. Or maybe they're both out there."

"But I thought Calvin sent the hit man," Turner said. "Why would he come himself?"

"Obviously, Hyman's plans don't work out too well. The fact is we have no idea who's shooting." Where was the guy? Maybe he'd left the area. A small grassy clearing in front of the ice fishing house led down to the lake. Behind, the small structure backed up to the woods. Too many places for a gunman to hide. And if they didn't get Torelli out of here soon, he might very well go into shock or bleed to death.

"But—" Turner started.

John came to a decision. "Wait here. I'm going to take a look around."

Torelli forgot himself and swore again, but John was already out the door. He made a running dive for the trees, the muscles in his back twitching with the expectation of a bullet.

Nothing happened.

He hunkered, Glock held ready, just inside the woods and listened. The tree branches rustled overhead in the breeze. Somewhere, a ways away, a woodpecker was knocking on a tree, reminding him of the last afternoon he'd been here—when the hit man had nearly killed Turner.

John inhaled silently and rose to a crouch. He moved through the trees flanking the ice fishing house, being very careful where he placed his feet. The ground was littered with dry leaves and sticks, just waiting to give him away. Dappled sunlight shone through the trees, beautiful and deadly. There was hardly any cover. He felt exposed. And then he saw it.

A flash of red fabric.

John froze, then slowly hunched at the side of a mature tree. Someone had just disappeared behind a bush up ahead. He slid forward toward the spot, always keeping a tree between himself and where he'd seen the glimpse of red. His mouth was dry, his pulse beating in his head. He carefully placed another foot. The quiet of the woods was broken.

RO! Rorororororo!

Shit. Squeaky must've found the guy. He hoped the gunman wouldn't shoot the dog before he could get there. John started sprinting, no longer caring about the noise he made crashing through the forest. Squeaky's barks covered the sound, anyway.

"Shut up! Goddamn it, shut up, Duke!"

Duke? John rounded a tree in time to see Calvin Hyman aim a handgun at Squeaky.

"Drop it!"

Hyman squealed and leaped. He almost made the mistake of leveling his gun at a federal agent. John could see the thought cross the other man's mind.

"Don't even fucking think about it," he growled.

Squeaky was still barking, stiff-legged and intent, his upper lip pulled back to reveal nasty-looking fangs. He must really not like his former owner. Hyman's eyes widened, and he might've gulped. John couldn't hear the sound over Squeaky, but he saw the movement of the other man's throat. Hyman's fist opened and the gun fell to the ground. John had Hyman facedown in the grass before the weapon could hit. He knelt beside him and pulled his arms back to cuff him, reciting the Miranda code, all the while aware that there might be another gunman in the woods. Squeaky stopped barking and came over to sniff the side of Hyman's face.

"This is a mistake," Hyman started babbling. "You don't understand. This is my property. I have a perfect right to be on my own property—"

"Shut up."

"My gun is registered and—"

"Just shut the fuck up."

And Hyman did. Which was good, because John's attention was on other matters.

He smelled smoke.

Chapter Forty-nine

$\mathcal{I}$nside the ice fishing house, Turner glanced worriedly at the door while she tended to Dante. Where was John? Dante's wound was still bleeding. The blood had soaked through the T-shirt bandage and started dripping down his sides, gluing his shirt to his skin. Her hands shook as she fumbled at his back. The blood brought back images of yesterday. Victoria's wound; the dark-haired woman staring at her with wide, accusing eyes. The memories were too fresh.

She tried to keep her face calm. John's partner might be an FBI special agent, but she didn't want to alarm him. He was lying down now, his handsome face pale against the drying, rust-colored blood on the collar of his shirt. He was younger than John. That was very apparent when his eyes closed, dark eyelashes brushing against his cheek. She checked her watch again. It felt like hours, but John had left the ice fishing shack only a few minutes ago. She hadn't heard any shots, but she still worried. He might be out there with a killer.

And then Squeaky started barking. Deep, purpose-ful barks, like the ones he'd given when he'd cornered Dante. Turner half rose.

"Stay here." The man might have been weak, but he still had an air of command. Especially with his intense gaze trained on her. "Mac can take care of himself."

She frowned, distracted. "Mac?"

"John MacKinnon. Everyone calls him Mac. Didn't he tell you?"

She shook her head.

He smiled rather charmingly, his chocolate brown eyes crinkling at the corners. He really was a beautiful man. "No reason he should."

She studied him. "Why don't you like John?"

"What makes you think that?"

"Oh, come on. You two are barely civil."

He looked sheepish. "We had a, uh, professional differ-ence of opinion on the last case we worked together."

"And?"

"That's it." He groaned theatrically. "Man, this bullet is killing me."

She gave him a look. The pain was no doubt real, but he was obviously trying to change the subject. "Tell me."

"God, you're persistent," he muttered. "Okay, we were on a case and I felt that Mac was behaving like a royal—" He shot her a look. "—jerk. He wasn't keeping me informed, he was going out and doing his own thing, and he kept blowing me off. So I went to the SAC—Special Agent in Charge—and let him know what Mac was doing and that I thought he shouldn't be heading the case."

Turner sucked in her breath and stared at Dante incredulously. "You told on him?" Even she could see that would be a very stupid move with John. What had Dante been thinking?

"No." He tried to lever himself up and grimaced instead. "No, see, I was just worried about the case—"

"Uh-huh." She raised an eyebrow sympathetically. "So, did he slaughter you?"

He winced. "Close. Turned out he was good buddies with the ASAC, who went to the SAC for him—"

"Duh."

"Yeah, so I don't play politics well." If Dante were a little boy, she'd say he was pouting. Turner bit the inside of her cheek to keep from smiling. "And he kept me off every case he's worked since then. This is the first one he's let me on."

"Can you blame him?"

"No. But he really is a—" That quick glance at her again. "—jerk. Even if he just saved my life."

Turner laughed. "You two—"

But Dante interrupted her. "Smoke." His expression suddenly sobered as he looked past her. He tried to lever himself up on his elbows. "I smell smoke."

Turner swung around to look behind her. White smoke was curling up from behind the tiny bar. As she watched, there was a pop, and flames leaped toward the ceiling.

The ice fishing house was on fire.

"Come on." She wrapped her hands around Dante on the side that wasn't wounded. "Let's get out of here." She pulled with all her strength, but he came only to a sitting position.

"No." He must've inhaled sharply, because he started coughing, each rasp shaking his frame. He gasped, "It might be a trap."

She stared at him. "Well, if it is, it's a darn good one. If we stay here, we're going to be roasted alive."

"Then let me go first." He had his gun out and in his hand.

"You can't even stand on your own!" She wasn't sure he could stand at all. Right now, he was leaning against her shoulder.

"I—"

The door burst in and Dante jerked his gun toward it. John crouched in the doorway. "Come on!"

"He can't stand, John," Turner said.

"I can—"

John cut Dante off by simply walking over and wrapping his arms around him. He hauled him to his feet but then staggered. Dante was making a valiant effort, but his head lolled on his shoulders. He had to be almost a dead weight on John. Turner tucked the laptop under one arm and came up on Dante's other side. Together, she and John half dragged, half walked him out the door. Outside, the air was fresh and the sun bright in her eyes. Turner coughed and looked back. The ice fishing shack was billowing black smoke. As she watched, a whoosh of flames burst through the roof.

"Christ," someone exclaimed. "Do you have any idea how much that ice fishing house cost?"

Calvin Hyman was standing by a tree, his arms behind his back. It took Turner a moment to realize he must be handcuffed. Squeaky was in front of him, apparently guarding the man, although the dog looked anxious. His tongue was hanging out, and he panted. The fire probably had him on edge. The fire had her on edge, too. She glanced around. The forest was bone-dry. There hadn't been any rain for weeks.

"We need to call the fire department."

"Already have," John panted. "On Hyman's cell."

He pivoted them toward the path leading up the slope to the cabin. Her instinct was to run away from the fire—she felt her arms prickle at the danger—but they couldn't run. Not with Dante. John's partner was leaning more heavily now. Turner wondered if they'd be able to get the man up the slope. If he passed out, could they carry his dead weight?

"Squeaky, come on," John called.

The dog hustled over. He evidently thought leaving the fire behind a great idea. Already, the leaves on the trees shading the ice fishing house were burning.

"You, too, Hyman." John didn't bother looking back to see if the bank president would follow.

"You have to let me go," Calvin whined. "I can't climb with these things on."

"Try," John said unsympathetically.

The gravel on the path slid beneath Turner's feet suddenly. She went to one knee, painfully pressed into the rocks. John grunted as Dante's full weight fell on Turner, pulling him over.

Crack!

Calvin screamed. Squeaky took off again, tail between his legs. *Oh, Lord!* Turner flinched and fell facedown, shaking. She knew that sound. Someone was shooting at them. Again. She dropped the laptop and tugged at Dante, trying to drag him into the woods with her.

Crack! Crack! Crack!

The shots started echoing in her head. The smell of smoke filled her nostrils. Turner whimpered. She didn't want to be here, going through this again.

She didn't want to be dead.

Calvin swore loudly, profanely, and dove into the woods on the opposite side of the path.

Crack! Crack! Crack!

She dug her heels in the soft, dry dirt and heaved at Dante with all her might. And he moved suddenly, toppling her as John shoved them both into the safety of the trees. She panted into the dusty leaf litter, still shaking. John fired his gun next to her, the sound so loud she thought she'd go mad. She had her hands over her ears, trying to press the percussive shots out, but they still came.

The shooter was returning fire, as well. Bark jumped off a tree in front of her. Dante groaned. He had his gun in his hand but couldn't bring it up.

All around them, the smoke was choking and thick. The woods were on fire, and the only path out was blocked by a killer. "Oh, Lord."

John didn't respond. His whole attention was on his opponent, somewhere out there, still firing at them.

"Stop! It's me!" Calvin shouted from the other side of the path. "Dammit, Hank, it's me, Calvin Hyman. Shoot them, not me."

John grunted. "Knew he hired this asshole."

Crack! Crack!

Was the gunman following Calvin's instructions? Turner tasted ashes in her mouth. John shifted and felt along Dante's body. The younger agent groaned. If he wasn't unconscious yet, he was close to it.

"Here," John said. "Take Torelli's gun. The safety is off. All you have to do is point and shoot." He turned fully toward her for the first time since they'd dived into the woods, and Turner saw . . .

Blood.

Blood painting half of his face, clotting over his eyebrows, clumping his eyelashes together, dripping onto the ground. She thought she smelled the copper scent, mingling with the smell of smoke.

John was bleeding.

No. Not John. She reached for him, ignoring the gun.

But he shoved the weapon into her hands. "Pay attention. If I pass out, you have to continue shooting. You have to keep him away, make him think I'm still here."

The blood. She whimpered.

"Turner." His pale eyes bored into hers, grim and intense, deadly serious. "This guy is wacko. He likes to shoot things. You need to keep him off if I can't. Because he'll kill you. He'll kill all of us."

He meant to say more, she could tell, but the shooting resumed.

Crack!

She ducked reflexively and felt the grit of dirt in her mouth. She blotted out the image in her mind of John drenched in blood. Her eyes stung from smoke, and her chest was tight. How long before the fire reached them? How long before they couldn't breathe or were burned alive or shot dead?

"Jesus! Let me through, Hank," Calvin yelled from the other side of the path. "I can't breathe. Too hot."

The only answer was another volley of shots.

Beside her, Dante started coughing, his chest shaking convulsively. He groaned, the sound making her more anxious. Turner was sure that had he been aware, he would've smothered the sign of pain.

"Goddamnit!" Calvin yelled again. Branches on the other side of the trail waved frantically as he thrashed around. "I'm coming out!"

The bank president ran out into the middle of the path, coughing. His hands were still behind his back, bound by the handcuffs, and he was having trouble keeping his balance. He started up the path, then seemed to notice the black laptop case for the first time. Turner could almost see his mind debating. Calvin turned and carefully squatted as if he were doing an intricate curtsey. He was trying to pick up the laptop from behind.

John swore. He raised his gun, but he was beaten to it by the hit man.

Crack! A shot kicked up dirt a foot away from where Calvin bent. He yelped and toppled over. Then a flurry of shots danced about him, hitting dirt and rocks and making a haze around Calvin but not touching him. Evidently Calvin had ticked another person off.

Beside Turner, John took careful aim and fired three shots so quickly that they seemed like one sustained explosion. Her ears rang, and she covered them reflexively. She thought at first that he'd shot Calvin, but his target was farther up the trail in the trees. Something large crashed in the woods, and from behind a tree a man's arm flopped onto the edge of the path. The rest of the body was thankfully hidden in the shadows of the trees. In the sudden silence, the crackle of the fire was loud. Nothing happened for several seconds. Turner stared at the arm, waiting, waiting, for it to move. But it didn't. Instead, flames began marching down the trail.

The fire had cut off their escape route.

Chapter Fifty

We need to get to the lake," John said and then burst into a spasm of coughing.

Turner nodded. She didn't trust herself to speak. The smoke grew denser, creeping into her throat, clogging her chest, stinging her eyes. Sparks danced through the air. One lit on the back of her neck, and she slapped at it in instinctive panic. John took Dante's right arm, and she took the other. They pulled in unison, muscles straining. The young man hung, a dead weight between them. She hoped his lack of response was from loss of blood, not something more serious. Not that loss of blood wasn't serious.

They dragged Dante back out to the path. Turner tripped over the tree roots now obscured by smoke. Calvin had already righted himself and was hobbling down to the lake. There was no sign of Squeaky. Turner briefly worried. Would the big dog know to get out of the forest? Animals weren't always smart about fires. She'd heard tales of cats hiding under beds in burning houses and horses that refused to leave barns on fire. But she couldn't worry about the dog now. It was all she could do to hold up her end of Dante. They edged their way slowly down the path to where the laptop lay in the dust. Turner quickly bent and grabbed the black case, looping the handle over her forearm, where it hung like a bowling ball.

John shot her a glance but didn't comment. The lake lay up ahead, blue and serene, the sun sparkling off the water as if nothing had happened in the last few minutes. As if John hadn't just saved their lives by taking another. As if the forest wasn't roaring behind them like a demon intent on devouring its prey.

A few more careful steps. The path was steep. A birch sapling by the water's edge exploded into flame, the fire popping and leaping into the air. Burning leaves floated merrily in the breeze like miniature firecrackers. John stumbled, caught himself, and stumbled again. Dante sagged against Turner with his entire weight, and they all went down like a house of cards. Turner skidded on her rear. Dante slid a couple of feet on the trail, head pointed down, gravel rattling after him. He swore weakly, and Turner managed a small smile. At least he was still alive.

She scrambled to her feet, then doubled over coughing. The wind, so light and playful earlier, had turned malevolent. It swept toward them, bringing the fire and the asphyxiating smoke with it. She looked up, still coughing, and saw through a cloud of tears the lake's bright blue water just out of reach.

"Go on," John commanded. But when she looked at him, he was still on hands and knees. His head hung down, dripping scarlet blood into the khaki dust beneath him. "Go on. I'll follow with Dante."

And she knew.

John wasn't going to follow with Dante. He didn't think he could make it to the lake. He was telling her to save herself.

To go on alone.

Turner felt tears that had nothing to do with the smoke stinging her eyes. How could he even think, after all they'd been through, that she would just leave him? That she wanted to be alone now? Did he think her the same isolated woman she'd been only six days ago? She wasn't that woman.

Not anymore.

Turner dropped the laptop into the dust and went to pull at John. "Come on."

He looked at her. "Go."

She shook her head. "No. I'm not leaving you. We'll make it to the lake. Together."

She pulled again and John heaved to his feet, a colossus rising. The blood on his face was streaked with dirt and sweat, and he swayed as he stood. But he grimly bent to pull at Dante while Turner took the younger man's other arm. She strained with all her might. There was no point in trying to get Dante upright anymore. They simply dragged him on his back. Slowly, agonizingly, the muscles tearing in her shoulders and arms, they pulled toward the blue lake. Toward safety.

Toward life.

Turner didn't once look back to see what had become of the laptop. Everything important to her lay ahead and beside her, no longer behind. And when they finally made it to the water's edge, the lake embraced them like the cool kiss of a welcoming mother. Turner felt the liquid wet her feet, calm and soothing. It rose to her thighs and then up to her waist as she walked into the water. They waded out until the lake lapped gently at her chin. John held Dante's head above the water.

Only then did she look back.

The shoreline was a holocaust. Flames climbed the trees, licking and devouring, and leapt toward the sky as if seeking more fuel. The path where she'd dropped the laptop was obscured by smoke and fire. A black pall hung over the sky as far as the eye could see, shrouding everything in death.

All except the lake. The lake was still quiet. Still cool. Sanctuary and life, it enveloped them in safety.

"Ha," Calvin gasped from where he struggled to stay afloat in the water. "The laptop's gone. You have no evidence on me."

"Premeditated murder," Dante mumbled. "Contract killing, bank robbery, assault on a—" He drifted off again, but John took over.

"And generally being a pain in the ass," he drawled. He smiled crookedly at Turner. "Hyman's going away for a long time."

Turner smiled back. Just as Squeaky burst from the trees, made one giant bound, and splashed them all with water.

Chapter Fifty-one

*J*ohn looked at the dashboard clock and groaned. It was close to midnight, and Turner was just now driving him home to his apartment. The hospital had wanted to keep him overnight for observation, but he had stood firm: he wanted to sleep in his own bed. Fortunately, Turner wasn't hurt. He wasn't sure the ER doctor would've let him go, otherwise, but since there was an able-bodied driver, the doc couldn't very well refuse. Thank God. John'd had enough of monotonous medical procedures and hospitals by that time.

They had been in the lake over an hour before being rescued by helicopter. The minute they'd landed, Hyman was taken into custody, John and Dante had been medivacced out in another helicopter, and Turner was left to follow by car with Squeaky. He still wasn't sure how she'd found a car to drive back to Milwaukee. His Chevy Silverado, along with much of the surrounding forest, must have been ashes by that point. He'd been worried about Dante and the delay in getting him help.

The younger man had been unconscious by the time the helicopter rescued them. He'd lost quite a bit of blood, and his shoulder blade was cracked, but the docs were cautiously optimistic that with care he'd fully recover.

"Turn here," John directed Turner. She'd been silent most of the ride.

Squeaky, a little singed and a lot smelling of lake, snored in the back. The glow from the dash softly lit Turner's face. John watched her. She had a red welt on the side of her neck, probably a burn spot. She'd been so strong today, so fearless. And in the end, she'd relinquished the treasure in her grasp—evidence of Hyman's crimes—for him.

What could a man say to a woman who'd sacrificed so much?

He opened his mouth, but then they turned into the parking lot. John frowned and decided what he had to say could wait until they'd gotten inside and had a chance to sit down. They parked, and he climbed out of the car carefully. They'd given him a painkiller at the hospital, but his head still felt like a semi had hit him.

"Are you okay?" Turner watched him worriedly, probably afraid that he'd fall down and she'd have to drag his sorry ass up a flight of stairs.

"I'm fine."

She didn't look convinced, but she made no reply. They went in the building and up the stairs, and he tried to find the right phrase for what he wanted to say. He halted in the hall beside his apartment.

"Turner . . ." He grimaced and fished in his pocket for the key.

She looked at him. "What?"

"I—"

"Dad!"

My God. He swung around at the feminine voice. Rachel was behind him. Taller, her blond hair longer. His first stunned thought was that she looked so mature.

"Rachel?" he asked stupidly.

She frowned—scowled, really. "Who is this? Is she why you haven't been answering my calls?"

"Rachel, why don't you come inside?" He fumbled at the door.

"I want an answer, *John.* I want one now. She—"

"A bullet grazed your father's head today," Turner said evenly. "An inch over and he would be dead right now."

Rachel swung her scowl to Turner. "What right do you have—" The meaning of Turner's words seemed to hit her. Her face opened, her eyebrows drawing up, her mouth widening. "Daddy?"

John grimaced. "Come inside—"

But then a strident voice interrupted him. "Rachel!"

They all turned. Well, shit. This was just perfect. Amy was rushing toward them with, yup, Dennis the asshole in tow. His head felt like it was about to explode.

"Rachel!" Her mother skidded to a halt in front of the girl, hands on hips. "What were you thinking to come here without even telling me or your father?"

Dennis, behind Amy, lifted a hand and mouthed *hi* to him. John nodded wearily. The guy was really all right. For an asshole.

"Is this something you cooked up, Mac?" Amy narrowed her eyes at him. "I would expect that—"

"She wants to know why you two divorced," Turner said.

"What?" Amy blinked. "Who the hell are you?"

"She's his girl," Rachel sneered.

John felt his temper spike. "Turner," he said clearly and loudly, "is the woman I'm going to marry."

Rachel's mouth dropped open, Dennis blinked, and Amy—for once—evidently couldn't think of anything to say.

"Um," Turner cleared her throat in the silence. "You all have a lot to talk about, and John needs to sit down. Rachel, why don't you take your father's arm before he keels over?" Against all expectations, his daughter rushed to his side. "I'll just go down and get Squeaky." She nodded at Amy. "Nice meeting you."

And the one person he wanted to stay left.

John sighed. Fine. This was going to be a painful discussion no matter when it happened. Might as well get it over with while he was high on codeine. But then Rachel put her shoulder under his arm and helped him into his own apartment like she really thought he needed support. That was gratifying in a bittersweet way. He could smell some kind of perfume in her hair. His little girl used perfume.

"Maybe we ought to come back another time," Dennis said. "John's obviously been hurt—"

"No, no, stay." John made himself smile. "Let's go inside and talk."

"I'll go get you a glass of water," Amy said, oddly subdued.

Dennis excused himself and disappeared into the bathroom. John sat on his boring beige couch with his daughter beside him. He already missed Turner.

"What happened to you?" Rachel asked. "Was she right? Did you get shot at?"

"Yeah, but the other guy missed. I'm okay, really. The bandage is a lot bigger than it needs to be."

She seemed to think about that for a moment. Amy was taking longer in the kitchen than she needed to. Maybe she was giving them some time alone.

"Are you really going to marry her?" Rachel whispered.

"Yes."

"Oh." Her lips trembled at the corners.

"I'll always love you, no matter what," John said carefully. "You'll always be my daughter."

"No. You gave me up three years ago." But despite her words, she huddled more closely to him.

John sighed. "That's what you wanted, sweetheart. You said you thought of Dennis as your father and you didn't need me in your life anymore."

"Maybe . . ." She took a deep breath. "Maybe I changed my mind."

He felt his lips curve as giddy hope swam in his veins. "That's allowed."

Amy came back into the room. She gave him a glass of ice water and sat down in a chair across from them. "You worried the hell out of me, Rachel. What's this all about?"

John took a sip of the water and was silent.

"She was right," Rachel finally said. "Dad's . . . fiancée. I want to know why you and Daddy broke up."

Amy looked wary. "You already know—"

"No, I don't! Not the truth. There's more, I know there's more—"

"Your mother and I were sleeping together," Dennis said. John hadn't even noticed him reenter the room.

"Dennis," Amy said faintly.

He didn't look at her. "It was pretty tacky of us, because Mom was still married to Mac. But we were in love, and sometimes even adults make mistakes in that state. When Mac found out, he divorced your mother."

John winced. "The infidelity happened because of many things. I was gone frequently—"

"But it wasn't my fault," Rachel murmured.

"No, of course not!" her mother exclaimed.

John watched Rachel thoughtfully. "Why did you think it was your fault?"

She shrugged and looked down at her hands. "I always felt there was something you all were keeping from me. A-and I remember that I cried a lot when I was little. Before you left."

He frowned. "So?"

"I thought maybe you didn't like it." She stared at him with her big, lake blue eyes.

It took him a second to get it, probably because it was late and his system was full of painkillers. She thought the normal tantrums of a small child had driven him away. How could she? Rachel was an intelligent girl—he knew that, even if he was biased, being her father. How could she think he'd leave because she'd thrown a hissy fit now and then? But was anyone smart when it came to their own family? And he and Amy had held back the real reason for the divorce. No wonder she'd jumped to the wrong conclusion.

"No." He was shaking his head even as the thought crossed his mind. Amy still looked confused. "Nothing—*nothing*—you did broke us up, Rachel. If anything, your mother and I stayed together longer because of you."

Amy frowned, an odd look dawning on her face. "Rachel, darling . . ."

Then they started talking. Explaining and reassuring. Something they all should've done a long, long time ago. It took only an hour, but it felt like a lifetime of tension had been broken. By the end, John was drained of whatever stamina he still had left, but he'd come to a new understanding with his daughter.

"We'll e-mail you the airline confirmation," Amy said briskly at the door. They'd decided that Rachel could come visit him in a week or so—after she'd gone home and sorted things out with her mother and adopted father. "She'll only be able to stay a few days. School begins right after Labor Day."

"That will be a good start," he said, trying to keep his eyes open. Where was Turner?

"Bye, Daddy." Rachel looked awkward a moment, then lunged into his arms and hugged him painfully. Not that he let that show on his face. "I love you."

"Love you, too." He leaned, he hoped casually, on the doorway and watched them walk away down the hall.

The moment they disappeared around the corner, he went looking for Turner, even though he felt like warmed-over shit. She'd said that she was going to get Squeaky over an hour ago—where was she? He hadn't meant to blurt out a wedding proposal in front of Rachel. If you could call such a blunt statement a wedding proposal. John winced. It hadn't been the time or place. He'd been envisioning something along the lines of a candlelit dinner and white wine. Instead, he'd shown all the finesse of a bull rhino. He hurried down the stairs and looked out at the lit parking lot.

Her car wasn't there.

He stared for a moment more in disbelief, then turned back inside. The stairway going up looked longer than it'd been going down. Turner was skittish of intimacy, of getting close to other people. Maybe she'd used the excuse of his daughter showing up to make a run for it.

Christ.

His head was pounding dully by the time he reached his door. He knew her home address, but she was so squirrelly that she might've gone into hiding again. He'd have to find out—

The phone rang from inside his apartment. He swore and fumbled with the door, having somehow forgotten how to work the knob.

He got it open, slammed it behind him, and dove for the ringing phone. "Yeah?"

"Special Agent John MacKinnon?"

He shut his eyes in relief and came close—very close—to crying. "Yeah, baby."

Turner cleared her throat, the small sound erotic even over a phone wire. "Has your family gone?"

"They've gone. But only Rachel's my family. And you."

She didn't comment on that. "Would you mind if Squeaky and I turned ourselves in now?"

He sagged against the wall. "I'd like that. Where are you?"

"Open your door."

He straightened and looked at the door he'd just shut. Hardly believing, he opened it.

Turner stood on the other side, phone to her ear, humongous dog beside her. She smiled at him.

Chapter Fifty-two

$\mathcal{J}$ohn looked so tired when he opened the door. That was Turner's first thought. She should have saved this for tomorrow. Should've found a motel room and let him sleep in peace. The bandage they'd used to cover his head wound at the hospital looked large and white against his salt-and-pepper hair.

But then he reached out and pulled her into his arms. The cheap little cell phone she'd just bought at an all-night convenience store fell from her hand and clattered to the floor. And she forgot about her worry. John was kissing her as if she were the elixir to everlasting life. As if she were the most important thing in his world.

As if he loved her.

She knew tears were running down her cheeks. She could taste them on his lips, but she didn't care. She'd come home. She'd finally come home after four long years of isolation. Four long years of living on the outside, peering in on her own life. She could let Rusty rest, let her anger at Calvin settle, and finally look around. She could get on with her own life.

With this man.

John somehow got her inside his apartment, his mouth all but devouring hers. His phone began ringing, but she ignored the sound. They bumped against furniture, careened off a wall. Neither one of them wanted to break the kiss. She hoped his eyes were open, because hers sure weren't. Somewhere Squeaky sighed, and there was a thump as he probably lay down. Then she forgot the dog.

John had maneuvered them into the bedroom and was busy stripping off her T-shirt. To do that, he had to lift his mouth from hers. "Never leave me," he muttered as he threw her T-shirt on a chair.

"I won't." The phone kept ringing. "Are you going to answer that?"

"I don't want to chase after you all over hell and back." His fingers were on her front bra clasp. He seemed to be having trouble with it. "Did that already. I don't need to do it again."

"Of course not. Um, the phone?"

He got the bra off and triumphantly tossed it over his shoulder. She didn't see where it landed. He was still muttering. "I thought you'd gone."

"I hadn't. I just went to the store to get Squeaky some food and to buy a cell. Speaking of which, are you going to answer that phone?"

He swore violently and lunged for the bedside phone. *"What?"*

Turner busied herself pulling back his brown bedspread. She was going to have to get him something with more color—maybe red?

"Fine. Good. Thanks." John hung up the phone while whoever it was on the other end went on squawking. He pulled the phone cord from the wall and turned to her purposely. "You're not going to jail."

"What?"

"That was my boss—"

Turner's eyes widened in horror. "You hung up on your boss?"

"Yeah." His eyes were narrowed on her breasts. "He says the bank isn't pressing charges against you, and under the circumstances, Mrs. Hyman won't, either."

"But how—?"

"I called Tim—my ASAC—from the hospital to see if he could fix it. He could."

"Why—?"

But he wasn't listening. He'd opened his mouth wide over her breast. It was like sinking into a hot, humid cavern. Turner gasped and gasped again when he wrapped his big hands around her rib cage and lifted her against him. He walked with her to the bed, his mouth still on her breast, and placed her on the end. Her legs hung off the edge. He knelt there on the floor between her legs and licked his way down her bare torso.

Turner tried to prop herself up on her elbows. "John, shouldn't you come to bed, too? You've got a head injury."

"It's only a scratch." He grinned boyishly from between her thighs as he unsnapped her shorts. "I've always wanted to say that. Besides, I'm feeling better now."

And he yanked her shorts off.

Well, she'd made her token protest. If he was determined to make love to her, she saw no point in dissuading him. And he'd already parted her legs. John bent his head and licked her, right between the folds of her vulva. Turner flopped back on the bed and closed her eyes. My, oh my, the man knew what he was doing. She reached down and ran her hands through his short hair, feeling the strands like silk against her palms. Her hands brushed against the bandage at his temple. And once again she felt tears prick at her eyes. Which was silly, considering what he was doing to her and how much she liked it. She had come so close to losing him. Had the bullet been an inch over, he would've died. She would've lost this bond, this love with him.

John circled her clit with his tongue. She gasped and jolted. Then he began deliberately licking her, over and over again, relentlessly torturing that small nubbin of flesh. She bit her lower lip. The feeling was almost too intense.

"John." She arched against the hands holding her hips, but he held her firmly. "John . . ."

She'd never let another man do this to her. It had always seemed too intimate. And it was. It was. But she spread her legs wider and welcomed him. Him and his love.

Because this was John.

She felt so warm. So hot. She couldn't take much more of this, and she didn't want him to ever stop. "John—"

He slowly pressed his thumb into her and at the same time bit gently, firmly on her clit. She shook, her head thrown back, her hips arching. A wave of intense light spread through her, widening, widening, until she simply lay there, gasping. She was sublimely at peace. She was with John.

She felt the bed move as he took his hands away from

her, and for a moment she was cold. Then he was back. He lifted her and pulled her up until she lay fully on the bed. She felt him grasp her hips again, and his cock nudged against her sensitive flesh. She opened her eyes. He was poised above her, his pale eyes grave, the lines on his face looking as if they were carved.

"I love you," he said as he began to enter her. "I want you to know that. Now and forever."

He thrust heavily into her. She opened her mouth at the intrusion, at the feel of his penis in her.

But he wasn't done.

"You don't have to respond now. I know it's too soon. We've only known each other a week." He lay, his pelvis pressed fully into her, warm and heavy.

She tried to move against him—he wasn't thrusting—but his weight prevented her. "I—"

"Just give me time to get to know you. To court you. I won't force anything."

She doubted that. After all, he'd chosen to make his declaration when he was inside of her. And John was the kind of guy who couldn't help but coerce, even when he tried not to.

He frowned a little. Beads of sweat glistened on his forehead. Holding still was costing him, she could tell. "I want you to know—"

She smiled and touched a finger to his lips, quieting him. "I love you, John MacKinnon."

The lines eased a bit on his face. "You're sure?"

"Yes."

He moved his hips, readjusting his weight. Oh, my, that felt wonderful. She almost let her eyelids fall, but she kept them open with an effort.

He withdrew slowly. "Because—"

"John?"

He froze. *Not* what she'd been hoping for.

She took a deep breath and concentrated. "I love you with all my heart and soul. You are the sun and the stars to me. I feel whole when we're together. And, just for the record—and even though you didn't officially ask me—yes, I will marry you and be your wife until the day I die."

He blinked. "Uh, well . . . good."

She wrapped her legs around his hips. Tight. "Now. Is that settled?"

"Yeah."

She looked him sternly in the eye. "Good. Please make love to me until I scream."

A slow grin spread over his face. "Yes, ma'am."

And he did.

Chapter Fifty-three

Meanwhile, somewhere in northern Wisconsin . . .

"Dude, this is depressing," Fish said, as the prison van bumped over a rut in the road. His chains rattled.

"This is, like, worse than at the end of *The Lord of the Rings*," Nald moaned. "Nine stupid hours, and then Frodo gets his finger cut off and has to go to the land of unfun with what's-his-face the wizard."

"*This* is unfun, man." Fish shifted on the hard seat.

"Liver and onions," Nald muttered.

He was still, like, stunned. Who ate liver and onions? They should tell everyone that's what they served in jail. That would keep guys like him from robbing banks.

"The guy next to me had seconds," Fish groaned in horror. "It looked like he was eating alien brains."

"Gross! Alien brains."

"And there's no cable."

"No Sci Fi Channel."

"No Cartoon Channel."

"No World Wrestling."

"Dude, that's a regular channel," Fish pointed out.

"I don't care," Nald yelled, suddenly losing it. "They probably won't let us watch it, anyway! We're probably going to have to watch *Jeopardy!* and Martha Stewart!"

"Martha Stewart?"

"Christ!" the guard guy yelled from the front of the van. "Will you two just shut up?"

The guy had a short temper. He'd been yelling that at them ever since they'd left the jail, an hour back. The van bumped again—really hard this time—and stopped.

Guard Guy swore and got out of the van, slamming the door behind him.

"I think we're stalled," Fish said. He looked out the window, but Nald doubted he could see anything. It was black outside.

"I don't care," Nald said. He slumped in his seat.

Headlights glowed in the side window where Fish peered. The guard shouted from outside and thumped on the van door.

"Man," Fish said. "That dude ought to switch off his high beams."

The light was nearly blinding now. The guard pounded on the door harder. The van started to shake.

"Do you think we should open the door?" Nald asked.

Then a really loud horn blared really close. The door opened. Guard Guy stomped in looking very pissed and grabbed them by their orange jumpsuits.

"Hey—" Fish started.

The guard dragged them out of the van violently.

Forty seconds later, Nald and Fish were at the side of the train tracks watching the prison van get hit by a train.

"Awesome!" Fish screamed as the train went *bam!* and the van flew up into the air.

"Dude!" Nald agreed in between jumping up and down. It was the best thing he'd ever seen in his life.

The train slowed after a while, and the van driver went to yell at the train engineer. A bunch of cop cars and ambulances drove up with flashing lights even though no one was hurt. Nald stopped jumping and glanced around. Everyone was over looking at the van wreck and talking on their radios and stuff. No one was paying any attention to them.

Nald had his first idea since Saturday. "Dude—"

But Fish was still thinking about the van getting hit. "Did you see the windshield pop out?"

"Dude—"

"And the look on that guard's face. He was all, like, *Oh, shit!*"

"Dude—"

"And the tire that bounced off the back of the train?"

"Dude!" Nald yelled.

Fish stopped. "What?"

"Which way is Canada?"

About the Author

The author of the *New York Times* bestselling Maiden Lane series and the Legend of the Four Soldiers series as well as the Princes trilogy, Elizabeth Hoyt writes "mesmerizing" (*Publishers Weekly*) historical romances. She also pens deliciously fun contemporary romances under the name Julia Harper. Elizabeth lives in central Illinois with three untrained dogs, two angelic but bickering children, and one long-suffering husband. Central Illinois can be less than exciting, and Elizabeth is always more than happy to receive missives from her readers. You can write to her at: PO Box 17134, Urbana, IL 61873.

Maisa Burnsey must track down her infamous ex-mobster uncle who may be back to his old habits. But when she's pulled over by the sexiest sheriff she's ever seen, the real crime would be to let him get away...

Please see the next page for an excerpt of

Once and Always

Day One

*S*hit. Maisa Burnsey's heartbeat did a little stumble as she watched the familiar police car halt behind her. She pushed up her chunky black glasses. Every damned time she passed through Coot Lake, Minnesota, she got stopped.

In her rearview mirror she watched the tall trooper climb from the squad car. He sauntered toward her Beetle, loose-hipped and long-legged, as if he had all the time in the world. And like the good guy in a black-and-white western, he wore a stupid cowboy hat.

Maisa snorted softly.

He stopped by her car door, his pelvis framed by her window exactly at eye level, as if he was showing off the bulge of his package.

Not that she was looking.

There was an American flag on the left breast of his padded navy uniform jacket, a metal badge on his right, and below that a name tag that read *WEST*. One gloved hand rested on a lean hip, behind a holstered gun. His upper face, obscured by mirrored sunglasses and the cowboy hat, was stern and intimidating. His lips, though, were wide and almost soft, the top just a little fuller than the bottom. The man had a mouth that was beautiful enough to make a woman ache just by looking.

Maisa straightened her spine and glared at him. Okay, she could do this.

He twirled his gloved finger to tell her to roll down the window.

She opened it, letting in the freezing January wind. "What?"

He nodded. "Hey, May."

His voice was deep and gravelly, like he smoked, though she knew for a fact that he didn't.

"*Maisa*," she snapped automatically. She wasn't going to think about the last time he'd called her May. "This is the fourth time you've stopped me here."

"Maybe you should quit speeding." That beautiful mouth quirked. "Or quit running away."

"I'm *not* running away," she lied, poker-faced.

"Darlin', you've been running away from me since last August."

Maisa felt her teeth click together. "*I'm* talking about pulling me over for speeding."

His wide mouth curved. "I'm not."

She breathed deeply. Evenly. God damn it, meditation was supposed to make her *less* angry. "This is entrapment."

"Now," he drawled, his small town accent broadening, "I don't have any fancy un-*ee*-versity learnin', but I'm pretty sure entrapment is if I *falsely* lure you into breaking the law—"

"What do you call a speed trap, then?"

"—*which*, since I didn't *make* you drive well above the speed limit—"

"And that's ridiculous as well." She scowled. "The limit's seventy everywhere else but this stretch of highway."

He shrugged. "Still fifty-five here."

"Well, it shouldn't be. There should be better things for you to do than lie in wait for some poor driver who hasn't noticed that the speed has gone down so you can pounce." She stopped to inhale.

He looked at her. "Like what?"

"What?"

"What should I be doing instead?"

She licked her lips. God damn it. Did he have to stand so close? "Doing your job."

"This *is* my job."

"Following me isn't your job." She could feel the heat mounting her neck with her anger. Oh, to hell with it. "Speeding isn't why you stopped me and you know it. You're harassing me, Sam West."

There was a pause as if she'd broken some obscure rule in their game. The wind whipped icy snow against her car, making the vehicle sway.

He didn't even flinch, steady as a granite monument to male stubbornness.

"That right. You know, you don't *have* to take this route every month when you drive up from Minneapolis." His voice was terribly gentle, and she had a flash of him straight-armed over her, his mouth wet, his voice a gravel whisper as he'd murmured, *Like that?* And shoved inside of her, quick and hard and confident.

One night. One night last August she'd let him in. It'd been hot and muggy, and her uncle's cabin hadn't had any air-conditioning. She'd booked a room at the Coot Lake Inn and then gone to the only bar in town to have a cold beer. Sam had been there, looking way too sexy in faded jeans and a T-shirt so thin she could see the outline of his nipples when the condensation on his beer bottle had dripped on his chest. He'd bought her another beer and flirted and she'd thought, *Why not?* Why not just one night? So she'd brought him back to her tacky motel room and let him undress her and kiss her and make love to her, and in the morning she'd woken with her heart already beating too fast in panic. She'd dressed without showering, grabbed her bags, and left him there, still asleep on his belly, his wide shoulders bare and erotic in the stark morning light.

It'd been a mistake. One terrible, unforgettable mistake.

She exhaled through her nose, glancing away from him, feeling suddenly sad and vulnerable.

She hated that feeling. "This route is the easiest way to my uncle's house."

"Uh-huh." He didn't even bother to sound like he believed her, which was just insulting. "And me being the cop on duty most of the time along this stretch of highway has nothing to do with it."

"*Yes.*" She was going to chip a tooth if she ground down any harder.

"May—"

"*Maisa.* Look, just give me the goddamned ticket and I'll be on my way."

She could see him shift his weight from one leg to the other out of the corner of her eye. "Your brake light's out."

She swung back. "What?"

He nodded his head at the back of her car. "Right rear."

Maisa started to crane her neck to look before she realized how silly that was. "Oh. I'll get it fixed."

"'Preciate that," he drawled. Did anyone else *drawl* in freaking *Minnesota*? "But I'll have to cite you in the meantime."

"Oh, for God's sake, Sam!"

That got a gloved finger sliding his mirrored glasses down just enough to see the flash of his electric blue eyes. "Well now. Glad to hear you remember my name."

She didn't give herself time to think, just slipped the knife between his ribs, quick and nasty. "Of course I remember, *Sam*. It's not a big deal, you know. You were a good lay, but that's all you were."

For a moment everything seemed to still along the stretch of lonely highway. The land was nearly flat here, rolling farmland broken by small clumps of trees. The wind was relentless, blowing across the prairie in winter. In order to survive it those trees had to be tough, hardy, and tenacious.

Maybe tenacious most of all.

Sam sighed and took off his glasses and she thought obscurely that he'd never hide those eyes if he had any idea what the sight of them did to women. He was thirty-three, but he had lines around his eyes as if he'd been squinting into the sun—like Clint Eastwood looking for the bad guys on the open plains. Except Sam had already found the bad guy and was too stupid—or too bullheaded—to know it.

"You practiced that in front of your bathroom mirror, didn't you," he said, flat.

Of course she had. No way was she letting him in again. Sam West was just too dangerous to her peace of mind—and heart. "Just give me the ticket."

He leaned one arm on the car roof just over her head, bending to look at her through the window. The position put his face close enough to hers that she could smell mint on his breath.

She tried not to breathe, refusing to look at him again. If she could just get away, if he'd just let her go, everything would be okay.

She could freehand a dozen dress designs in one night, she could set a dart so perfectly it'd make any woman's ass look like gold, but she couldn't deal with the emotions Sam West made her feel.

She. Just. Couldn't.

"Listen, May," he said, too near, too damned *intimate*, "I won't give you a ticket this time. Just be—"

The sound of a revving engine came from behind them on the highway.

Sam looked up.

"Fuck," he murmured, and in one graceful movement vaulted onto the hood of her car. He slid spectacularly across the surface on one hip, just as a little red car tore past, so close it rocked the Beetle in its wake. The red car's taillights flashed as it braked for the curve, tires squealing. But the car just kept going straight. It slapped into the packed snow at the outer curve, climbing the embankment, nose skyward, engine squealing before suddenly cutting.

In the silent aftermath Maisa stared, open-mouthed with shock.

Then she remembered Sam. He was no longer on the hood of her car. She couldn't see him anywhere. Panic crowded her chest as she began battling the car door handle.

Oh, God, oh, God, please don't let him be hurt.

When free-spirited Zoey Addler
hijacks Special Agent Dante Torelli,
she doesn't expect to be dodging bullets
and an inconvenient attraction to the
sinfully sexy federal agent.

A preview of Julia Harper's

For the Love of Pete

follows.

Chapter One

*T*hings finally came to a head between Zoey Addler and Lips of Sin the afternoon he tried to steal her parking space.

Okay, *technically,* her upstairs neighbor's name wasn't really Lips of Sin. She knew the guy's occupation but not his name. Since the man was drop-dead gorgeous, Zoey had taken to calling him "Lips of Sin" in her mind. And yes, *technically,* the parking spot in question might not legally have been hers—she hadn't paid for it or anything—but she *had* shoveled it. This was January in Chicago. In Chicago in winter, shoveling out a parking spot made it yours. Everyone knew that.

Everyone but Lips of Sin, that is.

"What the hell are you doing?" Zoey screamed at him. She body slammed the hood of his black Beemer convertible, which was sitting in her stolen parking spot.

Lips of Sin, behind the wheel of said Beemer, mouthed something she couldn't hear. He rolled down his window. "Are you insane? I could've hit you. Never get in front of a moving vehicle."

Oh, like he had the right to lecture *her.* Zoey straightened, planted both Sorel-booted feet firmly, and crossed her arms. "I shoveled this parking spot. This is *my* parking spot. You can't take it."

Her words emerged in white puffs into the frosty late-afternoon air. They'd already had eight inches of snow the night before, and it looked like it might very well snow again. All the more reason to keep this spot.

The Beemer was at an angle, half in, half out of the parking place, which was almost directly in front of their apartment building. Every other parking space on the block was filled. There was a yellow Humvee, hulking in front of the Beemer, and a red Jeep to the back. Her own little blue Prius was double-parked next to the red Jeep. It was a sweet parking spot. Zoey had gotten up at five freaking a.m. to shovel it before she went to work at the co-op grocery. She'd marked the spot with two lawn chairs and a broken plastic milk crate in time-honored Chicago tradition. Now, returning after a long day of work, it was too much to find Lips in the act of stealing her space.

"Jesus," Lips said. "Look, I'm running a little late here. I promise to shovel you another parking place tonight. Just get out of my way. Please?"

Obviously he wasn't used to begging. Gorgeous guys didn't beg. He had smooth, tea-with-milk brown skin, curly black hair, and bitter-chocolate eyes, framed by lush girly eyelashes. Except the girly eyelashes helped emphasize the hard masculine edges of his face. In fact, the only soft things on his face were the eyelashes and his lips of sin. Deep lines bracketed those lips, framing the cynical corners and the little indent on the bottom lip that made a woman wonder what, exactly, the man could do with that mouth.

Perfect.

He was perfectly perfect in his masculine beauty, and Zoey had hated him on sight. Gorgeous guys were always so damn full of themselves. They strutted around like they were God's gift to women. *Please*. Add to that the fact that the man was always dressed for corporate raiding in suit and tie and black leather trench coat, and he just was not her type.

Lips was getting out of the car now, looking pretty pissed, his black trench coat swirling dramatically around his legs.

Zoey leaned forward, about to give him what-for, when the front doors to their apartment building burst open and a middle-aged guy in a red puffy jacket came running out. He had a baby under his left arm like a football. Zoey froze, her heart paralyzed at the sight. In his right fist was a gun. His bald head swiveled as he caught sight of them, and his gun hand swiveled with it. Zoey's eyes widened, and then a ton of bricks hit her from the side. She went down into the frozen gray slush on the street, and the ton of bricks landed on top of her. An expensive black leather sleeve shielded her face.

BANG!

The shot sounded like it was right in her ear. Zoey contracted her body in animal reaction, trying to make herself smaller beneath the heavy bulk of the man on top of her.

"Get behind the car," Lips breathed in her ear, and she had the incongruous thought that his breath smelled like fresh mint.

Then a flurry of shots rang out, one right after the other, in a wall of sound that scared her witless. The weight lifted from her body, and she felt Lips grab the back of her jacket and haul. She was on hands and knees, but she barely touched the ground before she was behind the Beemer on the driver's side. She looked up and saw Lips crouched over her, a black gun in his hand.

"Don't shoot," she gasped. "He's got the baby!"

"I know." His gaze was fixed over the roof of the car. "Shit."

The word was drowned out by the sound of a revving engine. Zoey looked around in time to see the yellow Hummer accelerate away from the curb, the bald man at the wheel.

"Come on!" She grabbed the door handle of the Beemer and pulled, scrambling ungracefully inside. There was a moment when she thought she might be seriously tangled in the console between the seats, and then she was on the other side, pulling out the passenger-side seat belt. She looked back, and Lips was still standing outside the car, staring at her. "What're you waiting for? We'll lose him."

He narrowed his eyes at her but thankfully didn't argue. Instead he threw back his coat and suit jacket, holstered his gun in a graceful movement Jack Bauer would've envied, and got in the car. He released the emergency brake and shifted into first.

He glanced at her once assessingly and said, "Hold on."

The force of his acceleration slammed her against the Beemer's lush leather seat. Then they were flying, the car eerily quiet as they sped through Evanston.

"Do you think he's a pedophile?" She clutched at the car armrest anxiously.

"No."

The yellow Hummer had turned at the corner onto

a medium-sized boulevard lined with small businesses and shops. Zoey was afraid they would've already lost him by now, but two stoplights ahead, the Hummer idled at a red light.

She leaned forward. "There he is. Up ahead at the stoplight."

"I see him." The words were quiet, but they had an edge.

Well, too bad. "Can't you go any faster?"

He sped past a forest green minivan.

"The light changed. He's moving again." Zoey bit her lip, trying to still the panic in her chest. "We can't lose him. We just can't. You need to go faster."

Lips glanced at her. He didn't say anything, but Zoey heard a kind of scraping sound, like he was grinding his teeth. She rolled her eyes. Men had such delicate egos. She hauled her cell out of her jacket pocket and began punching numbers.

"What're you doing?" he asked. The Beemer swerved around a Volkswagen Beetle in the left lane, briefly jumping the concrete divider before thumping down again in front of the Beetle.

Zoey righted herself from where she'd slid against the passenger door. "Calling 911."

He grunted, and she wasn't sure whether that was an approving sound or not. Not that it mattered.

There was a click in her ear and a bored voice said, "911. What is the nature of your emergency?"

The Hummer had turned right at the light onto Dempster. Lips steered the Beemer into the turn going maybe forty mph. The Beemer's tires screeched but didn't skid. Points to BMW engineering.

"A baby's been kidnapped," Zoey said to the 911 operator. "We're chasing the kidnapper."

The operator's voice perked up. "Where are you now?"

"On Dempster, near uh . . ." She craned her neck just as Lips swerved again, nearly sending her nose into the passenger-side window. "Shit."

"I beg your pardon," the operator said, sounding offended.

"Not you. I know we've passed Skokie Boulevard—"

"We're on Dempster and Le Claire," Lips said tightly.

Zoey repeated the information.

"Tell 911 that it's a yellow Hummer," Lips said as he accelerated around a postal truck, imperiling the paint on the Beemer's side. "The license plate's obscured by mud, but there's a dent in the back left panel over the wheel."

The Hummer suddenly swerved into the right lane and took a ramp onto the Edens Expressway.

Zoey gasped in the middle of her recitation. "He's gotten onto the Edens going north."

The Beemer barreled up the ramp and abruptly slowed. In either direction on the freeway, as far as the eye could see, was a four-lane-wide trail of cars.

"Shit," Zoey muttered.

"I beg your pardon," the operator said again. Must get sworn at a lot in her job.

"Not you," Zoey replied and then said to no one in particular, "This is why I never take the Edens after three. They've been doing road construction for, like, ten years here."

"I'll be sure and tell the guy that when we catch up with him," Lips ground out.

If they caught up with him, Zoey thought and bit her bottom lip. The Hummer was already several cars ahead and moving, whereas their part of the traffic jam was stopped dead. There was a good possibility that they'd lose the Hummer in the traffic. She kept her eyes firmly fixed on the massive lump of yellow steel. She wasn't letting it out of her sight. That truck contained a kidnapper with a gun and a very important little piece of humanity. 'Cause the kidnapper hadn't taken just any baby.

He'd taken Pete.

Fall in Love with Forever Romance

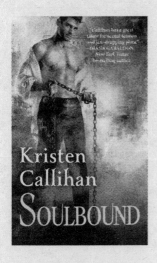

SOULBOUND
by Kristen Callihan

After centuries of searching, Adam finally found his soul mate, only to be rejected when she desires her freedom. But when Eliza discovers she's being hunted by someone far more dangerous, she turns to the one man who can keep her safe— even if he endangers her heart...

WHAT A DEVILISH DUKE DESIRES
by Vicky Dreiling

Fans of *New York Times* bestselling authors Julia Quinn, Sarah MacLean, and Madeline Hunter will love the third book in Vicky Dreiling's charming, sexy, and utterly irresistible Sinful Scoundrels trilogy about a highborn man who never wanted to inherit his uncle's title or settle down...until a beautiful, brilliant, delightfully tempting maid makes him rethink his position.

Fall in Love with Forever Romance

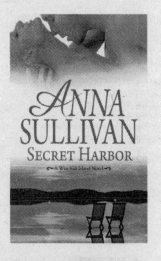

SECRET HARBOR
by Anna Sullivan

Fans of *New York Times* best-selling authors JoAnn Ross, Jill Shalvis, and Bella Andre will love the last book in Anna Sullivan's witty contemporary romance trilogy about a young woman who left her beloved home in Maine to become an actress in Hollywood. Now a star, and beset by scandal, she wants nothing more than to surround herself with old friends... until she meets an infuriating—and sexy—stranger.

MEET ME AT THE BEACH
by V. K. Sykes

Gorgeous Lily Doyle was the only thing Aiden Flynn missed after he escaped from Seashell Bay to play pro baseball. Now that he's back on the island, memories rush in about the night of passion they shared long ago, and everything else washes right out to sea—everything except the desire that still burns between them.

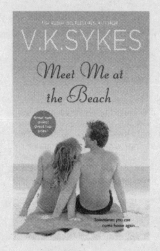

Fall in Love with Forever Romance

HOT
by Elizabeth Hoyt
writing as Julia Harper

For Turner Hastings, being held at gunpoint during a back robbery is an opportunity in disguise. After seeing her little heist on tape, FBI Special Agent John MacKinnon knows it's going to be an interesting case. But he doesn't expect to develop feelings for Turner, and when bullets start flying in her direction, John finds he'll do anything to save her.

FOR THE LOVE OF PETE
by Elizabeth Hoyt
writing as Julia Harper

Dodging bullets with a loopy redhead in the passenger seat is not how Special Agent Dante Torelli imagined his day going. But Zoey Addler is determined to get her baby niece back, and no one—not even a henpecked hit man, cooking-obsessed matrons, or a relentless killer—will stand in her way.

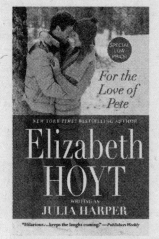

Fall in Love with Forever Romance

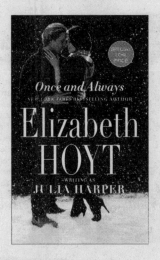

ONCE AND ALWAYS
by Elizabeth Hoyt writing as Julia Harper

The newest contemporary from *New York Times* bestselling author Elizabeth Hoyt writing as Julia Harper! Small-town cop Sam West certainly doesn't mind a routine traffic stop. But Maisa Bradley is like nothing he has ever seen, and she's about to take Sam on the ride of his life!